DAYBREAK

A gripping thriller full of suspense

(TITAN TRILOGY BOOK 3)

T.J. BREARTON

Published 2017 by Joffe Books, London.

www.joffebooks.com

© T.J. Brearton

ISBN-13: 978-1-912106-44-8

For my wife.

PROLOGUE / SIX MONTHS AGO

She said life with an addict was like living with a time bomb. For some reason this was what Brendan was thinking as he felt the gouge of the knee in his back, the hand clamped over his neck, pressing his face into the ground. You never knew when the addict was going to show up at the back door in the middle of the night reeking of booze, you couldn't be prepared for when their temper snapped and the poison forked out.

That was what Angie had said, years ago, when they were married.

And while it may have been true, what went unseen was the suffering beneath the defensive actions of the addict. The pain that led up to the breaking point. Because he kept it hidden. He hid it so well sometimes he lost it himself.

Which was the idea.

Cue, routine, reward. The basic equation of the habit. The formula that these animals in prison, these murderers and thieves on top of him, would never know about. They were mercifully free of introspection, most of them. Running on the three primary drives of the human

1

condition: avoid pain, conserve energy, and pursue pleasure.

It was that last one that had them all hopped-up on neurotransmitters at the moment, the addictive release of peptides from their throbbing, massive prison-inmate glands washing through the cells of their body, washing through the cells of the state penitentiary, sucked up by the furious, deprived eyes of the cons clanging in their cages as they watched the fight taking place in the middle of Motchan Center.

The guards will come any second now. They'll break up the fight.

Some time ago, back before he'd lost his wife and child, back before nearly completing his own suicide, long before Rebecca Heilshorn was found dead in a farmhouse and was alive and turning tricks as a high-priced escort, Brendan might have believed his own desperate mind. The guards — who hated to be called guards, never call them guards to their faces — would rush in and take these three throbbing thugs piling on top of Brendan and throw them to the corners of the room, and punish them. Prison wasn't as bad as the rumors, right? It wasn't like the way it was in the movies; that was sensationalized. Prison was a part of the justice system, and there was oversight and responsible people and the rest was a bunch of hype.

Tell that to the guy shouting in Brendan's ear, his full weight on Brendan's back, making it impossible to breathe. *Go ahead and tell him. Before he snaps my spine.*

"How's that feel? Huh? You wanna dance on the blacktop? You little terrorist bitch? Feel good?"

No. It didn't feel good. It felt like a ton of molten lead had been poured over him and was hardening there, and he would be forever flattened to the ground. The air was crushed out of his lungs. If he could speak, he would tell them what he had already told them, that he wasn't a terrorist, he wasn't a traitor to his country; that this was an ugly rumor probably started by someone in the jail who was paid to start it. That the people who put him here wanted him to suffer every kind of torture.

Probably the guards had been instructed to stand down. There was no one coming to help him. For that matter, there was no Seamus Argon to yank him out of the garage, pull him from the cloud of carbon monoxide. No Rudy Colinas to rush in with the State Police and save his life moments before it ended.

In here, he was on his own.

Brendan flexed every muscle in his body. He used his chest and his chin and his knees, and tried to buck the terribly large convict on top of him. It didn't do any good. The other two cons were working on his shoes; he could feel a tug and one of them — Velcro-fastened — popped off his foot. Then the other. A second later and they were pulling off the bottom half of his green fatigues.

Were they going to rape him? He couldn't imagine they would do such a thing right here, right in front of the whole block. Even perverted sex acts in prison were usually done with a little more privacy than this. If you were lucky, you got a meal first.

"You like that, cho-mo? Is this what you liked to do to them little kiddies? All you terrorists like them little kiddies . . ."

Brendan tried to speak. His face was mashed into the ground, his pancaked cheek interfering with his speech, but he managed to draw a thin breath as the weight on top of him shifted. "I never hurt a child." It came out: *I nee-ah hoot a shy.* He realized as he spoke that his mouth was bleeding. A quick flick of the tongue revealed a blank spot in his teeth. One of his molars had been knocked out.

"Yeah," the convict cooed. "Yeah, you liked that, *inmate.*"

His shoes gone, his pants gone, all that was left was his underwear.

* * *

3

Baker, one of the newer corrections officers who'd started after Brendan began his time, came jogging into the open area amid the cacophony of hoots and catcalls from the cell soldiers. As he did, two other guards suddenly appeared, as if some invisible force holding them at bay had at last released them.

They pulled the three men from Brendan and got him on his feet. Brendan bent and pulled his pants up, his entire body shaking, but feeling incredible relief. As Baker hauled him away from the scene, Brendan turned and looked back at the aggressors. The inmates watched him go; the guards who had suddenly materialized watched him too, their expressions not much different. Mocking.

"The Deputy Warden wants to see you," Baker said as he hustled Brendan away.

* * *

"You've been here three weeks," Deputy Warden Grimm said. Grimm was in his sixties and had a face to match his name.

"That's correct, sir."

"Came in on November nineteenth."

"Yes, sir."

They were in Grimm's office. The space looked like the inside of a giant locker, with thick paint slabbed on slate-gray walls and an equally gray popcorn ceiling. There were three sets of file cabinets, a coffee percolator that looked a decade old, and a dying fern slumped in the corner. The one window in the room overlooked the Rikers Island complex through bars. The Deputy Warden had Brendan's file splayed out on his desk in front of him.

Grimm watched Brendan for a moment and then his eyes dropped to the papers in front of him. "You're in here, still pending trial for first-degree murder." His eyes rolled up. "Why are the other inmates saying you're a nonce? Was there a kid involved?"

"I don't know why they're saying what they are."

4

Grimm gave Brendan a hard look. "I think you do."

"Sir?"

"I've heard about you. You have some story about how the government is messing with you. Drawing out your trial, keeping you here, making you sweat."

Brendan said nothing.

"I don't like that," Grimm said. "I don't like that at all. That's what terrorists do, that's where uprisings come from, everybody going against their government. It's scumbag shit and I won't tolerate it. You can be sure of that."

Brendan didn't argue. Better to let the man talk, say his piece. He still felt the cold shock of his assault. The convicts of Motchan Center had been shuffling back from jug-up. As the men were filing up the stairs and returning to their cells, one of the aggressors had tapped Brendan on the shoulder and started to talk to him. His name was Tony Laruso. He was built like a truck, Italian, from the Bronx, and had been a gang member since he was a boy. Brendan had been managing to keep a low profile, though he'd heard the rumors that he was a domestic terrorist; conjecture ranging from how he'd tried to blow up a hospital in Manhattan with babies in the building to how he was an assassin hired to kill a prominent, do-gooder doctor. He'd never found the source of the rumors, and rumors had been all they were, whispers and hard stares and cold shoulders, until Laruso.

Laruso had come in just last week. Brendan had overhead Laruso say to another inmate that he was only in for a short nap. He had been hit with a slew of racketeering charges, a medley of identity theft, fake IDs, passports and credit card fraud. In the cafeteria, he asked Brendan about his offense. Brendan didn't know everything about jail etiquette, but you certainly didn't talk openly about your crime, especially if you thought you'd gotten a bad beef, no matter what lies were told about you. So Brendan just said, "It's complicated," and Laruso had replied, "I don't see nothin' complicated about being a baby-killing fuckin' terrorist."

By the time Brendan had noticed that the rest of the cons were entering their cells, and the guards were looking over their shoulders as they disappeared, it was too late to get away, too late to do anything to save himself.

"I haven't met with my lawyer for a while," Brendan said to Grimm. "So I'm not updated on my case, sir."

"Guy probably came to his senses and left." Again, Grimm fixed Brendan with a look that suggested Brendan was more than just a burden, an unpleasant part of the Deputy Warden's job, but a brush with complete filth. "Listen to me. I looked at your jacket. You copped to the whole thing."

"Yes, sir."

Grimm exhaled in frustration, sat back and rubbed his face for a moment, regarding Brendan with that same dull hatred.

"It's not good what happened to you today, is it?"

Brendan looked back, unblinking. "No."

"I didn't think so; I didn't take you for a puff tart. You're an educated man, with a background in law enforcement. So you can appreciate when I tell you that this jail complex has an annual operating budget of eight hundred and seventy-five million. Holy shit, yeah? I've got a staff of nine thousand officers and fourteen hundred civilians to control an inmate population of thirteen thousand. Know how much we spend on each inmate annually?"

Brendan shook his head. He suddenly felt very far away from everything, as alone and adrift as the first night the cell door had slammed shut.

"One hundred and seventy thousand dollars. That's right. Per inmate. Each year. A lot of people to be responsible for, and at quite a cost, don't you think?" Grimm was in the habit of asking rhetorical questions. "Not only that, but we've got inmates serving sentences for up to one year, guys like Laruso, the one who was on top of you in the commons. We've got many men here pending transfer to another facility. And we've got men like you, awaiting trial, not granted bail by the judge. You're just sitting here, your trial gummed up in bureaucratic bullshit. Costing me money, and your beef is going to take its sweet time getting to trial. You know what? You piss me off, Healy."

Brendan felt a quick jolt in his stomach. He'd been keyed-up since the attack, the adrenaline still squeezing his heart, but with Grimm's comment about being pissed off, he went from feeling tense and racy to a kind of nervous excited. The guards were being manipulated by the Deputy Warden. He suddenly felt sure that even if Grimm were getting pressure from outside the prison to make Brendan's life hard — with Staryles behind it — something in Grimm's demeanor read like he had his own demons pursuing him. Something other than the weight thrown by the CSS. Brendan felt the first small ray of hope, a dangerous thing to have in a place like Rikers.

Grimm was watching him. "You know, used to be that only the most hardened and dangerous criminals got sent up. But these days we got pansy first-time offenders doing mandatory terms . . . and with so many incarcerated in general — Jesus, over 1.6 million in the US — normally they luck out without encountering real violence. But Rikers is an older institution, not phased out yet, lot of traffic, lots of flux. It's the northeast Chain Gang. I want you to remember that, Healy."

His last sentence seemed to hang in the small room, as if inviting Brendan to challenge it.

Brendan nodded, and licked his dry lips. He was thirsty. His body was sore, his lower back aching from having Laruso on top of him, breathing into his ear. *You like that, cho-mo? Is this what you liked to do to them little kiddies?*

"You gotta get cleaned up," Grimm said with an air of distaste. "Anyone from the outside, your lawyer, that

Kendall detective from your beef, you tell them you slipped in the shower. Something. But what you're not going to say is what happened to you this afternoon. Are we clear?"

"We're clear."

Grimm continued to clock him, hunting for any signs of bullshit. He was staring at Brendan so directly that Brendan started to feel self-conscious. The man's lips parted. He took a breath. His eyes were cold, calculating. "As a former cop, you know how tough it is . . ."

The pause at the end of Grimm's statement demanded an affirmation.

"Yes."

"You know that you're around the criminal element so much of your life. It can mess with you. It can change you, right? It changes most people."

Brendan nodded. Something was happening, something was coming.

"You've got to do what you've got to do. You have to survive." Grimm tapped the side of his head. Brendan noticed the man's hands were like paws, the knuckles swollen, the fingers thick and calloused. "I've been part of the New York Department of Corrections for twenty-seven years. Heard it all. You, Healy, you're going to stop this bullshit about how you got a bad break, about how some ridiculous conspiracy got you where you are. You hear me? The only thing that got you where you are is you. Your actions. That's all you have. Action."

Grimm tented his large fingers on the desk in front of him, and struck a sage pose, as if he were the chaplain and not the disciplinary officer and had just dispensed some wisdom. He turned and gazed out the barred window. He was silent for so long that Brendan started to think that there was no pitch, no opportunity or ray of hope, he'd been mistaken, this was just some sordid display of power, some pointless sermon. Then Grimm's head slowly swiveled back, and his gaze bored back in.

"So now, the action you can choose, is to help me. You see what I mean?"

"Help you . . ."

Grimm's face twitched, the upper lip curling ever so slightly into a sneer, as if the word *help* created more bad taste in his mouth. "Shut up," he said, "and listen."

Brendan was quiet. He listened. If anything, it was good just to be out of Motchan Center for a little while.

"We're the second largest jail system in America," Grimm said, "and we're being investigated."

Brendan raised his eyebrows, but stayed quiet.

"Let's just say the New York City Department of Investigation has been looking into us for matters of violence and other illegal conduct. It's shaping up to be a massive probe, an unprecedented joint, tactical search and operation. I've got so much pressure on me from the Commissioner and Corrections Commissioner right now, it makes Laruso look like your girlfriend lying on top of you in the park. I'm talking serious pressure. And I'm not going to go out like this. I've got two years until retirement on full pension. My wife and I are moving far, far away from here. I've been looking out over this island for too many years. Decades. And I can't have it all come down around my ears at the last second, just before I get free. Because one thing about those of us who work in the jail system, Brendan; we're in here, too. We're caged, just like you."

Brendan cleared his throat. "What can I do for you?"

CHAPTER ONE / TUESDAY, 8:58 AM

Jennifer Aiken took the stage in the Robert F. Kennedy building and everybody clapped. The auditorium seated over a thousand people with a main floor and the mezzanine. There were just about fifty people present but their enthusiasm made it feel like a stadium. She walked to the center of the stage and stood at the glass podium. She smiled at the group and felt generally good that she was at last back in DC, but it was hard to feel like a whole person. She'd lost something, and she knew it, and she wasn't sure she'd ever be able to get it back. Innocence wasn't exactly the right word, she thought, but it was close.

Three weeks in a hospital in New York. Three months of convalescing and physical therapy followed by a month of preparation and then two months in courtrooms and in offices with walls of glass overlooking the city. It was uncomfortable, at times, being that high up, and she wondered if she'd be forever scared of heights.

Back in the offices of the Justice Department — which smelled perpetually of new carpet, ink toner and perfume, washing her in nostalgia — Jennifer had prepared her presentation. She felt like she'd had to rebuild the XList case from near scratch. For two weeks, she'd had a small entourage with her, a gathering of assistants buzzing around. When she went somewhere it was in a veritable motorcade, with her own driver, bodyguards, lead and follow cars. The Attorney General was taking no chances with her; they said she was to be prized and protected.

Not for their lack of trying, Jennifer didn't feel prized. She felt older, she often felt tired, and part of her dreamed of faraway places. Places like Cotuit Bay in the summer, with its ivory stucco buildings and crushed shell walkways spread out beneath the overturned bowl of blue sky.

It seemed hopelessly beyond reach.

"Hello everybody, I'm Jennifer Aiken, special prosecutor with the Human Trafficking Prosecution Unit."

They had gathered near the front, an even split of men and women, all wearing sterling but conservative ensembles, average age about forty-five. As Jennifer surveyed them, a man in a dark suit stepped into the room through the back door, and leaned against the wall and watched her from beneath the mezzanine. She looked away from him, momentarily flustered.

"Let's get started." She used the clicker to call up the first slide. Jennifer's laptop was wirelessly linked to a projector hanging in the middle of the room. When she pressed the button a face appeared on the screen: pretty, with strawberry blonde hair, and a light constellation of freckles.

Rebecca Heilshorn loomed over them, her eyes filled with pain, her lips forming a sham smile. Standing on the stage, Jennifer's body was about the size of Rebecca's nose. The image had been cropped from a professional photograph, the kind still taken at a few department stores in rural areas. It had once stood proudly framed in Rebecca's house in the country. Jennifer had pulled it from the files.

"This is Rebecca Heilshorn, murdered at age twenty-seven."

She clicked the button and the image changed to a different young woman: dirty-blonde hair, sharp cheekbones and a square jaw. Beautiful, but tough.

"This is Sloane Dewan, twenty-eight, and quite the survival story."

Another click.

"And this is a woman named Lana Mazursky. Whereabouts unknown."

A third pretty face commanded the screen. Mazursky had an equally square shape to her features, while still feminine. Large eyes, dark hair pulled back with strands twirling around her ears. The more Jennifer looked at them, the more she saw how much Mazursky looked like her daughter.

She advanced to a slide which paired the faces of Sloane Dewan and Lana Mazursky side by side. "Lana is Sloane's mother."

Mother was the operative word. She imagined the scene as she'd pieced it together: a young Mazursky writhing in an alleyway as the rain poured down, giving birth. Seamus Argon later darkening the mouth of the alley when he heard the abandoned infant's cries coming from a storm drain.

She gripped the podium with both hands again and gazed out over the expectant faces of the crowd. "These three woman have something in common. In unique ways, they're each a part of the black market prostitution ring called XList. Lana there at the beginning, Rebecca in the middle of it, and Sloane a product of it. In my investigation, which started over a year ago, and which I recently resumed, I traced the evolution of XList from its origins to what it is now, a massive black market in the United States and into Canada and Mexico."

Jennifer observed the man standing at the back. He pointed a finger at the door, and then turned and let himself out.

* * *

She studied him as he sat across from her in the back of the large SUV. The driver whisked them away down Pennsylvania Avenue, leaving behind the squat, gray Justice Department headquarters.

"I thought we were meeting later today," she said. "You stalking me? Checking up?"

"Been a long time," Rascher said. "That was a good presentation. Sorry I couldn't stay to the end."

She looked out the window as they sped down Ninth Street.

He tilted his head to the side, sympathy working its way into his eyes. "How are you feeling?"

She looked at him, perhaps too quickly, her gaze too sharp. She realized some part of her would have loved to boot him out the door and watch his body bounce down the road. Maybe get run over by one of the huge tourist buses circling the Smithsonian.

"I'm fine," she said, debating on whether to say any more. If she should tell him how hard it had been since that day in Manhattan. That despite everyone's sympathetic smiles, three different specialists and a physical therapist, she still dreamed of Jeremy Staryles at night. Or Agent Apollo, taking his own life in front of her.

No, she concluded that the simple *I'm fine* was sufficient.

"Jen, you've really pulled it together. And after all you've been through. It's remarkable."

"What I've been through? What about what they've been through? Sloane Dewan. Lana Mazursky. Heilshorn's daughter. Brendan Healy." She raised her eyebrows on the last name. "He's the main reason I'm even alive right now." She wanted to say more but held off. *Why wasn't I protected? Why wasn't I told the FBI was going to play possum while the Justice Department sent me into the lion's den?*

Rascher looked at her like he was reading her thoughts. She felt irritated, as if it somehow made her a transparent person. She decided instead it was because she and John had spent three years together in law school. And that, like it or not, people didn't really change. She thought she'd bring that up if the situation called for it. Surely John thought he'd come a long way and had changed since those days. Didn't everyone think that?

"Hey listen," he said in a voice she recognized. It was the same voice he would use after his temper flared and he'd yell and berate her, all the while telling her he was challenging her to become a more astute observer, a more critical thinker. A better person. She rested in the idea that men like him were a dying breed. That was harsh, she knew it was harsh — probably harsher than imagining him kicked out of a moving vehicle — but she couldn't help it.

"Listen," he said again, and shifted his weight. *Dear God, he's going to put a hand on my knee.* But he didn't. He said, "I stepped in because I had to. You have been in no condition. No one faults you for that. But there's no sense in . . . I just don't want you to think that way, that you're always on approval now."

"Of course I think that. It's true."

"Can we bury this thing between us?"

"That's got nothing to do with anything."

"If this is a conflict, us working together on this, we need to address that now."

"It's not a conflict."

The problem is that in seven months you've done nothing with my task force except tell me to hold tight, she thought.

He raised his eyebrows at her. His irises sparkled a royal blue. His hair had thinned out, though, and this gave her some small satisfaction.

She wondered if she was being irrational. Overly negative. She chalked it up to the morning's talk. She never

14

much cared for getting up in front of people to speak. It had a way of desiccating her, her throat scraping through the words. And her headache had teeth in it. She needed to take one of her pills.

"Let's forget it," she said of their personal history.

He sat back and looked out the window, as if disappointed. Ninth Street became the expressway and cut past the Department of Homeland Security. It was all here. One building after the other in mostly off-white, tombstone gray, or pale, ecru colors. The curved architecture of the Housing and Development building in L'Enfant Plaza, the red brick of the Smithsonian Castle against the bright morning sky. And then they shot beneath the 750 Building, amber lights of the short tunnel flashing past like a strobe. Was he expecting something else from her? Some gushing about how great it was to have him back in her life? If so, it pissed her off. She couldn't hold back any longer.

"What I want to know," she said, "is how much you knew, how much anyone knew, of what was going on when I got sent up to New York to look into Alexander Heilshorn."

His eyelids flew back in a *Who, me?* expression. "Jen, you know that my hands were completely tied. I was only dialed-in to a small part of what was going on, and that was what I'd been doing for five years, and that was human trafficking, on my own cases. We'd barely shared a phone call in ten years until this happened. Anyway, what did we even have that would've suggested a link between Heilshorn and XList?"

"What did we have? We had the Oneida County Sheriff's Department murder investigation. If we didn't think there was any connection, then how — or why — was I privy to personnel files on ex-special forces like Ewon Parnell and Ursula Galloway?" She could see Parnell as he stood in front of her, the 9mm in her face, nothing in his eyes but her own ragged self, reflecting back at her.

Agent Apollo. *Apollo Helios, God of plagues.* He'd turned the gun on himself. *Boom.* The shot echoed in her mind.

"That was a mistake," Rascher said. "Wyn Weston was all over the place with his research . . ."

"I was working a whole other case and I didn't even know it. I knew *something*, John, I knew that Heilshorn was into something even dirtier than money laundering, and that it has to do with where Titan's money is going. But every question I've asked since then has been shut down."

The mention of Titan seemed to suck the posturing right out of John Rascher. It would have been enjoyable to see, if she hadn't felt the awful presence of it, too. Suddenly the roomy SUV felt claustrophobic, and she reached over and opened the window beside her as the tunnel flushed them out and back into the bright day.

They were both silent until she spoke. "I feel like I got hung out as bait."

"No," he said immediately, as if he'd been anticipating the remark. And he leaned forward and this time he did put his hand on her knee. She could smell the cologne he wore — *Christian Dior* — same as he'd worn in college. She glanced at his hand and he took it away. She dipped her head toward him and bared her teeth. "Hung out as bait to see what would come crawling out. And now that we've seen what came out, what are you doing about it?"

He sat back, the leather seat squeaking under his legs. "That's not true, Jennifer, and you know it." For a moment, he couldn't meet her gaze. "But you're right; we did learn some things," he said.

"And it almost cost me my life," she said.

"Well now, come on . . ."

Fuck you, she wanted to shout, but she bit her tongue.

Jennifer leaned over and got her bag. She took out her pills and a bottle of water. She hated the idea of taking them in front of Rascher, even if that was irrational, too, but she couldn't wait any longer. The heat was rising within her, and her hands were starting to shake. As she swallowed she avoided his eyes by looking out the window. They were nearing the townhouse where she'd been staying for the past few years, recently standing at her window and staring out towards the construction of Gangplank Marina which seemed interminable, cranes forever scraping the sky, fences and gates surrounding everything. It felt like an apt metaphor for her life.

She tipped the bottle back and drank some more water. She felt more settled.

The SUV had driven past several blocks of townhouses and now stopped out in front of the ones closest to the Washington Channel, the waterway partially hidden beyond the concrete roadblocks and piles of steel girders.

She put her bottle away in her bag and reached for the door handle. Rascher grabbed her wrist.

She opened her mouth to tell him to let go, but she stopped when she saw the dark look in his eyes. Rascher was all-business now, pleasantries — such as they were — dispensed with. "Jen, there's a chance for you to find out what happened. And it might reveal where Titan's money is going, which is what you seem most interested in—"

"What I'm most interested in, what I have been most interested in, is my *job*. To find out the role Alexander Heilshorn played in XList. To find out who is running it now. How to shut it down."

He held up his hand. "It involves a domestic terrorist threat. A major one."

She stared at him. She knew how his mind worked, how careful he'd been to deliver the news in such a way for maximum impact. But she was intrigued. "Okay. Where's it coming from? Titan? Why would a giant multinational company fund domestic terrorism?"

He let go of her wrist and sat back. "We're not sure. It's complicated. The point is, let's get to the bottom of it before something bad happens."

She held his gaze for a moment, then took her hand away from the door handle. "First of all," she said, "we're not a counter-terrorism group. So you're obviously leaning hard towards something already, and that's why you're here. We're not spit-balling for old time's sake; you want to recruit me for some dirty work. Fine. But I find it very interesting how I'd be any help illuminating a terrorist threat when all I've gotten from the FBI and my own Department over the past half a year — particularly when it comes to Titan — are sympathetic looks and instructions to chase my own tail until further notice. What could I possibly do for you?"

He folded his hands on his lap. His eyes retained that intent look. "The Justice Department and the FBI have been asked to work together with the Department of Defense on this. And there's a Senate Select Intelligence Committee meeting in a week. This is big, Jen. What we're looking at is Titan possibly channeling some XList revenue into a group called Nonsystem. They're a revolutionary group. Libertarian-types. Hackers."

"I've heard of them."

"What we would like — what we feel is the best course to take here — is to smoke them out of hiding so we can see who they are, learn what they are planning, exactly. And since we have some overlap in the players; and you're the biggest proponent of that — Staryles, Argon, Heilshorn — we have a parallel opportunity with the HTPU case on XList."

She thought about this carefully. They were asking her to take part in a sting. Or, at least, find an in for a sting through her XList investigation. But Staryles was elusive, and Argon and Heilshorn were dead. Titan was massive and multifaceted. Money flowed from Titan into rat-holes where it disappeared, offshore accounts gobbled it up, slush funds, shell companies; it was a chimera. An entity too big to fail, too big to prosecute.

The kind she couldn't resist.

"Alright," she said.

His eyes seemed to clear and his mouth jerked into a tentative smile.

"One condition," she said, halting the smile in its tracks. "I want to bring in Brendan Healy on it."

"Healy? No way."

"He's the one who cracked open the XList case in the first place."

"He's in prison on murder charges. No."

"John, I just spent an hour telling a group of people in a very nice way that we don't know shit about how to take down XList after two years. You want to piggyback this threat on the XList case? Okay. Then I need a jumpstart."

Rascher looked uncomfortable. He turned his head and gazed out the window at Jennifer's housing complex, the marina beyond, white yachts bobbing in the slate blue water. She could sense him calculating. She thought she even caught a whiff of jealousy beneath the fug of his cologne.

"Alright," he said at last. "But there's no way the US AG or the Director are going to agree to that unless Harlan Doherty is there, at least. And I'm sure the New York City District Attorney will be interested — or harangue us if we don't at least notify her. God, Jen."

Fine, she thought. Whatever it took.

She offered a smile and slipped out the door. Before she left the SUV she leaned back in and said, "See you tomorrow."

It was already time to go back to New York.

CHAPTER TWO / FIVE MONTHS AGO

Louis Tremont was a bank robber. Unlike most of the Rikers population, which was pretrial, Tremont was doing six months for a parole violation. He was obese, with dark, glossy skin and hair that sprouted from his ears. He became Brendan's new cellmate when Brendan was transferred to the West Facility, and not by coincidence. Deputy Warden Grimm wanted Brendan and Tremont together.

Tremont said he was going to spend his time inside dropping the extra weight. "When I was on the job," he told Brendan at lunch, "I was in shape, man, positively svelte. I was a smokin' hottie, you hear me?" Tremont was also an avid reader. He claimed he'd read every book on safe-cracking ever written, even though he'd never been a cat burglar and never had to enter a bank safe without assistance from a teller and a key. He also told Brendan that though he hadn't robbed a bank or armored car in more than seven years, he never stopped casing. He cased everything, he said, all the time. And, true to his word, while he sat at the cafeteria table, he seemed to watch the comings and goings of the food line and the kitchen behind it with great interest, computing something in his mind.

The two men sat alone at one end of a cafeteria table. West Facility was sparsely populated compared to Mothcan Center, or any of the other ten buildings on Rikers Island, which were all overflowing.

"What are you doing here, Healy?" Tremont stuck a piece of apple in his mouth and bit down, squirting some of the juice. It was breakfast in the chow hall. Other than apples, there was cereal, toast, milk, coffee and the scrambled eggs that looked like Play-Doh and tasted like mouse shit. "West Facility is for contagious inmates, protective custody, and a few sentenced cons, like me. You're pretrial. What do you got — witness protection?"

Brendan took a piece of toast off his plate, looked at it, and dropped it back down. No one was supposed to know what Brendan was doing for Grimm, not even Tremont. When Brendan didn't respond, Tremont shrugged and picked up another slice of apple. There were wet-smacking sounds as he popped it into his large mouth and gobbled it down. He said, "I heard of you, you know."

Brendan raised his eyebrows. He decided at least the tea was tolerable and he took a sip. It had stayed warm because the chow hall was probably ninety degrees with the heat blasting. Tremont was sweating, runlets coming down the stubbly sides of his wide face. Now the large man nodded his head. "Yup. You held some big league doctor at gun point last year. Ran through a hospital, turning the place upside down; had practically the whole NYPD come looking to blow your porch light. Amazed you made it out of there alive."

They weren't the only ones after me, Brendan thought.

He got to the point. "What do you know about what's coming in to Rikers? Chieva, tina, amidone, bug juice, any of it."

"That's an awfully coppish question," Tremont said, sucking the juice from his fingers now. "You still on the job in here? What're you, on the bumper for Grimm? What're you getting?"

That hadn't taken long.

"Maybe I just want a taste," Brendan said.

Tremont's eyebrows raised again, ridges of skin cutting through his forehead deep enough to jam slices of the apple. "You? Nah. You ain't a drinker or a drugger. Your eyes are too clear. Bet you used to be, though."

"Probably three quarters of the population of Rikers are ex-users. I'm curious about the people who are still using while they're in here."

Tremont took some more apple from his plate, playfully, pinching a slice, like Gulliver holding up a Lilliputian. He tossed his in his mouth, sat back, chewed, and looked Brendan over.

"Come on. What did they do in that movie? The one with Jodie Foster. 'Quid pro quo,' baby. Feed my brain. You were a druggie? Or a drunk. I'm thinking a drunk. The odds are good, but the goods are odd, right? You got that Irish hothead thing in you, I can see it. Mixed in with the Italian fuckin' attitude." Tremont started to laugh. They had one half of a long table to themselves, but he was drawing looks from the other end, and surrounding convicts. "Boy, didn't you get a nice mix, huh? Probably can't keep a relationship for shit, either. Keeps em guessing, though, huh? I bet you got a lot of tail on the outside. I bet you got one waiting for you . . ."

"I was studying neuroscience before I became a cop," Brendan said, to shut Tremont up. "Yes, I'm an alcoholic." The more he could throw at Tremont and redirect the big man's attention from Brendan's motives, the better.

Tremont absorbed the information silently. His expression sobered up and he leaned forward, put his elbows on the table, took a napkin, and started cleaning the sticky apple juice from his fingers.

"Science, huh? Thing with the sciences," he said, "it's like being a cop in a weird way. Right? Because with either of these things, when you look for explanations, you look for things that are never too complex. There's no great mystery; nature vies with itself, so does the street. And just like there's no sweet old man, no god behind nature, there's no mastermind, no arch-criminal behind crime. If you got a dead body and you think your little old lady neighbor did it, then she probably did."

"Sounds about right, I guess." Brendan pushed his tray away and gazed across the table at Tremont.

Tremont was enjoying himself. Brendan waited patiently, but the garrulous, bank-robbing convict wasn't through.

"I heard rumors."

"Oh yeah?"

"Yeah. That you're in here because of the CSS."

Brendan felt a sudden chill despite the cloying heat. He was instantly angry with himself, tired of feeling this way.

"I find that intriguing."

"Good for you." Brendan pulled his tray back to himself, and made ready to leave. Maybe now wasn't the time to work Tremont. It was going the wrong way.

"I mean, for one thing, it's the fucking Central Security Service. Not every day you meet a detainee who agrees, you know, nature and crime are simple, there are no great conspiracies, and it's the Central Security Service put him here."

Brendan's eyes cut over to a Corrections Officer walking around the room. He couldn't help feeling anxious the way he and Tremont were talking. This had been a bad idea. If Tremont knew anything about the drugs moving through the prison, he was going to be an ass about it. It was the wrong venue for such a discussion, anyway; they were surrounded by other convicts, any one of them could be tuning in.

After fondling it forever, Tremont popped the last slice of fruit in his mouth and talked around the white juicy flashes of the apple. "What do I get?"

"Huh?"

"You want me to tell you what I seen. What I know. I'm askin', it's the only question anyone asks, really — what's in it for me?"

Healy stared at Tremont. He could feel his pulse elevating. "If I gotta tell you, then it isn't worth it."

Tremont tossed his head back and laughed like a bullfrog, his neck throbbing in and out. He slapped his hands together, hands both thick and nimble-fingered. A safe-cracker's grip, though he claimed he never laid a hand on a combination lock. "That's rich. That's juicy. What're you, a bleeding heart? You gonna ply me with social justice concerns?" He grew straight-faced and angled his sweaty forehead at Brendan. "Yeah, the Left is always going on about social concerns. Meanwhile, the Right says, 'Okay . . . but how you gonna pay for that?' That's what I'm asking, Healy. Pay to play."

Brendan's teeth were on edge. When he spoke his lips barely moved. "Tell you what, Tremont. Like you figured, I was a cop. But I wonder if you know something."

He held up his hand. His fingers were long and slender, unlike Tremont's. "According to the Department of Justice, if you're missing any of these, you go on the terrorist watch-list." Brendan wriggled the three fingers he had left.

Tremont swallowed the apple. He knuckled down onto the table, leaned forward, pressing into it with his large belly. He got an eyeful of Brendan's hand, inadvertently bumped his silverware, which bounced out of his tray and clattered onto the ground. The convicts near them frowned and drew inward.

Tremont spoke in a low voice now. "You're the one they said was a terrorist."

Brendan stared across the table. He lowered his hand. "Yeah," he said. "That's me."

* * *

Their shared cell was eight feet wide by ten feet long. They had a small steel sink, a steel toilet, and a desktop that could be folded up into the wall. There was one chair, and one set of bunk beds. Convicts referred to their bed as a Cadillac. Tremont was on the bottom, Brendan on the top.

"Alright," said Tremont. "What do you want to know?"

Brendan was on his back, hands on his chest, looking up at the ceiling. He was silent for a moment, feeling a wave of relief. He'd gambled with that little bit of drama in the cafeteria, hoping to push the right buttons with Tremont. It had worked. In years of things mostly not-working, it was a small victory. "I've seen how you look around this place," he said to Tremont.

He could feel Tremont adjust himself on the lower bunk and again the whole apparatus shook with the man's movements. Brendan continued in a low whisper. "You're always watching, right? When you're not obsessing about your prison diet. You know there are drugs here, you know how they're getting in."

"I like you, Healy."

"Stay on your bunk."

Tremont laughed. "Inmates want drugs, and COs profit from the trafficking. It's a no-brainer. Some COs are paid to look the other way, to gloss over the cavity searches on new inmates smuggling things in, in dark places, if you know what I mean. Other COs are bolder; they come right in on the ferry, driving the shit in, in their personal vehicles."

"Where does it go when it gets here?"

"Alright." There was a tremendous quaking as Tremont got off the bunk bed. He moved across the small dark space and sat in the single chair. Brendan looked down at him, half of the man's heavy face limned in the corridor lights, points of it glinting in his eyes. "There are common areas that are staging points for sale and distribution. Like the guard locker rooms. And in the chow hall. There's stuff that comes in, in the food trucks, which goes right into the kitchen and is distributed from there."

"How would that work?"

"Prison food is from corporations like Sodexo, or it's military surplus. My last celly spent three months working in the kitchen. He told me about boxes labeled 'for institutional use only,' labeled, 'not for human consumption,' and 'Desert Storm.'"

"You're kidding."

"Nah. I've seen a whole day in here go to shit after everyone got sick from the chicken. Boxes labeled 'beef tongue' ain't much better. Sometimes we get special meals, that's what they call them. But I've always noticed the pigeon population decreases right after one of these 'special meals.'" Tremont started laughing again.

"Shh," said Brendan, glancing out into the corridor. "Now you're messing with me."

"Am I? Okay, I don't know about the pigeons, but everything else is true. Like you said, I'm obsessed."

"Desert Storm? That was over twenty years ago."

"Doesn't mean a thing. There are DOC food service administrators all over the country under investigation for taking kickbacks to accept outdated food. At least three people I know of have been indicted by the feds. But that was years ago. Anyway, before Gallo walked out of here, that's my old celly, he told me he saw the other stuff coming in. So, I watch. I sit at jug-up and I watch, see if I can see anything. And then you show up, and start asking your questions."

"The contraband."

"Right. You watch close enough, you'll see guards come and scoop up certain boxes whose content never made its way onto the food trays. That's probably the biggest pipeline."

Brendan soaked this in. Tremont had just given him what could be very helpful information.

Tremont seemed to rest after the disclosure, his eyes shining faintly.

"It's a cottage industry," he said quietly, as if to himself. "You got forty percent of Rikers inmates diagnosed with mental health disorders; guys come in addicted to drugs. Like you said. But, then you gotta deal with all this shit. Monotony, isolation, aggression, overpopulation. The correction system ain't equipped. So you've got stressed-out guards going crazy. Deputy Warden losing his mind."

"I have a hard time feeling bad for the Deputy Warden."

"Yeah. No shit. Want to hear about Grimm? Okay, not long ago an inmate poisoned himself with disinfectant — it was being used to treat cells after a raw sewage back up — be glad you missed that one. They knew he was taking the disinfectant, and a guard told Grimm, and Grimm said, and I quote, 'Don't bother me if you have live breathing bodies. You only come to me if you have an extraction, or if you got a dead body.'" Tremont's eyes flared white as more light caught them. "You believe that shit? The medical examiner ruled the death a homicide, citing negligence. Denial of medical care. Now Grimm's got that hanging over his head. Not to mention the city suit a guy filed for getting the shit beat out of him by two guards. Ass kicked so bad he's got fused vertebrae and a plate in his neck. Dumbass gets himself thrown back in jail because of a parole violation."

"Here?"

"Yeah, he's in the RNDC. Other side of the island."

"Not protective custody?"

"Nope," said Tremont. He turned his head to look out into the corridor. Brendan heard the noise; a CO was

27

on his way, making rounds. They had to end the conversation.

"So Grimm has more than a single problem."

Tremont grunted. "One strike of a match could burn him down entirely."

CHAPTER THREE / WEDNESDAY, 11:12 AM

The plane flew into LaGuardia airport. As it banked to land, Jennifer could see Rikers Island out the window. Rikers was New York City's main jail complex. It was on a four-hundred-acre island in the East River, between Queens and the Bronx. The flat land mass was green and brown, strapped with roads and parking lots, populated with white, X-shaped buildings that looked like targets. As the plane's tires barked against the macadam Jennifer realized she was gripping the arms of the seat hard enough to turn her knuckles white.

They left the airport in a convoy— three SUVs and two NYPD escorts; a lead and a follow car. They drove up 81st street and onto 19th Ave. As they turned towards the bridge which spanned Queens and Rikers Island, she found herself wishing the drive was longer. The sign on the road leading to the bridge read: *City of New York Correction Department. Rikers Island. Home of New York's Boldest.* It suddenly felt like it was all happening too fast.

She realized her anxiety was caused by a sense of guilt. It had been seven months since Brendan Healy had made the call to the authorities which had resulted in the FBI busting down the door to the room where she'd been held captive. Recovering from her injuries in the hospital, she'd vowed to see Healy right away. To thank him. To help him. But the time had never come. And the Justice Department and the FBI had warned her off a visit.

The train of vehicles crossed the bridge. Jennifer looked out over the choppy waters of Bowery Bay. John Rascher told her that, for a time, Healy had acted delusional, spewing conspiracy theories about the government. Wild conjecture to the New York Police that the CSS was somehow involved in the black markets, the private equity firm Titan, and working with Heilshorn himself. But then, suddenly, Healy had "dropped the act," and took back any accusations.

Rascher concluded that Healy had deep-seated issues. This whole thing was a shot in the dark.

They closed in on Rikers Island. The buildings seeming to grow in the windshield as the caravan of feds and cops crossed the bridge. On the other side, they passed through a massive parking area and came to a stop at the entry gate. The guards gave everyone's credentials a cursory look. In a short time, they were waved through. Jennifer felt her stomach lurch as the gate lifted and the vehicles continued their march along Hazen Street, further into the massive complex.

It was like its own city, in some apocalyptic vision of the future. They said it was the world's largest penal colony, a prison compound of drab, colorless buildings. In a strange way, it wasn't much different from DC, if it hadn't been for the endless coils of razor wire.

They turned into the lot for Mothcan Center and at last the vehicles came to a rest. The group of federal agents and city cops milled around in the parking area for a moment. Detective Kendall, who'd been on the Alexander Heilshorn murder case since day one, lit a cigarette. The New York DA had sent him and another NYPD detective to audit. She liked Kendall well enough; he seemed to have his head on straight. He caught her looking at him and smiled. Feeling the blood rise to her cheeks, she looked away towards where Rascher was standing with Harlan Doherty, from the FBI. She approached them.

"I need to see Healy alone."

"Not going to happen," Doherty said. The summer day was warm and bright, the sun directly overhead, draping Doherty's face in deep shadows around his squinty eyes and beneath his handlebar mustache. Since Doherty had met them at the airport, he'd assumed command of the situation. He was a big man, broad shouldered, looked like he could've been in a biker gang in another life.

Rascher was studying her, giving her a skeptical look. "Why?"

"Come on, this is my thing," she said, focusing only on Rascher and trying to ignore Doherty's ill-concealed look of contempt. "Healy's been in there, pretrial, for seven months. It changes people; waiting, incarceration. This calls for a friendly face, not an overwhelming gang of cops." She glanced at Doherty. "No offense."

Rascher continued to stare at her, as if trying to pry loose some underlying motive. He was the same way he'd been in college, she thought; at once possessive and emotionally unavailable. She knew he was thinking this had to do with some romanticized notion she had of Healy. But he had to know she was right, and not just because she'd studied penology as an undergrad. You couldn't just steamroll a guy who'd been in jail for this long with half a dozen cops and expect to get good results. Healy would've learned to be careful in there. He would be on the defensive. It didn't matter who a person was on the outside, it happened. It was survival. And the nicest fell the hardest, once the doors slammed home. They changed the most.

"A human-to-human talk," Doherty muttered, off to the side. "There's a national threat we're concerned with, here, Agent Aiken."

"I know that," she said. "Which is why this is critical. Healy doesn't owe us anything."

Doherty broke out in a gravely mirthless laugh. "Jesus," he said, translation: *Get a load of this chick*. She looked into his eyes which were a dull, fingerprint-gray color.

"He owes his country," Doherty said.

She could sense the others; Kendall, smoking and watching them from a few yards away with the other NYPD detective, more uniformed police, looking decidedly out of their depth, gawked around at the buildings, the sky, their feet. The day was mild and breezy, but it felt like a lie. In the air was the scent of men in cages. The bricks and mortar baking under the sun, the odor of metal, of pent-up bodies and aggression.

* * *

After they passed through the security checkpoint with the metal detectors and went through several sets of large, steel-piston doors, Doherty fell in astride Jennifer as they were led down the hall by a CO and the Deputy Warden, a man named Grimm. Jennifer noticed the way Doherty walked, his pelvis thrust forward, his shoulders back, swaying side to side. "You get off on this stuff, huh?" he said.

"I'm sorry?"

"Last year. You went to Bedford Women's Facility to speak with the woman who murdered Rebecca Heilshorn. That psycho shrink."

"That's right." She wondered where Doherty was going with this, but he said nothing further. It made her think about the encounter with Olivia Jane. At the end of the Heilshorn murder investigation, once behind bars, Jane had told Brendan Healy that Titan was entwined with the government. It seemed like the feds wanted to throw Brendan into the same padded room as Jane; a criminal crackpot, making desperate claims. So why were they so averse to her seeing him alone?

Ahead of them, Grimm, heavyset, turned to look back at the group following him. Grimm had dark circles beneath his eyes that burnt into his cheeks. He was flanked by two corrections officers. He seemed to be studying the team of law enforcement, as if taking mental pictures. He looked uncomfortable, Jennifer decided. This was his facility, his house, and he was wary of outsiders.

They turned down a corridor and came to a room reserved for special meetings. Jennifer was familiar with these types of rooms. Defense lawyers usually met with their clients in more visible places, either in the visitation center, or sometimes in the cells. The majority of Rikers was pretrial, so there was a lot of legal traffic as inmates awaited their fate. This was a room where defense lawyers caved and prosecutors struck deals, cops interrogated prisoners who sweated under the pressure, seeking ways to end their nightmare. It was equipped with a one-way mirror so that others could look on as the offender was worked over.

The group, composed of Jennifer, Doherty, Rascher, and the two NYPD detectives, filed into the room. Grimm nodded at the CO standing with Jennifer and then he slipped into the viewing room as the CO jangled his keys and opened the main room next door. Everything seemed to echo: the footfalls, the keys, the metal door swinging open. Like it was all happening at the bottom of a well.

There was a long desk, with at least a dozen chairs crowded around. Some of the chairs were different from the rest, the folding-kind brought in to augment the supply in the room. Probably inmates didn't usually meet with six cops all at once, even in rooms like this. The domestic terrorism threat had forged a nexus of law enforcement.

All of the chairs faced the back wall. The one chair for the inmate faced the door. It was just one more prison precaution: keep the prisoner as far from the exit as possible.

Everyone took their seats, no one talked. Jennifer tried to keep her heart rate down; she took long, deep breaths. She envisioned Grimm on the other side of the one-way mirror at the end of the rectangular shaped room watching her, but she didn't look that way. She didn't want to see her reflection.

She rested her eyes, straight ahead, at the back wall. The walls were painted darker than the rest of the prison. The enclosed space smelled of disinfectant, which did not entirely mask the other odors lingering beneath. The acrid tinge of sweat. The stink of bad breath and old coffee. But mostly the smell of concrete, that cool, dank aroma of a cave.

She put her hands in front of her on the table and enfolded the fingers. She was just about to say something to Rascher, break the awkward silence which had descended, when the keys hit the lock behind her. Her heart jumped. The door opened and she was suddenly gripped with fear. Here she'd been thinking that she knew prisons, she felt she understood Healy, yet in that moment one thought crystallized out of all others: she knew nothing.

She wondered if she should turn to look behind her, but she waited. She heard the shuffling of feet and the rattle of chains. These sounds moved around to her right side and then he came into view in her peripheral vision. She turned her head to watch as Brendan Healy shuffled around the table and sat down. His eyes were on her the whole time.

CHAPTER FOUR / WEDNESDAY 1:03 PM

Healy was wearing jail fatigues, institutional green, with INMATE 909896 stenciled on the front and back. He looked bigger than she'd envisioned, more muscular. She'd conjured his appearance from pictures, a few shots gleaned from the media during the Rebecca Heilshorn case, where Healy, appearing reluctant, would be partially hidden behind Lawrence Taber and Ambrose Delaney, the lead investigator. She'd seen earlier pictures taken during his graduate study at NYU Langone in Manhattan, publicity photos for the medical center. In those, Healy had been thin, his eyes often hangover red. He'd dressed in decent suits. Though his ties revealed that he was a bachelor, no wife would choose those colors. Now, his dark hair had been cut short, and he was at least ten pounds heavier than she'd expected, solid on his tall frame. There was a faded purple bruise around his left eye and yellow discoloration along his jaw.

He looked at her across the table, unblinking, his lips pressed into a straight line. He seemed to be waiting for her to make the first move. They all were.

"Hello," she said. Her voice sounded funny to her ears and she cleared her throat. "I'm Jennifer Aiken."

"I know."

Of course he knew. But what other way was there to begin? On the drive to the Island, on the flight in — hell, from the moment she'd first decided to meet with him — Jennifer had thought about what she would say. Any sense of preparedness deserted her now.

"How are you?" she asked.

She watched him calculate a response. It was just something in his eyes, alive and alert, which suggested he was going through some rubric in his mind. He was guarded, of that there was no doubt; but there was more. She felt a renewed pang of guilt. Surely he questioned why it had taken her all this time to come. Or was that self-centered? Maybe he hadn't been thinking about it at all.

"I'm good." His voice was rather toneless. "What can I do for you, Agent Aiken?"

"Well," she began. At the same time she pulled her fingers apart. She realized she had lost feeling in her hands, a strange sensation, and she dropped them to her lap. "First, I want to thank you. You saved my life."

It felt rehearsed, insincere, but it was the best she could do. So much time had passed. "Without you," she said, fumbling a little over the words, "I wouldn't be sitting here right now."

He remained expressionless, cutting through her with that studied glare. She waited for him to respond, but it didn't seem like he was going to. And now she began to feel exasperation. She needed to know why he'd thrown himself under the bus for the Heilshorn murder. Why he seemed to prefer going to prison for the rest of his life rather than any other alternative.

"I'm sure Sloane Dewan thanks you, too," she added.

Now something seemed to ripple his unemotional demeanor. His expression changed and his lips parted slightly. Then he turned his head away.

Jennifer spoke quickly. "Has she been to see you: Sloane?"

"No," he said.

"Probably because your trial is still pending. Your date is in three days. I'm sure her attorney advised her that it would be best not to come. Just as I've had my hands tied, too."

He looked back at her again and just for a moment she felt like she'd used a cheap ploy; she was trying to get herself off her own hook, assuage her own sense of guilt. But he didn't seem to take it that way.

"I told her to stay away," he said. "I wouldn't see her."

"Why?"

Jennifer didn't need a response, and Healy didn't give one. He had confessed to the murder of Alexander Heilshorn, claiming he'd acted alone. He said he'd brought Sloane Dewan with him against her will. Either he feared Sloane would try to get him to change his story, or that seeing her would be too difficult, or both. Jennifer changed the subject.

"You've waived having your own attorney here today."

"Yes."

She took her hands from her lap, lightly gripped the edge of the table and leaned forward a little. "But I can help you, Brendan. I want to help you. I want to make things better for you. Maybe even keep you from trial. Get you out."

"With all due respect, I don't want your help."

"Brendan, you're facing—"

"Thank you, Agent Aiken," Doherty said gruffly, yanking his chair forward closer to the table. He settled his large body and glared at Brendan Healy.

"So here you are," said Doherty. "What a pleasure to finally meet you. I'm sorry to interrupt your banter with our Justice Department Agent, but we have a national crisis here, and you're gonna help us."

Brendan withdrew his hands from the table, chainlinks chattering again. His gaze brushed over the cops, and then landed back on Doherty. He sniffed. "Okay," he said. "I'll try."

Doherty slapped a large file on the table, then clicked on a digital audio recorder he slid over towards Brendan. "Mr. Healy, tell us everything you know about a group called Nonsystem."

Jennifer glanced at the recorder. "Brendan, at any time you decide you'd feel more comfortable with your lawyer here, you let us know."

Doherty shot her a snide look. "We've already established that Mr. Healy has waived his right to counsel." He returned his attention to Brendan. "Besides, we're just talking. One professional to another. Mr. Healy seems to have been up front about everything so far. Right, Mr. Healy?"

Brendan spoke. "I don't know much about them. I think they're something like the Anonymous group. But that their focus is on digital currency. It's not really my field."

"They're hackers," Doherty said, "cyber-terrorists, libertarians, pick your precedent. They specialize in crypto-currency. Know what that is? It's digital currency, virtual currency, that's been concealed. Hidden from the public ledger."

Brendan nodded. "Okay. So they write software to secure digital currency."

"Secure? That's a hell of a way to look at it. We're talking about hiding transactions where people pay for things with bitcoin. Like when they buy drugs online, or hire murderers, or buy friggin' body parts. You name it. They want to keep it hidden, so they use cryptocurrency. Nonsystem is preeminent in that area."

Brendan said nothing. Jennifer was watching him closely. She thought she read something behind his eyes, a reaction to the mention of bitcoin.

Doherty pressed further. "Are you familiar with any member of Nonsystem, personally?"

Brendan shook his head. "No."

Doherty and Rascher exchanged looks.

Now Doherty looked around for the NYPD detectives. "Okay, Healy. Let's put a pin in that for a second. I'd like to introduce you to . . ."

One of the detectives spoke up. "Detective Kendall." Kendall had a medium build, thinning reddish brown hair, hazel eyes. He wore a light gray trench coat and looked overheated. "We've met," Kendall said, nodding at Brendan. Then he glanced around with a half-smile. "FBI," he said, "DOJ, NYPD. Any letters of the alphabet we're missing?"

Jennifer suppressed a smile, finding the humor in it nonetheless. The air was tense and the levity welcome, as far as she was concerned. But then she refocused on what Doherty was saying. Bringing in the NYPD detectives had been his idea. He was not only piggybacking her interview with Brendan, he seemed to be co-opting it entirely.

Doherty went on, "Of course you've met. You met when you were arrested for the murder of Alexander Heilshorn."

"Correct," said Kendall. "I took Mr. Healy's statement when he—"

Doherty cut him off. "I want to clarify a couple of things, Mr. Healy." He leaned in and sort of hunkered down, dropping his head between his broad shoulders. "After you were first arrested, and you were questioned by NYPD detectives, by Detective Sergeant Jim Kendall, you were taken to a holding cell. Ordinarily, arrestees first talk to their own lawyers, or to a public defender. But, you were visited by someone else."

Doherty opened the file. He started pulling out photographs. "These are still images taken from the video camera in the holding cell where you were for several hours before arraignment. As you can see, it's not easy to get a clear picture of his face. Who did you meet with?"

Brendan looked at the photos, then glanced up at Doherty. "Wouldn't the jail have that on record? Don't visitors have to sign in?"

One of the other detectives, the woman, leaned forward. "Detective Connors," she said. She spoke loudly and looked at the audio recorder on the desk, as if making sure her voice was picked up. She was dark-skinned with an athletic build, and bullshit-detector eyes. "We determined the identification provided by the visitor to be forged. He provided credentials that allowed him to pass through the system."

"What sort of credentials?" Brendan asked.

"Let's let this side of the table ask the questions," Doherty snapped. "What's important here is that shortly after meeting with this man, you changed your story about what happened at Roosevelt Hospital, with the murder of Alexander Heilshorn."

"I didn't change anything."

"Well, you suddenly became very adamant about falling on the grenade for Heilshorn's murder. You seemed to want to make sure any and all blame was shifted away from the girl, Sloane Dewan, and onto yourself. Why?"

"Because the blame is mine. Because I was the reason she was there. She didn't do anything wrong."

"And you maintain that you were the one to kill Heilshorn. With this." He pulled another photo and placed it atop the pile; a fire extinguisher lying on the carpet in Heilshorn's office, blood spattered on and around it.

Brendan didn't look at the photo, but stared at Doherty. Jennifer watched Brendan's face, the muscle twitching in his neck, the set of his jaw. He was almost close to having convinced himself of it; it was nearly his reality. She didn't know why it wasn't hers.

"Yes," he said. "That's correct."

"It was found resting next to Heilshorn's body, after being hurled through the air and delivering a fatal blow. Sloane Dewan's fingerprints were on it."

"She touched it when she moved it aside in her attempt to revive him. I've already gone over all of this with the lawyers."

"Uh-huh." Doherty was unconvinced. He ran a hand over his slicked-back hair. "Then you claim you yanked her out of there, and the two of you ran through the hospital, evading law enforcement until your capture in the hospital basement parking garage."

Brendan looked from Doherty to Jennifer. It was hard to make out what was in his mind, but it seemed clear he wasn't going to sit here and take this much longer.

Doherty leaned back a little. "So what did you and this man talk about? Your visitor in the holding cell?"

Brendan didn't respond.

"Because we have *other* pictures, Mr. Healy," and Doherty took them out quickly, tossing them on the pile, almost throwing them at Brendan. The photos slid over one another, spinning and coming to rest. One had rotated around so Jennifer could see it clearly from her angle. Her stomach eddied.

"These are photos taken when people enter and leave the jail. We've accounted for everyone that we have pictures of for the few hours you were there, before your first court appearance, when you pled guilty to murder. The only person we couldn't account for was this man. Because of his falsified credentials. But we found out who he is."

Jennifer felt her heart beating above her swirling stomach as she stared at the pictures. She couldn't help but flashback to the time she'd spent locked in the Manhattan skyscraper.

Jeremy Staryles had stood in front of her. He'd placed the vial of thallus sulfate on the floor. He'd been gentle, well-spoken, but completely insane. A sociopath.

Doherty glared at Brendan. He tilted his head. "Anything, Brendan? You want to tell me what you and Staryles chatted about? Because this man is a fucking fairy tale. The Defense Department can only tell us so much, to protect national secrets, but we know he was in black ops. Part of special surgical teams on night raids in Central Asia, and other parts of the world. But then, he disappears. We can't find anything on him, nothing in the DMV database, no social security, nothing. It's like he never existed."

Now Jennifer saw Brendan looking down at the picture. His expression remained inscrutable, his eyes unwavering. He kept silent.

"There were more deaths at Roosevelt Hospital than Alexander Heilshorn," Doherty said. "And as much as you'd probably take credit for those too, I don't think you killed two security guards." Doherty jabbed his finger down on the picture of Staryles. "I think he did."

Brendan at last looked up at Doherty. "Okay."

"Okay? That's all you have to say? You like being in here, Brendan? Maybe you do. Because I think you're dangling a limited hangout. You're taking the brunt of the Heilshorn murder and you're acting crazy and calling on government conspiracies as a cover. Why don't you tell me about Nonsystem?"

"Why do you think I know anything about them?"

"You want things to get worse for you? You think this is bad? This place?" Doherty suddenly looked around, waving his hands at the room, the jail. "This is a walk in the park, my friend. A friggin' lead pipe cinch compared to where people go who threaten national security. You need to open up. You need to work with us."

"Funny," Brendan said at last. "That was the same deal Staryles offered me."

Doherty slammed his hands down on the table so abruptly that Jennifer and half the rest of the room jumped. "Hallelujah!" Doherty cried, his mouth twisted into a rictus smile. "It speaks!" He leaned forward again and turned his volume down. "That's what I'm talking about, Healy. That's it right there. A little professional cooperation. You fucking psycho."

"Alright," said Jennifer, feeling the heat rise in the room. Her own anxiety was revving up — this was another blindsiding by the FBI and her own Justice Department. She'd had no idea they were going to spring this.

Doherty jerked his head to look at her, his body still facing towards Brendan, his eyes like a diamondback's. He turned his searing gaze back on Brendan then pushed back from the table, the feet of his chair grinding across the floor. He got up and paced the back of the room.

Brendan visually tracked his movement. Then Rascher, sitting next to Jennifer, leaned in.

"Mr. Healy, we have reason to believe that Nonsystem is planning a terrorist event. Within the next couple of days. Maybe sooner." Rascher's eyes dropped to the photo of Staryles. "We don't know how this man is involved for certain, but we strongly suspect he's working with them. We thought you could shed some light on that, help us to clarify. Considering the oddity of his visit your first night in jail."

They all watched Brendan. Jennifer realized she was holding her breath. She wasn't sure what she was expecting him to say. Maybe to revert back to his initial claims. Maybe to say of Staryles, *He works for the Central Security Service, you asshole*. Something. Anything.

"I'm sorry, I don't know what I can do for you."

Rascher opened his mouth to speak, Jennifer thought she was on the verge of stepping in and saying something too, when Doherty bolted around the table to where Brendan was. His expression was cyanotic with rage. His hands were out. He looked like he wanted to throttle Brendan.

Brendan stood up, chains rattling. He braced himself as Doherty came for him. But Doherty stopped short, like a dog caught by a leash. He remained within an inch of Brendan's face, seething.

"You're unbelievable," Doherty hissed. He cocked his head again in that insulting, aggressive way. The two men stared into each other's eyes. Doherty's face contorted into another humorless grin. "What? Huh? Tough guy? You're a tough guy now. Did a little time in the stir. You make your bones? Join the Aryan Brotherhood? Maybe you like being in here. You like having your pants pulled down. Huh? What's the matter, Healy? You look like you want to hit me."

"Stop it," said Jennifer.

"You want to hit me? Huh? You paranoid faggot? Go ahead? Go ahead and—"

And Brendan did, slamming Doherty in the face with the top of his head.

* * *

Two COs rushed in, the Deputy Warden close on their heels. Grimm looked both mortified and filled with hate, and the COs wrangled Brendan like an animal. Doherty was doubled over against the far wall, both of his hands on his nose. As they dragged him back around the table, Brendan met eyes with Jennifer. She didn't see an animal there, she saw a man fighting for his life.

The COs worked Brendan towards the exit as Grimm sputtered apologies at Doherty and Rascher and the rest of them, all the while jamming murderous looks at Brendan. The COs yanked open the door and ushered him out of the room, his feet shuffling and anklets clanking.

"No," Jennifer said.

Everyone stopped and all eyes pinned her, including Doherty, bent over, looking up at her over the hands protecting his nose. She saw a runnel of blood course down his wrist and disappear beneath cuff of his shirt.

"Wait," Jennifer said. She held her hand up, she turned her eyes on Grimm. "Okay? Just, hang on here for a second." From the doorway, the COs looked to Grimm for guidance. Grimm, chest heaving, paused reluctantly. Jennifer pushed past the others and took Rascher by the arm and led him a few steps to where Doherty was standing against the wall. "Listen," she said in a hasty whisper. "This is why we're really here, right? Why you agreed with me to do this? You think Brendan has a connection to Nonsystem—"

"Forget it," said Rascher. "I told you."

Jennifer let go of Rascher's arm and stared at Doherty, who was getting himself upright, still covering his face. "Let me look," she said.

She thought she heard a muffled *Fuck you* through his hands.

"Harlan. Let me look." She reached up and pushed his hands out of the way. His nose was bleeding profusely. "You're not going to want to ride out of here like that. Go to the infirmary. Let me finish up with him."

"You already tried," Doherty said in a nasally growl. His eyes looked past her to Healy.

"Hey," Jennifer said, trying to get the big man's attention back. "Hey, listen to me." She looked around for Rascher, standing behind her. "Both of you. You want answers, but he's in the dark," she said, pointing to Brendan. "He's been in here seven months. The paperwork I got last night says he spent two months in the SMU. That's solitary confinement; segregation. Before West Facility he was in Mothcan Center. An overpopulated jungle. You just cornered him, Doherty. Now let me talk to him. Let me get you what you need."

Doherty looked at Rascher. She resented their silent exchanges, she was furious about not being shown all of the cards, but at least she had a few things she could work with.

She expected more bristling from the two men, another *No way, forget it, it's over* from Doherty, but it didn't come.

"Fine," he said.

She felt a rush of confidence that she tried to keep under wraps.

Only this time, she thought, *you don't get to be here.*

CHAPTER FIVE / WEDNESDAY, 2:41 PM

The room was cleared. Jennifer asked Brendan to sit at the end of the table, so she could sit at the corner next to him. After Doherty and Rascher had agreed to her continuing the interview, Grimm, who'd been watching from the viewing room, still required further convincing. The Deputy Warden was simmering, his rheumy eyes filled with resentment at her summary of Brendan's time in prison. Jennifer felt like there was something more to the relationship between Brendan and the Deputy Warden.

She took Grimm aside in the viewing room and spoke to him quietly. "I would remind you that I'm a special prosecutor with the Department of Justice. The US Attorney General and Bureau of Prisons are in my phone contacts."

It was tacky, a trump card, but she felt like it was the right way to deal with a bull like Grimm. He skulked out of the room after that. The NYPD detectives agreed not to watch so long as the audio recorder stayed on. They left, presumably for coffee and more cigarettes and to talk over how Jennifer had just basically told the Deputy Warden of Rikers Island to go shit in his hat.

Jennifer entered the room. Alone with Brendan finally. She took her seat. "I'm very sorry about that. I'd make excuses — we're all under a lot of pressure here — but there's just no excuse for the way Agent Doherty antagonized you."

"That's nice of you."

Already she could feel him closing down. There was a fresh red mark on his forehead from where he'd head-butted Doherty. She realized Brendan could've broken Doherty's nose if he'd wanted. Her mind rifled through the options. She needed to connect to him somehow. And fast.

Whatever she was scared of, whatever guilt clouded her, she had to face it.

"Brendan," she said, "I'm sorry."

He looked at her for a moment, then turned his eyes away.

"I left you in here," she said. She felt the emotion rising in her, unexpectedly. "But I didn't leave you, okay? Not in my head. I just didn't know what to do." She felt her lip trembling and realized she was on the verge of tears. It was all catching up with her; the trip here, seeing Brendan for the first time, the violence in the room, so much she could not control.

He still wasn't looking at her. She turned away, too, took a moment to gather herself.

After a little while, she found herself smiling. "I can't believe you hit him."

Brendan met her gaze this time. "Neither can he."

She laughed softly then grew serious again. "I need you to be honest with me, Brendan."

"And I need to be able to trust you."

She nodded, biting her lower lip. "I wasn't aware of this thing with Staryles, just like you. They've been keeping me in the dark, telling me it's for my own protection. Because if Staryles is in with Nonsystem, probably so is Ewon Parnell. That's the man who . . . the one who held me captive on Staryles' behalf. He interrogated me while I was under the duress of thallium poisoning, and then he committed suicide when the feds broke into the room."

She watched him carefully, and could read in his face that he wasn't convinced. She played to that for a moment.

"But," she said, "the ensuing investigation ran contrary to the information Wyn Weston had found on Parnell. Weston's investigation suggested that he worked for Titan. Both Parnell and Staryles."

Now she seemed to have Brendan's full attention.

"For Alexander Heilshorn," she added. "Weston found that Parnell had been military, special forces, but that after he'd been dishonorably discharged, he'd begun thug-work for different private corporations, private groups." She looked at him closely.

Brendan gave a subtle nod of his head. "Yes. Staryles worked for Heilshorn."

"Can you prove it?"

"I can't."

"Did Staryles tell you himself?"

Brendan leaned back and looked at her coolly. She knew she was dangerously close to losing him, having him clam up. "I'm sorry," she said. "We have to be sure. Conjecture will get us nowhere. My people are pretty convinced Staryles works for Nonsystem, not Titan."

"Maybe Staryles can be anyone he wants to be, look like anything he wants to."

"I haven't ruled that out," she said in a low voice. It gnawed at her though, despite the way he seemed reasonable, that he was just going to lead her into far-fetched territory after all. They needed to stay concrete. She glanced down at the audio recorder, and then impulsively reached out and shut it off. She met Brendan's eyes, and caught him deciding whether or not she'd done it for show.

Brendan looked down at the table for a moment. Then he gazed up at the one-way mirror. There was no one on the other side of it now.

She hoped.

"The FBI has been after Nonsystem for a while. Their ways of stealthing bitcoin transactions online is a significant step towards the decentralization of money in our country — in the world. If you look at what's happened in Greece, who are drowning in debt, it's possible this kind of Bitcoin virtual currency could solve our financial crises. But Nonsystem would need to come under control, and they've been fighting the FBI in a silent battle for months. Years. They pop up, and the FBI pounces. It's a game of whack-a-mole, and with each hit, groups like Nonsystem get smarter and more sophisticated, and the FBI redoubles its efforts. So the thought is that Nonsystem has a plan to change the game. Put the ball completely in their court and keep it there. That's the FBI's position. That's where Doherty is coming from."

"How? What's Nonsystem's plan? Or yours?"

She was silent, considering. She didn't have an answer, but another question for him.

"Brendan, what did Staryles say to you?"

He sighed. He leaned forward to touch his face, rattling the chains. "He told me I had one hour."

"One hour." She raised her eyebrows. "For what?"

"To decide whether I was with him, or against him. You met him. You know what he's like."

"Yes. He's a sociopath."

Brendan looked away again, wearing a grim expression. Then he abruptly returned his focus to her.

"Remember Staryles is a chameleon," he said. "Can become anything he wants. He's done it for years. It's who he is."

"Maybe you're right." She unconsciously reached up and touched her neck. She could picture Staryles standing in the unlit studio in Manhattan, placing the tiny white vial on the floor. "We really have no idea where he is or what he's doing right now. But I'm sure it's not good."

CHAPTER SIX / WEDNESDAY, 3:13 PM

He drove the Cutlass into a low-ceiling parking garage off Thomas Street in Manhattan. He parked, got out of the vehicle, and shut the door with force, listening to the slam reverberate off the mortar. His hard-soled shoes echoed as he walked out into the sizzling daylight.

He turned right and walked to the corner of Thomas and Hudson Street. Hudson was one-way heading north, and Staryles took that direction. There was minimal traffic; mostly small trucks — a Fed Ex, a white cube truck, one small tractor-trailer reading *Skyline Windows*. A few cabs bounced on soft shocks up the road, these merging to get around the half of the road that was blocked off. Concrete barriers and a four-foot-high chain link fence sheathed in green plastic separated two whole lanes. In the middle of the segregated area was a large yellow excavator with the word LIEBHERR written across the long hydraulic arm. Beside the excavator were large rectangular dumpsters for construction refuse. Piles of gray brick. A squat, yellow KAESER generator. There were no workers out this afternoon; the piles of material and the hulking excavator sat unattended. A sign hung from the fencing read

"Crosswalk Closed Use Other Side." The air was dry and smelled of dust and oil.

Staryles crossed to the other side. Through his Ray Bans, he looked up at the expanse of the 55-63 block opposite the construction zone. The block was bracketed by Jay and Duane Streets. The building was nine stories tall, classic red brick construction and large multi-paned windows. A fire escape zigzagged up one side of the face, air conditioners rattled and dripped from windowsills. Staryles looked up at the top floor. Then he entered the building.

The first floor was the Downtown Arts Development. A frigid blast of air hit him, in sharp contrast to the baking heat of the city outside. A pretty young woman was sitting at a high desk just inside the doors, which served as both a foyer for the Arts center and the lobby for the elevators. There was another desk, much smaller, just a podium, really, in between the two sets of elevator doors and a security guard standing there, watching Staryles.

Staryles ignored the guard at the back of the room and smiled at the young woman. He flirted with her for a moment, making idle chat about the hot weather outside, asking her if she had ever eaten at *Caliu*, a restaurant further up Hudson Ave. She had, and she'd really enjoyed their traditional tapas, and then she asked him if he was interested in the Downtown Arts Development, if he was a collector. He looked like a collector, she said.

Staryles beamed. However, he was not, he informed her, an art collector, though he had the eye for the market. What he was, he said, was curious about the history of the building. What did she know about it?

The young woman, who said her name was Jimena, blushed and stalled for a moment, glancing around the empty foyer before launching into what sounded like a well-rehearsed speech, something she'd recited when interviewing for her front-desk position.

"Well," she began, "Sixty Hudson has long been a major communications hub. The building was completed in 1930. It started off as the headquarters of Western Union."

"Wow," said Staryles.

"Yeah. It was Western Union until . . ." she turned to look at the guard, who was a distance away, by the two elevators. "Randy, when was Western Union out of here?"

"Seventy-six," said Randy in a monotone. His dark skin contrasted with the whites of his eyes, which were locked on Staryles.

"Seventy-six, right, yup, that's it." Jimena smiled prettily. "But, all during the time Western Union was here, the building's facilities grew and adapted, you know, keeping up with the pace of technology. First there were pneumatic tubes, then the telegraph cable. At one point this building had seventy million feet of copper wire, if you can picture that."

"Hard to imagine." Staryles almost winked at the girl, but forced himself to keep a straight face.

"Yup," she chirped, "Then telephones, and then, now, you know, fiber-optic cable."

She finished up and her expression changed a bit, like someone who had just inadvertently strayed onto a dicey subject and wished they hadn't. He wondered what they'd told her — how much she knew about what was up there, on the ninth floor, and its significance.

Jimena glanced at Randy, and Staryles looked at him, too. Randy knew what was up there. At least, old, minimum-wage, rent-a-cop Randy knew that it was important, incredibly important, more than a few MacBook Pros and office supplies to protect. And yet his job was largely for appearance — just a run-of-the-mill friendly neighborhood security guard here, not even armed, perfunctory.

The real security was upstairs. There would be half a dozen of them, maybe more, on the ninth floor. They would be specially trained, armed, some plainclothes, meant to blend in with the other hipsters who would be bustling about.

Sensing the awkwardness, Staryles jumped back into the conversation. "Sure, fiber optics. That's the new way of things, right?" He sounded like a shmuck with no clue about technology.

Jimena nodded eagerly, but still, the initial bit of flirtation and carefree conversation seemed to have gone. More than that — the way she acted reminded him of time-lapse footage he'd seen somewhere of flowers closing down at the end of a season; vibrant, full bulbs one moment, withering and furling as the sun plummets in the sky. It made him angry, when he got these reactions. He didn't understand them. What was it with women? All smiles and batting of the eyelashes when you first met, appraising your wardrobe, your chiseled face, your wavy hair. They looked into your blue eyes and then shyly glanced down and you had them.

But then it happened. Suddenly they switched off, like they'd smelled something bad in the room.

It didn't happen with all women, he reminded himself. Just last night he'd been with a beautiful Ecuadorian with cheekbones as sharp as scythes, small upright breasts, full lips, long legs. This Jimena, she had no idea what he could do to her.

"Yup," she said again, and nodded. "The way of the future. Everything is digital." She kept nodding, and now she avoided eye contact, and he realized something. His problem was that he just lingered too long. And it only seemed to happen stateside. His timing was fine in Yemen or Afghanistan. There he would pull away from a job before the body hit the ground. He'd disappear into the night before the family — what was left of them — awoke inside the dusty, stucco rooms. As if back here he was making up for lost time. Taking things more slowly, trying to get somewhere with people, trying to remember how to be human. He hated himself for it. Their conversation had ended, and he needed to walk away.

"Well, thanks for the little history lesson," he said, and ripped open a huge smile.

"Oh, sure . . ." She looked puzzled. Fine, he thought, let her wonder. Without another word, he turned and strutted across the space to Randy, who watched him come over with the kind of wariness reserved for Jehovah's Witnesses at the door.

Forgoing the small talk now, Staryles strode up to Randy and said, "Ninth floor."

Randy blinked. "You have to be in the book. What's your name?"

"My name is Jeremy Staryles," he said, already pulling out his credentials. He held up the wallet with the ID inside the plastic window. He tapped it with a manicured fingernail. "Five Star Securities."

Randy glanced at the ID. His gaze dropped to the book sitting on the podium in front of him. He dragged a finger down the page. "Yeah, okay, I got you here. I'll phone up."

"That's very good, Randy."

Randy's eyes flashed. "Excuse me?"

"I think you're a helluva guy, Randy."

They held each other's gaze for a moment before Randy looked away, scowling, and picked up the phone at his small, high desk. As he called, Staryles took the opportunity to think about how nice it would be to kill Randy. Then he glanced over his shoulder at Jimena. Maybe he would have her watch.

CHAPTER SEVEN / WEDNESDAY, 3:21 PM

Jennifer looked around at the gray walls of the small room. There was a dance of light along the edge of her vision she could only chase by turning her head. She stopped and closed her eyes for a moment. Then she opened them to stare at Brendan.

"Look; what we're working with is that Nonsystem is ramping something up. Doherty claims there's enough to get them on what happened to me last year. That's why they've had me keep a distance. Get some of them to cooperate, turn in the others, in return for leniency. But they're holding off, because they want to fry them for what they're planning now. Catch them in the act."

Brendan sat up a little straighter. He studied her. "Who's lead prosecutor? Are you?"

The question struck a deep cord with her, made her feel hollow. Her muscles recalled the effects of the poison, twisting them into gristle, liquefying her organs. Over the ensuing months, she'd gotten the feeling her superiors and colleagues considered her a permanent wreck. They thought her integrity was compromised.

They thought: *Thank you for playing, but thallus sulfate poisoning deprives you of further privileges within the Department. We'll be managing your career until further notice.*

No, she was not lead prosecutor.

So what was the FBI really doing by coming to her like this? Were they freeing her, or was it just more of the same, more close-watch, more shackles? Sometimes it felt like she was still trapped in that room, high up in the city. Not much different from Brendan, sitting there, chained.

"John Rascher is prosecuting. What the prevailing thought is, you know, the FBI do what they do best. They draw Nonsystem out. They get them talking, supply them with what they need, learn their full intentions."

Brendan was quiet, perhaps considering this.

"I've spoken with the US Attorney General," she went on. "Everyone is in agreement. They've got me taking a point position on this."

"But they're limiting your information." He raised an eyebrow.

"That's how it has to work some times."

"So how am I supposed to help you?"

"We believe there is crossover between what's happening now, and the XList investigation. And since you were the one to really bring XList out in the open with your case, I thought we could pick each other's brains."

"Ok," Brendan said, relenting. "Fair enough. Let's do this: tell me how you got into XList in the first place."

"Well, now we're going way back." She winked at him, and then felt foolish for it. She took a drink of water. "Okay, let's start with Wyn Weston. Weston was one of the first Justice Department investigators to look into the Rebecca Heilshorn murder during the trial of Olivia Jane. Reason being, county prosecutors alluded to a criminal enterprise surrounding Rebecca's death. It grabbed the attention of the HTPU. Weston obtained the data from the case, including the financials on Alexander Heilshorn."

"Which were relevant because of Rudy Colinas," Brendan added.

She looked closely at him. "Because of *you* and Colinas. You had good instincts on that case."

She saw the blood rise in his cheeks. He seemed tempted to look away, self-consciously, but he maintained eye contact and said, "If you say so."

"You're welcome. Then Weston left the case."

"Why?"

She leaned back and lifted her shoulders. Her neck and back felt stiff. "We don't know. Weston has been MIA for almost a year. He's officially a missing person. As is a medical examiner from Westchester County. One who initially did the postmortem on Seamus Argon's body."

Brendan seemed to drift off for a moment. No doubt he was thinking of Argon. Brendan had been locked-up the day of Argon's funeral. His focus came back, sharp.

"Argon's death was staged."

She swallowed, feeling a lump in her throat. "Well, the assessment is nowhere to be found."

"I don't think Argon died in that collision as intended. I think Staryles had to finish him off. Then adapt the body postmortem to appear more consistent with the plan."

"But, why?" She was getting slightly frustrated. It seemed like he kept trying to lead her somewhere, but then would back away. Of course, to be fair, she'd been explicit with him about not dwelling on anything unsubstantiated. "Why take these other people and toss them into the abyss, never to be found, but kill Argon? Let the funeral happen, risk interfering with his body, involve a second medical examiner, all of this?"

"Maybe too many missing shows a pattern. Maybe you've got to mix it up," Brendan said, looking closely at her. Then his gaze wandered over her shoulder. "But as far as those missing go, I don't think they're alive. I think they're missing because they're dead and buried somewhere."

She thought maybe part of her agreed, which worried her. She steered the conversation back to Wyn Weston. "When I made the call to the Justice Office to get the files on the Heilshorn case and the financials on Alexander, it took about two weeks. They arrived where I was staying in White Plains. The next morning, I was kidnapped."

It still felt strange to hear, strange to say.

"The files stayed behind."

"I didn't take them jogging."

Brendan smiled. She thought it was the first time she'd seen him smile since she'd gotten to Rikers. The smile faded as he stared at the table between them, at the switched-off audio recorder. Then he lifted his head and looked into her eyes. "The copies I had were still in the apartment where I was staying, yes. The people who abducted me didn't bother going after copies. They knew the originals were kept safe somewhere. And now the FBI has them."

"Heilshorn's personal bookkeeping only? Or was there Titan information in there, too?"

"Both. Yes."

"Alright, then tell me what you remember."

She clasped her hands together on the table. "Heilshorn was a founding partner of Titan. Titan is one of the world's largest private equity firms. A huge investor in leveraged buyout transactions over the past five years."

"I'm sorry . . . English, please."

She smirked. "We're talking about mergers and acquisitions. Titan often serves as a financial sponsor acquiring a company. In some cases, like when they acquired a large, but struggling construction company called G. Hanson Construction, they renamed it Titan Construction."

"What about Titan Med Tech?"

"Same thing. I forget the original name, but it was acquired and rebuilt, with a huge R&D department added in. These transactions, partially funded by borrowing, usually occur with private companies. But, they can occur as a public to private transaction."

"So, Titan can acquire a public company, buy it out, and take it private. Are there solid examples?"

"A few," she said, running a hand over her hair. "Most of which we already know; there was a money trail leading to Titan from companies which did not generate sufficient cash flows to service their debt. Which means the equity owners swap control of the company to the debt providers."

"The banks."

She dropped her hand to the table. "Yes."

"This happen a lot?"

"A lot. The companies are bought, over-leveraged to insolvency, then turned over to the banks. But the banks aren't all Titan was feeding."

"Money going to something else," Brendan said. "And *from* something else. From the debt-to-equity swaps, and subsequent liquidations, but also from the black markets. From XList. And then following the same pattern. Funneling into . . . what?"

Jennifer took a beat. She was familiar with Brendan's hypothesis that Titan was behind XList; she'd seen his case files on Rebecca. She had even used the theory when interviewing Olivia Jane, hoping to bait the murderer into revealing something she never had. Alexander Heilshorn had first mentioned Titan in a phone call with Brendan. Heilshorn of course denied any involvement with XList, displayed shock and fear over his daughter's involvement, but stayed transparent about his relationship to the large firm. She decided to let it lie.

"The current belief is that the money was going into Nonsystem."

"I don't think so."

"No?" she asked, feeling her skin prickle. "Well, again, all we have is conjecture; we don't have proof. Titan's money disappears into a black hole. That's the thing with cleaning money — it's moved around, disseminated — it gets sheltered in Switzerland or the Caymans. Places like the Ugland House. Where it winds up after that is just a guess."

"So, what's your guess?"

She glared at him, his unmasked stubbornness getting under her skin. "I don't guess. What I see is what's in front of me. *You* taking the fall for Alexander Heilshorn's death. And Staryles' visit when you were first arrested. We want to get the bottom of this? We've got to figure out what Staryles is doing right now. That's my guess."

CHAPTER EIGHT / WEDNESDAY, 3:21 PM

The elevator doors opened on a cool, dark floor. Staryles could immediately sense a change in the environment: the lobby had smelled of new carpet; up here the air reeked of clustered electronics and hot plastic. Like a Best Buy in 100 degree heat, despite the whirring air conditioning circulating in drafty currents.

There was a high, wide desk dead ahead in front of a glass wall, flanked by two blackened, thermal-paned doors. This time it wasn't a perky grad student at the desk, but two men, security guards. Both gave Staryles the eyeball, utility belts saddling their waists, semi-autos a thong-strap away from their clutches. Then the door opened to the right of them and another man stepped through, dressed in a suit and tie. He put on a fake smile and approached Staryles. He was in his fifties, gray-haired, his face creased with dignified wrinkles. The suit was silver and shined beneath the overhead lights.

Time to smile again. Staryles offered his hand and gave the silver-suit a firm, three-pump shake, finding the man's grip dry and cool. He snuck another glance at the armed guards before giving the suited man his full attention. The greeter looked him up and down.

"Mr. Staryles?"

"Yes."

"Cal Riggins. Nice to meet you." Riggins let go of Staryles' hand and reached up to the rimless glasses perched on his nose. He gave them a push with the tip of his finger while his eyes jerked toward the two security agents. Upon his wordless communication, the two men left the desk and came over. Big boys, one of them at least two hundred pounds of muscle, the other a little flabbier and heavier, built like a linebacker. He was holding a wand that connected to a battery pack clipped to his belt.

Riggins looked at Staryles with a curl of a smile. "You understand we have to follow procedure."

"Absolutely," Staryles said, raising his arms and biting back the bile that rose in his throat. He needed to play his part, and play it convincingly. And that meant, for the moment, letting himself be molested by security like any other helpless citizen.

The second security guard went about riffling up and down his pant legs while the linebacker feathered the wand along his arms, across his chest, around his waist. Then they switched positions. It was some kind of awkward, heavyweight ballet. Staryles could smell their sweat, and turned his head to the side to stifle a gag. He could feel Riggins watching the whole thing with a kind of churlish pride.

When it was finally over, and no knife, no SIG automatic with sound suppressor was discovered, nothing but a wallet with his credentials, the fake picture of his wife and daughter (it was an idea inspired by Brendan Healy), the two meatheads took a step or two back, and Riggins pulled his face into a disturbingly pleased smile.

"Right this way," he said.

* * *

Inside, the temperature was another five degrees cooler, but even beneath the air conditioning the smell of baking electronic gear was pungent, the white noise louder as aisles upon of aisles of servers all busily whirred away in the darkness. The cavernous space was dimly lit.

"We keep the lights low; they add heat," Riggins explained.

Just inside the room was a warren of offices. Their walls also tinted glass, less opaque so that Staryles was able to peer in. A see-through office on the right contained a woman in an attractive pantsuit pacing with a Bluetooth attached to her ear, her lips moving and her hands gesturing in the air. She didn't notice Staryles. Next door to her, a younger woman seated in an ergonomic chair behind a handsome desk looked up and tracked Staryles as he passed. He smiled at her. He looked at the offices on the opposite side. One was empty, another featured a conference table with men and women gathered round, some catching his eye, some not. One man watched him while sipping a beverage, then averted his gaze. The last glass wall was occluded, completely screened in and private.

Staryles focused ahead. One very long aisle of servers bisected the massive room. Shorter, perpendicular aisles were off to either side, each humming with stacks of chrome-and-black servers, each of these behind a glass door, telltale lights — green, amber, traffic-signal red — blinking at different intervals.

"Kind of like a space ship, right?" Riggins blurted happily. "This facility is fifteen hundred square feet. That's why we call it the Meet-Me-Room. When you're a convergence point of multiple layers of local, national and global fiber-optic cables, you've got to keep it human. Because this is all about humans, after all. It happens right here, the place where everyone and everything meets."

Riggins took the right side of the central aisle, and Staryles followed just behind and to the side of him. It was an old habit, not walking abreast. Riggins didn't seem to notice as he chatted away, gesturing with flicks of his wrist as he spoke. He pointed at the ceiling, twenty feet above, where the fans spinning in the gloom would've looked completely anachronistic if it wasn't for how big they were, like helicopter blades.

"There's nothing like this in the country," Riggins said. "I mean, One-Eleven is another super-data center, so there's two right here in the city." He tossed a glance back at Staryles. "By One-eleven, of course, I mean . . ."

"One-eleven Eighth Avenue. And there is One Wilshire, Los Angeles. And a data farm in Miami."

"Correct." Riggins resumed his attempts to dazzle Staryles with information as they walked. "But these two centers really support the whole northeast." He pointed at the main trunk in the middle of the room. "This is where each carrier's server resides." Then he indicated the rows they were passing along the right. "And here we have networking equipment. On the other side of the center galley; storage. At the back; arrays of optical terminations, a few coaxial terminations, some vestigial copper terminations."

Straight ahead, the world of glass and dark machines gave way to a bunker-style room, windowless and squat. Riggins stopped near the formidable, sealed room. "In there is where the connection panels are, allowing the carrier's colocation units to connect with other networks."

In the center of its concrete façade was a steel door, bolted, gilded by another beefy security guard. The guard offered a wan smile to Riggins and then glowered soberly at Staryles. Staryles noted the holstered firearm, same as the others.

Riggins turned and spread his arms like a showman at a carnival. "There you go. This is the physical hub of the Internet. Essentially a giant Ethernet switch. The whole thing is powered by a ten-thousand-amp DC power plant."

"And where is that?"

Riggins swallowed and glanced at the guard before saying, "Right this way."

They left the bunker and turned down a corridor. Another steel door, red with chipped paint along the edges, was locked ahead of Riggins. He pulled out a bunch of keys. *No guard personnel here,* Staryles observed, accumulating mental notes for his non-existent security report. *Just a guy with keys.* Riggins opened the door and stepped through into a pitch-black room. He fumbled for a moment before flipping on a switch. The place lit up.

"Wow," Staryles said, adding a touch of childish wonder to his voice.

"Gets the job done," Riggins said. He spun slowly around, marveling as if he was seeing it for the first time himself.

Staryles walked in and touched a hand lightly to one of the distribution shelves. "This a LORAIN?"

"That's right."

"Excellent heritage, LORAIN. A large vortex power platform. I see you've got the bulk output shelves, integrated distribution shelves, and that looks like it leads to an externally mounted distribution panel system."

Riggins nodded, clearly impressed. "Backup. On the roof."

Staryles regurgitated more of the information he'd read over that morning. "Right, right. And these here, you've got rectifiers; these provide, what? Sixteen-hundred watts at sixty-five degrees Celsius? This is top notch stuff."

He'd read over the specs before sunrise, the Ecuadorian lying in bed beside him, still asleep. Staryles didn't sleep. He was awake at four, sometimes three AM no matter what. One of those people who simply didn't require lots of rest. Like his father. He had ample time to read. To him, the utility room with all of its metal boxes and shelves and cooling fans was as obscure as HAL, the computer in *2001: A Space Odyssey.* Except with more cables. Cables bound together and rambling up the wall and disappearing into the ceiling. Feeding into the concrete bunker on the other side of the wall; he understood at least that much on his own.

"Well," said Riggins. "This is actually NetSure 700, here; we just upgraded, so we're talking about two thousand five hundred watt constant power rectifier providing up to a hundred and four amps at plus twenty-four vdc."

Riggins was looking affectionately at something, which to Staryles resembled a propane heater with little post-office mailboxes tucked beneath. He felt an uncomfortable tug of nerves, a creeping of heat along his neck. He'd reached the limit of his crammed knowledge. Some incompetent analyst had given him old information; they'd upgraded their power supply at the Meet-Me-Room. Not that it would change anything. Explosives were explosives, and would take care of whatever nerd-device, regardless of the chain of letters and numbers used to describe it.

"Very nice," Staryles said, and then squared his shoulders with the door, indicating that they leave.

Riggins scowled. "Don't you want to see the cameras?"

"I already saw them," Staryles replied curtly. And he pointed, still looking at Riggins, at the four different spots in the room where partially concealed cameras monitored them. He might not have been an electrician, but he knew surveillance. Which suited his cover story well.

"Very good," said Riggins. He slapped his palms together to dispel the little bit of humiliation Staryles had intended. Another courtesy smile and then he stepped in front of Staryles and opened the door. He paused there and cocked his head. "So then you've already seen all of the security in the rest of the place?"

It was meant to be rhetorical, a barb. Poor Riggins, he really just oozed pride. But he was only a glorified office administrator.

"I've seen ten cameras," Staryles said, "three uniformed security, one plainclothes security sitting at a conference table, and another behind her desk." He walked out of the giant, thrumming utility room past Riggins.

Riggins closed the door behind him and they were back in the main warehouse, alongside the half-story bunker. "That's very good. I appreciate the time and expense to do this. You can never be too car—"

Staryles stopped abruptly and turned around. "Mr. Riggins. I know what you think you know. That we've been asked to take a look at security here; just routine. But you seem like a smart man. You know I'm not here for a cursory checkup. This is in the interest of national security. This facility is a global destination. What Times Square is to tourists; an internet Babylon. So, now that the tour is over — which was really unnecessary anyway — let's stop wasting time, let's go sit down and talk. And I can tell you what we need to be prepared for. What the Known Knowns are, and the Known Unknowns. Okay?"

Riggins was nodding. Twenty years older than Staryles, and reduced to a bumbling teenager. "Y-yes. Absolutely."

* * *

An hour later, after more tedious playacting and listening to Riggins drone on, comforting him, asserting the national-security platitudes and shaking more hands, Staryles left the massive data center.

He glanced at his watch as he crossed the street back to the construction site, and then looked at the building above the *Cloudsplitter Scaffolding* which caged the sidewalk on that side. There were two stories visible above the top of the long scaffold chain, two banks of windows dark and apparently empty.

He rounded the corner back onto Thompson Street to retrieve the Cutlass, reflecting on his tour of the Meet-

Me-Room. It had gone perfectly. He had to repeat the procedure for One-eleven Eighth Avenue and then the first phase would be complete.

He thought of Riggins and all his jangling keys. It made him think of guards like Randy, and corrections officers in a jail.

CHAPTER NINE / WEDNESDAY, 3:50 PM

Brendan leaned back in his seat. He had to lift both hands, chained together by the metal bracelets, in order to rub one of his eyes.

Jennifer took another sip of her water. The pain was already cycling back. She needed another dose of the meds. "Brendan, I need something from you. I know I don't deserve it. But you've got to give me something on XList. Anything. Any moment everyone's going to be back in this room."

He lowered his shackled hands and placed them on the table between them and looked at her. She searched his eyes. She found herself momentarily distracted by how bright and engaging they were. "I've told you the play; I keep doing exactly as I'm doing with the HTPU. Rascher is still my supervisor, only now he's working the parallel Nonsystem sting. The task force becomes my cover. My work dovetails with the sting because of the connection between the two."

He was silent a moment longer, and then shook his head. "I don't think it's a good idea. Not for you."

"Excuse me?"

"You should back off. Tell them you can't do this. You're in too much pain."

She flinched at this, as if struck. "I'm what?"

"What have they got you taking?"

She felt a flare of recalcitrance. What business was it of his what pain meds she was on? But she quickly realized her defensiveness had more to do with vanity; she didn't want to seem vulnerable, and here Brendan was seeing through her bravado like it was nothing. She continued to gauge the situation, deciding her answer. Best not to alienate him now. She knew he had something for her. She could sense it.

"Tramadol," she said.

"Tramadol? That's usually prescribed for things like phantom limb pain. Or diabetic neuropathy." He looked deeply into her eyes. She had never felt so clearly seen. It was both unnerving and pleasant. "Immediate release or sustained release?"

"I usually take it with acetaminophen. Immediate release."

"Four hundred milligrams?"

She nodded. "Four times a day. I hate it."

"You've got central neuropathic pain. Some complex polyneuropathy. Do you see any strange things? Bright lights? Visual tics or trails? How's your sleep — lots of dreams?"

He had affected an affectionate bedside manner, and she could see him running through some medical calculus — thinking about her wellbeing, perhaps, more than just the clinical questions that he was asking. It was charming. It was . . . attractive.

"Brendan, I appreciate what you're trying to do . . ."

"What am I trying to do?"

She looked at him, and felt a sudden, unexpected rush she hadn't felt for anyone in so long she couldn't remember. *You're trying to protect me*, she thought, but the

72

sentiment traveled no further than that. Instead she said, "I'm here, and I'm in it. End of story."

"Alright," he said. "So, you continue your work as special prosecutor with the HTPU, and, what? I help. How?"

She narrowed her eyes at him. When he was discussing her health, he was being genuine. But he danced around XList. He knew as well as she did that there was an overlap of the players — Heilshorn, Argon, Staryles. They had just sat together and put forward XList as a black market that fed Titan's coffers. What was he holding back? Was he waiting for a deal?

"I'm counting on you to give me something," she said. "And maybe, maybe if you do . . ." She was careful to lower her voice until it was barely audible. "Maybe then we see where else it all leads. You get me?"

"I don't want that," he said.

She sat up straighter and brought her voice back within normal range. She was empowered to make a deal with him. Maybe he was already negotiating — acting uninterested. "You're in here for murder one, Brendan. Your trial is in three days. You start out with a second degree charge, reckless homicide, which carries some jail time with a conviction but not nearly as severe as murder-in-the-first. Yet, two days after you're in, you give the cops a very convincing confession that shows the requisite intention to kill the deceased. Yet you say you didn't know, upon entering Heilshorn's office, that he had had anything to do with the death of your wife and child until that moment? That's not usually what people do, Brendan, come to a place like this and then try and add to their time. You almost want to make it look like premeditation. I can offer you a lifeboat."

"I haven't been sentenced yet."

"Brendan, has anyone been here to see you? Anyone besides Kendall from NYPD, or your lawyer?"

"No."

"How about contact from the outside in any other way? Anyone? Anything at all?"

She watched him become still. He looked at the cup of water Jennifer had set down, looked at his own. But he wasn't paying any attention to the water. He was elsewhere. She gave him the time he needed, just a few moments, watching him weigh the options. When he looked up, she read anxiety on his face for the first time since she'd been in there with him. Maybe not for himself, but someone else.

"You need to speak to Philip Largo," he said at last.

"Former Assemblyman Largo?"

"I'd heard about him, but didn't recall anything right away. No one pays attention to the state legislature." His mouth curved into a wry smile, but the fear was treading water behind his eyes. The smile dissolved. "I came across his name while looking into Argon's death. At first I thought, you know, Argon has this list going of crooked politicians. And he did. But Largo was different. Years ago, Largo was with an escort. But he didn't know; or, that's his claim, and has been his claim all this time — she was an XList pro."

"How do you know this?"

"Just talk to him. Not everyone was cowed by Alexander Heilshorn, no matter how much influence he peddled."

She felt a tiny electric pulse through her chest. "Tell me."

"The escort was known as Danice," he said. "Real name, Rebecca Heilshorn. That's your way in."

The key hit the lock to the interview room.

Jennifer's heart tried to squeeze into her throat. The revelation about Largo was major, and had her ears ringing. She needed to know more. This wasn't in the case files on Rebecca Heilshorn; how did Brendan know?

But there was no more time. She needed to scrap her plans for the day and scramble a meeting with Largo as soon as she could.

The corrections officer entered first, holding a cluster of keys. Grimm followed on his heels, his eyes suspicious, flicking little looks at Jennifer but offering Brendan a cold stare. John Rascher and FBI Agent Harlan Doherty came in next. Doherty had a bandage plastered across his nose. He jabbed a finger in the air, pointed at Brendan. His eyes were shining with fury above the swath of white gauze. "You're fucked, Healy."

"Okay . . ." Jennifer said, rising.

Doherty turned his high-beamed hate towards her. "Tell me you got something useful out of this shit bag."

Jennifer ignored him and turned to Brendan. She could feel the eyes of the men boring holes in her back as she leaned towards Brendan. She knew Brendan hadn't told her everything. She knew she needed more evidence to proceed. She knew she hated the men standing behind her now, breathing down her neck.

"Thank you," she said to Brendan.

The CO got behind him and hoisted him to his feet. His manacles clacked together and the chains rattled.

He kept eye contact with her as they stood him up, the same way he'd looked at her when he first walked into the room. There was so much there to unpack, she thought. There was pain, there was resignation, but there was also resilience. Strange for these things to coexist, but somehow not strange, either. Somehow right. She suddenly realized that Brendan had a plan.

He shuffled away, passing by her, his eyes turning away. She stayed standing with her back to the rest of them for a moment. She overheard Grimm speak in a low tone to Brendan. Grimm told him that they would be dealing with the head-butting incident very soon.

She turned around quickly then, too quickly, and her back muscles seized, and she gritted her teeth against the pain. She wanted to tell Grimm to stand down, that Brendan was now a potential witness for the prosecution in a federal case, but bit her tongue. There was an appropriate venue for that; it would only inflame things here.

Doherty glared at Brendan as he left the room. She watched Brendan walk out the door, a large corrections officer filing through after him. She watched his stiff movements. She noticed again the faded bruise on his cheek, the scar that ran down the other side of his face. Between her pains and his bruises, she thought, they were ready for a vacation. Once it was over, they needed a break. Maybe forever.

The door closed.

Rascher was looking at her. Not in the empathetic way Brendan had, but like she was a liability. "You alright?"

"I'm fine." She tried to keep her posture casual, though her lower back was mutinous, threatening collapse.

"Did he give you anything?"

Now Doherty drifted over to the two of them and hovered, listening.

"I need to see Philip Largo tomorrow morning."

Doherty grunted and scowled behind his bandage. "Largo? What for?"

"Jennifer," Rascher pressed, "did Brendan give you something we can use?"

She made an effort to raise her eyes to look at him. "Maybe."

"Then let's get you moving."

He and Doherty stepped back as she walked out of the room. She'd been in there with Brendan for only eighty minutes, but it seemed like longer. It seemed like she'd shared a part of her life with him now. She needed to get outside. Out of these walls. Into the fresh air.

CHAPTER TEN / WEDNESDAY, 4:09 PM

The first blow to his stomach knocked the wind out of him. The second and third, he barely felt. He got numb. Unable to breathe, unable to stand, but, numb.

Brendan dropped to his knees in front of Baker and Ephraim, the two COs. Grimm loomed behind them, darkening the doorway to the isolation cell.

"Far as I'm concerned you can rot in here until your trial," Grimm said.

Brendan's head hung forward, his chin resting on his chest. He closed his eyes. He pictured Sloane. Then there was a bright burst of light as one of the guards kicked him in the head.

When he came to, sometime later, he was lying on his side. He could see beneath his cot. The book was there. He reached out and pulled it to him. He rolled over onto his back, wincing at the pain in his abdomen, cramping the muscles, in his skull, cutting through his thoughts like saw blades. He held the book up over his face and looked at it.

It was *The Great Divorce* by C.S. Lewis.

He hadn't been completely honest with Jennifer Aiken. He'd had some contact with the outside world since he'd been in here. Minimal, but some. A man he never expected to hear from again, Rudy Colinas. Colinas had been his partner on the Rebecca Heilshorn murder case. He'd blown the whistle on Brendan when Brendan had gone off on his own, and it had saved Brendan's life. He'd helped him, too, while Brendan had investigated Argon's death as a private citizen, and then he'd felt the need to stop, for fear of his career, his life, his family. But then after Brendan had been inside Rikers for two months, Colinas had sent this book and a short note.

Brendan took the note out now and read it for the hundredth time.

"Thought you'd like this," Colinas wrote. "Remind you of the good old days. Ha ha."

Another C.S. Lewis book, *The Screwtape Letters*, had been found at the scene of the Rebecca Heilshorn murder. It had helped Brendan to crack the case. Colinas was referring to that with his typical black humor.

"Check out page 98. That's my favorite. Makes me think of you. Makes me think of the future. Keep your head down in there. Reject any marriage proposals. Hey, at least you're ugly. That should help. Stay strong, my brother. — R."

Brendan kept the note tucked into the passage Colinas had mentioned. Now he read the text highlighted in the book, as he did nearly every day.

> *"Son," he said, "Ye cannot, in your present state, understand eternity . . . That is what mortals misunderstand. "They say of some temporal suffering, 'No future bliss can make up for it,' not knowing that Heaven, once attained, will work backwards and turn even that agony into a glory.*

The page shook; his hands were trembling. He dropped the book to the floor and covered his face. He let the anger pass through him, a sensation of flames licking the channels of his body, the belching heat of a furnace somewhere deep within.

Every day, he was grateful to Colinas for that book. He didn't think Colinas could know the extent to which it would not only release a flood of feelings in Brendan, but grant him insights, too.

He related the passage to himself, to his own life. There was no doubt about that. He was haunted by what he had done wrong and he had to make things right. But he wasn't alone. Philip Largo was another man, like him, who'd strayed from the path and suffered the enduring consequences. The two men were tied together by fate.

CHAPTER ELEVEN / THURSDAY, 9:41 AM

Philip Largo looked terrible. His skin seemed pulled too tightly over his face, which was otherwise handsome — he had sharp cheekbones and full lips. He had the look of a governor, despite the smudges of fatigue and the bent corners of his mouth. Since John F. Kennedy, what a politician really needed most was a camera-friendly face. Beneath the strain, Philip Largo had it. Jennifer wondered why someone like him, with a beautiful wife and children, and a bright future ahead of him, would have ever wanted to sleep with a prostitute.

They sat at his small lakeside home in Western New York. The place was no great shakes — a one-bedroom cabin that looked like the kind the guy might have fixed up in more robust times. The high grass had gone to seed, swishing against the shiplap siding of the house in the breeze from the lake. It was as if Largo had just decided to let it all go.

He regarded Jennifer with wary suspicion.

"Thank you so much," she began, "for agreeing to meet with me."

He fidgeted for a moment, in a boyish way, before he looked up at her. "You're persuasive."

80

She smiled at him. She felt a bit better after a night's rest, after leaving Rikers Island behind. She'd even gone for a walk that morning, feeling some relief in her joints and muscles, grateful for a temporary reprieve from the headaches and unnerving visual anomalies. She knew it wouldn't last forever, though.

He watched her, seeming to examine her, in a similar way to Brendan. They sat in a pair of wooden chairs, and faced each other in his overgrown yard. Jennifer's security detail was nearby, one standing next to the vehicles in the driveway, another walking the perimeter, a third down by the cattails along the lakeshore, looking decidedly out of place there, a large man in a black suit framed by the silvery water.

"See these guys?" She twirled her finger, loosely pointing at the security detail. "I went for a walk this morning . . . I used to be a runner. They've got me at a Marriott Courtyard just south of Rochester. Not a bad place. Nothing around, though. I guess it's where Xerox used to have offices, warehouses, and they're all gone. Anyway, I go for my walk and these guys are driving along behind me. They follow me everywhere."

He turned his wounded eyes on her; now she saw the frustration deep within him. The worst kind — the knotted, twisted, obdurate kind that resisted its own resolve. The kind of frustration a person could lose themselves to, because they knew not trying to fix it somehow gave them license to do other things. To let the anger roil to the surface. It was a dangerous state to be in. She could see why Philip Largo had tucked himself away here, away from everything. He was afraid of what he might do.

Or, there was something else. Something more.

She tried to coax him out of his shell. "The reason I have them pasted to me like three overgrown kids is because of what happened to me. I was abducted in broad daylight, back when I was a strong runner." She watched him countenance this and continued. "I was taken to a building in Manhattan and dosed with thallium nitrate. I was interrogated, and the idea was if I gave the other side what they wanted, they'd administer an antidote. But I never really believed that, because they never really meant it. They wanted to find out what I knew and then kill me. So, you can trust me, Mr. Largo, because I'm not dead. Because after seven months of hiding out in New York and Washington, I'm back out in the world." She paused, thinking better of tacking on the phrase, *and you can be, too.*

His expression softened and he gazed out over the lake. The way he sat in his chair, with his hands out on his knees, he looked like a person sorely out of place. He belonged in office. It killed him to be here like this, to be purposeless.

"Nobody has been on my side for a long time," he said, not in a self-pitying way, but matter-of-factly. He nodded to himself, then lifted his hands from his knees and looked down and studied them as if there were answers there to the riddles of human nature.

She leaned in slightly. "Why don't you tell me what happened? In your own words. Not the words you were coached by your people to say to the media."

He looked up from his hands. "They did a good job of delivering me from all that, pretty quick, don't you think? For a scandal, it had less publicity than others. You would've thought they'd make hay."

"Maybe you shouldn't discount that there were people in the media who actually liked you and what you stood for, and couldn't bring themselves to get in on the lynching."

He watched her for a moment and then looked away again.

She steeled herself and took a breath. It was one thing to talk over the phone, it was another to do this sort of thing in person. "Mr. Largo . . . Can you answer something for me?"

"I can try," he said, looking out over the lake again.

"Can you verify that the name of the escort was Danice?"

He slowly turned back to her. "I can."

"Do you know what Danice's real identity was?"

She saw him draw a deep breath, marshaling the will to tell his story. "It was a long time ago."

"I understand."

"It's best if I just tell you what happened."

"I would like that."

He closed his eyes for a moment. "Celia, that's my wife, she knew it was going to be hard for us, the life of a politician." His eyelids drifted up. "I didn't think it would be that hard, though. I'm from out here, you know? I was born in Almond. She's from the Midwest. I thought, okay, I'll spend the time in Albany and I'll be home every other weekend and we'll make it work." He tilted his forehead down, his sad eyes peering up from beneath his furrowed brow.

She nodded in encouragement.

"Well, it's never what you think. You get pulled away for weeks at a time, you miss one weekend and you realize it's a month since you've been home. You're missing things with your kids, your wife is becoming a stranger. And then, ramping up to campaign, forget it. You're raising money, looking at all the initiatives, budget talks until six in the morning . . . I'm not making excuses, I'm just saying — I jumped at the chance to run, if only because if I won, we could all live together in Albany, and it would solve so many problems. Not to mention, you know, I would be governor."

He smiled and she saw some of that old Largo, the charmer in front of the cameras, the impassioned, rising star transcending the broken legislature. She saw his sincerity, too. She didn't question whether the office itself was more a motivating factor than his desire to bring his family back together. He would have done a great job, if not for that reason alone.

"And then one night, it's late, I've been out with some of my staff, it's been two months since I've been home to visit . . . Ceal and I are in this long, quiet fight, on and off over the phone. And there she is. This girl who's been sort of popping up all night; I thought she was a friend of one of my staffers, maybe an intern I hadn't met, but by now my staff have all gone home and I'm sitting there at the bar and I know I've got to turn in but it's just . . . in that moment, I didn't want to. You know? One of those nights where going to bed just means waking up the next day and having to start all over again and I don't know. . . I needed a break."

Largo leaned forward and put his head in his hands. "God," he said, "she was barely in her twenties." He was silent for a moment and Jennifer didn't press him any further. She looked around at her security detail. Much as she'd bemoaned their presence, she already felt a fondness for them. The one by the pond had gotten up and was further away along the edge, turning to where a path led into a section of woods.

"Philip," she said softly. He looked up. She saw tears in his eyes. "Do you know who she was?"

He gave her a long look. "I read about it, saw a few things on TV. And I heard, from a few close friends."

She waited for him to say the name. Instead he looked down again, and she realized he was trying to hide his fear from her.

"I understand the need for discretion. You knew you had to step out of the race, and disappear from politics altogether, or that the information you were with . . . someone . . . it was going to be made public."

His head snapped up to look at her, and she saw that fear burning together with a savage protective look.

"More than that. I had a family. Still do. Even if I'm not with them."

84

If someone had put this hook into him, they still had him on a taut line.

"Okay," she said, thinking. "Let me ask you this — why? Why do you think someone would want to bring you down? An issue you dug your heels in on? I've gone over your bio, I know what you did as an assemblyman. There's no one obvious tack you seem to follow, you really acted bipartisan. Something I missed?"

He gathered himself together and sat up straighter. His eyes narrowed into a hawkish stare.

"You work for the Justice Department?"

"Correct."

"As a special prosecutor."

"Yes?"

"You'll say I'm nuts."

"I doubt it."

"You'll say its conspiracy-theory bullshit."

"Try me."

He lifted an arm and pointed behind her. "Are your men . . . what are they doing?"

She looked behind her. Two of her security detail were trotting away from the house, down the dirt driveway, while the other guy remained by the vehicles, speaking into the transmitter attached to his sleeve cuff.

CHAPTER TWELVE / THURSDAY, 10:23 AM

Jennifer and Largo stood up and watched as the security guy by the vehicles turned and came across the yard towards them. Jennifer's heart pounded. He called over to them.

"Sorry," he said. "It's okay. Couple kids back there tromping through the woods, I guess they're just kids being kids, trying to get a closer look at us."

Jennifer saw the two other security guards coming back down the driveway towards Largo's property. They looked grim, perturbed by the intruders, harmless kids or not.

Still, she felt her pulse easing. Largo said, "I should have warned you about that. The nearest neighbor is about a quarter mile away, and there're always kids out there. This is really their turf."

She offered Largo a smile and gestured for him to sit down. She could see how frayed his nerves were. Hers didn't feel much better. Once they were facing each other again, she tried to recover the openness they'd started to get going.

"You were saying?"

He cleared his throat and seemed to find his bearings. "Part of my job as assemblyman involved looking into land development in rural areas. There's a lot of farm country in New York, more than a lot of people know. And the UN's report on future global food shortages has prompted policy ideas from the Pentagon."

She nodded. "Eminent domain. I'm friends with the director of the Bureau of Land Management."

"Then you know that it's controversial. People are worried they're going to be shipped off to high-density housing in cities while the government takes over all the farmland." He looked at her with pleading eyes. "I'm not an alarmist, Agent Aiken, or a conspiracy theorist. I'm not. But I came across something while I was doing my research on rural land use."

"Please."

He gripped his knees. "Okay. What you won't find, even as an agent for the Department of Justice, what you won't find, declassified, are the no-bid contracts Titan Med Tech and Titan Construction got with the US Military. And I'm talking military, armed forces, but I'm also talking about local, county, state, and federal law enforcement. There's been the push since 9/11 to have all law enforcement bodies speaking the same language, cooperating. And armed to the teeth. We're talking military tanks in the sheriff's department. Drones in the Texas sky."

"That's pretty drastic." But she found herself thinking about Seamus Argon. About people who believed only militias could resist the US government and military taking total authoritarian control of the country.

"You wanted me to speak plainly."

"I did, I do."

"Titan subsidiaries get exclusive contracts, in one case for all medical supplies for this conglomeration of state, local, federal law enforcement, and a huge chunk of armed forces. Billions of dollars. It was my job to look into Titan because of land development in Albany. Specifically, the UAlbany campus."

She knew the building. Titan Construction had erected a new campus building for UAlbany. The New Business School was where Brendan Healy had waged his showdown with Reginald Forrester and Jerry Brown. Brendan had been searching for Rebecca Heilshorn's killer.

"So you were . . . generally suspicious of Titan, due to what you found with the Titan Med Tech contracts for US military and police. And so, what, you moved to block the construction at UAlbany?"

"Generally suspicious? Yeah. You could say that. I started looking at the specs for the building. That was my job. And I found something."

"What?"

"Part of the design for the building was for a massive data center. Like the kind only found in a few places around the world. London, Paris, Los Angeles. There are two in Manhattan. They call one of them the Meet-Me-Room."

"Why would Titan . . . why would UAlbany want to build a data center there?"

"My question exactly. And where would they get the money? That's hundreds of millions. Maybe more. So I spoke to the president of the college. Or, I tried to. He was evasive, to put it nicely. Nobody seemed to want to talk about it. I wanted to know who was in charge of making this kind of a decision for the state — for the country, really. And, again, who was funding it."

"What did you find?"

"Closed doors, mostly. I uncovered a labyrinth of money that was moved around through dummies and shell corporations. I saw a word, once or twice: Altnet. And then I received a memo from US Cyber Command, a division of the CSS. Telling me to cease my inquiry. That there were matters of national security at stake."

She felt something cold twist inside of her, and shivered in her light coat despite the fact that the sun was shining on a warm June day.

She was at a loss for the moment. Largo had seen something the government didn't want him to. It was possible the government could have been already on to Nonsystem back then, and didn't want Largo inadvertently screwing up a covert operation. It happened more often than people liked to admit, unanticipated crossover in the government that made a mess of things.

"Philip," she said. "I want to thank you for your candor. In return, I'm going to be frank, too. Please know that I understand your concerns. Your fears. But I can help you. The escort you were with, about seven years ago now, you know Danice was not her real name. Her name was Rebecca Heilshorn."

Largo's face drained of blood. He looked like he was going to be sick. "I don't want to talk about it anymore," he said in a small voice.

"Please, Philip. I know this is hard. For a while, through Oneida County's investigation, it was believed Rebecca didn't find her way into the business until later, coerced by a woman named Olivia Jane, but it seems like she was positioned quite early on. Maybe even starting with you."

He shook his head, with his eyes closed. He gripped the chair. His knuckles were white, and she was reminded of flying into Rikers, her trepidation at facing Brendan Healy.

"I can't . . ." he said. He was about to get up and leave.

"The detective on Rebecca's murder," she hurried, "Brendan Healy. I believe he knows, because during the investigation he encountered Rebecca's personal driver. The one who probably brought her to the hotel you were staying in that night, picked her up the next day. Eddie Stemp."

Largo opened his eyes. His expression hardened. "I agreed to see you, Agent Aiken, because I couldn't just sit here anymore. But, you're not thinking about the cost. You're not seeing the whole picture. It's not just my reputation, for God's sake. They wanted me gone — Alexander Heilshorn wanted me gone — *Titan* wanted me gone, and to stay gone, and to sit here, and to suffer. Because I opposed him." He leaned towards her, dropping his head.

Bent over like that, Largo muttered something. "There's a disc."

"What, Philip? What do you mean?"

"There's a disc," he said. He raised his head. His face was one of terror, after many years of fear settling in and making a home in the soul. "A compilation, ten years' worth, or so, of Titan's backdoor deals, along with just about every other piece of political malfeasance you can think of. A kind of bottom-up monitoring of government."

"How do you know this?"

"Argon."

"Seamus Argon?" She remembered Brendan telling her he'd first become interested in Philip Largo while investigating Argon's death.

Largo nodded. "We talked. Just before he died."

"What did he tell you?"

Largo sat back, and his chest expanded with a deep breath. He blew out the air forcibly, and wiped at his eyes as he composed himself. "He said that this was all going to be over soon. That everything was going to come out, at last."

She took this in, and then asked. "Where is that disc now?"

But Philip Largo just looked at her with his sad eyes. He didn't know.

CHAPTER THIRTEEN / THURSDAY, 11:11 AM

In summer Laurel Grove was as pretty as a picture, Staryles thought. White limestone radiated calm and cool. As lazy June summer days came to an end, nothing was more languorous than the atmosphere on the retirement home campus. He could just sense it as he drove into the parking lot in his dark blue Oldsmobile Cutlass.

As he popped the trunk of the car, his feelings were confirmed when a nurse — or orderly, or personal care giver, whatever they were called — came rolling an old-timer out at a snail's pace. Staryles exited the vehicle, went around to the trunk and pulled out a small duffel bag. He headed to the front entrance.

The nurse smiled and the old timer — a white man with even whiter hair, and veins and liver spots showing through his parchment skin — waved a knobby hand as Staryles approached. Staryles waved back. There was no hurly-burly here, no urgency. The dusty summer air, the stillness of the maple trees by the river, the ease of the low Hudson itself, Pepsi-colored water purling unhurriedly down towards the city.

Staryles passed the nurse and the old timer (*bet that corn husk saw the beaches of the Pacific or Normandy so close and personal he could count the grains of sand*) and reached the entrance. The automatic doors swung inward, inviting him in.

He stepped into a vestibule with a bank of locked brass mailboxes, and then to a second set of doors. Lettering on the glass declared that *These Doors Are Locked 7 PM to 7 AM*.

But they swung open now, friendly and welcoming. Laurel Grove was not some squat concrete building with a few fake plants in the lobby in some rundown district of town. Laurel Grove was top-notch and pricey.

But their security sucked.

Staryles maintained his leisurely pace, admiring the plants — not fake — which decorated the front lobby, the low benches that were sort of Art Deco with cushions, the mosaic stone walls with their shining specks of mica.

The front-desk nurse smiled at him and he smiled back. He noticed how her eyes dropped to his clothes. No suit today, but a pair of M3 Safari designer jeans, a vintage-fit white t-shirt from Hugo Boss, and a pair of sandals Christ himself would envy.

For just a second he felt a pinch in his gut at the blasphemy, and almost lost his smile. But then he watched how the nurse's eyes lingered on him — it was only a second, barely a second, but that was all it took — and he regained his full presence.

"Hello," he said in a voice which he'd carefully cultivated, even practiced during morning sit-ups. He set down his bag.

"Hello," she said back, failing utterly to hide the fact that she was single and found him intriguing, if a little intimidating. The usual.

"Here to see Philomena Argon," he said.

"Oh wonderful," she chirped, and then something in her changed. Her smile faded and her eyes grew suspicious. It was happening again, this metamorphosis which occurred in people whenever he got close.

As she gathered up the log book, he turned away. He decided it was less pleasant in here than he had first thought. It was more like some smug Ivy League library, or some fancy home where the uppity rich wife never lets the kids touch anything. It was stuffy in here.

"Here you go, just sign in right here and I'll page the home worker to bring you in."

Mmpf. Staryles thought. *A home worker.* The term was nonsensical.

But he didn't share this insight. Instead he gave the nurse behind the desk another full-veneer smile and bent forward over the log book.

The front-desk lady turned away, giving Staryles a chance to fan the pages of the logbook. He already knew Healy had been here. Seven months previously, late November, Healy had stood right here, right at this desk. But he just wanted to see. When he had flipped to the appropriate date he scanned the page. Sure enough, there was Healy's scrawl. Staryles felt a small thrill and sense of self-satisfaction. He would have made a good detective himself, if he weren't in such high demand for a different vocation.

He quickly returned to today's page, signed and turned the book around to face the nurse who stood up and took it without so much as a glance at it. She put it back beneath the countertop, gave him one more fake smile and then turned her shoulder to him as she went back to whatever she was doing on the computer. Probably Facebook, or Pinterest.

These women. The same thing kept happening. They didn't recognize him. Didn't seem him for who he truly was, what he really could do.

He looked through the glass doors. The nurse pushing the old-timer in the wheelchair had only just made it to the end of the front walk, heading towards some elm trees where there was a picnic table.

The picnic table sparked a memory of a family picnic, the only one they had ever had as far as he could remember. His father had lectured the young boys about how the nation was founded on the family structure, with the father meting out proper discipline and punishment. *It's the mother's job to bear children and nurse them*, he'd said, *the father's job to straighten the spine.*

Their mother had not been happy with the conversation. Staryles remembered how she had looked as if she'd rather be anywhere other than sitting with her husband and these three boys she had somehow rented a womb to for nine months a piece, only to lose them to the father the moment they'd dropped off the nipple. His mother's face haunted the expressions of the women he encountered.

"Sir?"

Staryles snapped to attention, his spine rigid, his hands ready. Within the span of a breath, however, he caught hold of himself and turned on a smile.

"All set for you, sir," said the home worker who'd come to escort him.

"Great," he said, slipping the strap of his duffel bag over his shoulder.

They walked down the hallway together.

* * *

Philomena Argon was in her room. Everything was exactly the way it had been the last time Staryles had seen it. The quaint furniture, the framed picture of her parents in their Scottish getups. The roll-top desk, not so unlike the roll-top desk Olivia Jane had kept in her house. Stupid Olivia Jane. Unable to keep her mouth shut in the end.

Mena sat quietly at the edge of her bed, watching Staryles as he softly closed the door behind him.

He walked across the room and squatted in front of her, relishing the way his thigh muscles felt taut and ropy, the way his spine was straight as a board.

94

"Hi, Mena. I thought we'd talk a little bit. I was wondering if you knew the story of King Midas." He looked at her, perhaps the way his father had looked at his mother that day. His mother hadn't been around for long after that picnic. "It's a good story. The god Apollo calls King Midas an ass and touches him and gives Midas the ears of a donkey."

He searched her foggy eyes. It was hard to say, but he felt like she was emanating a little hatred towards him.

"Midas is embarrassed — I can only imagine — and covers up the ears with a huge hat. But guess who knows about the ears? His barber. Those town barbers have all the juicy secrets. Midas warns the barber never to speak of it or he'll be beheaded. But the barber is just exploding with this intel, he's just bursting."

Staryles looked around the room, out the window, and then back at Philomena. He opened his bag and took out a pair of black gloves.

"So you know what he does? He runs out and digs a hole in the bank of the Pactolus River, checks to make sure no one is around, and then whispers the secret about Midas' ass-ears into the hole. Boom, done, got it out of his system. So he fills up the hole and leaves. But, Mena, the next spring, the reeds sprout. One grows up from the hole, and it whispers to the other reeds. The reeds tell the insects, and the insects tell the birds, and a bird lands on Midas' window. Guess what? The bird declares that Midas has the ears of a donkey hidden beneath his Phrygian cap. And so you can imagine what happened then."

Staryles reached into the bag and took out a small vial of white powder. He cocked his head to the side and licked his lips, just a quick dart of the tongue.

"You're kind of a blabbermouth, Mena. Let's face it. Kind of a barber-type. It's people like you that make regs what they are — who make security have to be as tight as it is."

Staryles brought his gloved hand an inch from her skin and feathered his fingertips down the side of her sagging face. His eyebrows knitted together in mock compassion.

"See? Your admonishment was poetic justice, I'll give them that. You can't talk because of your stroke. But I'm the next generation. I don't have that sense of mercy, Mena. No stroke for you this time."

He looked out the window again, his face a carefully built expression of serious contemplation. He practiced this face in reflective surfaces; he wished he could see himself now, but the room was gloomy and the day bright outside. No reflection.

He took the vial of thallus sulfate and tapped it against his thigh, cutting his gaze back over to her. Her eyes, milky with glaucoma but still intelligent, dropped to glance at the vial, then met his stare.

They remained like that for a few moments, Staryles squatting and looking directly into her eyes, Philomena looking right back.

Then he spoke, "Where is it, Mena? Is it in your room here somewhere?"

She mumbled something unintelligible. He got up and sat down on the bed beside her. It was a soft mattress, way too soft for his tastes. He cupped his free hand around his ear. "What's that, Mena?" He pulled the hand away and then tilted his head to the side. "Did you give it to your brother? Is that what you did? You've been sitting on that IMF data, like a hen on an egg, for a long time." He clucked his tongue, and shook his head with parental disappointment.

She said something again. It sounded like there was some suction in her mouth, like she was at a dentist with that tube hanging from her lips. Was she playing dumb? Surely she could speak better. Her muscle memory had to have come back somewhat after all these years.

"Because I wonder," Staryles said, lifting the vial to his face. He tapped the tip of it against his jutting chin and rolled his eyes to the ceiling. "I wonder if Lawrence Taber, that old son of a gun, if when he sent Brendan Healy down here last year to look for something . . . I wonder if he was hoping Seamus Argon had taken all your hard work, and stashed it somewhere." His eyes found her again. "You think?"

This time she made no effort to speak. Staryles pursed his lips and puffed his cheeks out like a chipmunk, then blew through his lips. He sucked air in through his teeth and then stood upright. He turned his head to look back out the window. "Yeah. That's what I think, too." He considered things for a moment, striking a thoughtful pose, gazing into the rolling green yard outside. Sun dazzled the chrome and plastic of the vehicles in the parking lot. The nurse pushing the old man in the wheelchair was off to the left, turning back this way.

It was so quiet here. So peaceful and still. You could lose all sense of time, really. There wasn't even a television in Philomena's room, or a computer, nothing. How did she stay in touch? He looked at her. This woman who had once been plugged right into the very heart of it. Secrets swarming around her like a vortex.

Secrets necessary to keep people safe? Staryles wasn't so naïve. Midas should've just come out with his ears instead of burying his secret beneath that ridiculous cap. Because soon the reeds would know, and the insects would know, and the birds would know.

Philomena was like the barber. Lawrence Taber was one of the birds. You could hardly blame the bird, really. But you could — and you should — behead the barber.

He sat shoulder to shoulder with her and carefully unscrewed the vial. It would be an hour or so before anyone even checked on her and he would be long gone. With her failing health, Mena wouldn't last as long as the

97

others. A few hours of necrosis, maybe one night, and her heart would give out.

"Philomena," he said in his best stern-but-warm voice, "if you have it here, tell me. Otherwise, I'm pretty sure I know where it is, anyway."

A nerve fired beneath his eye. He felt it, and it triggered a flare of anger. He brought the vial up to her lips. He expected her to start babbling, to cry for help, but she was motionless and silent. She actually turned her head away. He followed her gaze and together they looked out the window.

She remained silent, and he pressed his fingers against her cheeks and forced open her mouth. Her skin felt as thin as tissue paper, her lips parted easily, as if she didn't care. He felt her slump against him, the two of them watching that still, unmolested world through the glass.

CHAPTER FOURTEEN / THREE MONTHS
AGO

By the time Louis Tremont finished his time at Rikers Island, he had dropped twenty-six pounds. Brendan could imagine the man he once was. He saw Tremont sitting in a boxy old Crown Vic outside of a Manhattan bank, casing the joint for access points and timing the rotation of the security staff. A younger Tremont, fit, top of his game, the world as his piggy bank. He'd smoked cigars in those days, he said, so Brendan pictured the younger Tremont puffing on a Rocky Patel as he watched the bank like a predator.

It was a Sunday, a quiet day in the West Facility, when Tremont offered the final piece of information Brendan needed. It had nothing to do with the channeling of drugs through the jail system. He was folding his spare set of sheets; Tremont often folded and refolded his bedding when he was thinking about something, or when he was nervous, a habit developed from all the time he spent in the laundry. And he was getting out in less than forty-eight hours. Brendan thought Tremont was worried he would slip back into crime and wind up in Rikers again.

"I know you don't want to talk about it," Tremont said. He made a careful, ruler-straight crease in the sheets and folded them over. "But I gotta tell you, I heard something."

Brendan was rereading *The Great Divorce* and tonguing the cavity where his molar had been knocked out not long before. *Heaven will work backwards and turn even that agony into a glory.* He looked up. "I don't want to talk about what? Your weight loss? I think we've covered it. You look great, boss. The ladies will be lining up."

Tremont laughed, but there was little humor in it. "You're kind of like a celebrity," he said.

"Oh yeah?"

"When you came in here, there was a buzz about you. High-profile beef. You know?"

"I guess."

"Well, big shit, there have been some other celebrity-types through here," he said. "You're not so special."

"I'm dying to know."

Tremont set down a perfect square of a folded top sheet, laying it gently on his top bunk. "Lil' Wayne, was here. You know? That rapper. 'Motherfucker' this and that. Tupac, too. Then Plaxico Burress, NFL receiver, he took a short nap here. And back in the day, Sid Vicious. Can you believe that?"

"I'm not sure I fall in the same category."

"No. Maybe not. But you fall in with who's here now."

Brendan was keeping it light, but he sensed the shift in Tremont's tone. They did a bit of goofing around to pass the time. This wasn't part of that.

"Alright. Who?"

"Someone who really takes the cake."

"Enough of the suspense, Lou. Let's have it."

"Okay. So, just the head of the IMF."

"Alright, now you're fucking with me again." Brendan put his nose back in his book. He felt the hairs on his neck standing up. "This more about the pigeon population dropping just before the cafeteria serves chicken cacciatore?"

"Didier Lazard. Here for an alleged sexual assault of a housekeeping employee at the Waldorf-Astoria. Awaiting trial, just like you. Though I imagine his will get moved to the head of the docket, no offense. Guy's loaded."

Brendan looked up from his book. "He's been in protective custody?"

"Yep. For two weeks."

"Okay. So what? And this guy is in the same category with me, how?"

Tremont stepped away from the bunk and sat down on the toilet. He'd lost weight, but he was a still a big man, getting on in years, and the flesh seemed to hang on his bones. He turned his dark face to Brendan, who sat on the bottom bunk, tucked into the shadows. "Word I heard was that Lazard was here to meet with the head of the CSS. Guy named Wick. That's why he was in town. But, seems he got touchy-feely with the maid and is taking a ride for it."

Brendan felt his skin crawl. It wasn't exactly fear or distaste, it was the sense of something coming together, like an electric charge turned up in the room.

"How do I get to him?"

"You don't. He's in the protection wing."

* * *

"What is it, Healy? You've got something for me?" Grimm looked desperate. The pouches beneath his eyes could hold pennies. The heat in his office was stifling. Outside, the late March afternoon was gray and cold. It looked like it was about to snow.

"I need to see Didier Lazard."

Grimm blinked, straight-faced. "That's funny, Healy. I didn't know you were so funny. The fuck do you think you need to see him for? Get an autograph?"

"Because of the smuggling going on in here."

Grimm pursed his lips and exhaled through his nostrils. "Healy, goddammit. Three months I get nothing from you. You want to fuck around with me? Fine. Let's see how you fair out there in gen. pop. with Laruso after you."

"Just hear me out, sir."

Baker appeared in the doorway. Brendan turned to look at CO Baker's mouth curled into a sly smile, as if he'd been waiting for Healy to screw up and to get the opportunity to punish him for it. He entered the room and Brendan turned quickly back to Grimm.

"It's not because Lazard is involved directly," Brendan said quickly. "It's the facility. The protective custody cells in West Facility are your major gateway."

Grimm's expression shifted from rage to interest. He held up his hand, and Brendan sensed Baker come to a stop just behind him, looming there, ready to pounce.

Brendan hurried on. "Think about it, sir. The rest of your facility is overpopulated. Men everywhere — guards and inmates. West Facility is far less populated. You've got special ingresses and egresses for inmates in custody — places where the security is isolated."

"Then how is it being distributed?"

"Through the laundry," Brendan lied. "You've got all those cots set up to handle the overflow. The machines there are running practically around the clock, so you've got laundry service making trips over here to wash that extra bedding and fatigues. Then the washed stuff goes back to the other facilities, and contains a little something besides clean sheets."

Grimm leaned back in his chair, which squeaked beneath his considerable weight. He skewered Brendan with his glare. "And how do you know this?"

Brendan took a breath. "Sir, I've been quietly interviewing dozens of inmates. I've been taking all this time to build a case that gives you everything you need. But if I give you information now and you, in turn, do a little in-house cleaning, stave off this tactical search probe — which you and I both know is going to hit the jackpot with all the bug juice running through this place . . . You've got, what? Two years until social security and full pension, you said? You really want the Corrections Commissioner pulling you two years before retirement, the whole thing splashed all over the media? Because that's what will happen."

Grimm was as silent as a tomb, unmoving, watching Healy with dead mackerel eyes. For a moment Brendan thought his life might be over. Grimm would just do away with him. Change his mind on the whole thing and have Baker drag him down into the laundry where the rest of the guards would beat him to death. Or stick him in segregation and let them pay him visits over a period of weeks, maybe months. He'd already threatened as much.

"Who was talking?"

Brendan felt his heart thumping. "I would like to protect my sources if I could, sir."

"What are you, a fucking journalist for the *Times*? Protect your sources? What do you care about what happens to some other scumbag in here? I put you together with Tremont for a reason . . ."

"I don't, sir. I care about myself." He paused and swallowed down the bile rising in his throat. If he involved his cellmate in the scam, Tremont's nerves would prove accurate, his obsessively folded sheets auguries — Grimm wouldn't let him go anywhere. He would trump something up to keep Tremont inside until things were resolved. "If I disclose my sources," Brendan said, "I'm as good as dead. But you let me do this, let me go to the protective wing, it circumvents the source. We can say you put me there, for whatever reason you want to come up with, and I found things out on my own."

Grimm took all of this in. He even brought his hands up and tented the fingers together, as if he were the Godfather. After a full, ostentatious, thirty seconds of this, he nodded. Brendan could feel Baker breathing down his neck. The man's desire to throttle Brendan was palpable, as if it were the source of the heat in the room rather than the clanking radiator.

"Alright," Grimm said at last. "So we send you into the protective wing to talk to Lazard. First of all, what's your cover? And second of all, if we already know the contraband is being distributed via the laundry, what are you going to find?"

"Glad you asked, sir. Good questions. My cover is that you're moving me into protective custody."

Grimm changed his posture to sit up straighter and was waving his hands in the air. "I don't like that. Too much paperwork. It will look suspicious if we get a probe audit, which we're bound to, because if they're waiting to pounce on the raid, and I've got to tell you, I can feel the cocksuckers ready to pounce, and when they do and they find nothing, they're going to know I beat them to the punch and then they're going to get their paper-pushers in here and look through every one of my files . . ."

"You won't do the paper work on me, sir."

"Excuse me?"

"Inmates bounce in and out of the protective wing all the time. No one is going to notice I'm gone for two days. Three, tops. Then I'm right back to my Cadillac."

"Your celly will notice."

"Tremont will go along with whatever story you feed him, sir. He wants to do right by you, wants to do his time and be out of here tomorrow."

Grimm laughed. It was a wicked, humorless laugh. "Everyone wants to get out of here." He grew straight faced again. "So if this happens and if you get in, what indisputable evidence are you going to get for me so I can move on this?"

"I'm going to get you contraband."

Grimm blinked. "How?"

"Lazard. He has the one occupied cell in your private wing. And that's where they're storing it right after it comes in, before it gets moved down to the laundry with his sheets. Storing it in the other cells would be recorded — every time one of these cells opens or closes, you have an account of that. So it's the one cell that's occupied. The one you usually reserve for these celebrity-types. No one bats an eyelid when their cell is opened. And they're not complaining that they've got the freshest bedding in town; they expect it, they're used to being treated like royalty. That's probably why Lazard figured he'd pinch a little tail and get away with it."

Another chuckle from Grimm, a sinister sound. Brendan felt a surge of nervous excitement. It might work.

But Grimm frowned. "And how are you going to get the contraband from Lazard's cell? If I put you in there, then I've got to move him, and we're back to the whole paper trail problem, Healy."

"I'm going to talk him into giving it to me."

Grimm's eyes remained glassy and serious. "You are?"

"Yes."

"And just how are you going to do that?" Now Grimm's face contorted into a violent mask. "You're telling me your plan is to have the director of the IMF turn over the illegal contraband in his cell to you? What if when he gets out of here in two months, he decides to tell the whole goddamned world that drugs were being stored in his fucking cell at Rikers-fucking-Island?" Grimm was shouting.

"He won't. Or, even if he thinks he can, he's the *former* head of the IMF. No one is going to give a shit about what he has to say about his time in jail for sexual harassment, especially not the global organization he used to represent."

Grimm sat back again, slowly, never taking his eyes off Brendan. Outside, the first flakes of snow started to drift down.

"Okay," Grimm said. He looked at Baker. "Let's make it happen."

CHAPTER FIFTEEN / THREE MONTHS AGO

If the West Facility was a quiet, less-populated building than the rest of Rikers Island, the protective custody wing was a morgue. Baker led Brendan along a narrow corridor which pitched gradually down into nothing but the echo of footfalls and odorless pumped air.

Brendan was to wait two hours until yard-time when he would be able to see Lazard.

The time passed as slowly as his first night inside. He'd been transported by bus after being processed out of the 11th precinct in Manhattan, driven in the back of an NYPD cruiser to another jail in midtown where he'd spent three nights, and then from the midtown jail up to the bridge over the East River to Rikers. He remembered the way it had looked in the haze, like some medieval island fortress. The flat, grey buildings, the chain-link fences bent on top with an interminable coil of cyclone wire. As the bus had drawn him across the long bridge, he felt a deep ache in his chest. He was utterly alone. He'd always been an outsider, even when he was married to Angie he would exile himself emotionally. But there was a time when he'd had a wife, a mother, a father. He'd had a child. And it had all been over in ten minutes, a flurry of scrapbook images he'd filed away to perhaps appreciate later, sometime down the road when he arrived in some elusive place.

Here it was. Doing time in an island jail complex, a place of lost souls, violence, and desolation. A place he knew he deserved to be. A place where the present would find him at last and unfurl into painstaking eternity. This new purgatory even lonelier than the last. No cellmate, no noise, no life.

It had been so long since he'd studied a picture of his wife and child that their images had left him. He tried to trace their faces in his mind and found he couldn't.

He suddenly wanted a cigarette. He fantasized about lowering his head to light the cigarette, the flash of lighter flame in his eyes, cupping it in his hand. The taste, the smell, the moment, the relaxation. The time-out from the torture.

He tried to focus on something else. He decided to mull over what he knew about the IMF.

In their own words, the IMF promoted financial stability around the world, sought to reduce poverty, promote economic development, high employment, and facilitate international trade. They called themselves "financial firefighters," and sought to put out the economic fires around the world by deploying emergency loans. The IMF was composed of 188 countries worldwide, and the organization described itself as working to foster global monetary cooperation and to secure financial stability. Didier Lazard had been its head.

And then there was the other point of view about the IMF, probably one Tremont would share. Seamus Argon, too. Detractors considered them economic slave masters, that the loans deployed were highly conditional, unrealistic for the struggling nations they were supposed to be helping. They would drag the indigenous workforce into endless debt and wage slavery while exploiting the natural resources and fleecing those nations dry.

Claims were made that the monetarist policies of the IMF towards low inflation and low budget deficits prevented developing countries from being able to scale up public investment in public health infrastructure. Indebted countries were also said to damage their own environments to generate cash flow from oil, gas, coal, and forest-destroying lumber and agricultural projects.

It was global economic slavery.

Brendan heard a guard approaching, the whispering of starched fabric and the jangle of keys. The sound roused him out of his reverie. The time had passed.

A shape appeared outside of the cell, a dark face, eyes shining.

"Healy. Yard time."

The door opened.

* * *

As if he'd been waiting for him, Didier Lazard watched Brendan emerge from the jail and into the yard. He had thick, black eyebrows and silver hair. He probably weighed over two hundred pounds, filling out the jail-issue winter coat, his thick legs stretching the fabric of his pants.

He was smoking a cigarette.

Lazard looked Brendan up and down, and then took a pull from the tobacco. Brendan couldn't help but stare at it.

The yard was nothing but a dirt square surrounded by three stories of brick and barred windows. The sky was a low, bruised rectangle of clouds. Snow flurried down and dusted the ground. Brendan stood a few feet away from Lazard, but he could smell that cigarette.

Lazard pulled a pack of Dunhill from his pocket. He pulled the lid back and shook the pack so that a few cigarettes slid halfway out. He thrust the pack in Brendan's direction. "You want?"

Brendan practically licked his chops.

"I'll pass, thanks."

His inner voices screamed in protest.

Lazard shrugged and tapped the cigarettes back into the pack and returned the whole thing to his jacket pocket. "Probably think I'm a prima donna — smoking, special privileges." Lazard had an accent, French, though Brendan had read he was of Hungarian descent. He took another drag and squinted through the smoke pirouetting up from the glowing tip. "So, who are you?"

"Brendan Healy."

"Okay, Brendan Healy. I'm Didier Lazard." The last name sounded like *Lassald*. He looked upwards towards the sky. "It's pretty, you know."

They stood like that for a moment, looking up, Brendan suddenly full of doubt, wondering why he had done this, what he thought he was really going to get out of it. Grimm was going to expect results and he would have nothing to show. The whole thing had been a ruse to get in here and talk to the ex-head of the IMF. All based, really, on the rumor that Lazard had been in the city for a defense department meeting, one that had included the Deputy Chief of the CSS.

Brendan watched the falling snow as Lazard smoked. He decided the best route was the direct one.

"I'm in here because of the CSS."

Lazard turned and looked at Brendan with the same detached expression he'd maintained since they'd met. "You don't say."

"Were you in the city to meet with them?"

The big man narrowed his eyes. "And how is this your business?"

"Did you do what you're accused of?"

Lazard broke into a smile, and then he laughed. He had a jolly laugh, like someone's uncle. Then Lazard pursed his lips and looked down and shook his head.

"Ah," he said, "the prisoner's taboo question: 'Did you do it?'" His shrewd eyes focused on Brendan again. "Maybe I was a bit intoxicated and I made a pass at one of

110

the hotel staff. Hmm? Beautiful woman. I have a weakness for women, you see. I can never get enough. And so I think, this woman, she is something quite special. Honey-colored skin, big eyes, the perfect figure; she is in the hallway and I am coming in from dinner where I drink too much. I see her and I say, 'I have lost my key card. Can you let me in?' And we go to the door and she opens it. And I ask her to come in for a drink. And she says — polite, she is very polite — no, she prefers not."

Lazard shrugged and inspected the ash on his cigarette. "So I take her by the arm, I lean into her and I give her a little kiss on the neck, and whisper in her ear. You know, I say, 'you won't regret it.' And I feel her swell against me. But then she pulls away. The blush is off the bloom. And I reach for her and grasp her arm firmly, and I try to persuade her. But now she is unhappy."

Lazard lifted his shoulders again and then, with the hand holding the cigarette, pointed around him in the air, into the sky. "Cameras. Cameras in the hotel record everything. She tells her superior, and the police come and take me later that night, knock on my door while I sleep."

"Don't you travel with security?"

"Well, yes. But, they are not going to go to jail, too. So, the police come in. And here I am."

"You weren't set up."

"I admitted my mistake. I'll do a little waiting, deprived of women here in this stone city of hard men, I'll go to trial, I will pay, and pay some more, but, it will be alright."

"Will you get your job back?"

"No."

Lazard dropped his cigarette into the dirt and stepped on it with his Velcro prison shoes. After he was finished he put his hands in his pockets and drew a whistling breath through his nose and looked up at the sky. Snow had collected in his hair and bushy eyebrows. "It's definitely coming down."

Brendan glanced up again. The snowfall was intensifying. Lazard was watching him with a little smile playing on his lips.

"Now you tell me why *you're* here," he said.

It was amazing, Brendan thought. Here was Lazard, and the man was charming, friendly, if perhaps a misogynist pig. Brendan had expected a razor-sharp financier, inaccessible, dry as toast, probably uncommunicative. Lazard had a natural warmth to him, it seemed, or, he was a good actor. It wasn't that long ago, Brendan reminded himself, that Alexander Heilshorn had seemed like a decent man, caring, even vulnerable. And look where that had gone.

Brendan began to tell Lazard his story, censoring himself a few times, but otherwise laying out the tale, omitting the personal details and delivering an improvised résumé, including his three years as a beat cop for Mount Pleasant, and the blink of an eye he'd spent as a homicide detective in Oneida County. He described the Rebecca Heilshorn case, and how it had led to the human trafficking and prostitution rackets, but didn't share how he felt the evidence had coalesced around Titan. He skipped ahead to the showdown with Heilshorn at Roosevelt hospital.

"Heilshorn," Lazard interrupted in a musing tone.

"You've heard of him."

"You were the man who killed him?"

Brendan had a flashback to the office at Roosevelt Hospital, and saw Sloane running through the door and hurling the fire extinguisher at Heilshorn, hitting him square in the chest, a blow he had never recovered from. It was Sloane who had killed him, but Brendan said, as he had been saying for months, "Yes."

With this information in the open, Brendan relaxed. He decided it was time to do what he had come here to do. Ask what he needed to ask.

"So as I said, I believe you met with the Deputy Chief of CSS."

There was a twinkle in Lazard's eye. "You believe correctly."

"A man named Wick."

"Yes."

"Why?"

"Why?" Lazard looked thoughtful. But it seemed put-on. "Business. The IMF has a long relationship with the CSS."

"New York Police took me in after Roosevelt Hospital. But the CSS were there. I met with one of their agents. A man named Staryles. They've been around, in some way, since I first investigated the murder of that woman three years ago. Tell me about them."

Lazard scowled. "That's a piece of string."

"Give me the basics."

"Okay. The Central Security Service are cryptologists. Signals intelligence, tactical information assurance. It is an agency of the US Defense Department."

The wind swept through the yard, spinning the snowflakes. Brendan glanced at the guard standing at the entrance to the yard who looked back briefly before returning his attention to the phone he was poking at. He was beneath an awning by the door, somewhat sheltered from the storm.

Lazard didn't seem bothered by the wind tousling his hair. He turned his face into the breeze and smiled. "Here it comes," he said. Then studied his palms as the flakes landed on them and melted. "The CSS was founded after World War II, following the deactivation of the Army Security Agency." He glanced up at Brendan. "AFSA became responsible for all US communications intelligence and security. But at the physical, tactical level, it was the army, navy, and air force performing intelligence tasks, and these entities were not willing to accept the authority of the AFSA. So, the National Security Agency was created."

"Okay . . ." said Brendan, thinking it seemed like these intelligence agencies kept mutating into larger, more powerful bodies.

"Now, again, the tactical, on-the-ground forces, these are the specialized soldiers, sailors, and airmen. These are marines, coastguard. Men and woman doing the work. And as they're working independently, information is lost. There needs to be cohesion. There are increasing cryptologic requirements as the enemy upgrades, there needs to be unification of signal intelligence among these Service Cryptologic Agencies — the SCAs. Otherwise it is a . . . how do you say it, a 'pig roast.'"

Brendan thought the usual expression was cruder, but he let it go. Lazard went on, and Brendan was beginning to see where it was all headed.

"NSA was meant to integrate with these Cryptologic Agencies, but there was resistance. So, the CSS is formed as an inter-service organization. A way of merging all the armed services, all the intelligence, promoting full partnership with the NSA and the SCAs." Lazard took a breath. "It was conceived this way, executed this way — on paper."

"But in the end," Brendan said, picking up the thread, "the CSS is really a fourth service. Right? There is the army, the navy, the air force, and the CSS."

"Yes. A tremendous organization with all of the resources of the three other services, the intelligence of the NSA, both under presidential directive and free to operate independently. The best of all worlds, and unknown to most people. With one particular aspect that is perhaps the most elusive."

The wind cut through his clothes and stung his skin. "Tell me."

"US Cyber Command. They're the ones really responsible for the development of the internet. Alongside the Department of Defense — or, really, as a silent partner, Cyber Command built the initial World Wide Web."

"How do you know this?"

Lazard shrugged. "It's public information. It's all public information, if you know where to look. But many people in your country don't know. Or, don't want to. And, okay, also because the CSS has been the service used by the International Monetary Fund for more than ten years. The Fund leads geopolitics. The CSS enforces, so does the CIA, so does everyone, really; all foreign policy efforts come down to money. The CSS recruits from black-operative covens like the Joint Special Forces Command. A few navy seals, some marines. Men and women who have seen the agenda first hand. Men and women who have given up all semblance of a normal life."

"Staryles."

"Yes. Staryles is one of them."

"But Staryles was working for Heilshorn."

"Assigned to him, yes, most probably."

"Why? What does Heilshorn have to do with the Central Security Service?" Brendan had his own theories, convictions he had already shared with Sloane Dewan, beliefs he had already spat into the face of Heilshorn himself, and seen them confirmed in Heilshorn's eyes, but he wanted to hear it from Lazard.

"Liquidity, for one. Underground capitalism. The existence of the black markets to prop up the economy. But, ultimately, control. Control of the money. What else?"

The two men faced one another through the windblown swirls of snow, the CO watching them from inside the door to the yard.

"The US wants to maintain itself as the world power, Mr. Healy. It must maintain control of the money supply, of the petrodollar. When contractors like Halliburton, amongst others, cost the taxpayer billions, fresh revenue is needed to maintain the status quo. Your country is the largest financial contributor to my former organization, the

IMF. So of course we must talk together with the biggest politico-military organization you have. Shame, I just couldn't resist that little maid."

His eyes glassed over as he looked beyond Brendan, into the weather. "You see? I took a chance. Like any good businessman, any good investor, I must calculate risk. I must look ahead to the future. I must see several steps ahead, and then I must act, even against that risk."

Brendan realized they were talking not just about the housekeeper who claimed sexual assault, but Lazard's responsibilities with the IMF, and perhaps something else.

"I'm wondering if you're really here in Rikers because of something you did to a housekeeper," Brendan said.

Lazard grinned. Melting snow coursed down his expressive features. "Maybe not," he said. "Maybe we are both here for greater reasons than the allegations suggest." He raised his considerable eyebrows, then grew serious. "I see the decentralization of money as the biggest threat your country faces. Not being able to control the money supply. Not to regulate, tax, and control."

The storm intensified. Brendan glanced once more at the CO who remained beyond the door. He was watching the two convicts, with an amused expression. Perhaps he liked seeing them pummeled by the wind. Brendan turned back to Lazard.

"Most people dismiss these attempts to decentralize money as libertarian junk. Or the idea of the government controlling the population in these Machiavellian ways as wacko conspiracy theories."

Lazard stepped closer, the snow a thick, shifting curtain between him and Brendan. "Maybe so. And then again, most people thought *Mein Kampf* was a fairytale when it first came out."

CHAPTER SIXTEEN / THURSDAY 2:20 PM

Eddie Stemp sat on top of a red tractor at his sprawling farm in Barneveld, NY. The two black SUVs pulled into his driveway, churning up the dust. Jennifer exited the first vehicle and started over towards Stemp. She raised her hand in a wave. He stayed where he was on his tractor, clocking them like a sniper. She knew he was a former soldier, from the information collected during the Heilshorn case, though she hadn't been able to find records of it in the State Department files. She kept her hand in the air.

"Edward Stemp?"

"Good morning, sister," he said, and put on a big smile. He climbed down from the tractor and suddenly he became friendly. He wiped his hands on a rag hanging from his belt and offered his hand. She took it, his grip was rough and calloused.

Two security guards flanked her. Stemp turned his high-wattage smile on them, and his eyes darted to the third, who remained by the vehicles.

Stemp was shirtless, well-muscled, tanned, and sweaty. He had short dark hair, pearly white teeth. There was something about him that recalled an experience she'd had in college. She'd once met the head of one of the religious groups on campus, and he'd emitted a cultish vibe, a stoned-immaculate look like he'd drunk the Kool Aid. Stemp's demeanor wasn't exactly that, but there was a reach to his gaze she found discomfiting. "Good morning, gentlemen," he said to her bodyguards, raising his voice for the benefit of the one furthest away.

Stemp watched him for a moment, his head still, his eyes following as the security guard started a sweep of the property.

"I'm sorry about all of this," Jennifer said. "I'm not used to an entourage."

"Oh not at all," Stemp said, but she thought it was a false decorum. And she knew her detail was on edge after the scare at Largo's place.

"Would you like some coffee?" He gestured towards the small, quaint farmhouse behind him. The house was surrounded with fields. Green shoots poked up in furrows of soil, pointing through the wavering heat towards the horizon. "My wife is taking the kids to Bible study, and then she has her errands. The place is ours for an hour or so." Stemp gave Jennifer a look. He was telling her that it was all the time they had.

"Coffee would be great," she said.

He nodded, wiped his hands again and glanced at each of the three guards.

Jennifer turned to the men standing beside her and said, "Thank you, gentlemen." That was their cue to remain outside. "Ma'am," said the guard on her right.

She and Stemp went into the house.

* * *

The house smelled like bacon and coffee. The kitchen was small with a faded linoleum floor, white washed cabinetry, a breakfast table against a wall and a window with a view out over the property.

Jennifer was looking out at the cornfield when Stemp put a steaming mug of coffee in front of her. She pointed to the earth with rows of green shoots. "Knee-high by the Fourth of July?"

He nodded and sat down across from her. "Corn grows very well here."

"How long have you been working this land?"

His eyes rolled up to look at the ceiling as he considered. She could smell his sweat. He had pulled on a cut-off flannel shirt. His dungarees were stained with paint, oil, and dirt, and he wore large work boots with the steel toes worn through the leather. "Seven years," he said, and dropped his gaze to her. "Yep. Seven lucky years." He sipped his coffee. When he was finished he said, "In all that time I've never been visited by anyone from the US Department of Justice."

"I apologize for the unscheduled visit."

He waved a hand in the air, grime under the fingernails, dirt caked into the creases of the skin. "It's a welcome break from all the work."

"I can't even imagine. What prompted you to get into farming? Family business?"

He was shaking his head, no. "My family business is military. My father worked for NORAD for thirty-five years." It was a frank statement.

"You were in Iraq?"

He nodded. "Briefly. Early on."

She looked him over. "You must've been young."

"I was in the multinational force. Coalition forces." He seemed to look into the past.

"But that wasn't all for you. You stayed in Iraq, but you went into something else?"

Now his eyes snapped into place and he gave her an edgy look. She flinched.

"I did," he said. "I went into private security."

Jennifer tried the coffee, which was strong and sweet. This was a significant link in the chain, but she didn't want to betray that and make Stemp nervous. She acted like it was no big deal. She thought of Largo talking about Titan's no-bid contracts in the Middle East.

"And you . . . what job did you do when you returned stateside? Before you started farming."

Stemp grew rigid. "Ma'am," he said, "you told me on the phone this was about tying up loose ends on the Heilshorn murder. Now, I'm happy to reiterate what I told the detectives back then. But if you're looking for more than that, I think you need to be forthcoming."

She set her coffee down and sat back a little. "Of course, Mr. Stemp."

"Call me Kim."

"Kim?"

"My given name."

"I'm not trying to conceal an agenda here, Kim. I am following up on the Heilshorn murder, absolutely. I know you're a smart man. You've been forthcoming about your time in the military and, as you said, private security. I appreciate that very much. What I'd like to ask is whether or not your transition into working as a driver for XList escorts was facilitated in any way by your employer in Iraq. And who that employer was: Meecham, Blackwater, or someone else?"

He set his coffee down on the table beside him. He remained straight as a board, and placed his hands on his dusty knees. Like a diligent parishioner in a church pew, perhaps. Jennifer caught sight of movement outside as one of the dark shapes of her detail moved past the window.

"I stayed in security when I returned home. It was enough to provide me the start-up capital for my farm. To provide for my family."

"I don't doubt your integrity or your devotion to your family, and your finances are none of my business. But, Mr. Stemp, I've just visited Philip Largo. So if you're uncomfortable revealing your Iraq employer, I wonder if we could talk about Largo instead. And Rebecca."

Stemp said nothing. He remained statue-like at the table. His eyes, Jennifer saw, seemed to gray over a little.

She could hear the ticking of a clock in the other room. It was hot and sticky in the kitchen. A bowl of fruit, pestered with fruit flies, sat on a hammered chest. The window beside the table was open but there was no breeze coming through the screen. It was the type of humid summer day that soaked clothes and frizzed out hair. The sky had been open, but she could see a wall of hazy clouds on the horizon.

Stemp had gone mute, so she continued.

"My understanding is that you were in the business of driving escorts, while Rebecca Heilshorn was still involved."

Something passed behind Stemp's eyes. Then he blinked, as if awakening from a daydream, and he turned and looked out the window. His posture seemed to relax and he picked up his coffee.

"Rebecca has a child named Leah, correct?"

She watched this register in his expression and continued. "During the course of the investigation, the detectives considered you as a possible paternal match for Leah. But that's not the case."

His gaze was cool, and growing cooler in all the heat. "No, ma'am."

"But you know who her real father is, I think. Do you, Mr. Stemp?"

He brought the mug of coffee to his lips, never taking his eyes off her. His crow's feet deepened as he concentrated on her. The moment became uncomfortable. Then he lowered the mug and spoke.

"Yeah, this is a great plot of land for corn. Potatoes, lettuces, carrots — just the right PH balance to the soil. You've got to regulate soil temperature, though, that's key."

"It was Rebecca who brought the trouble to Philip Largo," she said, ignoring his non sequitur. "Largo believes it might be related to his move to block construction of a building in Albany. That and he just didn't step to the tune someone wanted him to. Alexander Heilshorn. Who, if I may make a rather circuitous connection, is affiliated with your employer in Iraq. And I believe that employer was Titan."

Nothing at all now from Stemp. He only watched the rippling heat over the cornfield; she saw his eyes seek out those same shouldering thunderheads in the distance. Perhaps she'd pushed too hard too soon, but time was running out.

"Just about seven years ago," she recapped, "about when you started here on your farm, Largo was caught with a prostitute. He claims he didn't know she was a working girl, but the media didn't care, his opponent for governor didn't care — it was chum in the water. So nobody bothered to publicize his version of the story. There were no criminal actions because the girl hadn't, in fact, ever declared herself a pro."

"You seem like a nice woman," Stemp said.

"Mr. Stemp, Philip Largo can identify you picking up the escort after the night that brought him down."

"I told you, ma'am, I admitted it. I drove for XList. I'm not proud of it."

She felt a minor relief, but she didn't think his statement was accurate. He hadn't admitted working for XList, specifically, until just now. "Is that all you did, drive the escorts? Protect them?"

"Mrs. Aiken, I have a family."

"We can protect you."

He shook his head. "No you can't."

"Mr. Stemp. Kim. We are the Justice Department. We coordinate with the FBI, with Homeland Security. My task force is set up so that we can do exactly this — obtain critical information and protect our sources."

"Ma'am . . ."

"I'm pretty sure you were a bagman. In addition to picking up and dropping off the women, you picked up money. I need to know where that money was going, Mr. Stemp. I need to establish a chain of custody, follow the money up to the top, and I want you to testify before a grand jury."

He laughed.

She ignored it. "Can you at least tell me how you went from working private security abroad to here in the states? Is it the same company? Is Titan putting ex-soldiers to work as escort bodyguards?"

He looked out the window, his mug of coffee hovering above the table in his grip. His laughter faded into a smile. Then he blinked, his humor evaporating, his eyes losing their focused aspect as he looked inwards.

At last he spoke. "One of the top managers of the firm I worked for threatened to kill a US Department of State investigator," he said. "There was a probe coming. Evaluation of the firm's performance."

His eyes found her again, and they were haunted. She could see her reflection in the dark irises. He reminded her of Ewon Parnell, and she felt her stomach knotting.

Easy. Easy now.

(Agent Apollo, Apollo Helios, God of Plagues)

"Two weeks later, twenty-three civilians were shot and killed in Nisour Square, in Baghdad."

"I remember."

"Yeah? Do you remember that the embassy sided with the firm? The State Department investigators were ordered to leave. And it looked to Iraq and to the whole world that private security firms on the US payroll could do whatever they want, with impunity."

"If I recall, four members of the firm went to trial here in the States."

"And what happened?"

Jennifer tried to remember exactly what the outcome had been, but she'd been under pressure at the time to finish her thesis in order get into the DOJ, which had offered her a position pending graduation. But she could assume where Stemp was going with this.

"They're above the law," he said. "You don't stir up that kind of liability and negligence protecting a few diplomats. That was dirty from the start, and continued to be dirty, and when it came time for me to stand in front of the jury, they buried me up here in farm country and gave me the job driving XList girls, in exchange for my silence." He looked at her, and his eyes were burning coals. "I say anything, and what will happen to me will be worse than what happened to those state investigators. Much worse. That's why you're never going to get what you want. I can't give it. Largo can't give it. No one can. They've got us all, right where it hurts. They got to Argon, and they're toying with Healy, too. You should know that."

She ignored the remark about Healy, though it pained her. "I know there are lives at stake. That's exactly why I'm here. Your family's lives, but also others. In order to keep everything flowing and everything hidden away, sacrifices are made. Women are exploited. Children are used like tools."

There was a loud crash, the table shook, and Jennifer was splattered with hot coffee before she even realized what had happened. Stemp had brought down the hovering coffee mug with tremendous force, shattering the mug against the kitchen table and spraying the coffee everywhere.

"Don't you think I know that? I tried to get Rebecca *out*. We were *both* trying to get out. She didn't want to be the one to entrap Largo. She was against it, she was going to come out with it — her brother was trying to help her — and look what happened to them. They manipulated her like a slave. You know what they do? They give some of the girls fake birth control."

She could think of nothing to say. She was dimly aware her guards were running towards the house due to Stemp's outburst.

Stemp was shaking with rage. She thought she could smell his breath wafting over to her. "Because sometimes they want the girls to get pregnant," he went on. "The babies provide all sorts of opportunities . . ."

"Okay," she said, holding her hand up for him to stop. "It's okay," she said softly. "It's alright—"

Jennifer's security burst in the front door. She saw another blur of black from the same window, but headed in the other direction, as the second guard ran around back. The third she could hear running up the driveway.

She started to stand up, when a rough hand pushed her back down. "Hey, wait . . ." she said. Stemp was upset, okay, yeah, but she could handle things; what were they doing?

This was the only thought she had time for as Stemp launched himself out of the chair at the bulky guard who'd just busted in the front door.

No, she thought. *No no no no . . .*

Stemp was fast, amazingly fast, and she felt the rush of air as he blurred past her and burrowed into the big man standing to the side of Jennifer. The men slammed into a set of shelves, and then the dishes on the shelves fell and exploded against the floor.

Not only was Stemp quick, he was nimble. In one swift move he disarmed Jennifer's guard and had the semi-automatic pistol in his own hand, the big man in front of him like a shield. At that moment there was a clamor in the back of the house as a second guard came in. Stemp held out his arm and turned his head and pointed his gun through the rear door of the kitchen and into the gloom of the house.

"No!" Jennifer cried out. "Kim, I'm on your side. We're here to help—"

Stemp fired. The gun was so loud in the room Jennifer's ear drums felt like they had burst. She didn't hear the sound of the second guard as he fell to the ground, but instead felt the floorboards shake as his body landed in a heap.

CHAPTER SEVENTEEN / THURSDAY 2:48 PM

They say life with an addict was like living with a ticking time bomb. Tick, another day goes by. Tick, another struggle to stay sober. Tick, the daily irritants accrete on the soul, like barnacles on the skin. Tick, the soul grows restless, resentful of the limitations of its cage. Tick, the minute hand on the timer jerks towards the zero hour, rigged to the packed C-4 explosive. Tick, it's just a matter of time. A matter of time and triggers become more sensitive, the resolve deteriorates, rotting away, porous with insect-eaten holes. Tick, and we're seconds away now, seconds away.

"You're free to go, Mr. Healy."

As much as he had been longing to hear the words, as much as he'd been dreaming of his release, they sounded foreign to him, uninterpretable. Brendan's head felt wadded with cotton. His eyes were puffy, as if from a hangover. Across the desk from him, Menzaro, his lawyer, looked back. Also sat there were three members of the city's prosecution team with the Department of Investigation, and several members of the NYPD, including Detective Kendall. They were together in a private room, procured by Deputy Warden Grimm, who had been absolutely writhing with anxiety and contempt when he'd shown them in. Grimm was outside the room now, unaware of what was taking place inside, but no doubt in a wretched state of purgatory.

Brendan managed one word, "When?"

Menzaro nodded, as if he'd expected this. He was about to speak when the New York City District Attorney, a thin, frizzy-haired, severe woman named Melissa Craddock, cut him off.

"The city is willing to drop its charges against you, Brendan, provided you follow through with your end."

Menzaro leaned back.

"The proffer is contingent on my client's terms, District Attorney Craddock. No testifying in open court, just his deposition. And you have the recordings from yesterday and today. The Justice Department will come in if you don't make use of this immediately — now."

Craddock pinned Menzaro with her hawk-like eyes. "Provided that everything in Mr. Healy's statement proves accurate." Those eyes shifted to Brendan. "Mr. Healy, when we depose you, you are willing to swear, under oath, that you have knowledge that will lead to hard evidence of how contraband — to wit: heroin, cocaine, marijuana, and alcohol — are being smuggled into this facility by corrections officers, and being distributed by corrections officers as well as inmates?"

"Yes."

Menzaro piped up. "And the city of New York is willing to drop all charges against my client, and you have an affidavit showing that no charges will be bought against Mr. Healy by the state?"

"That is correct." There was a shuffling of papers. "As long as Mr. Healy understands that this does not immunize him from a civil suit. Greta Heilshorn may pursue a wrongful death case. That's out of my hands."

Brendan watched the proceedings with detachment. Didier Lazard's ideas were still stuck in his mind, three months later. This was a false victory. The only way his release was going to be allowed was because Staryles, and the people he worked for, were allowing it. Or maybe, they just hadn't caught up to it yet. Still, he was getting out, he had to be able to marshal some enthusiasm for that, for God's sake. He was getting out of his own accord and he would be able to see Sloane.

But: tick, tock. All of the things undone. Tick, all of the compromises. Outside the walls, his addictions awaited. Pacing the grounds, looking in with hungry eyes. His own reflection, haggard, rangy, walking back and forth in his own, personal inmate's clothing. A quiver of the upper lip. Stalking back and forth, waiting to lead him.

"Mr. Healy?"

He brought his attention around to the District Attorney, who was looking at him with her humorless eyes. He watched those eyes crawl over him, taking in his scars, his missing finger, the fading bruises on his face from his beatings in segregation. Meted out by the guards, and by Tony Laruso, the fake-ID criminal sent in by Grimm to have his fun.

"Mr. Healy," she said again, and he thought he heard something softer in her voice, something almost human. "Mr. Healy, is there anything we can do for you before we proceed? Anything you need?"

"I need you all to leave this room," Brendan said, and poked his tongue into the cavity where his molar had once been. "And bring in Inmate 910721. Tony Laruso. I need ten minutes in here with him alone."

The DA held Brendan's gaze for a moment, and then looked around at the others in the room, perhaps wondering if any of them had understood the absurd language Brendan was speaking. There was a silent communication going on, Brendan could see the transmission between sets of eyes, the unspoken words conveyed from pursed lips. It was the captain who spoke. "I'm sorry, Mr. Healy. That's just not possible."

Tick, another denial. Another obstacle thrown in his path, another restriction, another concession to make. Another notch forward of the clock towards final destruction.

Tock, another minute clicked past towards detonation, a minute propelled by self-loathing. On top of it all, he was selfish. Addicted, like the rest of his countrymen, to getting his way.

Tick — but, that need for freedom. That need to live unadulterated. What was the social contract? What was it for, if not to keep people from violence and fear? Men from taking whatever they wanted, killing whatever or whomever got in their way. Total mayhem, nothing but a dog-eat-dog world, only the strongest surviving.

But wasn't that what was going on anyway?

A distant part of Brendan observed that these thoughts were just chemicals in his brain, like sparks in a reactor. Electric impulses carried by neurotransmitters. Freedom had an opioid-like effect. He didn't want it taken away. He wanted it back.

This was supposed to be a triumphant moment. He'd turned the tables on his captors. He was going to take the information on the contraband enterprise in the Rikers system and bury Grimm with it.

He closed his eyes and shook his head so hard he felt he saw those sparks thrown against the backs of his eyelids. "This is the only way we have a deal."

He opened his eyes and saw Craddock looking back at him, her face hard. But he thought he saw something glimmer in her gaze, motes of recognition dancing in her stare. Maybe she knew. Maybe, at some point, before her razor-sharp suit and the determined set of her jaw, the whittling away to 120 pounds of bones, gristle, and a flawless record, she'd been there. Where he was. Maybe she knew.

"Mr. Healy—"

"In here you live day to day," he said suddenly. "As a detective you live case to case. If you're a fighter, you live fight to fight. And what you do in the meantime is prepare. You prepare each day towards that day in court, that moment in the ring. All of this preparation for one moment, the moment of judgment and exposure. To witness a truth. Maybe we prepare all our lives, from the moment we're born to that final moment, at the end."

Craddock exchanged looks with Menzaro, Kendall — everyone was looking at everyone else. They figured he was insane.

His mind called up a line from the C.S. Lewis book he had committed to memory: *The bad man's past already conforms to his badness and is filled only with dreariness.*

Craddock frowned at him, and closed her file. Whatever was kindred he had momentarily glimpsed in the DA was gone. She worked the file into her open satchel. "We'll be back tomorrow for the formal deposition."

If she didn't give him Laruso, then the whole second phase of his plan would fall apart.

"You don't really have a choice," Brendan said.

Her head jerked to look at him and her upper lip curled back. "Mr. Healy, you really think as the District Attorney for New York City I'm going to allow you some sort of revenge-time alone in a room with another inmate, full-well knowing your intent to harm? Or maybe, rather, your intent to commit suicide by his hands?"

Never breaking eye contact with Craddock, Brendan pointed at the door. "It's not your call, it's the Deputy Warden's call. I just thought I'd be nice and ask."

Menzaro reached over and touched Brendan on the arm, leaning in to speak quietly to him. Brendan shrugged off the arm and stayed eye-locked with Craddock.

Brendan knew Grimm would go for it, because Grimm figured Laruso would kill Brendan in a fight, the same as Craddock did. And Grimm would want nothing more. There was no way he'd be able to ferret out the real reason why Brendan wanted this.

Craddock sneered. "What are you playing at, Mr. Healy?"

CHAPTER EIGHTEEN / THURSDAY, 3:07 PM

The kitchen was filled with the pungent smell of gunpowder. Sounds were muffled in her ears. Sounds of choking, grunting, violence.

Morgan, the guard who had come in the front door moments before, was kicking and flailing. Stemp had a forearm hooked around his neck, his muscles bulging, his face an inhuman mask. Morgan's own face was bright red. He jammed an elbow back, catching Stemp in the ribs. Stemp howled and let go. A moment later Stemp ran out of the kitchen, disappearing into the rest of the house. Morgan took fumbling steps backwards, grasping at his throat and gagging.

His windpipe was crushed.

Jennifer's hearing was returning: Stemp pounded through the house for a few seconds, then a door creaked open and slammed closed. Morgan sputtered and clawed at his neck, his mouth working, as if trying to speak. He needed air. He took another backwards step, his knees buckled, and collapsed in a heap. She got up from the kitchen table and rushed to where he'd fallen. She pulled out her phone and dialed 911.

She crouched beside him and put a hand on his shoulder. "It's going to be okay . . . going to be okay."

"911, how may I help?" came the voice from the other end of the phone.

She put her fingers to his neck, feeling for an artery. His pulse was weak, but there. He pulled shallow, reedy breaths, barely getting oxygen. Unless he was intubated, he was going to die.

She gave 911 her location and situation while she looked around the kitchen for something — a pen, maybe, just the plastic tube around the ink — that she could stick into Morgan to get airflow. She'd never done anything like that in her life, and she realized it could kill him faster than if she left him alone.

She stepped away from Morgan and stopped in the middle of the kitchen, shaking. Suddenly, Prellwitz stumbled into the room and past her, through the short hallway, dripping blood as he went. Prellwitz was the guard Stemp had shot when Prellwitz had entered the house from the back. He stepped around Morgan and crashed his way out of the front door. She watched, too stunned to speak, as Prellwitz staggered to one of the SUVs in the driveway and got behind the wheel. It looked like he was trying to start the engine. He was in shock.

"Ma'am?" The 911 operator was in her ear. "Ma'am? Just stay on the line with me. Officers are responding. There's one very close by — be there in under a minute."

She heard a shot ring out. Then two more, in rapid succession. She instinctively ducked down, and ran bent over to the wall. She crouched against it, and waited. "Shots fired," she heard herself say into the phone. "Shots fired."

"Ma'am? Where is he? Where is the gunman? Is he still in the house?"

No, Stemp was not in the house. Stemp had alighted out back. Everything was quiet now. She steeled herself for a look, and then stood up just enough to see out the window beside her.

Davis was lying in the yard, not far from the SUVs, rolling on the ground, back and forth, gripping his arm. She saw a bright rose of blood blooming through the fabric of his white shirt.

"Ma'am. Is he still in the house?"

And then she saw him. A dozen yards from Davis, Eddie Stemp was sprawled in the corn. At least she thought it was him. She could see only his feet, those well-worn work boots, and part of one hand, palm up towards the sky. Davis had managed to shoot him back.

"He's not in the house," she said, breathless. "He's outside. He has one of my bodyguard's guns." And he could still be dangerous.

As the 911 operator advised her to stay put, she looked over at Morgan. She couldn't help him. But maybe she could help Davis and Prellwitz outside. If she just sat here and waited for the emergency response to arrive, they could die.

She left her phone connected to the call but dropped it into her pocket as she headed to the front door. She stepped around Morgan. His eyelids fluttered as she passed, and she felt her stomach twist. She pushed open the door, stepped off the porch and ran to the driveway, grabbing cover behind the vehicle in case Stemp was an active threat. She didn't think Stemp would hurt her, but he was obviously desperate. She thought he'd been more scared than anything. She approached the SUV. Prellwitz was slumped unconscious over the steering wheel, a pack of cigarettes on the seat by him. He'd been trying to light a smoke. She opened the door. Blood everywhere. She put her fingers to his neck to check his carotid artery for a pulse. There was nothing.

"Ma'am? Hello?" The small, tinny voice came from her pocket.

Thunder rumbled above and the rain started. She ran into the yard and crouched down next to Davis, whose grimacing face was turned up to the sky, his teeth gritted, eyes squinted shut. He'd torn off his formal shirt and was left in an undershirt. "Can you walk?" She looked at his arm, with the rain coming down, sluicing the blood from his flesh, exposing the dark bullet wound. She used his shirt to wrap around his arm and cinched it tight. He nodded, and she helped him to his feet. They started back to the house — keeping an eye on Stemp's unmoving feet.

Halfway there, Davis cried out and stopped walking. He dropped to his knees – he was too heavy for her to hold up.

"Get inside," he grunted.

"Come on." She strained and pulled on him. She actually managed to drag him a few inches through the dirt and mud. He twisted out of her grip. "Get inside," he repeated. "*Now.*"

She spared once more glance at Stemp's feet. Were they twitching? She left Davis and did as he said.

The rain clattered against the tin roof of Stemp's home, so loud it was as if the heavens were dumping barrels of dimes. She watched out the window as the first police vehicle turned into Stemp's driveway and pulled up to the house

The vehicle was from Oneida County. A well-muscled man with hair cropped so short it was barely there stepped out of the cruiser and slid his nightstick into his belt beneath a bright yellow poncho. He looked around and drew his service weapon. Jennifer could hear more sirens in the distance; the warble of the ambulance, the wailing of more police vehicles. It was going to be a mob scene in a matter of moments.

She watched as Davis was hoisted to his feet by the deputy. She didn't know whether to go back outside now or stay where she was. Jennifer felt immobilized by indecision. Suddenly it all hit her, and she was

136

overwhelmed by the reality of the past few minutes. She'd expected to touch on some soft spots with Stemp, but this thing had escalated so fast and unexpectedly that part of her knew she must be in a state of shock.

And after all you've been through, she thought at herself. It sounded curiously like something her mother would say. *Wouldn't you be used to this by now?*

Davis, standing once more on shaky legs, pointed to the house. The deputy in the yellow rain poncho looked over and seemed to catch Jennifer's gaze through the downpour. Half-aware she was even doing it, she raised her hand and twiddled her fingers in the air.

Yep. Definitely in shock. Maybe not even mild. You're losing it.

Maybe. Maybe she was. Maybe it was too much. Maybe meeting with a former state assemblyman who could have been governor, destroyed by a honey trap was a bit tough to take. Maybe it said things about her own abduction she hadn't wanted to face. Like that the naysayers were right; the United States was another corrupt empire in decline. Susceptible to the same entropy of past civilizations, in the final decadent stages before the death knell.

Something caught her attention and she looked out the other kitchen window. Two black crows were fighting in the chicken yard. One of them flew away through the silver rain with something dangling from its sharp beak. She was watching it flap towards a billow of dark clouds when someone entered the kitchen, startling her.

The deputy in the yellow poncho stood dripping in the doorway. He glanced at Morgan, slumped on the floor, and then he looked at Jennifer. He holstered his weapon.

"Ma'am? You alright?"

He looked like some sort of grizzled ex-NFL quarterback, she thought. A cop in his mid-forties, who could still kick down a door. She thought she'd seen his face in the Rebecca Heilshorn murder case files. The deputy who'd been first on-scene, perhaps.

"I'm okay."

He seemed to analyze her for a moment, then gave a curt nod. "Okay. State Police are en route, there's an ambulance in-bound, just another minute until it gets here."

"Thank you."

"Uh-huh." He turned and looked into the hallway. Then his head snapped back around and he held her again with his bright eyes. "Far as you know, no one else is in the house?"

Jennifer shook her head. "I haven't heard anyone. I don't think anyone was here but me and Stemp."

"Your bodyguard, Davis, told me that after he was shot, he returned fire. Shot Stemp in the back."

It should have been a relief, but it wasn't. Maybe because she felt like Stemp was more of a victim than a perpetrator. Or maybe it was because his wife and kids were due back from church at any moment.

The rain continued to hammer the tin roof of the small house. It sluiced from the gutters and eaves — the effect was like being behind a waterfall. When the ambulance turned in, followed by a state trooper and an unmarked car, Jennifer had to squint to see. The lights blurred and bled in the deluge.

"I'm Bostrom," said the deputy. She remembered the name now from the Rebecca Heilshorn case files.

"Jennifer Aiken."

He gave her a lingering look, then stepped back onto the front porch to greet the rest of the police and paramedics.

Moments later, a plain-clothes detective stepped through the front door. He threw a handful of something into his mouth, then wiped his hand on his pleated pants. He was wearing an old-fashioned beige raincoat which was soaked through. He was older, late fifties, the kind of seasoned cop who thought eating a messy snack on the job was OK. He glanced around the kitchen until he found the dishtowel on the stove. He took it and blotted his face and neck. Then he sniffed it, frowned, and threw it aside. He did all of this without ever once so much as glancing at her or introducing himself. He didn't need to. She knew who he was, too: Ambrose Delaney.

Delaney went over to the door and gave a quick look deeper into the house, keeping his feet planted in the kitchen. Then he pushed himself back and let go of the door. Looking at the body, he said to her, "Bad day, Agent Aiken?"

Deputy Bostrom, in the yellow poncho, was still holding the front door open after the paramedics had carted Morgan outside. He shot Delaney a curious look. He was probably wondering how the detective knew her name. So was she.

She watched Morgan being loaded into the ambulance. "These men were a security detail assigned to me by the Justice Department."

"Uh-huh. Looks like Stemp made pretty quick work of them."

"It escalated quickly," she said to Delaney.

"Oh, I know, I know," Delaney intoned. "I know Eddie. I know his wife and children. This is going to be devastating for them."

The blame in his voice was unmistakable. Jennifer decided that she preferred the way things had been ten minutes ago — alone in the house surrounded by the dead and the dying, rather than with this guy. She realized the phone was still in her pocket, possibly connected to 911.

"Something you want to say, Detective?"

At last he turned to look at her. He glared across the kitchen. "Yes, Agent Aiken. You just brought murder to my county. You come here on your highfalutin cloud, you take a good family man, a church-going man, and you turn his life upside down."

She looked at her hands, which were shaking, and clasped them together. There was blood on them from when she'd touched Davis. Or Morgan. She didn't know. She raised her head slowly. "We both know why I'm here. Don't we? What's your story, Delaney? I know Eddie's. Why don't you tell me yours?"

Deputy Bostrom, still holding open the front door, started to mumble something. "I, ah, I'm going to bring in Clark when he gets here. I ah . . ." and he made a fumbling exit, curling his eyes over to Jennifer as he slipped outside.

"How did they get to you, Delaney?"

Delaney tucked his chin back and widened his eyes in a dramatic expression of incredulity. "*Get to me?* How did they *get to me?*"

"I thought at first it was maybe an affair. Stepping out on your wife. But to look at you, you're going to be hard up to find anyone that stupid or desperate; I bet you just went in for the money. How much did Alexander Heilshorn pay you?"

He stepped toward her suddenly. "Lady, you watch your fucking mouth."

"Or what? You know what I think about Stemp?"

"Oh I can't wait to hear it."

"Maybe what just happened here happened because he's afraid of you. Afraid of what you might do to him or his family, with the truth out in the open. The truth that Eddie worked for the same private security firm back here that he did in Iraq. Only stateside, he was driving escorts. What I wonder is, who do you answer to now that Heilshorn is dead? Who's calling the shots?"

"I don't know what you're talking about."

Two state troopers entered the room, followed by a thin man Jennifer assumed was the deputy coroner, Clark. She saw Delaney had to make an effort to pull his hateful attention from her and turn and greet the arrivals. He spent a moment talking with them in low voices.

She felt herself seething. The shock was already wearing off, replaced by an anger she hadn't known was possible to feel. Delaney had walked into the room and belittled her, blamed her, when he was as dirty and corrupt as they came.

She looked out the window. The puddles in the driveway boiled and snapped as the rain poured down. The doors to the back of the ambulance closed and she felt something drop in her chest. Her breath caught in her throat, she thought she saw points of light glittering around the edges of her vision, like she was going to pass out. Poor Morgan. She barely knew the man. She'd resented her security detail, and look what had happened to them.

She spun around as Delaney neared her again.

"Know why I'm here, Detective? I'm following the dollar. Black markets like XList are laundering money, which ends up as slush funds to bribe politicians. So, do your job. See that my men are given the best medical treatment, and get the hell out of my way."

Delaney barreled over from the doorway, took a few large strides and was right next to Jennifer, breathing hot in her ear. "Listen to me, you cunt. I don't care who you work for. What you're fucking with here; you've got to get with the program. You're on the wrong side."

She turned and looked into his pasty face. He had dark eyes and a black mustache and sallow skin, there were sunflower seed casings stuck in his teeth. She decided then and there she would never eat a sunflower seed again. "I've heard that speech before," she said quietly, her heart pounding. "Now, if I could just speak to your sheriff, Lawrence Taber. Is he around? I'm sure he'd like to hear what I have to say about you."

"Everything okay in here?"

Jennifer looked past Delaney's looming face at the earnest young trooper, watching them from the other side of the room with wide eyes. She could feel Delaney's breath on her face. Her stomach rolled with nausea. Then Delaney slowly turned his head to the trooper.

"No," he said, "everything is not okay here."

And he pulled out his gun.

Oh God, said that voice in her head, then one that sounded eerily like her mother. *You've gone too far, Jenny. This time you've gone too far.*

CHAPTER NINETEEN / THURSDAY, 3:19 PM

Tony Laruso. Two hundred and fifty pounds of fat and muscle. Early thirties. Bronx bred, started out in gangs when he was eleven and grew up fast. At sixteen, hit a guy so hard he put him in a coma for a month. Brendan had done his research, in between the beatings.

Laruso would have served time in a juvenile facility for putting that guy down, but as he'd already committed other offenses — larceny, accessory to car theft, forging driver's licenses — he was sent to Rikers and did six months. He'd been in and out of jail ever since.

One thing that was unusual about Tony Laruso was that he didn't have a single prison tat. He believed the flesh was sacred, not to be desecrated. Six months ago he'd been on top of Brendan, pinning him to the ground — with a few other inmates helping out, although Laruso didn't really need assistance. Laruso had been following Grimm's orders, probably wrangling a deal of his own for special treatment of some kind. But he was un-inked, the granite muscles moving like plates beneath his thick skin.

Now, he stood in front of Brendan, chest heaving, ready for war. The corrections officers backed out of the room, closing the door and grinning like a couple of kids who'd just set a bag of shit aflame on some teacher's porch. Brendan turned and scowled at them and tried to look tough. But when the door finally snapped shut, he faced Laruso, his heart thumping against his chest.

Laruso had seventy-five pounds on him. He'd been in hundreds of fistfights. Brendan had been in less than half a dozen. If you counted grabbing Russell Gide by his tracksuit in a fit of fright and anger while Gide sat helpless behind the steering wheel of his BMW, okay, that was one. If you counted Laruso jumping him in the commons area, tackling him to the ground, screwing up his already screwed-up face, that was another. And maybe hitting FBI Agent Harlan Doherty in the face with his forehead made the list. What was not debatable was that, pound for pound, Brendan was outmatched.

"You ready to do this?" Laruso clenched his fists and bared teeth so white and square they looked fake.

Laruso took a step forward, bringing his hands up. He didn't raise them like a boxer, instead he held them near his hips, like a wrestler. Laruso shook his head. "You're one crazy motherfucker," he said, and lunged.

Brendan stepped back and batted Laruso's groping hands away. "I know Grimm put you up to it."

Laruso paused, scowled, and then lunged again. "Grimm didn't put me up to nothing."

Brendan leapt back, running out of room in the cramped space. His hip connected with one of the folding chairs, which ground across the concrete floor with a metal squawk. He kept backing away from Laruso, rounding the long table that had been the site of slightly more civilized interactions only recently. Laruso dove at Brendan, who jumped up onto the table.

"Oh, you think that's going to save you?" Laruso said and kept coming, and dear God, he was smiling. Brendan kicked him in the chin. The blow snapped Laruso's head back and spit flew from the inmate's lips. Two fat pearly drops of it.

Laruso lowered his head and glowered up at Brendan from beneath a hooded brow. "I'm gonna fuck you up, bitch."

"Stop," Brendan was saying, waving his hand, palm out, and backing up along the rickety table. "I have a proposition."

"Get down from there, you pussy," Laruso growled, and he swiped at Brendan's legs, his fingertips brushing one of Brendan's legs.

"No," said Brendan, his stomach dyspeptic, his skull throbbing in sync with his beating heart. "Listen."

"Fuck you." Laruso used a chair to climb onto the desk.

This was going to hurt.

CHAPTER TWENTY / THURSDAY, 3:22 PM

The state trooper in the room was quick, but once he'd drawn his gun, he acted confused. He stood pointing the weapon in the general direction of Delaney and Jennifer, but he seemed unsure of which one of them was the target. "Detective?" he asked, his voice high and raw.

Delaney had his gun pointed at Jennifer's shoulder, the barrel pressing into her. With his free hand he took the handcuffs from his belt and held them in the air. "This woman is under arrest for suspicion of murder. I have reason to believe she and her security detail tried to coerce and then murder Edward Stemp."

"You're out of your mind," Jennifer said. Her pulse was racing, her thoughts jumbled, but she couldn't help herself. Delany did not appreciate the remark and hit her in the side of the head with the handcuffs.

"Jesus!" the trooper called out. "What . . . ."

Getting hit with the cuffs was like a hot sting, with a thick, throbbing pain to follow. Silvery spots danced in her vision. At the same time, her clamoring thoughts settled, her mind calmed, and only one clear notion remained in the temporary stillness.

I'm not going through this again.

"Whoops," said Delaney. "Slipped."

He pulled the gun away from her shoulder and shoved her forward so she was bent over at the table just below her rib cage. "Cover her," he said to the trooper. He then pulled the gun away so he could rack the cuffs on her. Meanwhile the trooper was pointing his handgun at her, clearly conflicted, but following instruction nevertheless. The coroner, Stanley Clark, appeared in the doorway and looked into the kitchen with his mouth open in a confused oval, as if he were about to ask a question.

"You're going to arrest me?" said Jennifer. "I'm a prosecutor with the United States Department of Justice."

"I don't give a shit if you're Queen Cleopatra of Egypt. You want to see Taber? Ok. I'll bring you right to where he is."

She couldn't help but think of Brendan. *They're all dead and buried somewhere.*

Delaney slapped the cuffs home. Tight. Then he gripped her under her arm and yanked her painfully to her feet. She felt the business end of his firearm jab into her lower back. "Move," he said. "Outside."

He shoved her through the kitchen, past the coroner and the perplexed state trooper and out onto the porch. Petrichor and manure filled her nostrils. Everyone looked at her and Delaney, the other troopers and the paramedics sat in the ambulance with the doors open, tending to her bodyguard. Heads swiveled as Delaney marched her into the driveway.

"You really think this is going to work?" she asked.

The moment she said it, her security guard, Davis, broke away from the woman who was bandaging his arm in the back of the ambulance. He leapt to the ground, pulled his gun, and ran towards Jennifer and Delaney. As he did, the other troopers in the yard and the deputy, Bostrom, drew their weapons on him. Delaney pointed his own gun as the man charged.

Davis stopped in his tracks. Everyone froze, and the rain beat down on them. The air was dark and thundering.

"Let her go," Davis called.

"Arrest him, too," Delaney called out.

Bostrom started over to the security guard holding his pistol out, gripped in both hands. He took his cuffs out as he walked. Davis watched Jennifer through the downpour.

"Drop your weapon!" Bostrom shouted. Davis didn't so much as look at the deputy, but did as he was told, leaning forward and tossing his gun into the muddy yard. Bostrom reached Davis and took out his cuffs. Jennifer saw his lips move as Bostrom said something to the bodyguard she couldn't hear. As the cuffs were about to go on, a car slowed in the road and turned into the driveway, headlights shining and wipers whacking back and forth.

"Oh fuck," said Delaney.

The troopers, three of them, all turned and pointed their weapons at the vehicle. Delaney called out to them. "Stand down, stand down a minute, that's Stemp's family."

Jennifer could just see their faces through the windows, despite the rainwater streaking down the glass. Two pie-eyed children and one mortified-looking woman. Just back from church, coming home to this. All of the cops in the yard were looking at them, including Bostrom, who'd yet to wrap the cuffs around Davis. And Davis seized the moment. In one quick move he bent, scooped up his gun, and took off running, aiming to squeeze in between the ambulance and a trooper vehicle.

"Runner!" Delaney cried out. He aimed and fired his weapon. The explosion beside Jennifer's head was deafening. Davis was just about to slip between the two vehicles when the bullet took him in the shoulder. It threw him forward, and Davis stumbled and almost pitched all the way down onto the ground. Somehow he stayed upright and kept running. A second later and he was on the other side of the driveway, concealed behind the ambulance. All the troopers took cover. They shielded themselves behind the cruiser and the ambulance on the yard side of the vehicles and threw cautious looks over the hoods.

Delaney shoved Jennifer forward to get her moving again. He was cursing under his breath. When the gun came back to gouge her in the side, the barrel burned her. She cried out and jumped away from it. As she stumbled through the silver rain she saw her life flashing forward. Delaney was going to shoot her. She was going to fall to her knees and die here in the middle of this farm, just like Eddie, his wife and kids looking on.

And then she felt arms grabbing her, and she looked up and saw Deputy Bostrom.

"I've got her, I've got her," Bostrom said to Delaney. Her ears felt wadded with cotton, but she heard him. "I'll take her in."

Delaney hesitated for a moment. Then one of the troopers shouted. "There he is!"

Jennifer saw Davis, just a sketch of his shape, running into the corn near the barn. The troopers opened fire. The explosions sounded like depth charges. Davis disappeared into the corn stalks a second later. One of the troopers left the cruiser behind and started running after him. Delaney had edged in that direction too, and the last Jennifer saw of him was his back as he stood watching the corn, his trench coat dark with the rain, and then Bostrom grabbed her head and shoved her into the back of his vehicle.

Bostrom slid into the driver's seat, sparked the ignition and backed out. Jennifer looked out the window as they reversed past Stemp's family. The little girl had her face to the window, taking everything in as the mother got out of the car.

Jennifer saw Delaney turn his gun on Eddie Stemp's wife.

"Oh my God," Jennifer breathed.

Then they were on the road, and the tires spun on the oily asphalt as Bostrom threw it in drive and they sped away.

CHAPTER TWENTY-ONE / THURSDAY, 3:22 PM

Tick. Tick-tock.

Tony Laruso jumped up onto the desk. The entire thing shook beneath Brendan's feet. It was a desk meant for coercion and coffee mugs — for criminals to bargain with prosecutors; for lawyers to bullshit their clients into thinking there was light at the end of the tunnel, in order to stay on the payroll. It wasn't meant for two-hundred-pound, convicted identity-thieves squaring shoulders with damaged ex-scientists/ex-cops.

"Tony, the only reason Grimm let you in here is because he knew you'd tear me apart. That's what he wants."

"That's what he's gonna get."

"But I'm the one who suggested it."

Laruso swiped at the air in front of Brendan with both hands — like a bear — and he smiled. He was enjoying himself now, and completely missing the irony. Brendan tried to drive it home. "Why would I ask for this, Tony?"

The convict shrugged, cocked his head and stuck out his lower lip. "Cuz you're a freak, man. Anybody can see that. You probably get off on this shit. You probably liked it when I was on top of you. You probably wanted me to do more than give you that little spanking. Huh?"

"I'm not a terrorist. That was a rumor Grimm started to get me working for him. Because of what's going on in this place."

That got Laruso's attention. He lowered his hands and his grin faltered. Brendan rushed on.

"I know you're a part of it, Tony. I know how the liquor comes in with the cleaning supplies, so the dogs can't smell it. I know how the drugs come in with the food, and with the COs. I know how the kitchen is the main distribution center. And I know how you're one of the distributors."

Now Tony Laruso's face, which had been slack while he listened, built into a rictus of anger. "You're fucking snitching to the cops?" He leaned close and the table trembled beneath them.

"Like it or not, there's an investigation pending; a probe that's going to come through here with a fine-toothed fucking comb, Tony, and take down every single person involved. And yeah, I made that happen."

Laruso paused, considering this, his expression vacillating between anger and confusion. Maybe he was starting to get it. Brendan drove it home.

"I can either retract my statement, stay in here, branded a terrorist, look forward to monthly beatings, and go on trial for a murder I didn't commit; or I can let Grimm and this whole place go down while I walk away." He paused for effect. "Which one do you think I want, Tony?"

Laruso, for just a moment, looked like he was back in the fourth grade, put on the spot by his social-studies teacher about some historical event he knew nothing about. Brendan could almost see him sitting at his little desk back by the window, this kid from the Bronx with a few ounces of innocence still left in him, just a year or two away from the gangs that would initiate and corrupt him with their coarse mimicry of corporate structure. Then his forehead creased with a scowl and his eyes glinted fierce. "You want to see it burn," he said.

"Tell the man what he's won," said Brendan softly, adrenaline corkscrewing through him.

Laruso, instead of backing down, as Brendan had hoped, finally launched himself into a full tackle. Brendan saw him coming, just a blur of teeth and slashing arms and open fingers ready to rip him apart, and at the last second as his hands closed around Brendan's face and neck (*he's going to pop my head off like a bottle cap*) their combined weight flipped the table.

The end where Brendan stood collapsed, the legs cracking and folding beneath them in a flat drop that made his stomach float for a fraction of a second before the hard, unforgiving ground shocked his legs. But for Laruso, the momentum of his lunge flung him past Brendan and catapulted him into the wall. Laruso hit the wall and fell to the ground after catching a handful of Brendan's fatigues, pulling Brendan on top of him on the floor.

It was just possible for Brendan to get his leg up, to bring it in between himself and the raging convict. He brought his kneecap down squarely on Laruso's neck, and as their two bodies fully impacted the floor together, Laruso expelled the air from his mashed throat in a wheeze, and his eyelids flew open.

Brendan wasted no time. He'd wanted to reason with the man. He'd wanted to hatch a deal with him, but Tony Laruso was either too stupid or too conditioned to not hear reason. And now, after this tumbling turn of events, he would be even more livid. He would be unstoppable. He'd been on top of Brendan in the middle of Motchan Center. He'd had his knee gouging into Brendan's body just like Brendan now speared into his. He'd whispered death threats in Brendan's ear, he'd ripped his pants down, for God's sake. He'd been let into segregation with other cons who took turns taunting and cat-calling to Brendan in his isolated cell, pledging his destruction, pledging themselves to a lifetime of his torture. And then his door had been opened by unseen hands, and they'd entered his cell to carry out their threats.

Laruso had scraped him up, beaten him up, pulped his already ruined face, knocked out his tooth. But worse than any of the physical harm, he had made Brendan live in fear.

Brendan was tired of living in fear.

Striking Laruso was like hitting stone. The man's skull a bowling ball, and there was, in fact, concrete just behind the round shape of it. There was no give, and pain crackled up through Brendan's arm, the bones vibrating from the impact, the nerves like singed wires. His whole arm tingling and throbbed at the same time, he drew back to strike again. Laruso's stricken eye was shut and the lid fluttering. His other eye somehow remained wide and staring and filled with enmity.

One more punch would do it.

Yes, beyond corruption and greed there was human frailty, addiction, at work, but as Brendan raised his fist in the air and brought it down again, he felt justified.

Tick, anyway, tick-tock.

CHAPTER TWENTY-TWO / THURSDAY, 3:27 PM

"This is crazy," Jennifer said. "This is crazy, this is crazy."

"I know," said Bostrom. He was gripping the steering wheel with both hands, cutting the cruiser through a curtain of rain, really hitting the gas. Jennifer saw they were doing almost eighty miles an hour. The road rose and fell beneath them, shivering corn stalks blurred past on either side.

"My God. Did he just kill her? Would he have? Oh God." She felt the tide of emotion rising within her, the numbness of shock wearing off, everything threatening to spill loose, the twists of the past hour, the horror of the past few seconds. She tried to get away from it, to swim away from the undertow. She focused her mind on Bostrom. Could she trust him?

His eyes found her in the rear-view mirror for a split second and then he returned his attention to the road. The windshield wipers wicked back and forth at high speed. The rain was an unending dump of gray water.

"I've known about Delaney for a while," Bostrom said.

Jennifer felt a tingling at the base of her spine, a tremble of rawboned hope. The thrall of the undertow lessened just a little.

Bostrom went on. "Delaney has been a part of one shady deal after another. He was all over the Heilshorn investigation, trying to throw it one way or the other, looking to stick everything on the girl's brother."

Jennifer was still processing the events of the past few minutes, but a name surfaced. "You're talking about Kevin Heilshorn."

"Yeah. Him. Rumor has it Delaney was even sleeping with Olivia Jane at one point. He's a shit bag."

She could hardly process it all. Delaney turning the gun on Stemp's wife. State troopers and sheriff's deputies firing on her own security. Employees of the Department of Justice, for God's sake. How did they expect to get away with it? To reconcile it? Everything was mixed up. Nothing made any sense.

"What are we doing? Where are we going? Are you arresting me?"

They were coming to a stop sign and Jennifer could feel the brakes thudding beneath the car. Bostrom made a right turn. The corn fell away and they passed a large elm tree drooping in the rainstorm; and a teenager in a red raincoat, watching them from the driveway of a small house.

"I'm not arresting you," he said after they got up to speed again. "We need to get further away and then I'll take the bracelets off."

She shifted her weight at their mention, felt the steel of the handcuffs biting into her flesh. "Why are you doing this?"

Bostrom was silent for a moment. "I told him to run."

"Who?" But she thought she knew. She remembered watching Bostrom say something to Davis that she hadn't been able to hear over the rain and the ringing in her ears.

"Your bodyguard. I told him to get out of there. I didn't think . . . fuck, at this point, Delaney is operating completely outside of the department. He's insane, only hanging on there by a thread. Taber tried to have him removed from duty, but then Taber went on a so-called vacation, and he never came back."

"Who's running the department now?"

"The undersheriff. Usually runs the COs at the jail for Taber. Robertson's alright, but he's out of his league. Delaney walks all over him. Does whatever he wants."

Jennifer's head ached from the blow with the cuffs. Her hands were falling asleep and her arms hurt from being pinned behind her. Yet she felt alert, more alive than she had in days, maybe months. Maybe since she'd been abducted by Staryles.

She had to keep the thought of Stemp's wife pushed far away.

"Is he on the payroll? Heilshorn's payroll?" She took the next logical step. "Titan's payroll?"

Once more his eyes gauged her through the reflection of the rear-view mirror and then snapped back to the road. "Three years ago," he said, "A man named Seamus Argon met with me. You know who that is?"

"I do."

"He came up here to help Brendan Healy out. Healy was the detective on the Heilshorn case, but I'm sure you know that. I guess it was rough on him, and he relapsed; had a drinking problem or something. I'll never understand how someone can't stop drinking. I have one or two, I'm good."

"And you met Argon?"

"He found me. I didn't know who he was. But man . . . that guy was something else. Too bad what happened to him, but, his legacy lives on. You know what I mean?"

"Not exactly."

"I mean, maybe he wasn't the first, but he was really committed. He started paying attention years ago before anyone really realized the kind of corruption and cronyism going on. Before multinationals like Titan were basically buying politicians."

They went straight through the next intersection. Where was he taking her? She didn't know this area in great detail, but even in the rain she had a basic sense of geography. They weren't driving towards Oriskany, the headquarters of the Sheriff's Department. They were going the other way.

Bostrom's radio gurgled and a voice came over. He pressed a few buttons, silencing it.

"We have to ditch the vehicle. It's GPS tracked. They're going to come after us."

He slowed and turned into a driveway to a small, double-wide trailer home. It looked like any more rain would cave in the roof. Luckily, for the moment, the rain was tapering off.

"This is my house."

He put the cruiser in park. In the gloom, she discerned a pickup truck. "Don't worry, that's mine."

He got out, came back around and got her out of the rear of the vehicle. She met his eyes and looked up at him. All of the pain, adrenaline and rushed activity unbottled something she'd been carrying for quite a while.

"You're talking about some kind of revolution? Is that what Argon started? Some sort of an American resistance movement?"

She realized the idea scared her: the idea of a revolution, even if the cancer of corruption in her own government had metastasized beyond treatment. Not scared for herself, but for others.

He frowned and lifted a hand, twirled his finger in the air indicating for her to turn around. He removed the handcuffs. She spun back around, rubbing her wrists, trying to get some feeling back into them.

"What do you think?" he said.

"I think we have problems, okay. But that there are always peaceful solutions. Creating this kind of guerilla army — if that's what you're talking about, what Argon was doing — it won't achieve anything."

"You saw what just happened back there," he said somberly. "You don't want to resist that?"

She didn't answer. Her head was spinning with the new information. If Titan was funding Nonsystem, then Titan and Seamus Argon were linked. That didn't add up. Whatever it was, though, this resistance, this answer to the politico-military complex, she was being pulled right into it.

Bostrom stared at her. He stood nearly six feet tall. Built out of marble. Where was his family? Did he have one? Did she know anything about him other than a name associated with the Rebecca Heilshorn case? He'd been the first cop on the scene. A footnote in the investigation. And now here he was, whisking her away from the scene of more violence, going against his own department, like some kind of vigilante. Was he really her guide into this underground world, into Nonsystem?

She blinked in the drizzle. "I need to make a phone call."

"We need to keep moving. Call from the vehicle."

"And I need to pee. Is that alright with you, Deputy Bostrom? Or are you imposing on me the same fascist controls you're talking about fighting?"

He stared back at her for another moment. He held out his arm towards his house with the sagging roof. "I'm just trying to keep us alive. But, right this way, miss." Then his expression changed and he looked at her with a sudden compassion, his eyes roving as he evaluated her expression. "Maybe . . . yeah. You're going to want to wash that off, too."

In the bathroom she peed and rinsed the sticky blood from her face and ran her fingers through her mop of wet hair. She looked to see where the bleeding was coming from and found the gash just below the hairline, from where Delaney had whacked her with the handcuffs.

She left the water running in the sink and took out her phone, glancing at the bathroom door. The call to 911 had ended a while ago, but in her log she saw that it had been connected for almost fifteen minutes. She dialed John Rascher. As the phone rang, she looked around at the tiny bathroom with its stained cabinetry, warped flooring, and bathtub in need of a fresh grout. She took out her pain meds and shook two into her palm and swallowed them with a gulp of water from the tap.

"Where are you?" Rascher sounded more annoyed than worried.

"Where are *you*? Where was the follow unit? I was at that house for an hour. The thing exploded into a shootout, John . . ." She looked at her hand and saw that it was shaking. There were cuts on her knuckles, and her wrists were bruised from the handcuffs. *Calm down. Calm down.* "They shot at the security detail, John. They need to be arrested. All of them. A mother and her children were there. You need to pounce on Delaney right now. You hear me? It's all recorded. My phone was connected to 911. It was a mother, Rascher, a mother and—"

"Easy, okay, I hear you. Give me your location, Jennifer. Do you know your location?"

"I'm at a deputy's house. About ten miles from Stemp's. Deputy Bostrom. I don't know, we drove straight for about three miles, took a right, five, six miles, turned into a driveway. It's pouring with rain. I didn't stop to check the address on the mailbox."

She could hear the fear in her voice, masked by sarcasm. She didn't care. Rascher surely heard it, too.

"Why?" Rascher asked. "What the hell is the deputy doing pulling you out on his own?"

"Why do you think?"

He was silent. She realized it was sinking in. "Jen, I know this is bad. Okay? I know. I couldn't bring the

160

Follow Unit into it. Not right now. We're not ready for that. We're still building this. We take Delaney in now — what? We get him for ripping off the department, cheating on his wife, maybe murder, if any of the other cops talk, and my money says they won't. Neither will Delaney. He's not going to give us anything."

She couldn't believe what she was hearing. "You've got to be kidding me. Get the call from 911. Just listen to what happened, John."

Rascher sighed. She could heard the rain still coming down where he was, drumming on a metal roof. "Come on, you know how this works. Now we come get you."

She said nothing for a moment, her heart beating a steady rhythm as she sat on the toilet seat. A runnel of rainwater made its way down her neck, slipped beneath her shirt. She was bait again. They had anticipated this explosive scene at Stemp's farm. Maybe even hoped for it.

There was a knock on the door that made her heart jump. "You okay in there?"

"Yup," she called out. "One second."

"Jen," Rascher said. His voice struck a familiar chord. Like the way he sounded when he was going to explain himself, how his bitter medicine was really for the best. "Stay put, help is on the way."

"No."

Silence. Then, Rascher, incredulous, "No?"

"This is what you wanted? Okay. Fine. Then I'm going to follow this where it goes. Maybe this takes us right where we want to be." She felt like a kidnapping victim negotiating with her captors. It wasn't exactly unfamiliar territory, but it had a fresh twist. She felt like she was going to vomit.

He was quiet again. She could almost hear him calculating the risk, considering the liabilities. "No," he said at last. And she heard something in his voice she hadn't expected. Or maybe wasn't ready yet to believe.

Fear. "Let Oneida County pick you up. We still don't want to risk sticking our heads out to—"

She hung up. She slipped the phone into her pocket and then shut the water off and walked out of the bathroom. *They knew,* she thought.

They knew Eddie Stemp would jump out of pocket, and when he did, all the snakes would come out, like Delaney, worried old God-fearing Stemp would talk, shine the light on them. They sent me in to rile him up. Scare him. They never intended for me to get any closer to Nonsystem than that. Because of what I might find.

She knew that was the truth. The FBI was hiding something. She'd suspected it since they'd pulled her out of that building seven months before. They didn't actually want her getting close to Nonsystem. There was something they didn't want her to find.

Bostrom yanked her out of the bathroom a moment after she opened the door. Holding her by her arm, they passed through his kitchen, with a peeling linoleum floor, a lingering odor of burnt eggs in the air. He was holding a duffel bag in his other hand.

He shoved open the front door and the two of them headed for his truck, running through the overcast afternoon. She could hear the sirens rising in the distance. They were coming.

CHAPTER TWENTY-THREE / THURSDAY 3:27 PM

"Stop it," Laruso gagged. "Stop it stop it, motherfucker."

Brendan was straddling the convict. Tony Laruso's punished eye was red with burst capillaries. There was a dark gash near his eyebrow where the skin had split, glistening with blood. He'd gotten his hands in front of his face, where the fingers shook, feebly warding off further blows.

"I didn't want to do this," Brendan said. His voice sounded like it was coming from someone else. He felt wetness on his face and he took his hand — trembling just as badly and wiped at his skin and then examined his fingertips. No blood. Just moisture. For God's sake. Crying.

His other hand was suspended above Laruso's face. The knuckles were already swelling, fine drops of blood dotting them like freckles. He tried to open his hand, but it resisted. It was someone else's hand. He pushed himself off Laruso and backed towards the corner.

He watched, impassive, in shock, as Laruso rolled himself over, groaning. The convict got to his knees and up on his palms so that he was on all fours, his head lowered between his shoulder blades.

Brendan took an unsteady breath, exhaled, and fought to get himself under control, to return to his senses. If Laruso came at him now, it would be the end. One of them would wind up dead.

"You don't have to go down with this place, Tony. I can keep you out of it."

Laruso dragged himself away in the other direction, his knees shushing across the hard, bare floor, his palms slapping and pulling his large, muscular body along. He reached the corner and sat up against the wall. He kept his head lowered, brought his knees up and hung his forearms over the top of them. His tattoo-free skin was dirty and grazed.

"How?"

Brendan felt a flush of relief through his body.

"Grimm doesn't know you're involved; he'll never have to."

"I mean, how?" Head still down. "What do I have to do?"

"Just one thing. Just one thing for me and you have my word I'll keep you out of all of it."

Now the head came up. Laruso glared across the space with one good eye, the other already puffing up, the blood from the wound running down his face in a single rivulet, like a red tear, the eye itself filigreed with so many erupted vessels it was like a crimson ball in his head. "Motherfucker, I think you just blinded me. How am I supposed to trust you?"

"Because I stopped hitting you."

Laruso continued to stare at him, the rage mercifully draining from his features. Then he dropped his head into the palm of his hand.

"There are no cameras in this room, Tony. Nothing recorded. No one knows what's going on in here. So I'm telling you right now, you do one thing for me, and I won't

164

name you. You'll be kept out of the probe that's going to turn this place inside out, and you'll get out on time. Or, this thing sweeps through tomorrow and you're going to do a long stretch. Real long."

Silence. Laruso unmoving, his head in his hand. Surely it was throbbing as much as Brendan's hand. That hand was held in a loose fist, the tendons reluctant to release.

"Okay," Laruso said.

CHAPTER TWENTY-FOUR / THURSDAY, 3:48 PM

Bostrom's pickup was fast, a V-8, fuel-injected engine combusting under a gleaming red hood that rammed through the air, but when the first Sheriff's Department SUV came blasting through an intersection and swerved in right behind them, Jennifer was scared.

She gripped the armrest, her feet firmly planted on the floor. She glanced through the windshield at the sky.

"We're going to draw lots of attention." She was thinking helicopters. Police or FBI. News choppers. She was picturing the various events over the years with people on the run, dozens or hundreds of police on their tails as the media spied from above. Good God, was she going to be one of those stories? What was she doing? How had everything gotten so turned around?

"In less than twenty-four hours, no one will be paying any attention," Bostrom said.

She looked at the county cop in the side-view mirror. The vehicle was right on their tail. "What's going to happen in twenty-four hours?"

Bostrom gave her a quick look, and then pinned the road with his eyes again as they headed around a steep curve.

"You've got to think like the military; it's all chain of command, it's the careers of the people involved. Someone like Argon didn't want any of that bureaucratic bullshit hanging over him. Ever wonder why he stayed a beat cop for his entire career? He used the street to hold court."

She kept watch on the mirror. They were out in the sticks, with nothing but cornfields, barns, and telephone poles on long flat roads, glistening like silver ribbons in the rain. The sun was buried behind the dark gray clouds, making the siren lights stand out extra brightly. They had picked up another pursuer. Not an SUV, but a fast-looking county cruiser.

"Argon was right on top of it," Bostrom said. "And his sister was, too."

"Philomena?" She turned away from the side-view mirror, momentarily shocked out of her fear.

"Philomena Argon was recruited by the IMF. She was repatriated here. She brought her younger brother with her. Their parents were dead and gone."

Jennifer felt like a grenade had detonated in the reaches of her mind. Largo had told her that Argon had been in possession of damning information — data that could expose more political and corporate corruption than any recorded 911 phone call could. Now Bostrom was telling her where he'd gotten it from. Not only that, but the former head of the IMF had recently been in New York City. He'd been arrested and sent to Rikers. Now released, he'd been in there with Brendan for a time. She was sure of it.

"Mena stayed in DC for years while Seamus moved north to Westchester County," Bostrom said, his forearms bulging as he manhandled the wheel. "But after a stroke forced her retirement, he had her move to Dobbs Ferry to keep her nearby."

She was still reeling from the information. "What did she do? What department was she in?"

"Communications. Editorial and publications, plus internal."

Her mind spun with the possibilities. They were coming up hard behind a smaller pickup, taking it's time. Bostrom swung his big truck out and around the other, passing them almost as if they were standing still. The cops on their tail followed suit.

"Better grab the holy-shit bars for this one."

Jennifer reached up and took the handle above the door as Bostrom urged the pickup to a higher and more dangerous speed. The cops receded in the mirror, but only a little. The whole frame of the truck vibrated over the rough county road. "Philomena studied macroeconomics at Oxford. When she started working for the IMF, she was under-challenged. Her mind was always working. She watched the flow of money into the Fund — the IMF — and where it was coming from, and where else it was going. She had a heart doctor in Westchester County. Gerard Healy. She didn't just pick him at random. She'd seen his name half a dozen times working at the Fund."

Jennifer quickly added what Bostrom was saying to her own knowledge. "Gerard Healy sat on various boards and committees with Alexander Heilshorn . . . including one called 'The Foundation.'"

Bostrom suddenly threw on the brakes, and Jennifer lurched forward, the seatbelt strap cutting into her chest. "That's exactly right," Bostrom said. He spun the wheel hard left, gunned the engine, and the big truck leapt onto a side road, a dirt road. They rocketed towards a line of trees. Jennifer hung on for her life. "Opinion makers," he said. "Heilshorn was on that committee. Advising about medical technology, about the internet, digital currency like bitcoin."

Bitcoin, she registered. It was how she had found a credible link between Heilshorn and Nonsystem.

"Philomena was cultivating Gerard Healy, as an asset. Remember this is a woman from a military family, civic duty imbued in her. Probably would've been CIA if she'd been a natural-born citizen."

"That's how Argon came to know that Alexander Heilshorn had a daughter going to school up here," she said, fitting it together now, staring ahead at the dense woods. They were driving towards it, full speed. "Because Gerard Healy knew?"

Bostrom nodded. "When Rebecca was murdered, Argon came up and met with all of us — myself, Stemp, and his buddy Taber. Taber kept an eye on things, but Taber was under Heilshorn's control. Argon had essentially put Brendan Healy in place. Like a chess piece."

Brendan Healy: Gerard Healy's only child. In the middle of the maelstrom, just like she'd thought. Only now she knew how, and why. Because Argon and Taber had been friends. Argon had been onto XList from the beginning, and he'd sent Brendan up here because Argon had suspected how Heilshorn had trapped Assemblyman Largo.

But that meant Brendan had been manipulated. His wife and daughter had been killed to satisfy Heilshorn's vengeance. He'd escaped attempts on his life, he'd spent half a year in prison. He was at the center of this whole thing, and it was because he'd been put there. And now he was fighting his way free.

CHAPTER TWENTY-FIVE / THURSDAY, 6:07 PM

He tried to lose himself in the rush of the streets, the cabs frenetically jockeying through the traffic, the buses with blasts of exhaust fumes as they passed, the urine stink hissing up through the subway grates. Skirting the sidewalk plane trees and pin oaks in their little squares of soil, as he walked. And the people, exhausted, leaning forward, or listing to the side, or arched back with a laugh, the chaotic patterns as they weaved over the cement. Everything individual and collective at once. Large plate glass windows to the laundries, the dry-cleaners, the electronics stores, the cheap clothing stores, the doors wedged open to sticky yellow light, every third with Freon refrigerating the overweight tourists, scratchy *sarod* music playing from tinny speakers. The racks on the sidewalks and the tables with sunglasses and hats and bootleg DVDs. The hot, baking air, industrial air, like the whole place was a sweatshop, but it was okay.

The mercy of being out of that prison hell. The freedom. Nothing better than freedom. Nothing on earth. Brendan really felt like he could kiss the streets. They said no matter what, you had everything if you had your health. But healthy prisoners would beg to differ.

He couldn't sit in the hotel room. He'd tried. He'd checked in, taken a long hot shower, put on the TV, and promptly felt like an alien. There was a mini-bar in the room. He opened the door to the small fridge and crouched in front of it, staring in at the candy-colored liquors. He could taste the polish of the bourbon on his tongue, smell the sting of the vodka in his nostrils. He imaged the bitter taste of Heineken sliding down his throat, cutting through an unquenchable thirst.

He left the room, and went downstairs. He asked at the front desk if he could change rooms to one that was devoid of alcohol. The waifish, middle-aged clerk behind the counter betrayed a curious look he quickly quashed beneath cheery helpfulness. Of course he could have another room. Right *away* he could have another room. *Let me just check and see if one is available and then maybe you'll actually be able to go to that other room right* now.

As the staff busied themselves with the room change, Brendan left the hotel. He ended up walking for two hours and made three calls from three different phone booths. From the first payphone he found, he called the 914 number he had for Sloane, the one his lawyer had given him, the number for her adoptive parents. She wasn't in, but they promised to pass on his message. He told them where he was staying, including the original room number he'd been assigned.

He wandered, down Fifth Avenue, up Broadway as it cut over the other avenues, back down to Central Park, through it to Columbus Circle, back towards Seventh Avenue, then on the subway south to the Village. Third Street, Sullivan, McDougal, a bar called Duffy's, the jangle of music and clack of pool balls drifting up and out, the sylphlike shapes of the men curled around their drinks, the bright and intoxicated laughter of a woman.

He kept walking. No rhyme or reason to his direction, total autonomy, deciding he would keep moving until his legs were burning, a zigzagging path through a city grid.

At last, he noticed the two people following him.

A man and a woman. The woman he'd first noticed uptown, and then he'd seen her again in the reflection of a window back along Third Street. The man appeared as Brendan rounded Third onto Sixth Avenue and descended back down to the subway. The man came down after him, and Brendan was sure he'd sighted him, too, this time by Central Park, that same crewcut, the same gait, the same way one shoulder sagged slightly below the other. Dressed in civilian clothes which didn't fit right. A style that didn't match his haircut. The woman, too, with a low-cut blouse exposing her clothes-hanger collar bone, dangly earrings. Something wrong about both their appearances.

The 4 train rattled and squealed into place and he stepped on and watched as the faces flurry past, and he saw the crewcut man in the too-obvious hipster clothes and for a fraction of a second they locked eyes before the world outside the scarred subway window became black with the inside of a tunnel.

CHAPTER TWENTY-SIX / THURSDAY, 4:12 PM

Her phone rang. It seemed like the most bizarre thing. As she stared out the windshield, as Bostrom drove down a series of trails so off-road that some of them were just two grooves in the grass, roads he clearly knew well, and as the Sheriff's Department disappeared from their tail, the idea of her phone ringing was absurd. Phones rang when you were sitting at your desk, or walking down the street.

"Hi, John," she said, putting it to her ear.

"What the hell are you doing?" Rascher sounded furious and afraid at the same time.

She glanced at Bostrom. "I've gotten more information this afternoon than in the past seven months."

"Jennifer, this is insane."

"I agree."

Rascher didn't know what else to say. He wasn't used to this. She felt a perverse twinge of pride. No, he wasn't used to it at all. He was used to her being tractable. But that had started to end the day she was taken up into a skyscraper and poisoned. And what little remained of her pliancy, was circling the drain now after watching cops shoot members of her security detail, turn a weapon on a defenseless woman, and have her supervisor dismiss a possible 911 record of it all.

Bostrom gave her a quick glance. They bounced down the old logging roads, at times so hard she was lifted right up out of her seat. If it hadn't been such a dire situation, it might've even been fun.

"I've gotta go, John," she said, and ended the call. Then she lowered the window, and threw her phone out into a blur of pine needles. Bostrom glanced over again.

"I hunt out here," he explained after a moment. "Some of the other guys know this area. A few. But I think we're going to be in the clear."

True to his words, a few minutes later they emerged from the woods and were on a dirt road alongside an old cow pasture. There were two large boulders and a grove of small fir trees, huddled together like an oasis. They came to the end of the dirt way and the truck jumped onto the hard surface of a more major route where Bostrom cut a right turn. They got up to speed and were on their way again. No cops in sight, no one behind them. And nothing above.

"Bostrom?"

"Yeah."

"Where are you taking me?"

He piloted the big truck along at a sane speed of sixty miles an hour. The road was wet from the afternoon storm, the puddles evaporating, a mist in the air.

"Alexander Heilshorn saw multiple opportunities in XList," Bostrom said.

She took one of the water bottles he had stashed in his duffel bag and drank. "Such as?"

"Prostitutes gathering information, prostitutes causing scandals, even prostitutes committing murder." Bostrom raised his eyebrows. "You made it your career to investigate this stuff."

"I did and I didn't. I'm interested in the common denominator. In big black market busts, it's always the money that leads to the big players, never the product. That's what you follow. And, occasionally, you see that money go to the top, somewhere it really shouldn't. But when that happens, you're dealing with something dangerous; you have to tread very carefully."

Bostrom nodded. She sounded like she was convincing herself as much as him.

Jennifer amended, "But, in the end, it's about the people. The women involved, the children involved. You're right. That's my job."

"Argon was worried about them, too. I think baby Sloane triggered that for him, for sure. Really brought it home. As I'm sure you know, the more the FBI has been coming after black markets, organizations like XList go deeper underground."

They took an on-ramp and merged with the flow of traffic on an interstate. Jennifer was about to question the use of a major route, but Bostrom spoke first. "Plus, you have the money side, like you said. Only, bitcoin gets hacked, people lose millions, bitcoin gets tracked, people get arrested, what happens? That goes deeper, too. The way of transacting business online goes into total stealth mode."

Nonsystem, she thought. Hackers. People managing newer and more sophisticated ways to conceal the path of the money — the path which so often led to the answers. But who was Nonsystem? Libertarians paving the way for more ways to purchase drugs, guns, and humans outside the spotlight of government? If that was all there was to them, theirs was a dark crusade.

"The authorities make busts," Bostrom said, driving, "and you've got people who've invested millions into these black markets, and then are taken down. Drug kingpins arrested, accused of running illicit online businesses worth billions."

She ran a shaky hand through her still-wet hair and took a deep breath. "You're taking me to meet them."

"Philomena had compiled one of the most comprehensive lists of corruption, money-laundering, bribery, and black market scheming. A civilian's NSA, turned on the government. Seamus knew he had something valuable, but what do you do with that? He was either going to get it into the right hands, or he was just going to take things into his *own* hands when the time was right." He gave her a quick glance. "Yes, I am taking you to meet a few people in the Nonsystem group."

She felt excited and fearful at the same time, a paradoxical mixture that cycled through her system, jittering her nerves. "When Argon visited Brendan Healy in the middle of the Heilshorn investigation, he didn't tell him any of this? Why?"

"That's when I met Argon. That same time. Argon knew Brendan was being watched — figured he could've been bugged. So he was cautious. Plus, Heilshorn stayed deep behind the curtain until Rebecca's murder. That's when it all started to come out."

"How and why did Heilshorn push his business into this region? Proximity to Albany?"

"That's part of it. Here's the other: there's heat on XList in the beginning, the Feds are too close. There are a couple of busts, nothing that ties Heilshorn to XList, but they lose some of the girls. They need fresh recruits. So, Lawrence Taber is the key."

Taber, she thought. "You know about Taber and—?"

"Sloane, yes. Argon told me. Not that it's public information, far from it. Heilshorn has been using it against Taber for years, using it to manipulate the man and his department once XList moved into the region."

Jennifer was familiar with parts of the background story. She'd shared it with fifty people in the Robert F. Kennedy building just a few mornings previously, before Rascher had picked her up and this whole thing had started going crazy. Argon and Taber had been friends as young men — Argon the older and more cynical one.

Taber had made the mistake of falling for a girl who was trying to escape her pimp, a man named Jerry Brown. Brown had big plans, and he'd just gotten in with a financial backer willing to give his organization the cash to expand, but to also provide a very unorthodox service — Heilshorn would become the in-house obstetrician. It made even more sense now, darker sense; everything with the girls would be controlled, including pregnancies.

The whole thing had been sparked by a young woman Taber had become smitten with: Lana Mazursky, a Russian immigrant inducted into the sex trade by Jerry Brown. She and Taber were Sloane's biological parents. Argon had tried to help Taber, to find Lana when she went missing, but he'd ended up getting to her too late. He'd found her giving birth to the baby in an alleyway in a derelict section of the city. An intentional baby, a pregnancy she'd wanted with Taber, nearly destroyed by Jerry Brown, who'd tried to abort it with his fists.

Taber hadn't known, not for years. Argon had kept it from him. Taber was on his way to do good things, he'd already met someone new. But Alexander Heilshorn had known; it was what had given him the idea for XList. And when the time came to infiltrate Albany, he'd blackmailed Lawrence Taber with Sloane.

Sloane Dewan had been the birth of an idea for Heilshorn. A way of doing business, of ensuring his investments, using humans as collateral.

"Rebecca was really the beta phase," Bostrom said. "The Heilshorns are a twisted family. Probably she'd been abused growing up. Heilshorn sets her on Philip Largo when the assemblyman finds out about the data center. After that, Rebecca gets in deeper. But, willingly. Almost like an act of defiance. If she can't get out, she'll make an even bigger mess of things, who knows? Maybe she liked it, too. Eventually Reginald Forrester is called in to handle it, to put a scare on her. But Jane . . . Olivia Jane took it the extra step. I was the OSO on the murder."

"And now you're the one telling me all of this. Would you be willing to testify?"

"Testify?" Bostrom tossed her another look. Then he patted his sidearm. "That's the only testifying I'm gonna do."

She allowed the macho talk to stand for now, but all this bluster about Wild West justice — that was where she took issue, she realized. That was her sticking point. "Alright. Tell me why Gerard Healy trusted Philomena enough to furnish her with what he had on Heilshorn."

"She didn't ask. The woman was born to be a spy, I'm telling you. She raided Gerard's laptop, copied the hard drive."

"And?"

"Gerard had published a paper on processed foods causing inflammation of the arteries, for one. It flew in the face of the popular opinion that fat and cholesterol cause heart disease. That this is just money-making BS from the opinion-makers in bed with Big Agribusiness and Big Pharma who want to sell low-fat food and pills. His paper gets some reactions, stakeholders in companies who have been highly profitable for years making money off human disease. And it gets him booted from The Foundation which is advising private equity firms and multinational corporations on things related to medicine and technology, like you said."

"So he's upset? What? Wants to get back at them?"

"He's just a freedom fighter. I mean, Gerard Healy is a sophisticated guy, you know, liked his wine, spoke a couple languages, but a rebel at heart. They pushed him out so he started an anti-Foundation campaign, talking about how the government is run by corporations. Specifically, Titan's relationship to the government."

"Then he succumbs to a grand mal seizure."

Bostrom looked over at her as he slowed the car at a red light. "That's right. Titan is flexing its power."

"Can you prove they're responsible?"

He shook his head. "It's not until years later, not until Rebecca's murder, that Argon makes the connection. He starts to put it together at the same time Brendan Healy is working the case, like I said. I mean, Healy's the reason we're talking right now."

She scowled and peered out into the rain. "Right, because when Argon died, it drew Healy back in. The whole thing comes full circle."

"Taber really lassoed him."

Taber, she thought. *On permanent vacation.*

And: *They're all dead and buried somewhere.*

Jennifer took another deep breath. She glanced in the side-view mirror and saw headlights coming up behind fast them. It made her heart jump, until she realized it was a civilian vehicle, jockeying for position on the interstate. Traffic was thickening now as they drove southeast, towards more populated areas, and commuters headed home from a day at the office. The storm was moving off ahead of them. It felt like they were chasing it.

"Does Philomena still have the data?"

"No. We do."

"Where are we going, exactly?"

He wore a skeptical expression.

"Come on," she said. "I threw my phone out the window for God's sake. You can trust me."

His mouth twitched into a smile. "Cape Cod," he said.

CHAPTER TWENTY-SEVEN / THURSDAY, 6:09 PM

After the storm, the late afternoon was sun-splashed, cooler than before, the wind calm, as Staryles rode the Oak Bluffs Ferry over to Nantucket Island. Two Black Hawk helicopters appeared in the sky above a distant ridge of receding clouds. Staryles looked over the top of his newspaper and watched. Ferry passengers oohed and aahed as the choppers hammered the air. They were Air National Guard helicopters, equipped like ambulances. They could each carry as many as six patients and were able to fly speeds up to two hundred and fifteen miles per hour.

A young boy, held aloft by his father, pointed over the water. Cutting across the surface in the distance were two Coast Guard skiffs. Staryles knew they carried divers.

The whole rescue drill operation consisted of multiple parties: Barnstable County Regional Emergency Planning Committee; the towns of Sandwich, Mashpee and Dennis; Massachusetts Emergency Management Agency, Coast Guard, National Guard and private organizations such as Cape Air and MedFlight emergency air services. It would last into dark, simulating conditions that provided for a challenging environment for the rescuers to work in.

"Federal, state, and local partnerships are the key to preparedness," Geoff Tambour had told the press earlier that morning. *Indeed*, thought Staryles, watching the skiffs cruise smoothly over the Nantucket Sound. *The key to preparedness.*

There were three soldiers on the skiffs, divers who had a different agenda from the rest. No doubt those three were donning their gear at that moment, readying their Halligans — a mean-looking tool that firefighters also used, with a sharp ax-end and a crowbar end — for the trip underwater. They would plan to be there all night, ostensibly part of the salvage crew.

But not really.

The drill was a simulation of an airplane crash with one person seriously injured and a dozen more wounded. Airlifting the wounded was part of it, as was underwater searching for the two people who were launched out of the plane during the faux crash, and extricating the materials put in place ahead of time which would serve as the wreckage of the non-existent crash. The drill had been designed months ago, and called Operation Hopeful Lift. The Black Hawks would act as MedFlight and airlift the injured safely to Joint Base Cape Cod. From there they'd be taken to Falmouth Hospital by ambulances. Nantucket had been the chosen site of the drill because of its remote location. It was difficult to get to the island quickly, and presented a formidable challenge.

As the ferry neared the central part of the island, on the north shore, the Coast Guard skiffs began slipping out of sight behind the land. The site of the faux crash was on the south side, chosen because it presented just that much more of a challenge.

It also happened to be where a critical branch of the Mid-Atlantic Cable came into the United States, carrying the information from countries all over the world into the

US. The cable island-skipped from the south side of Nantucket over to Tuckmuck, across the sound to Chappaquiddick, then banked north and shot beneath the waters of Cotuit Bay before making landfall in Falmouth. But, after today, the information it carried would be lost, thanks to those three rogue divers.

He turned his attention to the Black Hawks as they circled Nantucket, watching them through his sunglasses, listening to the rapid chop of the tail rotors. The newspaper still in his hands, the article on the massive drill there on the front page: "This can be replicated anywhere," Deputy Fire Chief Brett Mason was quoted. "Heaven forbid, this was to ever to happen on the Islands. And if Route 6 ever got flooded, turning Provincetown into an island, we would be ready."

There was no mention of the cable. People rarely thought about such things. Most didn't know how the internet worked, how they were able to email an expat relative, play an online game with someone on another continent, or send money across the ocean.

Publicly-held companies that powered huge sections of the US stock market and world economies depended on international trade. The modern economy was global, and the cables linking the World Wide Web were its arteries, its nerves. The internet, in its physical form, was akin to the squid wrapped around the ship in *20,000 Leagues Under the Sea*. Cut off one of its tentacles and you could isolate America from the world and cripple the international economy.

The divers would work all night.

Staryles folded up the paper and wedged it under his arm. He and the other fifty or so passengers aboard the Oak Bluffs Ferry watched as the choppers descended. The divers would be throwing themselves over the bow and into the sea, holding onto their breathing regulators with one hand, clutching their Halligans in another, tools to extricate the imaginary people from imaginary wreckage.

The axe blades glinting in the bright sunlight as they splashed into the cool blue waters.

CHAPTER TWENTY-EIGHT / THURSDAY, 6:31 PM

The first rosy fingers of dusk painted the Eastern sky as the sun set behind them. Billowing clouds sat on the horizon, flat-bottomed, tinged salmon by the light. They were less than an hour from Cape Cod.

Jennifer's father had been a district court judge in Rockland County. He'd bought a small home in Cotuit years ago. She remembered her father telling her the story of how the town was settled. In fact, he'd told her more than once - he'd been getting to the age when men told the same story again and again and didn't know it. *Cotuit was purchased by Miles Standish in the mid-1600s for a large brass kettle and a broad hoe.* It had a ring to it, like a nursery rhyme.

"Why Cape Cod?"

"That's where Argon's place is," Bostrom said. "For one thing."

The 600 square miles of island cape jutting out from Massachusetts didn't seem the likeliest place a beat cop would vacation. But, maybe that was the point. "Who knows about it?"

"Nobody. His lawyer. Maybe Brendan Healy, who saw Argon's will, I think."

"No one looking to shut you down knows? Why risk it?"

"Argon's dead," Bostrom said. "He left the house to his sister in the will. Where is a seventy-something stroke victim going to go? As long as she's alive, the place just sits there. We watched it for months, swept it; it's clean."

He made an abrupt lane change. She checked his speed and saw the needling climbing to ninety.

"We're going to get pulled over . . ."

"How much do you know about the military installation there?"

"What my father told me, what I've learned on the job. Camp Cotuit trained units that eventually stormed the Pacific beaches in World War II, including New Guinea. But Cotuit was really a satellite camp for Edwards."

"Tell me about Edwards."

"Edwards is the largest part of Joint Base Cape Cod. Home to the National Guard and the Air National Guard; 3rd Battalion and 126th Aviation unit. It was deactivated after the Korean War. They faced a complete shut-down in the 90s but stayed open; there were strong objections from the military community to its closure. Now it's home to two training centers."

"And what about them?" It sounded like he already knew.

She took a breath, and looked in the side-view mirror. As they whipped past the other vehicles the low sun bounced bright off the chrome and steel, blinding her with shattering light. Time for another dose of the meds. She swallowed two pills.

"The training centers simulate war-torn villages," she said. "Some of the most extensive anti-terrorism exercises in the world happen there. Not just for the National Guard, but for special ops. Edwards' resources are used to practice rescue drills in the areas. By the way, slow down."

Bostrom glanced at her and raised his eyebrows. "Doesn't just seem like a vacation spot anymore, does it?" He took his foot off the gas.

"I spent summers on Cape Cod when I was young."

"I know."

"You do?"

"Argon told me."

"I never met Seamus Argon."

"Lawrence Taber gave Brendan your name. He and Argon knew who you were."

"Okay. What else do you know?"

He gave her another quick, tight look. "I know that the rescue drill underway right now off the coast is not just a rescue drill."

"What is it?"

"A sabo mission."

"Sabotage."

"That's right. Of the MAC."

"The cable for the internet? And you know this because—?"

"Because of everything I'm telling you. Because of everything Philomena learned over a decade of spying on The Foundation, learning from Gerard Healy. Because of every communication our hackers have seen. Because of eyewitnesses seeing Staryles enter the Meet-Me-Room in Manhattan. Because the rescue drill is going on right now in the exact spot where the MAC makes landfall. And it's no coincidence."

She took a moment to absorb the information. She decided the more she understood the past, the more she'd know why Argon had bought a house near Camp Edwards, and why the hell Bostrom was insinuating Edwards had something to do with sabotaging one of the world's most crucial internet arteries.

She went through the steps: Alexander Heilshorn learns about Gerard Healy's patient-relationship with Philomena Argon. He finds out who she is — the sister of the 'Baby Sloane' cop. But Heilshorn doesn't know exactly what she's doing on her own time at the IMF. He's distracted by other troubles. Namely, he's hired Reginald Forrester to murder his daughter.

Then, there's a wrinkle. Olivia Jane gets personal and throws things off course. She's the one to kill Rebecca. So Heilshorn comes up to Oneida County to keep a closer eye on the investigation and play the concerned father. Really though, he's dealing with Olivia Jane.

Of all the ironies, Jennifer thought, it's Brendan Healy who saves Heilshorn's life in that showdown at the unfinished college campus building. The new data center. Healy doesn't know what's really going on with Heilshorn, doesn't know he's just saved the man who took his father's life.

So, where did Argon come in? How did it relate to the destruction of a massive internet junction?

She spoke. "Okay. Bear with me a minute. Gerard Healy is assassinated for being too outspoken, threatening to divulge Titan secrets gleaned from The Foundation. But Philomena has already squirreled away a trove of devastating information. Only they don't know this yet? Their concern is Gerard's son, Brendan. So, they go after him."

"A clean sweep," said Bostrom. "Brendan's a heavy drinker and it will look like it's his fault as much as the truck driver who you paid half a million to swerve, hit the wife and daughter, claim to the cops he'd been awake for three straight days, and get five years for involuntary manslaughter, out for parole in two and a half. But, of course, Brendan's not in the car."

Jennifer shuddered. At the same time, she felt a light snap on in the back of her mind. A light that invited her to take another look at the time period Brendan Healy had disappeared. His father dies, and ten months later his wife and daughter are taken from him. But it is *four years* after that when Argon pulls him out of the garage, begins to nurse him back to health, and steers him into the police academy. All that time he still has his house and it's paid for and the taxes are paid up for half a decade and where is he? What is he doing? "Maybe enough time had passed that they figured he was dead," she considered aloud.

Then one day Brendan returns. He moves back into the house. Not long after, he's in the garage with the engine of his car running.

Seamus Argon saves the day and pulls Brendan out and takes him under his wing: gets him sober, into the academy, and on the Mount Pleasant police force, where he stays before transferring to Oneida County, promoted to detective. He's barely there two months when Rebecca Heilshorn is murdered.

"I think Argon wanted Brendan working with Taber," she said, feeling the exhilaration as it came to her. "Argon *did* make the connection to Alexander Heilshorn before Rebecca was murdered." She looked at Bostrom, held up her pills and shook the bottle for effect. "Back when an XList escort was seen with Philip Largo, a state assemblyman who had hit the campaign trail for governor of New York State and who was in Alexander's way."

She went on:

"Let's say Argon finds that Largo's politics are, prima facie, about civil liberties and restrictions and regulations on big business. But, he figures, there's got to be more. More than how he might just threaten Heilshorn's revenue streams. I've got to tell you, Bostrom, I've spent my life learning to replace my vague feelings of dread with specific concerns. Do you know what I mean?"

It was nice to see Bostrom grin. "I do."

"Because I met with Largo. And he said he moved to block the construction of a building at the UAlbany campus. It was for the college on the surface, but it was a data center."

Bostrom's smile hardened into the set of his jaw, becoming a grimace.

Jennifer stared at him. "Why is Alexander Heilshorn building a data center? Is he supporting Nonsystem? Or is there something else? I need to know, because I can't sit here a moment longer relying only on conjecture. I'm on the run, for chrissakes, from my own people."

But it was there, just eluding her — right there. Heilshorn, Nonsystem, the MAC offshore of Cape Cod . .

Bostrom nodded, keeping his eyes on the road. His jaw muscle twitched.

"Come on, Bostrom. What am I missing?"

Bostrom became grave. Then he spoke.

"There is a piece of software that can violate and evade all regulations. It can render government obsolete. And right now, as I'm sure you know, our banking institutions and our government institutions are inseparable."

"I won't argue."

"Then you know about Project Bullrun?"

"I've heard about it. It's NSA. A program built by defense contractors to defeat all encryption programs. To eliminate the public's ability to cloak their actions online."

"Yeah. Well, it failed."

She hadn't known about Bullrun's failure. That was a major program. If it had failed, then the people in the government who wanted to monitor all financial dealings — with bitcoin that path of transactions was called the blockchain — might have become desperate.

Bostrom continued, "Software, like Dark Wallet, that scatters the data, chops it up and combines it with others, also provides a stealth address which can receive the coins. All untraceable. This can include things like mortgage-backed securities. No more financial crisis and mortgage fraud and credit debt because it all goes away when the banks lose power. When the government loses control."

She struggled to raise a reasonable objection. She was no longer thinking of Nonsystem as only out to protect nasty black market transactions.

There were billion dollar bitcoin industries out there; it was becoming a huge chunk of the economy. Already unruly and causing a stir — a panic, really — in law enforcement. Now with Dark Wallet, or something like it, all those trails followed by the FBI and the DOJ would just disappear. Billions of dollars unaccounted for. Untaxed. Not factored into the GDP. Some would say, not unlike the mega corporations already banking offshore to get the lowest tax rate, to hide their own billions.

However, unlike the corporations and banks, who had their own lobbying industry, this was an underground world of money, with libertarian groups like Nonsystem acting as its guardians. They had no friends in Washington to keep the top tax rate low, or to write the tax law. This was huge sums of money, not hidden in offshore accounts, but underground. The government had been chasing it for years, learning on their feet. And the whole thing was about to go dark.

It was the kind of sea change that could topple an already unsteady government. And the transition would unleash complete havoc. She knew many men and women who worked in government who would consider this the doomsday scenario — for the country to lose its centralized financial power. They would do anything to prevent this outcome.

She felt something grip her, cold hands around her skin, everything tightening. *Oh God.* She felt choked. As though the poison was in her again, shutting her down.

CHAPTER TWENTY-NINE / THURSDAY, 8:14 PM

Brendan bought new clothes. A simple suit from Brooks Brothers; a Regent fit, black, with a white shirt. He lingered over the ties. He decided he hated ties, and didn't get one. He also bought a pair of jeans and a hooded sweatshirt. Crossing back through Midtown towards Grand Central Station, he stopped at a Duane Reade and bought hair dye and clippers. He boggled at the cosmetics section, confused by the sheer number of products, until he found some simple foundation make-up that he thought would work.

He put all his purchases in a new duffle bag, got on a train, and schlepped himself north to the Bronx. He kept one eye over his shoulder to see if he was being followed.

He wasn't.

It took twenty minutes walking around in the Bronx to find the address. He moved south along Courtlandt Ave in Morrisania, a section with low-rise brick buildings, sidewalk shops, fruit and vegetable stands. Everything was cast in the heavenly glow of a low sun. As he passed a tattoo parlor, Roma Pizza, and *Mr. Income Tax* the sun sank until it had slipped behind the buildings.

The traffic was thinner at the end of the avenue and few people were out on the streets. A stooped woman pushed a shopping cart full of rattling cans over the uneven sidewalk. Signs declared *King Steaks*, *E-Z Stop Deli*, *Bronx Laundromat*, some of the windows were broken.

At 146ᵗʰ Street a yellow sign read *No Outlet*. Brendan headed in and walked until he found the number 945 spray-painted on a single-story building, with a garage door open. Rap music thumped out into the evening.

Brendan walked in. The stained concrete reeked of gas and oil. A dark Chrysler minivan was up on a set of blocks. Tools were on the pegboards. A man emerged from the back, wiping his hands on a dirty rag. He was olive-skinned, built like Tony Laruso, without an ounce of flab. He looked Brendan up and down, his eyes crawling over Brendan's new suit, and he moved closer. The menace emanated from him as sharp as the smell of gas in the air.

"The fuck're you?"

The man had cold eyes, and Brendan stared right back, never breaking eye contact. If Laruso had been true to his word, things might be alright. If he'd been lying, Brendan probably wouldn't make it out of here alive. He took a step forward. "Tony sent me."

The man seemed to hesitate. According to Laruso, this guy was meant to be Bosco. Laruso was supposed to have gotten a message to Bosco by now. If he hadn't, there was a safe word.

A safe word, Brendan thought. Sure. With no gun on him, against a man who looked like he'd been born under the hood of a Mustang, there was nothing safe about this.

Bosco's menacing stare held for a moment, but then his lips split into a wide grin. "Fuckin' Laruso," he said. "How is that fat *chooch*? Come on in back; let's get you what you need."

* * *

An hour later Brendan returned to the Sheraton in Midtown. He stopped at the front desk and handed the clerk a small package. The clerk was someone new now; beneath her plastic smile, the young woman looked like she'd withstood hundreds of guest complaints already that day. The corners of her mouth turned up in practiced glee and she said she would be happy to mail the package out for him. She also informed him his room had indeed been switched to one with no mini-bar.

He thanked her and she handed him his newly minted room-key card. He noticed her eyes lag over his face for a moment. She caught herself and then looked away.

I'll start telling people I'm a cage fighter, Brendan thought.

He took the card from her outstretched hand and put it in his back pocket. He bid her good night and headed towards the elevators.

He spent the next hour sitting on a different floor from his new room, watching from the nook where an ice machine softly rattled and hummed. He kept his eyes on the door to the room he'd first been given. He drank a Pepsi from the vending machine next to the ice dispenser. By the time he'd finished it, no one had come by.

A couple in their fifties, looking like they'd had a good evening, walked to the room and keyed the lock, talking and laughing with one another. The door swung shut.

He waited. He'd gotten good at waiting.

At last the elevator doors opened and Sloane stepped off. He'd been alone for a decade, languishing in jail for seven months, standing in this same spot for a final few hours, and now there she was.

The way she was standing there, he was reminded of the first time he'd met her — in Argon's house in Hawthorne, when she'd had Brendan's gun. The one the New York Police Department had now.

"Hey," he said from down the hallway.

She turned around. She was even prettier than he remembered. She wore a Rugby shirt, jeans, and running shoes. Her hair was pulled back in a high ponytail. He took her all in: the slight tilt to her smile, her small ears and nose, large bright eyes taking him in. Those eyes looked sad.

"Jesus, Brendan," she said. "What did they do to you?"

He felt a childish blush of self-consciousness and almost put up a hand to obscure his face. He leaned against the wall, suddenly drained, as if all the strength he'd been building for the past months was just to get him here, and now that Sloane was standing there, he could collapse. Rest.

She walked down the hallway to him. Standing in front of him, she brought her hands to his face, and touched his skin. He jerked his head back — a reflex action. He forced himself back towards her touch. Her hands feathered over his skin, her sterling-silver rings shining in the overhead light of the hallway.

"Come on up to my room," he said.

She didn't ask for an explanation as they stepped into the elevator and took it to the next floor. They watched their thin reflections dance on the brass surfaces.

He opened the door of his room and stood aside so she could go in. He got the impression that something was different about her. She still looked like the Sloane he remembered, the one he'd imagined day in and day out for seven months, but something had changed. He couldn't put his finger on it. Maybe it was just the time that had passed — people couldn't expect things to remain the same with half a year gone. They'd known one another so briefly, even though they had been through such harrowing events together, time was time. Or, maybe it wasn't even her who was different. Maybe it was him.

He closed the door. Sloane ventured over to the windows and took in the view of the city at night.

"So what's with the smooth moves?" she asked. He remembered her voice so distinctly, the subtle impairment in her speech. Sloane's motor cortices sent slightly misguided signals to her pharynx, maybe her tongue. He had never asked her the extent of her injuries from being born the way she had. She was asking why he had given her the wrong room number — his old room — instead of this one.

"Two people were following me earlier tonight. All around the city. I lost them. Or, they're just hanging back at this point. They could be on you, too."

She turned around to face him, smiling. "Nobody's following me."

"They let me rot in there for seven months. They let me fight my way out."

"And you did."

"Yeah. I did. But they're allowing it to happen. Paying out the rope. Maybe seeing if I hang myself with it." He looked down, studying his hands, the one with the absent finger, the wedding ring long gone. "I don't know . . ."

Sloane crossed the hotel room. "Brendan," she said, stopping in front of him. She was six inches shorter than he was, so with his head lowered she looked right up into his eyes again. "You're a skeptic who wants to believe."

"Oh, is that what I am?" He felt a grin tugging at the corners of his mouth.

"Mmhmm. You're an idealist-pessimist."

"I see."

She moved toward him. They hugged, and he rested his chin on the top of her head. "Is this okay?"

"It's okay."

"It's good to see you."

"It's good to see you, too." She pressed her face to him, her words muffled. "They hurt you."

"They tried."

He could smell her — the shampoo in her hair, the detergent of her clothes, but something else, too, something anomalous. Like sea air.

"I can't believe what you did for me," she said.

195

"I did what I thought was right. I brought you into all of it."

She was silent. He tried some levity. "So, what have you been up to for the past seven months? Seeing anyone?"

It was a joke, but Sloane pulled away, and she turned her face up to him. He was grinning, but she remained serious. "How about we don't talk about it right now. Can we just not talk about any of it? For now?"

He stared into her eyes. "Okay."

She started to unbutton his shirt. "Always so sharply dressed, Mr. Healy."

He found himself still grinning, but the nerves were cycling through his body. This was what he wanted, this was what he had wondered about, fantasized about. This was what had helped him survive the inside. And now here it was, it was happening. There was just something not quite right — he knew she was brazen, that she was someone who didn't take orders, did what she wanted; he'd known that from the first moment he'd met her. But there was an even greater self-possession about her now that he hadn't quite expected. The Sloane he remembered and had conjured in his mind over the days, the weeks, the months, was a spitfire, intelligent, but also a bit dark and aimless. This woman undressing him was all those things, but she didn't seem aimless.

You're over-analyzing.

Maybe. People tended to misunderstand other people, and we made up the past every time we remembered it.

Brendan stopped resisting. He let Sloane pull his shirt off. He held his stance as she touched the scars on his chest before taking her own shirt up over her head. He helped her. Her breasts were small in the cups of her black bra. He bent over and leaned into her, kissing her. Her hands came around his lower back again, her tongue flickered in over his teeth, and he inhaled her scent, pulling her into him, lifting her up.

CHAPTER THIRTY / THURSDAY 8:14 PM

Cotuit Bay. The tug boats cut frothy grooves through the gray water. The long, dusty piers creaked in their pilings. Kayaks beached along the wet sand with scattered broken seashells. Million dollar homes rimmed the bay, lamplights flicked on as the sun set. In the distance, Jennifer thought she could hear the sound of thunder as the earlier storm continued to roll away. Or maybe it was helicopters.

The setting sun burned the beach sand a deep gold. She took off her shoes and walked barefoot through the long shadows down to the water's edge. Bostrom was just behind her. "See over there," she pointed across the water to a line of buildings on the other side, "that used to be The Cotuit Inn. Now it's all condos."

She glanced at Bostrom, his face dark in the eventide. She breathed deeply, inhaling the minerally smell of the beach, the saltwater air, the traces of gasoline from the motorboats trolling nearby. The whole thing was surreal, being back here, a place of sanctuary; taking a moment like this after the recent harrowing events, she could almost forget what was happening.

She looked up into his eyes, which caught the light of the late sun.

"Bostrom, I've decided: I like you. But if you're about to take me to a group of vigilante cops-turned-revolutionaries, some paramilitary group who thinks the US Military or UN Troops are about to occupy American soil, and trot out the second amendment for us all to rally around, I've got to tell you, I'm going to stay right here. Right here on this beach. Maybe never even let my own people find me. Maybe be done with it all. Because the only thing that's going to come from civilians fighting against our own military is the death of more civilians. Our women, our children, good men like you."

He gazed at her. "I hear you."

"Look. Right here. Right where we're standing. This is where children play. So I'm being straight with you — if you want me to be involved in some kind of revolution, despite everything you've told me, and even after what I've seen, I don't want any part of it."

"You have to trust me."

She cocked an eyebrow at him. *Trust* was a word a lot of people had been using lately, herself included. A breeze tousled her hair.

"I like you too," he said. "And there's one last thing you need to know. Maybe it will help you."

"What are you talking about?"

He watched the tugboats cut a path through the water. "One of the top people in Nonsystem. One of them is someone you've already met."

She stared at him until he turned to look at her. "Tell me."

He turned on one of his smiles. "Over dinner," he said.

She immediately opened her mouth to argue, but then thought better of it. She was starving. Her last meal had been a paltry continental breakfast at the hotel in Rochester. That seemed like days ago. But, she was a complete mess, her clothes still damp from the rain.

"I'm not going anywhere until I take a shower and change. Okay with you? My family's home is not far from here. Or, I guess you already knew that."

* * *

During the 1970s, a popular Cotuit restaurant called 'The Harbor View' was torn down, much to the dismay of residents and regular visitors. A private residence was constructed in its place. Years later, when the residence sold for a tidy sum, the new owners learned of the history and put a ton of money into a new restaurant for the town, which bore the unimaginative name of 'The Harbor View Too.'

Jennifer remembered the town debating the merits of the new name. But, eventually the people settled in to enjoy the Baked Stuffed Filet of Sole served with Lobster Newburg sauce, the Broiled Famous Boston Scrod (fresh from the waters of Georges Bank) or the Bouillabaisse a la Marseillaise — the menu declared that this famous French creation combined finfish and shellfish in a sauce made from fresh tomato, leeks, saffron and garlic.

"How about the steak?" Jennifer said, looking up at the waiter.

"Oh, our roast prime rib is especially succulent. Comes with a baked potato. The steak has been drizzled with a . . ."

"I'll take it," she said smiling and setting down her menu. "Rare."

"Excellent."

"Same," Bostrom said. He ordered a bottle of red wine for the two of them and the waiter nodded and walked off scribbling in his pad. A college kid home for the summer, Jennifer thought. The Harbor Too was as nice as she remembered. Floor-to-ceiling plate glass windows overlooked the Hyannis Bay, fifty feet below. It was dark now, the stars hazy motes in the sky, the lights of Cotuit village twinkling in the humidity off in the distance.

A ghost of herself looked back. Jennifer felt surreal again for a moment, disembodied.

At least she'd gotten to change. She was wearing clothes she hadn't put on in years, adding to the surrealness. And then there'd been the phone message from Brendan Healy. It had just about floored her. She'd checked her voicemail from the house landline to hear Brendan report that he was out of jail and in New York City. He'd given her the name of his hotel, and told her he'd be in touch.

She reached for her wine and slipped the stem between her fingers and cupped the smooth, round shape of it. The other patrons in the restaurant murmured contentedly, silverware softly scraping ceramic. She realized there was music playing, soft rock in the background.

The feeling persisted. Like she had stepped into a new existence. She looked at Bostrom, her palm still cupping the undrunk glass of red wine. He stared out the window. Down below, the bay waters turned white with chop as a wind swirled through.

"Okay," she said to him. "Talk."

His eyes met hers. "Alright," he said.

CHAPTER THIRTY-ONE / THURSDAY, 11:49 PM

"I got a book from a cop while I was inside," Brendan said. He and Sloane lay in bed together. Night had spread over the buildings outside, a haze holding the city lights in a greasy glow. "Remember Colinas?"

"Colinas?" She was burrowed in beside him, one arm draped over his bare chest. "Guy you were always talking to on the phone?"

"Yeah."

"What was the book?"

"Called *The Great Divorce*."

"Never heard of it."

"By C.S. Lewis."

"Isn't he a religious guy?"

"He wrote *The Screwtape Letters*, a book that turned out to be a big part of the investigation into Rebecca Heilshorn's murder." He put his hands behind his head and stared up at the ceiling. "Rebecca had two daughters. One, I saved: Aldona. She's back with her biological father. The other is Leah. She would be around six years old now. I think she's with Heilshorn's wife, Greta."

"Greta sounds like a witch in a kid's story."

"Real-life version."

Sloane shifted beneath the covers and propped herself up on an elbow, fans of her hair sliding across her forehead. She brushed it back and said, "So, wait a minute. Why did Colinas send you that book? What does it have to do with some little girl?"

"Well, she's not just some little girl. You were in trouble once, and someone helped you."

Sloane squinted, her expression severe, but her tone light. "You trying to pick a fight with me? After the first time we finally have nookie?"

Brendan laughed; it had just snuck out. Suddenly he felt like he and Sloane had been in a relationship for months. In a way, maybe they had. From a distance. She was frowning at him, angry he was laughing at her, and so he tucked his head to his chin and rolled into her playfully. She responded by hitting him on the shoulder and he cried out in mock pain. He stole a look at her and saw she was smiling. Then she became serious again.

"No, come on, tell me. What does a book have to do with Leah Heilshorn? What are you thinking?"

"I'm worried about Leah. I always have been."

Still skeptical, scowling slightly, "How do you know where she is? Or, how does Colinas?"

"It's not like he came out and told me. He marked a page in the book. It made me think about my past. And I think there might be a connection."

"Oh. I see . . ."

He gave her a close look. "What?"

Her eyes seemed hard. "Let's just say, hypothetically, now that you're out, you go and find this girl. What are you going to do then?" Her eyebrow arched. "Play house? You think finding her is going to somehow absolve you? You can forgive yourself for what happened to them? To Angie and Gloria?"

He felt struck. To hear someone else say their names aloud — he couldn't remember the last time that had happened. Years ago. A decade? Since the cops came to his house that night. Maybe in AA, maybe he'd spoken of them at some point sitting with Argon years ago in the group. He couldn't remember.

He thought about it, like he'd thought about it for the past ten years, and more recently, over the interminable nights at Rikers Island. He remembered the evening that it happened, how he had stayed behind at the restaurant after the argument with Angie, staying to drink while his wife and daughter drove away. He'd told himself they were better off without him anyway.

She turned over, as if she was going to get out of the bed, and he reached out and grabbed her.

"Hey," she called out, her forehead creasing with a scowl as she looked at his hand on her. He let go. He searched her face and she gradually softened. She eased back over to him, watching him, and then she curled back up beside him. "It wasn't your fault. And it's over."

Brendan couldn't look at her anymore. He stared up at the ceiling.

"Just tell me," Sloane said. "Get it out and let it go. Once and for all."

He waited. He thought of all the years struggling with the depression and the grief. Brendan took a deep breath, let it vent in a long sigh. Then he spoke.

He told Sloane how that night he'd finally drunk himself to the point where he wanted to leave the restaurant, grab a taxi, pick up more booze on the way home. He'd been convinced that he would be able to smooth everything over with Angie once he got there. Maybe she'd even have one with him. Gloria would be asleep, and he could coax out the old Angie. The one who would stay up with him all night, outrunning the dark right beside him, sitting there and listening to his theories with genuine interest and attraction. Angie, with her clear mind, who could distill what it took him an hour to express in a single moment, in one sentence.

Who had once told him that living with him was like living with a time bomb.

He'd ridden home in the taxi even thinking, in this fantasy scenario, that he'd be able to woo her into bed. They would talk, he would explain that having them leave the restaurant without him had been for the best — a wise decision, even.

But Angie hadn't been there. His wife and daughter had never come home.

"After that night, after it happened, I left. I was away for a long time. When I came home, I still had the house. I remember I had to break in. The car was in the garage, four years of dust on it. But it started up, I got in it, and I sat there, the windows down. I'd never followed the investigation. I knew that it was a truck driver, supposedly awake for three days, half asleep at the wheel, who lost control and hit them."

She propped her head up on an arm. "He went to prison, right?"

Brendan found it hard to meet her eyes. "He did. But he was out in thirty months."

"Where were you?"

"I traveled. Stayed in the mid-west. I even made it to Laramie. I went there again after the Rebecca Heilshorn case. But the first time I was there, that's where I was when I found out."

"About his release."

Brendan rolled over on his back and tucked his hands behind his head. He stared up at the ceiling. "Yeah. When I heard he was out."

"And you went after him."

Brendan was silent.

"Did you find him?"

Brendan didn't answer. He couldn't. Not right now. It was too much. His reunion with Sloane was something he'd been anticipating for months.

She got out of the bed. This time he didn't stop her. She pulled at the sheet as she stood up, attempting to spool it around her. Brendan had to lift up his butt to free some of it. He looked at her body as she pulled on the blankets. Her ribs, her protruding hip bones, her small breasts and nipples, the color of raspberries.

Her body reminded him of Angie's. Sloane had a scar running from her ribcage down to her pelvis which he hadn't seen before. Angie hadn't had any scars. She'd had skin the color of cream. Dark Italian eyes and hair, but light skin.

He'd actually thought he was going to get Angie into bed that night after the restaurant, when he'd showed up at the door with a bottle of vodka and a six-pack. Already ten drinks into the evening, swaying on his feet, grasping the doorknob to his home and turning it and finding it locked. Dark out now — it had still been light when they had left the restaurant — the hedges and trees jagged shapes, the insects buzzing and chirping in the grass. A locked door. No lights on. She'd locked up on him. She'd fucking locked his own house on him.

Enraged, he'd pounded on the door, rattling the windows, and lights had flipped on in the neighboring houses. Brendan standing there on his little suburban stoop, fishing around in his pocket for the keys, unable to find them, more furious as the minutes wore on, until finally he'd gotten the cops called on him when he'd turned and tossed his head back and screamed her name up at his house.

Angie.

His cry echoed in his head now as Sloane, fully cocooned in the bed sheet, standing in a hotel room in New York City all these years later, looked down at him.

"I'm going to get in the shower," she said, and walked off towards the bathroom, the sheet dragging along behind her like a bridal train.

She left him lying there in the bed. He was tired, everywhere he was tired. In his bones he was tired. But he also felt alive.

He closed his eyes. He forced out the other thoughts and replayed their lovemaking. His hands on her skin, the feel of her ribs, the supple skin, the sound of her voice when she came.

The man standing on the porch in Hawthorne, defeated, drunk, drinking from the vodka bottle when the cops showed up, not to arrest him for public intoxication or disturbing the peace, but to give him the news. To stand there — it had been a male cop and a female cop, exchanging looks with one another — and to tell him that the reason why his wife and child weren't home was because they were on the Saw Mill Parkway inside a twisted mass of metal that the rescuers were now prying open.

That man was still there. A ruined man undeserving of the two of them in the first place, he was still there. He would always be there. But it was as if that man belonged to another life now. That man was in his place. The time now belonged to this Brendan, the one possibly in love with the woman running the shower in the bathroom. The one standing there, her perfect bare feet on the hard white tiles, equally white sheet draped around her slender scarred fame, sticking her hand in the beading water as it warmed. This miracle of a person, who hadn't been meant for the world but yet was somehow still here, just like he was. He didn't want to ruin that.

He settled back into the bed, listening to the shower. He thought he even heard her humming a tune in there, and he drifted off to sleep.

* * *

The knock at the door woke him.

He sat up, half-awake, groping for his gun on the nightstand. There was no gun; he didn't have one any more. He cocked his head, listening — maybe he'd heard something else, like Sloane drop the shampoo bottle in the bathroom shower. But then it came again; someone was knocking on the hotel-room door.

He swung his legs out of the bed, his body lighting up with alarm, his skin breaking into gooseflesh. He found his pants on the floor between the bed and the wall, hooked a foot into the waist, and pulled them on. But he'd stood up too fast and his vision blurred. He lowered his head and hunched forward for a moment. He saw a plain white undershirt, pulled it over his head. Another rapping on the door, *knock knock knock*, soft but insistent. The shower continued to hiss in the bathroom; Sloane couldn't hear anything.

Sloane, he thought, both remembering the way they had messed up the bed he'd just climbed out of, and the self-possessed way she had entered the room an hour before. How she had come back into his life a different woman.

Brendan padded across the plush carpet to the door, and cautiously bent towards the keyhole.

A young man dressed in a hotel uniform was standing there. Despite the fact that it was the middle of the night, the employee looked as chipper as the front-desk clerks, standing at attention like a cadet at a military school, his face twitching as he practiced, no doubt, the apology he would offer for intruding at such an inappropriate hour.

Brendan put his hand on the knob, but didn't turn. "Hello?"

From the other side of the door, slightly muffled, the employee said, "Sir, I'm very, very sorry to be disturbing you at this hour. There is an urgent message for you, and I explained that it is NOT our policy to disturb guests at such an hour for *any reason* . . ."

Brendan thought that the employee's apologetic sermon was going to wake the whole floor. He reached for the bolt handle which he slid back with a click, realizing that despite the lack of sleep, he was still on a high; a high from being free, from being out, from being with Sloane.

It felt like being home.

He opened the door, the hotel employee's lips flapping, head tilted, hands folded together in front of his business-causal ensemble. ". . . There was some confusion with your room, and so there was a slight delay . . . Oh, hello, sir, I'm so sorry to wake you."

"It's okay," Brendan said. "What's the message?"

"Sir, I went and got my manager, as I was saying. The woman said it was a very important matter. You understand, our policy isn't to just disturb a guest."

"I understand."

"The manager said to take down the message and to bring it to you. The woman said she was an agent with the US Department of Justice." The messenger glowed with something like reverence, or maybe pride that he was involved in such an important communication.

The water was still running in the bathroom, steam drifting out from the crack beneath the door. He saw this as he looked down, for some reason dreading what was going to come next. He'd no reason to suspect the worst, but, then, he had every reason to expect the worst. Because the worst was what kept happening.

"What is the message?"

"I wrote it down," the employee repeated, and handed Brendan an envelope. His name was written on it in careful cursive, though misspelled. *Mr. Brandon Heely.*

"Thank you," he said, his head coming up. The employee stood there, and for some reason couldn't meet Brendan's eyes. *Do I tip or something?* But the kid seemed anxious to leave now that the task was done. He apologized again and wished Brendan goodnight and hurried off down the hallway.

Brendan eased the door closed and took a step back into the room, looking at the envelope. He turned it over in his hands a couple of times. Surely it was Agent Aiken returning his own call, giving him information where they could meet and debrief. Urgent matter? That might have been her way to make sure that the hotel delivered the message tonight, and not wait until morning. But, why? Couldn't it have waited a couple of hours?

He realized he was dancing around the obvious. She had made it urgent because it *was* urgent. He slipped a thumb along the edge of the envelope flap and started opening it. At the same time, the shower shut off.

He peeled back the envelope flap, reached in and pulled out the paper inside. He unfolded it and read the careful handwriting, same penmanship as the name on the front.

Sloane works with Nonsystem.
Now you understand the connection the feds made.
—J.A.

CHAPTER THIRTY-TWO / THURSDAY, 10:33 PM

Formed by glaciers, the Cape Cod peninsula resembled a flexing arm. From Cotuit to Chatham was a forty minute drive. Jennifer had time to further absorb Bostrom's disclosure in the restaurant about Sloane Dewan's involvement. She struggled to put the last pieces together now.

Chatham was where Seamus Argon had bequeathed a small house on a half an acre of land to his sister Philomena. The dwelling was tucked into the trees at the end of a road called Black Duck Landing, a quarter mile from the beach. It was where Argon had been coming with Sloane Dewan for years. Not as lovers, or proxy father and daughter, or as commiserative recovering drunks, but as co-conspirators in Nonsystem.

He had saved her as a child. The man who had a sister working for the IMF, feeding him information about corrupt government officials and unscrupulous businessmen and their twisted alliances. Sloane was the product of a heinous enterprise — XList. It was no wonder she had become who she had, hoping to use Nonsystem to have her revenge on the rich and powerful.

They passed the Chatham Lighthouse and several low, red brick buildings; they drove by an endless dark blur of lush greenery. The night air was blanketed with fog as Jennifer and Bostrom at last pulled into the driveway. There were several other cars parked, and the lights were on inside. Jennifer could see people silhouetted in the windows.

She found herself in introspective turmoil. How much further would she venture on alone? She might not be able to trust John Rascher — not that she ever fully had — or Harlan Doherty — but how long before she went straight to the US Attorney General? Or the President?

Bostrom shut off the engine to his SUV and turned to her in the gloom. This feeling of absurdity, this surreal sense that she was caught in some dream, or movie, clung tenaciously. Hadn't she been working on a task force designed to unearth some substantial component of the human-trafficking issue? Hadn't Sloane been an unfortunate victim, an innocent bystander born into a sordid world? Now everything had changed. Sloane being with Brendan — Healy just "finding" her at the Alcoholics Anonymous meeting, Russell Gide just happening to decide to bring him there. Sloane had been using Brendan to get close to Heilshorn all along. To kill him. And then she'd let Brendan take the blame. Maybe she hadn't planned it, but she hadn't stopped it either. And what about the other side? Sloane's involvement reinforced Brendan's belief that Staryles was following him, that the CSS was waiting for something. Perhaps waiting until Sloane emerged once Brendan was out. Because, when Brendan decided to take the blame for Heilshorn's death, Sloane had slipped through Staryles' fingers.

The other thing was, if Sloane had truly intended to kill Heilshorn, it finally and ultimately quashed the idea that Heilshorn was working with Nonsystem. It was what Bostrom had been waiting to tell her, preparing her for with all the other information.

This turn of events, everything lining up, had the feeling of fate again, of something much larger than she'd even suspected with XList, or with Nonsystem. It all smacked of inevitability. As if her life, a series of conscious decisions, was really not so independent. That everything was related, that she had been meant to arrive here, now, this night.

"You ready?"

She nodded at Bostrom. "Ready." She felt anything but.

He got out of the truck. There had been something melancholy about Bostrom since their late dinner. Did he know she'd secretly sent word to Brendan while at the restaurant? She got out of the pickup gingerly. She looked at Bostrom across the hood of the SUV. She tilted her head towards the house. "Who's in there?"

"I know you're out of your comfort zone here, okay? When I first got involved . . . you know, I had procedure drilled into my head. I love my country and it was hard to take all of that and listen to Argon, and to hear what he was saying. It was hard to see rebellion as patriotic."

Bostrom looked at the house, the figures in the windows. He appeared reflective for a moment, and then said, "Argon used to say, 'Don't waste your time looking at me. Look where I'm looking.' Argon's not some hero. He just grew up in unusual circumstances. Him and Philomena. It's not like they even had a choice, when you think about it."

She thought of her father again, a judge, and how she had gone to law school without a second guess. Once more, it seemed as though her life had been prescribed.

Bostrom's expression worried her, as he looked thoughtfully off into the dark.

"Mark?"

"It was tragic when Argon was killed. And now his sister . . . you know, now they're both gone."

"What?"

"You weren't the only one on the phone back there," he said, his face still turned away. "I got a call while you were in the bathroom. Philomena is dead. Found in her room at her assisted-care living facility in Westchester."

"Oh my God." Jennifer was still digesting the idea of Sloane as a central part of Nonsystem. Now Mena, Sloane's friend, former communication specialist for the IMF. Sloane wouldn't be happy — Jennifer was quite sure her affection for the older woman was genuine, even if the rest of the story painted them as co-conspirators. Bostrom apparently cared, too, which explained his recent mood shifts.

He snorted and spat into the dark. "Fuck."

"How did this happen? Does Sloane know?"

Staryles, she thought, without hesitation — *poisoned her.*

Bostrom looked at her. "Listen. Just accept it. Titan and CSS? Might as well be one in the same. Titan is not just entwined with the government, Ms. Aiken. Titan *is* the government."

He paused, and swiped a hand across his face. Had he gotten emotional just now, turned away in the dark? "Now they're cleaning house," he said. "Using their agents who can go anywhere, anytime, get away with anything."

And on the heels of that, an even more chilling thought. An immediate threat. She leaned close to him. "Mark, if Philomena is dead, and there is an investigation, this place is blown." She pointed at the small beach house. "You hear what I'm saying? I can't hold my people back. They'll be here."

"I know." He strode towards the house. "That's why we have to work fast," he said over his shoulder.

* * *

They looked like kids to her. As Bostrom took Jennifer through the house, she shook hands with a dozen people, tried to take in their names, but couldn't help but guess their ages. The average age was probably twenty-three. Tech start-up age. They were dressed casually, hooded sweatshirts, button-down short-sleeve shirts; she saw sandals and Crocs and sneakers — top brands. Hipster hair and beards for the guys, cropped-short Asian bangs for the girls, Paige jeans that looked painted on. It was what she'd expected, but not what she'd believed.

She counted seven females, five males. Every single one of them was attached to some sort of device — phone, tablet, laptop. There was a caffeine-fueled tension in the air, fear perhaps, and excited chatter.

Bostrom showed her around the place. The house was small and the nickel tour took one minute. The front room was the living room with two opposite facing floral-patterned loveseats, a leather recliner and end tables. Behind the living room a small kitchen with a back door led to a porch which then opened on a postage-stamp sized lawn, encroached with thick sumac. A bathroom off the kitchen, a shower stall, toilet, tiny sink. A wicker basket was stuffed with back-issues of National Geographic. On the other side of the kitchen a bedroom had been converted into an office, the bed upended and shoved aside, shelves lined with binders and manuals. A rickety spiral staircase led to a loft and more workspace, overflowing with atlases, encyclopedias; products of a bygone era.

In the living room, a young man approached Bostrom and Jennifer. He was slim, wearing charcoal gray slacks and a matching vest, a knit watch hat on his head. "It's happening," he said.

His eyes darted back and forth between them. He offered Jennifer his hand. "I'm Gentian."

Jennifer accepted the handshake. Firm, but brief. Gentian was one of the names on the FBI's list of aliases of suspected Nonsystem members. Here he was, standing right in front of her.

There was a tablet in his free hand. He moved beside her and presented the device so she could see the screen.

214

On it was a map of Cape Cod, centered on Camp Edwards. Jennifer drew a breath and held it. Her dinner sat uncomfortably in her acid stomach. She realized it didn't matter what anyone said, or what she might now know. Her training and conditioning were kicking in; this was a suspected domestic terrorist showing her maps of a military installation. Schematics of Camp Edwards. She was scared, and poised.

"This is also a training center for Homeland Security," Gentian said, as if picking up on her thoughts. He made some quick movements with his fingers and new images came up. Jennifer was looking at what she could only describe as some sort of supercomputer.

"And this is JANUS."

"JANUS?" Jennifer probed her memory. She'd heard of JANUS; seen something in one of countless memos that crossed her desk back in Washington.

Gentian elaborated, "State-of-the-art hardware, and software suite. You're looking at flexible-room configuration for a complete Battle Simulation Center."

More flicks of his finger, more images. Jennifer saw a soldier in virtual headgear and gloves standing in front of a war-torn urban scene on a giant, curved screen.

"Just the tip of the iceberg," Gentian said. "There's a whole outdoor arena constructed with entry control points and guard towers, two-storied structures built from connex containers, a layout that includes a full 360 degree world of residential, school, marketplace, and place-of-worship scenarios."

Jennifer nodded, her heart rate increasing, yet willing herself to remain detached. "I'm aware, yes. It's called Theater Immersion Training, and it's to simulate scenarios in military environments found during missions in Iraq, Afghanistan, the Balkans, you name it. Where did you get these pictures?"

"Grabbed them out of the ether, ma'am."

Jennifer thought he was dissembling. Gentian pointed at the screen. "Know who the contractor was for this whole Battle Simulation Center here, this whole cutting-edge set up?"

"I don't."

"Titan Construction," he said. He fiddled with the images, bringing back the supercomputer room. "Okay, see this here, this is another total immersion bay. Soldiers can learn how to clear rooms and buildings in built-up areas. They can, either in real-space or in virtual, conduct house-to-house searches in spurious, hostile urban areas. It's to teach them to distinguish between the characteristics of an innocent civilian and an embedded insurgent aiming to do harm."

Then he looked at her with large, dark eyes. An attractive young man, some remote part of her noticed. Effeminate, perhaps. It was so hard to tell these days. Was she standing in a room full of innocent civilians flexing their constitutional rights, or dangerous insurgents about to perpetrate an act of terrorism?

His eyes conveyed an understanding, as if he knew the conflict roiling within her. She returned her attention to the screen. "Why are we looking at this?"

"Because JANUS wasn't just built to train soldiers how to suppress and control any civilian environment in the world. This is a state-of-the-art system where a new internet will run."

"Altnet," she said quietly.

"Yes," he said. "Two days ago one of the largest data centers on the East Coast was assessed by CSS, under the guise of 'Five Star Securities.' It was probed for weak points. Tonight, a rescue drill is underway. There are CSS operatives on board, with the objective to sever the MAC cable." He looked at her again. "The internet cable that feeds the entire Northeast," he reminded her.

She fixed him with a hard stare and pointed at the screen, at Camp Edwards.

"Okay, so, what do you do? You and your friends are going to go into the belly of the beast there and try to stop the birth of Altnet? This is one of the biggest military bases in the northeast. They might not let you in."

Gentian lowered the tablet. Jennifer realized that the busybody activity in the room had stopped. The rest of the group were listening in.

The two of them played a game of eye-contact chicken for a moment, neither willing to back down. Finally, hoping for compromise, Jennifer said, "Let me go back to my people. Let me talk to my superiors. I mean, what am I supposed to think? These are hefty allegations. What's your proof?"

Someone spoke, from behind Jennifer. It gave her a jolt. She turned to see one of the youngest in the group, a kid with a straggly goatee and black, square-framed glasses.

"We have the information that Philomena Argon pulled from The Foundation. Everything she has on Heilshorn and the Titan private equity firm." He was holding up his own tablet, an iPad, slim as a comic book. "It's right here," he said. "It's what they've been looking for. And it shows how the very people you want to come help you are on the same side of the deal."

CHAPTER THIRTY-THREE / FRIDAY 4:13 AM

She studied the data late into the night, in the small sweaty loft workspace. It was a cram session like school finals, only with ten times the information, a thousand times the consequences. There was everything from Titan banks moving money from embargoed governments, phony charities, specious fundraisers, to the drafting of ex-military personnel.

While working for the IMF — "the Fund" — Philomena Argon had tracked Titan's money all around the world. Ultimately the data showed a stream of revenue coming from the most unsavory of places, where it looped through several rat-holes, was washed clean by shell companies, avoided the prying eyes of the IRS in offshore tax shelters, and then found its way home. What Jennifer had supposed about Titan was now concrete. And terrifying.

This was it. This was the Holy Grail for every conspiracy theorist in the country. But it wasn't conjecture. This was data, the financial trails exposed by Philomena, with research her brother Seamus had done on his own. Pages of names, from deadbeat cops to crooked US Attorneys, from corrupt mayors to leveraged governors.

Every man or woman on the take. Every back-door deal. Every piece of midnight legislation. Every scandal. Every covert operation behind assassinations, regime changes and banana republics.

There was no actual conspiracy, because there was no need to conspire. These were actions with two basic common denominators — an unquenchable greed, and a lust for power. Maybe, really, what even boiled down to one common denominator: addiction. People making their choices, ruled by bad habits.

But the further she read on into the night, going back over the Titan data, the more one pattern, at least, emerged from the chaos. Philomena Argon had uncovered the blueprints for a strategy that indicated some measure of premeditation. A document that outlined several strategies to keep money in the hands of powerful central governments. And contingencies against potential libertarian uprisings. When she got to the end of it, Jennifer realized that she had just read the mission statement for Lebensluge.

It was a German word which meant to live a lie.

She went downstairs. Nonsystem's members sat quietly, pretending not to wait, not to look at her, as she stumbled past them into the night air.

The air was muggy but cooler, fragrant with the trailing arbutus flowers. She wondered if Argon had planted the pink flowering plant himself. She tried to clear her mind.

She took a deep breath, drawing in the fragrance of the flowers and the salt air. In the faint dawn light, the white Hyacinth-like blooms of the Canadian Mayflower stood out.

Lebensluge: Titan using black markets to fund an ultra-secret project for the US Military.

The ultra-secret project a new fully-regulated internet; a complete corporatization of the global money supply, now including the digital currencies.

She suddenly looked around her. The house was still lit, late — or early — as the hour was. She turned and ventured further away, meandering in between the cars in the driveway. Bostrom's pickup was there, towards the back.

What was she going to do? She felt the urge to run; she wasn't cut out for this. She couldn't go any further. She'd wanted to shut down a human-trafficking organization, and somehow she'd wound up here, on the precipice of a civil war. But where would she go? Her own people — Rascher, Doherty — had they known about Sloane? Was what why they had let her bring in Healy? They must have known. Doherty and the FBI, at least. They'd been on damage control, smearing Brendan Healy's reputation at the same time they'd been using him to rein in one of Nonsystem's members.

A light went out inside the house, enveloping the yard in greater darkness. She froze.

After a moment, she walked back towards the house. Shimmying back through the cars, the sound of crickets loud. *Reet reet reet reet.* She stopped at the head of the overgrown brick walkway, holding a quick breath. She made out a figure on the stairs.

Gentian came down the front steps and onto the walk.

"Hey," he said.

He stopped and lit a cigarette. "Internet's down and power just went out," he said. "And it's going to get a lot worse." He moved past her, and Jennifer reached out and lightly gripped his shoulder.

"Why do you want me here? You know who I am." She suddenly couldn't stop herself. It felt like a confession. Maybe she shouldn't have come back. Maybe what happened with Staryles had done permanent damage after all, not so much to her organs or her blood but to her soul. "What you're doing is illegal. You've hacked the military and are spying on Edwards. Don't give me this 'pulled it out of the ether' bullshit. You're tapped into their secure system. Meanwhile, your groupies in there are working on new encryption software — I know code when I see it; you're the reason why Project Bullrun failed. And you're in possession of highly classified documents . . . these things are a threat to national security."

Gentian's eyebrows knitted together in a deep scowl. "A threat? No. This is a fight. This is a fight to remain human against massive, anonymous forces of discipline and control. We're under siege. Liberty itself is under siege. That's the reality which—"

"You have some compelling, damning evidence. But, Gentian, you have to understand, I can't act in the same manner. There's a way to do this. We can't just take this and say, 'alright, let's hit back.' I'm an agent of the US Government, for God's sake."

Gentian's scowl faded and he blinked, "You think I'm naïve." It had the slight intonation of a question.

"No. I think you're idealistic. But a resistance to the status quo . . . if it devolves into either totalitarianism or chaos, then you've lost something. You've lost that humanity you say is under siege."

Gentian took a half-step closer. "I think there are differing visions of what chaos is. Seems to me the conservatives and progressives are both lined up against a strong state authoritarianism. There's consensus here. Will it be messy to resist? Sure. Always is. Look, Ms. Aiken, Jennifer, you've gone over the data. You're just now trying to convince yourself. You want to arrest me, go ahead. You can take me." He flicked ash and pointed the cigarette at the house. "You can take everyone in there. But you can't stop this."

"Sure I can. You lead this group."

He was shaking his head, and in the soft light she could detect he looked compassionate.

"That's what you don't understand. You're used to this vertical authority." He sliced his hand through the air like an axe. "But ours is horizontal," and he spread his hands out, as if smoothing a picnic blanket. Then he brought the cigarette to his lips, dragged, and exhaled. "This is what the revolution is — it's a paradigm shift. Lateral means transparency, vertical means classification and secrecy. Lateral means equitable, vertical means concentrated power. We're not concentrated; there are those of us here, in this house, but we're everywhere else, too."

"You have to warn Sloane," she said suddenly.

"I will," he said. "But, she can take care of herself; we all signed on knowing what we were up against." He turned away and looked towards the dark house. "We're ready."

CHAPTER THIRTY-FOUR / FRIDAY 1:13 AM

Brendan hated lying to Sloane. He stuck as close to the truth as possible. He explained to her how he'd turned state's evidence in order to get out of Rikers. And about Tony Laruso, the fight, the deal with Grimm, Louis Tremont helping him to figure out the drug operation.

"My lawyer negotiated my release in return for my sworn statement."

"Oh my God," said Sloane, sitting on the edge of the rumpled bed with a towel wrapped around her. "I had no idea. I thought the Justice Department got you out."

"Why would you think that?"

She turned her head away for a moment. "Because of how you helped that one agent, Jennifer Aiken."

That's not what you were going to say, Brendan thought. *You thought I hatched a deal for the feds to penetrate Nonsystem. Because of you.*

What he said was, "So the DA is extremely ornery and set my first appointment for early this morning."

The lie created an almost physical pain in his joints, in his wounds. There was no appointment with the DA; he'd already given his testimony.

He used to lie to Angie like this. Little white lies, untruths he told himself were for her own protection, for the good of the marriage, their daughter, the future. He wasn't supposed to lie anymore — he didn't want to; it felt like a foreign invader in his body, like a sickness.

Sloane was sharp, though; when she turned back he could read in her expression that she didn't quite take the whole fib hook, line, and sinker. Not that Angie had been gullible. But when you were married to someone, something you took for granted after you said the vows was that any pretense was over, that lying was not permitted. You were a couple, a unit, and honesty was implied, expected, if perhaps taken for granted. When things were new, both parties tended to maintain a healthy skepticism.

She turned her head away for a moment. "Look, it's your personal business. You don't owe me any explanation. I just . . ."

"I know," he said, sitting down beside her. He put a hand on her neck. "There's a lot going on."

She turned her face to him without any hesitation and they kissed. Only when he opened his eyes, he saw hers were open too, and she was watching him.

They drew apart. "I've got to shower now, too," he said.

She scowled. "No. Come back to bed." She lay down across the mess of hotel sheets and blankets. She untucked the towel and let it slide off her body.

"Alright," he said. "Give me just a second."

He went into the bathroom and closed the door, sat down on the closed toilet and took the paper out of his back pocket. He turned on the sink faucet. He ripped the message into strips and flushed them down the toilet, watching them swirl down the drain. *Sloane works with Nonsystem. Now you understand the connection.*

Yeah, he understood. He understood why Staryles had stayed away from Rikers. He knew the reason why they

224

had let him out, why they were here now, in the city, waiting.

CSS wanted Nonsystem as badly as the FBI. In fact, CSS had likely been the one to enlist the feds in the whole affair. Why else let him walk out of jail and not intervene? Why let him go into jail in the first place, when they could have played any superior-authority card they'd wanted to and yank him right out of the whole thing after Roosevelt Hospital? They could've stepped in at any time. Sure, NYPD had played hardball and the captain had puffed out his chest and dug his heels in, saying, "Unless the President himself sends orders to let you go, you're staying right here," but surely CSS could have circumnavigated a police captain if they'd wanted, even the police commissioner himself. It was all about rank in the police and in the military, and CSS had their card to play any time they chose. But they'd left him untouched. Staryles had presented him with a deal that was laughable — come work for us —knowing full well Brendan would never go for it. They wanted him right where he was. Wanted to follow him to some prize — he'd already spotted the two people trailing him around the city. That he'd made two of them probably meant there were more.

The toilet gurgled, the paper gone. Brendan cupped his hands splashed some water on his face. He looked at himself in the mirror. Prison had made him heartier. At first he'd lost weight, but after regular workouts and the carb-heavy meals, he'd put on some pounds, gained some muscle. Despite the scars, he looked healthy. They said that by forty, a man had the face he deserved.

CHAPTER THIRTY-FIVE / FRIDAY 4:29 AM

The conflict within was going to break her. This was her job, this was her country, this couldn't be happening. There was right, and there was wrong. Before he became a judge, her father had served in the military himself. She couldn't live with this. She strode into Argon's house to collect her things. She was going to use the landline to call a cab. She needed to get to the airport and back to Washington. Enough of this shit.

"Listen," Gentian said.

She stopped in her tracks and spun around on him. She was dimly aware that the room was dark, illuminated only by candles. She could feel the eyes on her as she stuck a finger in Gentian's chest.

"Not another word," she said. "I'm done. This is not due process. This is not how things are done. Now give me a phone, or someone drive me to the airport."

"We've needed a backup plan for a long time," Gentian said hurriedly.

"I don't care." She closed her eyes. She could see floaters along the edges of her vision. Like flames.

"In the event of an internet meltdown, there aren't a lot of widely available alternate delivery routes. Okay, there are some, resulting in excruciating delays and a slew of other problems, but the worlds of business and communications have moved away from closed physical networks a long time ago . . ."

She opened her eyes. Where was Bostrom? He needed to get her out of here. Maybe she would skip Washington. Maybe she would go to her family home and lock the doors. It had been a long time in coming. Brendan Healy escaped when he wanted to. Look what Bostrom did — just up and left his Department. Why was she so loyal? Why was she the one always trying to fix the messes these men made?

". . . Business has opted for the open Internet, which breaks up data into small, unattached packets of bits, sends them around the globe by the most efficient route available, and reassembles them when they reach their destination . . ."

"I have no idea what you're saying."

Her thoughts were mashing together. She needed her bag. She had brought a bag, hadn't she? There was no more room in her mind. It was crammed.

"What I'm saying is, Ms. Aiken, no one has cared about a plan B because plan A has been doing everything they wanted it to. Except for the government. Plan A was not doing what they wanted it to. So, regardless of the dangers of a system scaled up beyond its ability to be maintained, with few significant alternate delivery methods, plan B was created: Altnet. For control. But it never needed to be this way. A backup could've been made by everyday people, by the people in this room — it didn't have to be a multi-billion dollar government project. Don't you see? There is no more real democracy. These decisions are made by an elite few."

She fixed Gentian with a look. Her peripheral vision was on fire. Her head buzzed like a broken machine.

"If you mess with JANUS, with Edwards, you are a domestic terrorist, no matter what your philosophy. Do you get that?" She turned and looked at the faces in the room, glowing in the candle light, watching. "Do you all get that?"

Gentian would not be deterred. "Let's look at the options for shutting down the net. First, political mandate. In 2010, a committee in the US Senate approving the PCNAA bill — Protecting Cyberspace as a National Asset Act — to grant the President the power to wield an internet kill switch. That—"

She snapped at him. "The kill switch provision was removed from the version of the bill that went on the floor—"

"But the act remained intact and *passed*. I'm sure you know this." Gentian arched an eyebrow. "The President has the authority to shut down private sector or government networks in the event of a cyber-attack."

She was barely hanging on. She needed to sit down, but she held her ground. "The shutdown idea is known to have major flaws," she said, her voice hoarse. "First of all, you could have all sorts of unforeseen ancillary effects from shutting down such a complex machine."

"Yes."

"And there are countless ways for an enemy to get around some kind of electronic fortification. There's no nation or legal decree which could possibly plug all of the holes."

"Correct."

Why was he just agreeing with her? "And if you create such a kill switch, all you've done is create a huge target. An enemy cyber-attacker would concentrate all efforts on that kill switch exclusively. That's why we backed off it."

"We did?"

"I can't sit here and entertain anymore unsupported claims! You've said political mandate — I don't see that as being factually possible, and I didn't see it in Philomena Argon's files. What else have you got? Can you show me something to support this?"

"Agent Aiken, let me be perfectly clear: This began long ago. The Roosevelt administration enabled the President powers of control over the media — given certain circumstances — back in 1934."

Some of the storm in her head abated. Okay, maybe there was something substantive here, something she could grasp. She'd read about this in school. "The 1934 Communications Act."

"Have you ever read Section 606 of the Communications Act?"

"Not lately."

"It's what gave The Foundation all the credibility it needed."

A young woman sitting on the couch who didn't look a day over twenty pulled a sheaf of paper from her bag. She crossed the room and handed it to Jennifer. The paper was creased and dog-eared and looked stained by coffee. Gentian reached out and pointed out the top page.

Jennifer felt like the worst of the fugue she'd just experienced was passed. She bent forward to read.

During the continuance of a war in which the United States is engaged, the President is authorized, if he finds it necessary for the national defense and security, to direct that such communications as in his judgment may be essential to the national defense and security shall have preference or priority with any carrier subject to this Act. Any carrier complying with any such order or direction for preference or priority herein authorized shall be exempt from any and all provisions in existing law imposing civil or criminal penalties, obligations, or liabilities upon carriers by reason of giving preference or priority in compliance with such order or direction.

Gentian seemed to be waiting when Jennifer looked up. He raised both eyebrows, looking suddenly fifteen. "Sound familiar?"

"I'll bite. Titan is 'the carrier exempt from any criminal penalties.'"

He nodded, then dipped his head toward the papers, encouraging Jennifer to continue.

Upon proclamation by the President that there exists war or a threat of war or a state of public peril or disaster or other national emergency, or in order to preserve the neutrality of the United States, the President may suspend or amend, for such time as he may see fit, the rules and regulations applicable to any or all stations within the jurisdiction of the United States as prescribed by the Commission, and may cause the closing of any station for radio communication and the removal therefrom of its apparatus and equipment, or he may authorize the use or control of any such station and/or its apparatus and equipment by any department of the Government under such regulations as he may prescribe upon just compensation to the owners.

The language reflected older technology — radio communications — but Jennifer knew it could stand in court that *digital* communication could supplant *radio*.

Gentian pulled off his hat and ran a hand through his hair. "'Upon *just compensation* to the owners,'" he repeated with emphasis. He'd apparently memorized the passage.

Jennifer waited for Gentian to finish his point, though she felt she knew right where this was going.

"Not only is the government going to create an event where the internet is shutdown, but it's going to be a watershed payday for major communications firms and all of their shareholders," he said.

"Fine. I'll accept that. You've done all of your homework. But you still haven't convincingly established what the event is going to be. Meaning, what the false flag claim is. So far the power is off and the internet is down. You've made accusations about rescue drills and a data center being sabotaged, but so far, nothing."

"You're looking at it."

"I'm not following."

"The reality is, we've spent years eliminating any and everyone in the Middle East who won't play ball with us so we can get what we want there. Take a close look, Agent Aiken, at the physical conflicts between India and Pakistan, the Israelis and Palestinians or the collapse of Yugoslavia, and you see a mirror of the cyberspace warfare reflecting back from the real-world violence. Up until now, the main cyberwar targets have been military. But attacks on multinational corporations are rising. You take one of these multinationals down, if only for a short time, and you've done more damage to your enemy's economy than a dozen bombings. What's more, you take out their utilities, you wreck their water, their power, their heat, and you bring a nation to its knees. But this is not done internally. This is done by hiring out rogue groups — just like weapons manufacturers — or in this case, hackers-for-hire."

Jennifer was silent. The dancing flames along the perimeter of her vision had retreated, but she could still feel their heat in her head. "They're going to say that you were hired by an enemy of the US to attack us."

"That's why you're here, Agent Aiken. Your superiors have placed you in the center of this. To go after a terrorist group. But you haven't done what they expected, have you?"

Jennifer felt a twinge of embarrassment, as if Gentian had seen right into her recent past. Throwing away her phone, running from her superiors, essentially disobeying orders to see what would come of all of this if she were, for a merciful few moments, unencumbered by procedure.

She took another deep breath, gathering her wits. She looked around the room at the youthful faces, and she felt the stillness surrounding her. In the distance she thought she heard a ship's bell sounding over the dark waters of the ocean.

She pushed the papers at Gentian. "Whatever this is, whatever is coming, it's going to cost lives. I want to minimize that. I want to warn people, I want to get people out of harm's way."

She walked to the front door, and everyone's eyes followed her. Gentian spoke. "When they were with you, when they had you in that building, they told you, didn't they? They said it."

"Excuse me? Said what?"

"What you saw in the data tonight, Ms. Aiken. Lebensluge. It's basically been happening for seventy years, since Alexander Heilshorn was born, you might say, and it's now coming together."

Suddenly the lights flickered, turning briefly on, then dousing again.

"The grid is taking hits right now," Gentian said. "They're going to be shutting down sections because the backup system is only capable of supporting a fraction of the power needs of the northeast. So they'll start isolating, keeping power going to where they choose. What house, what restaurant, or what military base. Like Camp Edwards. Backup power will stay on there."

Jennifer heard vehicles pull up out outside in the driveway, doors open and close.

The young woman who'd given Jennifer the papers now stood by the window, looking out.

"They're here," she said.

Gentian looked at Jennifer, and for the first time she thought she saw fear in his eyes. "You know now," he said. "Just remember. You know."

CHAPTER THIRTY-SIX / FRIDAY, 7:34 AM

The sun burst off the glass of the Midtown buildings. Brendan stood looking down on the city, the hotel room to his back. He picked up his bag and walked back to the door. Sloane sat watching on the edge of the bed, dressed. Her eyes were bright in the light blasting into the room, her expression tight, her angled, beautiful face hard, the way he remembered first seeing her in the Holy Ro' church basement.

He stood, gripping the door handle. He'd told her his appointment would last the better part of the morning, and he would get in touch after. He wasn't keeping the hotel room, he'd said. Too expensive. He needed to figure something out. She wanted to help him, she'd told him, in the hours before daybreak. They'd meet up later and figure it out together.

They both knew it wasn't true.

He closed the door as she turned to look out at the dazzling morning. When the door closed, he could feel it in his chest.

He rode the elevator to a random floor, stepped off, and followed the hallway until he came to the service stairs. He took these down to the kitchen, where griddles snapped and hissed with bacon, and hustling cooks served up eggs, orange wedges, sprigs of parsley, on white plates. Brendan moved through the kitchen to a back door and shoved it open. Outside two dishwashers in stained white aprons smoked cigarettes. They offered surprised smiles as he nodded his way past them, down a short alleyway out on to West 52nd Street.

On 52nd, he hailed a cab and told the driver to floor it for Penn Station, a few blocks away. He needed to keep off the streets. After five minutes of starts and stops, the city flowing all around him, he got out the cab and entered the massive station.

Despite everything, he felt good. At least, physically. He sensed the tautness of his muscles, the readiness in his ligaments. Six months of lifting weights had left him in better shape than he had been in years. Maybe his entire life. He'd beaten Laruso, he'd beaten Rikers. As he walked through the manic station, he felt like he could scale the walls. Grab hold of the steel girders and climb and get above everything and everyone.

He stopped for a coffee and an overpriced egg sandwich. He bought his ticket for the Adirondacker, and then had fifteen minutes to kill while he waited to board.

He wanted to keep moving, to keep feeling good, to stay ahead of his thoughts, so he walked. But now that he had his ticket and was waiting to board, the questions started rolling in, the sense of betrayal closed around his heart.

Sloane.

Sloane had lied to him.

But was it that fact which upset him so much? Or was it this idea that there was more to the relationship between her and Argon? As an investigator, his job was to grope his way towards the light. But now it was personal. He had a relationship, a close relationship, with someone involved in the whole Titan mess, and rather than be right there beside him, like he'd thought she would be, she was somewhere else. They couldn't be together.

"Going, somewhere, Healy?"

He stopped abruptly. A man was standing against a tiled wall, in between two blocks of cubicle shops. Brendan knew him.

Commuters and travelers were crisscrossing in between them. Brendan waited for a break in the traffic and stepped towards the man. He was dressed in black. Handsome, in a pinched-face kind of way, his hair wispy and thin. One of his shoulders stooped.

"Just out walking," Brendan said to him. He took a sip of coffee from his paper cup. In one hand he held the coffee, in the other hand his breakfast sandwich. His skin tingled around the base of his neck and his ears. He felt the scar that ran from his temple to his jaw pulse with his heartbeat. He'd been careful, watching his every move since leaving Rikers, but this felt unavoidable. Even though he'd left Sloane, they'd already gotten him in their crosshairs.

"People-watching?" the man added with a smug grin.

"That's right."

"Me too. Love to watch people."

"I'll bet."

"Been watching you for a while now."

"I know."

Brendan sipped the coffee, never taking his eyes away. He smacked his lips. He was making a show of the whole thing, and it felt good. Dammit, it felt good. "I saw you last night. On the Third Street subway platform. I noticed that hitch in your step. That from chasing me through Roosevelt?"

The smug look went away. "Then you know I'm not going to let you leave the city."

Brendan was silent.

"That wasn't very nice the way you left Ms. Dewan like that. She's upset."

This is where they want to put the clamps on me, Brendan thought. Now I'm supposed to break down, say, *Don't hurt her. I'll do anything you want.*

"She should be upset," he said.

The man raised his eyebrows. "That's not very nice."

"I'm not very nice."

"Oh, I think you're a good guy, Healy. We all do." Then the man's eyes flicked in a couple of different directions and Brendan looked around at the others closing in. One woman, another man. He'd seen the woman the night before. The second man was a new face. They moved through the zigzagging commuters, like wolves coming through the high grass.

Brendan took another showy sip of his coffee, which tasted bitter in his mouth. His skin had gone cold.

The man said, "Do you know who we are, Healy?"

Suddenly he conjured another one of the lines from the C.S. Lewis book Colinas had sent him. The words filled his mind, temporarily blotting out all else, like airplane writing in the sky.

The good man's past begins to change so that his forgiven sins and remembered sorrows take on the quality of Heaven.

Was that were Angie and Gloria were now? Were they in Heaven? Could they see him? Was his own past somehow a part of that Heaven, was everyone's past their Heaven or their Hell? Could they see him from those recesses?

Was Judgment Day simply a bright, incontrovertible, instantaneous burst of all days gone by, a life-flashing-before you moment that stretched on into eternity? Was he a good man?

The gun came out, just the tip of it, held casually by the man standing against the tiled wall as if it were his own cup of coffee.

With his other hand, he held up a badge. Brendan scrutinized it — metal alloy, pewter with brass luster, a crest bearing heraldic lion in its center. The badge went away. "You need to come with us, Mr. Healy. Rejoin your friend."

She's not there. She already left. She got away . . .

The woman reached Brendan and stood close beside him. He remembered her alias was Persephone. She'd tried to take Brendan and Sloane into custody in the parking garage of Roosevelt Hospital. "It's your only choice really; along with Ms. Dewan, you've now been designated as a national security threat by the FBI and the Central Security Service. Every uniform in the country from commissioners to traffic cops are going to have your picture. Come with us, now, Brendan. Help your country. Let's put this whole mess behind us."

"You're kidding me," he said. His words felt heavy — literally heavy, as if it took a great effort to speak. His lungs felt filled with wet sand. His body, throbbing like one giant muscle.

"We wouldn't joke about something like this," the first agent said. Hermes.

"Trust us," added Persephone.

"Trust you. You have a gun on me. Staryles offered me a deal. He wanted me to come work for you. When I didn't, he left me in jail."

"You made your own decisions," said Persephone. She was so close he could feel her breath on his ear. There was an announcement on the loudspeakers that the Adirondacker was now boarding.

"What you're feeling right now?" whispered Persephone. "That's your better judgment, trying to assert itself. Your loyalty to your country. Your rational mind, rejecting all of the paranoid ideas. They're becoming a habit, those ideas. And you know about habits, don't you, detective?"

He could smell her. Some kind of lilac shampoo, but not enough to mask another odor, like something exhumed from a chest or from inside the trunk of a car. Something stale, trapped.

He didn't look at her. He kept his eyes forward, kept the gun Hermes was holding low and mostly hidden in his vision. "I have somewhere I need to be."

Persephone slipped her hand around his wrist. "You need to be with us," she said.

CHAPTER THIRTY-SEVEN / FRIDAY, 7:44 AM

FBI agents in full tactical gear rammed into the place first. Other agents in dress suits streamed in behind them. The group of young people were yanked to their feet, read their rights. When Rascher came in through the front door he grabbed Jennifer, pulling her outside amid the commotion.

If the driveway had been choked with vehicles before, it was like parking at a rock concert now, only the majority of vehicles were black SUVs and town cars. As Rascher led her toward the front lawn of Argon's house and her eyes swept the scene, Jennifer counted at least three vehicles that belonged to the Justice Department, and five from the FBI.

Agents crawled all over the small property. Now that the bust had gone down, and the members were in custody — unarmed, unresisting — some of the agents stood around chatting. The rest of them were bringing out the Nonsystem group in handcuffs, parading them down the front steps of Argon's house. Most of the group slouched in submission, eyes downcast, but Gentian looked at her as he was hustled past, his eyes calm. The agent behind him shoved him to move faster.

Bostrom was brought out last. He looked at Jennifer, without emotion.

"God, what a mess," Rascher said beside her. "You start in one place, who knows where you're going to wind up."

"You asshole," she said.

She could feel him shrug against her, acting smug. "Yeah, well, you know, you went as far as you could go."

He stepped away, putting his hands on his hips. She watched Bostrom being placed in the back of one of the SUVs. Rascher's words stirred the bile in her stomach. As if he knew. As if he'd struggled to crawl out of the dark place she'd found herself in seven months ago. As if he'd been held captive in a Manhattan tower and poisoned nearly to death. "This was my call, John. This was my operation."

She saw Bostrom pass her a look from across the hoods of the vehicles smothering the small dirt driveway, a look that penetrated the core of her, before the FBI agent pushed his head down and Bostrom disappeared behind black-tinted windows.

He had driven her across half of New York State and into Massachusetts, evading his own department. Why bring her here? It had only resulted in Nonsystem's capture.

"You did well, Jen," said Rascher beside her. She could smell extra Christian Dior cologne on him this morning. And something else. A trace of booze maybe, a bit of Amaretto in the coffee. Or maybe that was her imagination. Maybe she just wanted to find some fault in him, something she could use against him, because he'd always been so friggin' meticulous. He covered his ass.

"It was scary there for a little while," he said. "We thought we'd lost you all over again. Bostrom going rogue like that; no one expected a kidnapping. I was worried, Jen." He gave her a compassionate look that was so contrived it seemed inhuman. "We all were."

She opened her mouth slightly, then pursed her lips. What was she going to do? Argue with him? Storm away? Have him put the cuffs on her, too? There would be weeks now of paperwork and meetings as everyone crawled out of the woodwork and warmed a chair. Rascher was already spinning his yarn; Jennifer had been kidnapped by Nonsystem. By their own personal maniac cop. And then Rascher had tracked her down, found her through an unfortunate — but lucky — coincidence. Philomena Argon's death. Which they would no doubt pin on Nonsystem, too. They'd find a way to make it stick. They'd implicate Staryles again, their stalking horse. Now the Senate Intelligence Committee would gather tomorrow, posture and congratulate themselves instead of demanding any kind of real investigation.

It had been a sting without any sting. Nonsystem had embraced her willingly, had brought her in and shared their beliefs with her, what they thought was happening. Something they even had a pile of documentation to corroborate, too. Why? Why had they let her in? And how were the Justice Department and the feds going to reconcile all of the IMF data?

She turned and looked at the house. She watched as a second wave of FBI walked out of the house, carrying armloads of wireless devices and data drives, resembling some twisted version of shoppers on Black Friday, but in white gloves.

You know now, Gentian had said.

They weren't. They were going to abscond with it. Every documented example of malfeasance, corruption, wrongful conviction, abuse of power, money laundering, bribery and coercion. Political scandals from Lawrence Taber through to Philip Largo, from mayors up to the President. Classified documents and memos which together formed a terrible picture of a bloated empire. Seized by the FBI.

"Power has been going on and off all night," she said softly. "And the internet is down."

"Parlor tricks." Rascher sniffed and looked away. "It's what they're playing at. These kids are tapped into major security systems. They're going down."

"I feel sick."

"That's normal," Rascher quipped instantly, as if he'd been waiting for her to say something like this. "It's totally natural to form some kind of sympathies in a situation like this. Stockholm syndrome. You can't help but get taken in a little; there's just a lot of conviction there." Rascher spoke like he was the preeminent expert on the subject.

They took me in willingly, she wanted to scream at him. But, the screaming part was over. She watched the vehicles jockeying to turn around and get out of the cramped space. It would've almost been comical in another context. Something you'd see in a romantic comedy that involved a wedding, and there was a scene when everyone left the wedding and got into matching SUVs and couldn't get their fat asses turned around to leave.

Stopping and starting in jerky three-point turns. The young agents at the wheels bristling with adrenaline at their first big sting. Taillights winking on and off. Down though the canal of trees, at the end of the dirt driveway, the neighbors would be surely gathering, watching as the dark vehicles with their blacked-out windows drove by, wondering who was inside.

Rascher was bent over his phone, frowning at what was on the screen. "Jesus," he muttered. Then he poked a few buttons and put the phone to his ear, making a call.

"What?"

"Healy. Just jumped three agents in Penn Station. He's on a train headed somewhere. Not sure where." Rascher raised his eyebrows at her. "Any ideas?"

"Excuse me? What kind of a question is—"

He stuck a finger in her face and turned away. "Yeah," he barked into the phone. "Right. That's right.

Stay on him, see where he goes. I'm sure CSS is five steps ahead of us anyway."

A pause, Rascher listening. "What? No, absolutely not. It's the same angle as before. We let it play out, see where he goes, where he leads us."

He looked back at Jennifer as he spoke. "That's right. We let these people fuck each other up, and then we just pick up the pieces."

"What do you mean 'CSS,' John?"

Be careful. Be careful now.

He regarded her in a way that made her feel like a tourist who didn't know the language, and who was very quickly wearing out her welcome. "Alright," he said, and hung up.

He squared his shoulders and looked down at her. "What do I mean? We've all got our orders, Jen."

"Orders . . ."

"You haven't been privy to certain things, Jen. To protect you."

She could say nothing. She simmered silently inside while she struggled to meet his eyes.

"We're going to debrief with Brigadier General Alan Wick in a half an hour," he said. "And you're going to play ball. Got it?"

"Where?"

"Here," he said, watching the last of the SUVs trundle out of the driveway. "On the Island. Camp Edwards."

CHAPTER THIRTY-EIGHT / FRIDAY, 7:52 AM

Brendan saw Hermes' gun come up, he felt Persephone's grip cinch around his wrist, he could even sense the heat of the third agent, coming up behind him. It was like something from a dream, the underwater kind, everything slowed down. Only, he felt he had complete control over his body. It was as if they were the ones lagging. He could see it all: the third agent would try to get him in a hold around the neck. Persephone would hold fast to his arm so he couldn't punch or claw at the headlock. And Hermes would step forward and, keeping his gun low, dig it into Brendan's stomach. If he resisted, the third agent would choke him until he passed out. And if the brief struggle caused a scene (even in New York, where people were conditioned to mind their business, someone might get involved) it wouldn't matter to the agents.

The agents could do anything they wanted to do.

As the heat closed in on him, he dropped low to the ground. Persephone had a vice-like hold on his arm, so he used this to his advantage, and took her wrist in his own hand, and bent her over as he dropped. Agent three ended up connecting with her above Brendan's head, a tangle that caused Persephone to cry out and release her grip.

Having evaded the headlock and free from Persephone, Brendan sprang forward, driving into Hermes like a linebacker, knocking him back against the tile wall. Brendan shoved with everything he had, and Hermes' skull hit the wall with a crunch.

Brendan leapt away as the third agent and Persephone were recovering. A few unsteady footfalls and he broke into a run, then a sprint, cutting through the throng of people — who all scattered, rearranging into a lane for him. He ran fast enough that the people around him just blurred together.

Shots rang out. His head reverberated with the noise; he hadn't been sure if they were going to fire or not; part of him had thought that they still would have limits.

They can do anything they want.

The idea became a mantra, a code for him to live by as he ran. *They can do anything.*

Another shot, and he felt a tug of air as the bullet tore past his face. People were screaming now, getting as far away from him as possible. They were high-pitched screams, the truly horrified kind, devoid of indignation or surprise, but sirens of terror.

He started down some stairs, taking two at a time. Another announcement boomed — last call for the Adirondacker.

Just like an addict, some untethered part of him observed, as if this was all just some sort of game, and happening to someone else. *Just like an addict, always last-minute, always late.*

Tick-tock.

At the bottom of the stairs, two cops, navy blue uniforms, worried but with determined looks on their sweaty faces. Brendan felt like his mind was running on high octane-fuel. He could see everything, hear everything, feel everything.

"Don't!" He called out to them halfway down the stairs.

The Irish cop on the left seemed to get it. He stopped. *Fuck this* his expression said, and then his eyelids flew back. The younger cop took out his gun and aimed it, but then his mouth fell open.

Two more shots, bap bap, and this time Brendan felt a searing burn as the bullet grazed his arm. The people on the stairs were crushing themselves against the sides of the stairwell, trying to get as far away as possible, but people still reaching the bottom aiming to come up, just a few, one kid plugged into his iPad, he wasn't aware of the commotion, and he dropped when the stray bullet found a mark.

Both cops hit the deck. Brendan reached the bottom and leapt over the younger cop who was reaching for the kid.

I'm sorry I'm so sorry I'm sorry I'm

He hooked right to get out from the line of fire and tossed a look behind him as two more bullets bit into the floor at the bottom of the stairs, chips of concrete flying. Everyone was on the ground, but at least no one else seemed to have been shot. The last thing Brendan saw before he made the next turn towards the loading deck for the train was the kid with iPad rolling himself over.

Alive. Thank God.

And then he was rushing down the concourse towards the train, into the stuffy, ammonia stink of it, the hissing as the brakes were released, towards the one conductor standing in the doorway, who was waving Brendan along, oblivious to the wreckage in his wake.

Oh, I'm coming.

I'm coming.

* * *

On the train, wet with sweat, he worked to control his breathing, to calm down — drawing stares. Waiting. Waiting for the station to contact the driver and for the conductor to come into the car with a worried look on his face as he approached cautiously thinking *I don't get paid enough for this shit* and tell Brendan he had to get off at the next stop. Or maybe no conductor at all, just no one coming anywhere near him, instructed to stay put, to steer clear of him, to not raise any alarm, stop the train at the next station and that's where they'd get him.

But it was an express train. The next stop was Albany, two hours away. If in two hours, no conductor came, he would know.

Of course, there was a third option, too, that his plan would actually work. He just needed to remain calm, and have faith that he would be able to pull it off. He needed to get moving.

Now that he had his breathing regulated and the sweat from his brow was evaporating under the cool air-conditioning vents of the train, he felt a little more stable. He stood up in his seat near the front. The train car wasn't full. A man with gray hair in a suit engrossed in a newspaper. Two older women sitting side by side, chatting quietly; one gave him a glance and then looked away. A kid with a large set of colorful headphones dolefully looking out the window at the city rolling by. Brendan glanced outside too; they were near 125th street.

He started towards the back of the car with his bag in his hand. He reached the back where the lavatory was and found it unoccupied. He slipped inside. In the cramped space, he set the bag on the toilet and unzipped it. He pulled out the electric shaver. He felt a quick trill of panic as he considered that the shaver wasn't charged. But once he got it out of the frustratingly tight plastic packaging, tearing it open with his teeth, he thumbed the button and it buzzed to life. He took it to his head and began making sweeping motions along his skull, hair falling away in clumps. He worked fast but meticulously, careful to make it look like a professional job.

He heard a clicking sound. He froze, feeling like an animal in the woods might, detecting the snap of a twig beneath a hunter's foot, his heart pounding.

Easy. Easy.

It was the conductor, punching the passenger's tickets as he made his way down the train car.

Brendan resumed the task at hand. His dirtied suit now covered in hair, and spotted with blood along one sleeve, he shuffled out of the clothes in the tight space. He examined the bullet wound, which had torn a shallow rut through his flesh. Incredibly lucky. There was just a minor welting of blood there. He washed it off, patted it dry, and then added a fresh paper towel as a compress. He pulled on the blue jeans and hooded sweatshirt he had bought in Midtown. They were a tighter fit than he'd expected. He realized he'd bought himself clothes the size he'd been wearing since he was eighteen. The sweatshirt fabric pulled taut against his bulkier body, the jeans skinnier than he was used to — he didn't even need the belt, but he looped it through anyway. He then stuffed the hair-strewn clothes into the bag and wiped up the rest with his hands. He wadded it all up and jammed it in the trash.

He unzipped the front pocket of the duffel bag and put on the tinted glasses he'd bought, and his new wallet. He reviewed the contents for a third time since he'd procured them. He riffled through the new driver's license and the fake credit cards. He'd even instructed Tony Laruso to have Bosco add in a couple of other personal effects, a gym membership card, a Subway card with a few holes punched in, a couple of phony receipts for purchases made over the past few days, dated before he'd actually gotten out of Rikers, and a picture of some people he'd never seen before — a woman and a little girl smiling, by a swing set. Too cheesy, he thought — if he'd been able to handpick the items himself, he would have opted for something a little less Hallmark. Plus, the woman was too old. So he built it into the story he had for his new identity.

This was his mother, and the child was his niece, and his sister — not pictured — was sick — cancer.

The conductor was very close — he could hear murmured talk that sounded serious. He stood frozen for a minute, looking down at the last item in the bag. It seemed crazy now, a lunatic idea, to wear bicycling gloves with a prosthetic finger attached. The get-up was meant to be seen at a distance, not this up-close and personal. He stared at them, debating whether or not to pull them on, or if he should step out of the bathroom now. People in the car had seen him as he made his way to the bathroom. If he came out looking completely different, it might draw attention, make them wonder, make him memorable. If he waited until the conductor passed, he could follow him into the next car and take a seat there.

He heard a burst of static, and then a voice too distorted to understand. It was the conductor's radio. The conductor spoke back into it. Just one word. "Alright." He was just on the other side of the door.

Brendan held his breath. *Easy.*

He waited and listened for the heavy doors to rattle open and close as the conductor went between train cars.

Knock knock. No such luck. Brendan zipped up the bag, forgoing the gloves.

"Hello?"

Brendan had locked the door. The little sign by the knob on the outside should have read *occupied.* Did conductors really do this? Interrupt someone in the bathroom in order to make sure they had a ticket? Probably. Probably, when Penn Station was the scene of frantic chases and gunfire.

"Yeah," Brendan said. "Someone's in here." He was careful to paint his voice with that mild annoyance people expressed when their privacy was invaded.

"Sir, I need you to come out of there, please."

There was no mistaking the seriousness of the conductor's tone. This wasn't just punching tickets or checking for stowaways. This was because he'd been told that there was someone aboard the train who was wanted by the police and would be removed at the next stop. It would no longer be an express — Brendan could bet that once they got to 125th street, the train would squeal to a halt.

"Okay," Brendan said, and immediately felt a nerve firing in his neck, a twitch signaling alarm. He'd left the ticket in the pocket of the suit pants now covered in hair and balled up inside the duffel bag. Hadn't he? He reached into the front pocket of the hooded sweatshirt. The ticket was there. He pulled it out and unlocked the door.

The conductor, an older man, rotund, with a bright orange Irish beard and freckles high on his cheeks, regarded Brendan with wary eyes. "Sir," he began, "I need to see your ticket."

Brendan slouched. "I'm sorry, man. Sorry about that."

The conductor looked him up and down as Brendan continued. "My sister . . . she's not doing so hot, you know? It's been a tough week." He handed the ticket over to the conductor who took it, still looking Brendan over, deciding something. "I'm going to see her and my mom," Brendan told him. "Get to see my niece, Chloe, too."

The conductor changed from authoritative to bored. His eyelids drooped as he clipped the ticket and handed it back. "That's great."

"Thanks," said Brendan. "Sorry," he repeated.

The round man in his blue suit tossed a glance through the window into the next car, as if he'd already moved on in his mind. He started to leave the car. He then stopped and looked at Brendan one last time.

"Ah, hey; good luck," he said.

CHAPTER THIRTY-NINE / FRIDAY, 8:40 AM

Jennifer looked at the trays of pineapple and oranges, piles of croissants and individually wrapped packets of butter. There were several coffee urns on the large table at Camp Edwards, cups, creamers, jugs of milk, and pitchers of juice. There was even a box of powdered donuts. No one, so far, had taken a single bite of anything.

When Brigadier General Allen Wick sat down at the long table, he leaned forward and poured himself a glass of cranberry juice. Wick had flown up from Fort George G. Meade in Maryland. He was not what Jennifer expected. Rather than the severe man with the hardened, clipped speech of the army and a painful-looking brush cut, Wick was soft spoken, smoother than the stereotypical commander, with limp blond hair. He had a focused attention that could cut glass, however, and when he looked her up and down with a flick of his eyes, she suddenly felt like the only person in the room.

She wasn't. Along with her in the sparsely furnished conference room were John Rascher, Omar T. Porter — from Company B, First Battalion, William Spalding, 45th Division — and the US Attorney General. They faded into the background as Wick sipped his juice and settled back into his chair. Despite his unconventional appearance, his presence filled the room. He set down his empty glass.

"Pleasure to meet you, Special Prosecutor Aiken."

"And you, General Wick." Formality always made her feel self-conscious. Their host, commander of Camp Edwards, Sainathan Agrawal, stood up at the end of the conference table. A young soldier appeared and engaged Agrawal in a brief conversation too low for Jennifer to overhear.

"I'm glad to have this chance to thank you in person," Wick said, "for all you've done."

Jennifer smiled graciously. "Fort G. Meade," she said. "US Army installation at the top of intelligence, internet and cyber operations."

"Affirmative, ma'am," Wick answered, shifting to get more comfortable in his chair. She wondered to what extent he had calculated sitting in that spot. She decided he had chosen it precisely. He wanted to face her directly; that high-powered focus was not going to leave her. He had arranged this meeting; he'd been the one to ask her here. She could feel Rascher, two seats to her right, fulminating with resentment, but his hands were clearly tied. Wick wanted to find out where she was at, mentally, before the Senate Intelligence Committee gathered the following Monday. This was more damage control.

"The installation includes a defense information school, and the United States Army Field band." He said the last part with a touch of pride.

She smiled. "You must get your share of trumpets warbling."

He laughed. It was an easy laugh, but practiced. As if Wick had a wife somewhere coaching him from behind the scenes. *Show them your teeth. No civilian is comfortable around a churlish commander.*

She crossed her legs. "It's also the headquarters for the United States Cyber Command."

"Correct," he said. "You know your US Army."

Jennifer nodded. So far, she thought she was doing ok. But there was tension in the air, she could feel the hairs on her arms standing up. At least her aches and pains seemed to have subsided.

Wick turned and looked at the others. She sensed that he was already done with her. She was inconsequential. Whatever she had seen, or thought she had seen, she would be loyal to the Justice Department. She would toe the line and do her job. Before long, Rascher would politely thank her for the tenth time, wearing that fake smile, and ask her to leave the room. Then they would get down to business without her.

The soldier moved away from Agrawal, who turned to the group seated around the table, as if he was about to make an announcement.

"General Wick," she said quickly. "As lovely as it has been to meet you, I wonder why the Central Security Service has sent *you* regarding this matter."

Rascher, listening in, opened his mouth to intervene. But Wick, light on his feet and without a wisp of defensiveness turned his attention back to her and said, "I am the Deputy Chief to the CSS and the NSA. I assist the Chief directly, who also serves as the Commander of the US Cyber Command and the Director of the National Security Agency."

"I'm familiar with your status. What I mean is—"

He ran over her like a speed bump. "I received my commission in 1995 through Officer Training School. I served on the Air Staff as the command briefer for the Chief Staff of the Air Force. I am a skilled and experienced advisor." He raised a silver eyebrow, thin as a blade's edge. "As surprising as I may be to you, you're also a surprise to me. A special prosecutor with the Human Trafficking Task Force Unit out here at Camp Edwards with quite a story."

Agrawal watched the exchange. Rascher leaned forward and turned to Wick. "We decided that Agent Aiken, already in the field investigating—"

Wick held up a hand, and gave Rascher a quick turn of his head and a flashy smile that said, *please, thank you, I don't need to hear from you yet* before turning the high beams of his eyes back on Jennifer.

She glanced at Rascher, who seemed to shrink back into his seat, his mouth closing with a click if his jaw, and then to Wick. "You're right," she said. "This is not my usual territory."

"Indeed. This case with XList was your first time in the field?"

"Yes."

Wick nodded, maintaining eye contact. "So you can understand my own incredulity when I'm told there's a matter of national security at stake, and counter-allegations by a group of cyber-terrorists about a false-flag scenario, by an agent of the Justice Department who has previous spent all of her time in academia — co-authoring the training manual for the HTPU, of course — but nevertheless at a desk before this XList affair."

"You're right," Jennifer said. "I am out of my depth, sir."

He leaned his head to the side and scowled as if it pained him deeply to be so misinterpreted. "That's not what I meant at all. What I meant was that we're both a surprise to each other. I'm an advisor, really, and you're an academic. Isn't that fair to say? I initiate policy, you criticize it."

The attorney general cleared his throat from the head of the table. She could feel the tractive force of him, wanting her to look at him, to defer to him. Jennifer ignored it. Agrawal had sat down at the head of the table, seemingly resigned to the fact that the meeting had begun without his inauguration.

Wick's eyes never wavered. "So, when your superiors tell me you have some sort of sympathies for the terrorists we've just captured, I can take it with that measure. You're uninitiated, Agent Aiken."

"Fair enough. Then can you explain to me, General Wick, what the Central Security Service actually *does*?"

"Agent Aiken . . ." said the US Attorney General.

Wick smiled. "Of course. The CSS promotes full partnership between the NSA and the cryptologic elements of the Armed Forces. We team up with senior military and civilian leaders to address and act on critical military-related issues in support of . . ."

She broke him off. "You said 'civilian?'"

"Yes."

"Can you give me a for-instance?"

He continued to keep eye contact with her, but now the charm was draining away. "The Central Security Service was established by presidential directive in '72 to promote full partnership between NSA and the Service Cryptologic Components of the US Armed Forces. By combining the NSA and CSS, we created a more unified cryptologic effort. Which is why the Director of the NSA is dual-hatted as the Chief of the CSS."

"That's not answering my question."

"Jennifer . . ."

"I am the principal advisor on military cryptologic issues and oversee the function of the military cryptology system. I manage and cultivate the partnerships, and I ensure military capabilities to fulfill the National Cryptologic Strategy."

"Which is?"

Wick moved his folded hands to his lap. "Can I tell you a story?"

Everyone else in the room was fuming. But as long as Wick seemed flexible and cooperative, what could they do? Jennifer felt a satisfaction in the way her superiors had been so easily dispatched. CSS had them by their balls. A story? Let's have it.

"Of course," she said.

"In 1996, a year after I was commissioned, the Director-Chief requested an insignia be created to represent both the National Security Agency and Central Security Service. As a result, a CSS seal was designed and adopted that year."

He turned his shoulder to her and tapped the round patch sewn into the clothing. Five different symbols balanced around a five point star.

The Cyber Command symbol was a heraldic lion. The same insignia as Titan Construction, LLC. Something few people would ever notice.

"This was ultimately the design chosen to represent the CSS," Wick said, feathering his fingertips over the patch to indicate its entirety. "The CSS provides the funding, direction, and guidance to all of America's Signal Intelligence activities, and fosters the fluidity of information between the branches." He rotated his shoulder back so his chest faced her once more. He sat primly, his gaze direct, looking more wooden by the second.

"Funding," she said.

"Yes," he said.

"You tap civilians for funding."

"I wouldn't put it that way. There are many aspects of government where the bulk of underwriting is from private individuals. That's obvious, I'm sure. In fact, the RAND corporation—"

"General, have you ever heard of Jeremy Staryles?"

"Agent Aiken, this is not a deposition of the Brigadier General." The attorney general grunted from the head of the table. "This will all be addressed in the proper forum at the Senate Select Intelligence Committee hearing in two days."

Wick barely gave him a sideways look. "It's quite alright. She's just doing her job. No, there is no Staryles, nor Ewon Parnell, nor Ursula Galloway. There may be terrorists who assume those identities, but as far as the Defense Depar—"

"Because I've been looking into this since I encountered Alexander Heilshorn during the investigation leading to XList."

A flicker — something registering in those cold eyes when she said the name Heilshorn.

She hurried on. "Is he one of the civilian leaders you speak of? Maybe involved in the funding? Maybe someone you met when you both served — as advisors, the way you describe yourself today — on a committee called The Foundation?" She turned her head the other way. "Is it possible someone like Heilshorn could be granted . . . oh say, certain powers, given a team of men and women to help him carry out his objectives — in the interest of national security, or, maybe, funding national security?"

She waited. She was aware she'd laid it on thick. She was aware that this might be her last hour as an agent for the federal government. And she was aware she had just insinuated that the CSS was paying for itself with prostitutes and sex slaves, among other things. She wondered, almost giddy now, if she should add anything else. Such as dead escorts, entrapped politicians, or illegitimate children as collateral.

Wick gave her a thoughtful look, some life returning to his eyes. *Amp up the charm. Blast another smile at them.*

"Alexander Heilshorn?"

"Correct. And his private equity firm, Titan."

"Titan."

"With subsidiaries in construction, medical technology, and defense contracting. Building schools and hospitals overseas. And doing a little business right here on American soil. Constructing a new college building that includes a data center, made to house colocation units; a massive fiber-optic junction for a new, government-controlled internet called Altnet."

"Do you consider yourself a patriot, Ms. Aiken?"

"Absolutely. I love my country and haven't a single doubt that we are a nation filled with good people."

"I see."

"Well-meaning people, guardians who want to protect the innocent, serve democracy, enable the market to work for everyone. I believe in justice, that's why I am here, and I believe to serve justice, and equality, you must be vigilant. Because corruption and evil can find its way in anywhere. And I mean anywhere. Even in our own military. And we are precisely at the point in our nation's history that we have to be more vigilant than ever."

"You're well-spoken, Agent Aiken."

"Thank you."

He leaned back slightly. "If I may be frank, you're conflating vigilance with lending credence to these ideas of a false-flag event perpetrated by our great nation. Keeping an open mind does not mean a wind-tunnel. I find this sad. Sad that you have allowed yourself to be taken in — to sympathize with a group of terrorists — misled children, really — who themselves are the threat we are facing. It's this kind of infectious, poisonous thinking, the same kind of outlandish ideas you're espousing now, that are the most corrosive and deleterious to an American way of life. We are a nation of principles. Of laws. And of leadership."

She was undeterred. "You and Alexander Heilshorn sat on The Foundation together." *I've seen records to prove it*, she thought, and then glanced at Rascher. *And he took them.* Just like the FBI had absconded with Heilshorn's financials, so now they were going to bury records that, among other things, linked the CSS to Heilshorn and Titan.

"Correct," said Wick. "Likely where Heilshorn must've gotten ideas that led to his involvement with Nonsystem."

"Bullshit."

"That's it, Jennifer," said the attorney general, rising. He turned to Wick. "General Wick, I'm so sorry. Agent

258

Aiken has been under a great deal of stress. I'm afraid we've pushed her too hard."

"It's my fault," Rascher chimed in, getting up. "I knew she wasn't ready to come back after her traumatic incident. But because of my own hubris, I pushed for it. I thought she was the best fit, since she had already established a rapport with—"

"Shut up," the attorney general snapped at Rascher. Rascher's face turned bright red and he tried to find somewhere to look.

Wick stood up as well and waved his hands in the air. "Please, there's no need. I understand completely."

Jennifer felt strangely calm. "You're right," she said, from her seat. "The fact that three men abducted me in broad daylight and dragged me off to a building in New York City to interrogate me, it rattled me a little."

"Agent Aiken," said Rascher, heedless of the attorney general's admonitions for him to shut up. "You're dismissed. Please see me outside."

"Of course," she said to Wick, "you would probably tell me that those soldiers were working for this group of — what did you call them — misguided children?"

"Outside, now."

"I wonder then where they came up with the term Lebensluge?"

Wick looked down at her, and she saw a tendon twitching in his jaw. His nostrils flared as he took a breath, the only betrayal of the aggression uncoiling inside of him. "They're very skilled cyber criminals," he said in a measured tone. "You did a commendable job bringing them in. Consider yourself as having been of vital service for your country."

"I have. I do. And since I'm so concerned, I just have to know — what *would* you do, General, in the event that these kids became such a threat to cyber security that lives were at stake?"

The attorney general put a hand on her shoulder. "Get out of the chair."

"How would you stop them?"

Wick's jaw kept tensing, but at last he was at a loss for words. In another second, she would be yanked out of her seat by her armpits. She was through. No more agent for the Justice Department; the only job she'd ever get in government again was maybe State Comptroller in North Dakota. She was finished. She stood up at last, on her own, before the attorney general could physically drag her away. She left the room, watching Wick as she went. Before she left she said to him, "It was very nice meeting you."

* * *

"I can't believe you, Jen. I don't even know who you are anymore."

"You never knew who I was. What are you going to do about Healy?"

"Healy? He's got a sign on his back bigger than Osama Bin Laden had. Let the local authorities pick him up, wherever he's going." Rascher pinched the bridge of his nose and shook his head. "God, Jen. You've lost it. You have no idea what you're . . . You're lucky all the Department is going to do is ask for your resignation. Charges could be brought against you for insubordination. Or worse."

"Worse?"

"Wick is a very gracious man . . ."

"You're sick," she said. "All of you. The Joint Services Cyber Command has a private paramilitary force. Probably Wick and Heilshorn put it together. How do you think it would be done? Is there an internet kill switch?"

"Listen to yourself!" Rascher was boiling now. He looked like he wanted to hit her. "You know the same as I do there is no unilateral control of the fucking internet, Jennifer. Like Wick said, you did well. Okay? You realize what we did? We may have prevented a major catastrophe here."

His composure was not merely slipping, it was gone. He'd cursed — John never used foul language, he felt far too superior — and he called her Jennifer. Just like her mother would, for God's sake. Her mother, whom she loved. John Rascher, whom she loathed.

"You keep telling me that. 'Listen to myself.' I am. I've spent years listening to other people. Years. I started by listening to all your bullshit. And I've listened to the bullshit of countless men after you. And now I was just stared in the eye by one of the highest ranking officers in the country and was lied to."

"You *attacked* him like you were in the courtroom and he was a witness on the stand you were looking to skewer. He's the deputy chief of the Central Security Service, for fuck's sake and—"

"And he denied knowing who Heilshorn really is because he's the one calling the shots with Heilshorn dead! He had to step in. Don't you see? This whole thing started to unravel when a woman named Olivia Jane and Reginald Forrester killed Heilshorn's daughter. Brown and Forrester wanted more than Heilshorn was giving them, and Jane was a jealous psychopath. They all screwed up and it started a chain reaction. Brendan Healy investigated. He found out about Heilshorn, who he was, how far back this thing goes. He killed Heilshorn — or, Sloane Dewan did, John. Brendan brought these players together, and Heilshorn wound up dead. It hastened this; this event. Wick himself has had to step in. He's just going for it. Crippling the internet in ways that will rock the economy, nearly collapse it and framing Nonsystem."

"No. That's ridiculous. You're wrong. You . . ."

She looked at him, and at last allowed herself to accept how unredeemable he was. Maybe, she thought, this was how everyone seemed once you'd turned that corner. She grabbed the car keys out of his hand.

He looked down at his empty palm. And he raised his fist — the same fist he'd raised and held above her once before, years ago — ready to strike her. Ready to hit her and call her a bitch. Because that's what men called women when they couldn't control them. He was gritting his teeth — he wanted to hit her. It had always felt like that with John, that things were just on the edge of violence. And now, here it was.

Before he had a chance to bring his fist down on her, Jennifer ducked, and hit John Rascher in the stomach as hard as she could. Not the balls — she could've gone there, but she had her principles — and she listened as the air burst out of his lungs. It was a good shot, just beneath the diaphragm. It dropped John Rascher like a rock. When he went down, clearing her view she saw the attorney general, watching her, his mouth hanging open.

She lowered her eyes to look at Rascher. He was on his knees, bent forward, gasping for breath. She looked out over the base, out at the simulated Middle Eastern village where the soldiers trained. Thousands of men and women serving their country. They got their target, they went after it. No question about it.

Like Brendan Healy.

Their loyalty was commendable. Their faith. Their strength. Their honor.

But it all just depended on whom and what you were fighting for.

CHAPTER FORTY / FRIDAY, 8:40 AM

An announcement came over the loudspeakers: "Ladies and gentlemen we're going to need to make an unscheduled stop on this morning's ride to Albany, Westport, and Montreal. We're very sorry for this inconvenience, and we'll be rolling back along in no time."

The train started slowing a minute later. Brendan stood back near the bathroom. He'd opted not to follow the conductor into the next car; he didn't want the man to even see him again, his gut told him to stay put. He reminded himself of studies done at NYU, research involving the frailty of human memory. He knew from both study and experience what unreliable witnesses human beings were due to the limitations of short term memory.

But none of that mattered anyway. By now the CSS was commanding Penn Station and the NYPD. They could have watched video footage confirming that Brendan had boarded the train a half hour ago. They knew he was here. Anything else was delusional. Yes, they might allow him to reach his destination, to wait and see where he was going, but surely an agent or three or ten were going to board this train at 125th street. Maybe some take-no-shit NYPD cops, too, who didn't care about the CSS taking command of anything. Someone causing a ruckus in Penn Station on the train headed north? Awesome. I'm fucking on it. Who knew how many were going to board?

As the train neared the station, he walked a few seats up the aisle, ducking his head casually to see out of the windows. He spotted at least two NYPD uniforms, a Metro Transit Authority worker with an orange vest on, and one guy in a plain black suit. In the distance, through the crisscrossing steel girders of the 125th Street Bridge, he saw more police arriving with their lights twirling.

No. Goddammit. Maybe they weren't going to keep the train moving at all. Maybe they were just going to let it sit here, despite all the griping that would arise from the disgruntled passengers, as they checked every person. If that was the case, he would just have to sit and take the scrutiny. Which he couldn't. Not with a fake finger.

Brendan realized he wasn't the only person on the train who was apprehensive. He spotted the kid with the headphones throwing nervous looks out the window. He wasn't so much a kid, really. Eighteen, maybe twenty. He wore some chains, a Starter hat cocked to the side, and large basketball shorts. Brendan blatantly profiled him, made a decision, and headed over. The train was almost stopped.

He kept his head down and then bent over when he reached the kid and leaned in. He had to tap him on the shoulder.

The kid turned with a jump and scowled up at Brendan. Brendan pointed to his own ear, and the kid reached up and pulled one side of the headphones from his head.

"A hundred bucks for those," Brendan said.

The kid just looked back. He had stubble around his chin and upper lip, and a thin line of it following his jawline, like a chin strap. His dark eyes were dancing. "Two," he said.

Brendan had already expected the bump in price and discreetly handed the kid two bills. The kid looked at the money, and, just as discreetly, slid it into the backpack sitting next to him.

"Can I sit down?"

Now the kid became standoffish. "Huh? Why?"

Brendan put the headphones around his neck as the train finally stopped.

He sat down and turned to the kid. "What are you listening to?"

The kid cut a sideways glance, his voice low but vehement. "Dude, are you fuckin' gay?"

"No," Brendan said. "Just looking for a little company, man. That's all."

"Last time some guy told me he needed some company, wasn't a good thing," the kid said, his eyes hard and direct.

"It's not like that."

The kid looked out the window, as if connecting the train's unscheduled stop with Brendan. Then his head swiveled back as Brendan spoke.

"Just thinking, maybe you got something else I can buy. Long trip; I'd like to relax, you know?"

The brakes hissed. The doors opened.

Brendan could see movement outside on the platform. He was careful not to make a show of looking outside to see who was there. He held his hands up, palms out, in front of him. It was becoming his new trademark gesture.

"Man, what I got ain't nothing for you." The kid glowered at Brendan. "Get the fuck out of here before I take my headphones back and keep your money."

"Alright, man," Brendan said. "I was just trying to be friendly."

Brendan got up and slipped back a few rows and sat back down. He watched the back of the kid's head.

A minute passed. Brendan put the headphones on and sat back in the seat, looked out the window, down at 125th. He bobbed his head slightly, moved his lips to non-existent music.

An eternity. Two minutes, five. What were they doing? They were checking every car. The passengers were getting riled up. One of the two women got up to use the bathroom. A man and his son were having a hard time — the son was bored, starting to whine. The kid with the Starter hat looked ready to crawl out of his skin.

Every minute that passed was one of doubt. Doubt that he had done the right thing, leaving Sloane. Doubt that the message from Jennifer Aiken was legitimate, when it could've been one of Staryles' tricks, aiming to flush Brendan out. Which it had. Doubt, even, that the book from Colinas had really been a valid clue at all, or if Brendan had been grasping at straws. To make the connection that Leah Heilshorn was now being kept near where Brendan had once tracked the paid killer of Angie and Gloria — where he'd met the ultimate darkness in his life — it was just an idea. Now, on this unmoving train, the minutes crawling by with agonizing slowness, it all felt insubstantial, like smoke. He was only getting himself in deeper; the more he struggled, the tighter the noose around his neck.

Ten minutes.

He continued to listen to imaginary music. He put on the gloves. He was a bike messenger from the city, an affectation of his new personality, as William Chase. William Chase, originally from Sarasota, Florida. Now living in Queens. Retired parents dividing their time between Sarasota and Lake Placid, New York. One sister, stricken with breast cancer at the age of thirty. A daughter, six years old, his niece. The name had been selected for him at random, but the backstory was his to invent. He focused on these details, aimed his mind there, sharpening his will to a point. He would not waver; this would be his new identity, and it would work.

The prosthetic finger looked terribly fake.

Now the first NYPD officer stepped onto the train.

Behind the officer was a plain-clothed agent. Brendan wondered what his code name was. Artemis, maybe. Or Zeus. He wondered if they fought over who got the best Greek-god names. He realized he was punchy. Punchy was dangerous. He needed to quell the adrenaline twisting in his veins, slow himself down, act a little stoned. Show his new ID with one hand, keep the other out of sight.

The agent was in his early thirties, short reddish hair. He tucked his chin in and spoke into his wrist for a moment, his gaze sweeping the train car. The NYPD cop preceded him, body language suggesting that this was his show, federal jurisdiction be damned.

"Hey what's going on?" said the passenger with the restless son.

"Everything is okay, sir, we ah, we're taking care of it."

"Yeah," the passenger said with a typical, New Yorker, no-nonsense tincture, "that's great, but what's the problem? We've been here a half an hour. This train ride is eight hours as it is."

"I understand, sir." The cop tried to keep moving. The agent was coming slowly behind him.

"You understand? What does that mean?"

"It means I'm not at liberty to discuss it."

"Not at liberty," the guy said with disgust. "Yeah, okay. Not at liberty. Thanks." He turned to his kid and in a lower voice sternly attempted to get the little one to *siddown and shaddup*.

The cop's eyes passed quickly over the women, the businessman, and then found the kid, where his gaze lingered. The agent loomed behind him, skeptical, at the ready.

Brendan felt badly, but it had been his only chance. If the kid was holding, he was going to pop.

The kid stood up. His face white as a sheet, he turned and walked stiffly down the aisle.

"Hey," the cop said. "Hey wait up."

"Better run," Brendan said under his breath.

The kid jammed one hard look at Brendan and got moving faster.

"Hey," the cop called. "Hey, whoa."

But the kid was going faster now, reaching the last of the seats. He leapt from the train onto the platform and took off running.

"Hey, hey!" the cop kept calling, now backing up. He pushed past the agent and ran out of the train, his handcuffs jangling on his belt. Brendan looked around, acting as if he was just now sensing some commotion, pulling one of the headphones from the side of his head, eyes wide. If the agent was clocking him, he didn't really know, because he didn't make direct eye contact. Instead he sort of half-stood in his seat, as people do when there is some drama happening, keeping one headphone pressed to his ear.

The businessman had set the paper aside and was craning his neck to look out the window. Brendan saw the cop run past. Finally he risked a glance at the front of the train. The agent was gone. He heard shouts coming from the platform. Then, nothing.

CHAPTER FORTY-ONE / FRIDAY, 9:17 AM

Staryles didn't want to look at the playback of Healy jumping on the northbound train out of Penn Station. He didn't need to. He knew Healy's mind, by now. He knew where Healy wanted to go. Staryles stood in the security room at Penn Station a half an hour after Healy had dispatched the three agents and outrun them to the train. Staryles was furious.

"Hey," said the security guard playing the video for the NYPD. The small room was messy with that morning's breakfast wrappers. The space was crowded, the wall was lined with soundproofing, like a recording studio. "Excuse me, but you can't just come in here," the guard squawked. That nasal, chirping version of the New York accent. "Who are you guys, anyway?"

Staryles didn't answer him but turned to leave. He was blocked by a fence of fleshy NYPD cops, standing shoulder to shoulder. They scowled at him as he stared back at their large hairy arms, looking for a way to cut through them. He debated, for a second, taking out his weapon and sticking it in their faces. Sharpened that morning, his knife would enter them like butter, and when he retracted it the serrated back edge would tear through muscle and sinew. Or a sideways slash, maybe just cut a smile in the fat stomach of the one in front of him, let the entrails slip out.

Grudgingly, they parted, and he slipped through them and out of the cramped quarters. He was wasting his energy in there, and he knew it. He was still off his game, just slightly. With Heilshorn gone, the last seven months had required a serious adjustment to the new order. General Wick was a fake bastard, as much as he tried to wear the mask of a real human. And he had terrible hair.

Staryles descended the stairs to the main concourse at Penn Station. He slipped into the crowd, becoming one of them.

But that was how these things worked. Nothing ever happened with everybody involved in-the-know. Each person had limited information, enough to play their part. The cop sitting beneath the Sky Watch tower with its Panopticon glare on the demonstrators didn't even know what he was guarding. The spies in the CIA were so caught up in their own convoluted operations that no one knew who to trust. The man driving to one of the CSS quarters in Pennsylvania in a Honda Civic with the lunchbox and the white hair and the glinting medals on his uniform never knew the ultimate decoded enemy message.

They knew only enough to effectively execute their specific orders. They were given assurances that any questions they may have, any concerns would be rightly addressed. And if, when certain events occurred, and they felt responsible, at least indirectly, and they didn't agree with the results, they could be dealt with. There were a number of ways to change a person's mind, to shut them down. It didn't always have to be by killing, in fact, in some ways it was best not to be.

He reached the station exit and pushed his way out into the bright morning. He wiped his arms, as if they were covered in the germs from all the people in the train station. And of course they were. The world was full of germs. Viruses. People. It would be a better place with the numbers reduced. After a little cleansing.

His earbud chirped and he listened as Agent Ares informed him of the developments at 125th street.

"He's not here."

"What?" Someone bumped into Staryles as he stood on the sidewalk. People rushing about every which way.

"He's not here. We searched the entire train. One guy got off and ran — not him. Some kid afraid we were sweeping for drugs. Had a gram of coke and two hundred cash on him. NYPD's got him in custody."

Staryles felt his skin prickle with perspiration under the rising, already blazing sun. He hated to sweat. Someone else checked him from behind. He didn't even turn to look at who it was.

Ares continued. "It's possible he got between the cars and jumped from the train before it came to a stop. NYPD is patrolling the tracks now, going back a mile. We had trouble, but we got a look at everyone at least."

Staryles gritted his teeth.

"Let it go."

"Yeah?"

Another pedestrian bumped into Staryles on the street, and he found himself fingering his knife.

Keeping hands off Healy had been the obvious choice to gain access to Sloane Dewan. Dewan had been working on software to update Dark Wallet, and they wanted it. First, however, he had refused visitation. So Wick had contacted the Attorney General and the two of them had set up the idea of the Nonsystem sting, and bringing in Jennifer Aiken. If she'd made it out of the last situation alive, maybe she could be of use. They had dangled a deal in front of Healy. But again, the stubborn bastard had refused. He'd gotten out on his own by turning the tables on the Deputy Warden, a slick move that even Staryles admired. And then at last they had her, coming to Healy at the Sheraton. But they got the room wrong. Healy had switched it on them. By the time they figured out where they really were, Healy had left.

But Staryles thought he knew where Healy was going. In fact, if he got going now in the Cutlass, he could beat the train.

"Let it go," he repeated, and cut the transmission.

He dialed a number on his phone. He brought the phone to his mouth, his gaze scraping over the people in his midst. He watched them as he gave the destruction order for two of the data centers. He watched them closely, less angry with them now as they passed by and bumped him and lived their oblivious lives. Less angry, more content. Many of them were now going to die.

CHAPTER FORTY-TWO / FRIDAY, 9:21 AM

"Ladies and Gentlemen, we apologize for the interruption. We're going to resume the express schedule of the 8:08 AM Adirondacker train to Westport, NY, and points beyond. Thanks for your patience."

The train began to roll forward.

The relief came as a blast of oxygen inflating his chest. Brendan wanted to stand up and shout and to grab one of his fellow passengers — the business man, the two older ladies — and hug them. But then the emotion passed, and he had a moment to reflect. He'd been nervous. But he hadn't been afraid.

He'd already been to jail. What more could they do? Kill him?

And the relief dissipated like a sudden flurry of wind becoming calm, still, and he realized something.

For the first time since he tried to asphyxiate himself in the garage, he wasn't afraid of death. If he'd died just now, his only regret would have been that he hadn't yet reached Leah, and what lay beyond her.

And Sloane. But Sloane would have understood. She was part of something larger than herself now, too.

He realized he was still getting glances from some of the other passengers. They looked away as soon as he returned eye contact. He felt himself smiling.

There was a distant, muffled explosion, and a roll of black smoke plumed into the sky further down in the city. Brendan stared out the window, smile gone, his heart sinking. The explosion had come from downtown.

CHAPTER FORTY-THREE / FRIDAY, 9:19 AM

The Liebherr yellow excavator across the street from 66 Hudson Street was moving. The body rotated and the claw-scoop end extended out over the single available lane of traffic. The cars in the street screeched to a halt, first two cabs, then a pickup truck, horns blaring. With the street already closed down to one lane, they were unable to pass. It wasn't long before the cab drivers were standing outside their vehicles and shouting towards the machine.

The driver of the excavator climbed down, lifted his hands in the air, and shrugged. Behind him, the engine of the yellow machine was smoking. In the distance, coming from around 8th Avenue, there was more smoke on the horizon, and the sound of sirens.

People walking along, on the construction side, stopped to watch. The pickup truck was trying to back up in order to go down Thomas Street, half a block back. But its reverse route was obstructed when an SUV came up behind it and stopped. More horns honked and the pickup driver got out and started shouting at the SUV to back up.

The rear door to the SUV opened, and the pickup truck driver fell silent. He started to back away. A second later, a bullet took him in the shoulder and spun him round like a top. He collapsed in the street and the blood began to spread beneath him. Still alive, he was trying to crawl to the sidewalk when a figure in full black riot gear stepped over him and up onto the curb.

Two more black-clad figures exited the SUV. By now the passers-by were shouting and running for cover. There were flashes of light from the dark building across the street from 66 Hudson. Sniper-fire caught several civilians and dropped them to the ground. One of the black-clad figures exiting the SUV entered the cordoned-off area where the Liebherr excavator now sat unattended.

Randy, the security guard from the Hudson building, stepped out into the bright day, looking around at the entrance to the Downtown Art Gallery. He rushed towards the pickup truck driver, shouting at the cabbies to help. But the cabbies had gotten back inside their vehicles. The driver of the excavator had disappeared. Everyone else had scattered.

The security guard reached the pickup truck driver and got an arm beneath him. He was trying to help him to his feet when one of the snipers shot him in the side.

Randy howled in surprise and pain, dropped the truck driver and fell to the ground where he tried to roll away from any more shots. As he rolled, one of the men from the SUV, face covered entirely in black except for the eyes, walked slowly towards him, the tip of a sound-suppressed submachine gun pointed at Randy. Three other operatives in black gathered where the first was extracting something from the back of the excavator. He handed them each a bundle, which they carried across the street and took inside the building.

They moved quickly to the elevator. The receptionist sat stunned at her perch behind the front desk, her hands in the air, her face a twisted grimace of fear and confusion.

In the elevator, Agent Zeus pulled off his mask and swiped a hand across his face. "This has to be quick," he said to the others. "Ninety seconds." They nodded agreement. Zeus felt the excitement pumping through him, and he was eager to get the job done.

The doors opened to the top floor. A hail of bullets pummeled the rear of the elevator car. After a few seconds, the firing ceased, and the four operatives in black peeled themselves off the walls of the elevator and returned fire. They began marching into the room, their ammunition pulverizing everything, shattering the glass wall behind the long desk at the entrance to the Meet-Me-Room.

There were screams from inside the room as the busted glass crumbled to the floor. Once the operatives reached the front desk they rounded it and riddled the two security guards, all three of them firing at once, until Zeus broke away and was the first one through the ragged glass and into the room, with all of those servers humming, their red and amber eyes glowing in the din.

CHAPTER FORTY-FOUR / FRIDAY, 11:54 PM

Jennifer weaved through the traffic on route 6 in Cape Cod in the SUV she'd boosted from Rascher. Her eyes flicked to the rear-view mirror. Coming up behind her was a military caravan of vehicles; cars, Jeeps and trucks. Gaining on her quickly. She watched them close in. The lead car looked like an ordinary police car, and then the lights began flashing.

"Oh, you got to be kidding," she said.

Two vehicles sped up on either side of the SUV, cops looking out at her. She tamped down on the gas pedal.

As she white-knuckled the steering wheel, and pushed the SUV past eighty miles per hour, she noticed something along the service road paralleling the three-lane highway. The streetlights were dark. Traffic had snarled around one intersection beside the highway and people were out of their cars. As she blew by them, she noticed one of the vehicles in the caravan on her heels break away from the back and take the exit to the service road.

She kept on the gas. The other cars and trucks on the road seemed to be slowing. It was getting harder and more dangerous to keep going around them.

"No, no, no, no," she said through her gritted teeth. She slammed a palm against the steering wheel, hitting the horn. "No!"

They were getting over into the right lane, which was mostly just a crawl. She glanced at the side-view mirror and saw one of her pursuers whip wildly around a slow-moving minivan. She felt her stomach flip. She was putting people's lives in jeopardy. For God's sake the very thing she wanted to do — help people — and she was endangering them instead.

She was only ten miles from Cotuit, according to the last sign. These were roads she had taken many times. On the other side of the service road were residential streets, small, narrow, like the ones where Argon's house was. Nothing she could navigate at high speed. She was screwed. If she kept this up on the highway she was going to kill somebody. If she tried to get off she'd only be switching one danger for another. She let her foot off the gas and the SUV started to slow. She passed a few more vehicles as the SUV decelerated. Of all things, it had to be the midday traffic of a holiday summer weekend that she was going through this, the highways choked. Vehicles everywhere she looked.

At the next exit, two cars collided, launching one into the air. Even from as far back as she was, she could hear — and feel — the metal-squealing crunch and earthquake vibration as the car came down and landed on another.

"Oh my God." She was unaware she was even going to speak. "Oh my God, my God, my God . . ."

Things were rapidly descending into chaos. A glance behind her revealed that she was no longer being pursued — the lights of the police cars were back several car lengths, stuck behind the clog of traffic she'd just made it through. In the left lane, she was able to pull off the road and onto the embankment. In a snap decision — no thinking now, no time to second-guess — she bounded down the grassy hill and hit the service road with a tremendous jolt that rattled the bones in her arms and threw her head back. The pain she'd been subduing with meds for the past months flared bright and cold in her neck and around the base of her skull as the rear wheels of the SUV came down next and landed on the road with a thud.

She was just past the intersection with the bottlenecked traffic and angry people outside of their cars. Throwing a terrified glance in the mirror she saw a cop car and a Jeep were following her path down the incline. She pressed the accelerator. She took a left turn off the service road. Careful as she could be, she rolled through the next stop sign making a right hand turn. She drove through a small neighborhood and out the other side. Up ahead was route 149 south, which would take her into Cotuit.

Maybe they would still follow her, she thought. Maybe they knew about her family home. But after going three miles south on 149, which was Cotuit Road, she was in Marstons Mills, a sleepy little residential community, and no one was behind her. She passed by the volunteer firehouse and saw that the doors were open, the fire trucks out.

She went over a bridge, slowing now, still checking her mirrors every five seconds, but feeling calmer.

After the bridge, she made the turn onto Old Post Road. Here the road was narrow and the trees thick and leaning in, the midday sun baking off the road.

She followed the road to the end, to the Point.

CHAPTER FORTY-FIVE / FRIDAY, 11:55 AM

Brendan looked out the window. The city streets were gone, the suburban residences were behind him. The Hudson River flashed in the distance through the trees. The passengers onboard the train were restless and chatting in quiet, pained voices. The explosions in Manhattan had left everyone in shock. One passenger, a middle-aged man, face flushed red, offered a brief and passionate call to action. We shouldn't take it anymore, he said; these terrorists — Al Qaeda, ISIL — whoever was responsible for the attack — needed to be wiped off the face of the Earth. Mostly the other passengers looked at their phones, out the window, or off into space — anywhere but at the man, who eventually sat down. Conversations went on more quietly along the same lines. Savages had done this. Another attack on American soil from Islamic terror groups.

Yet, somehow, life went on. People got off in Albany and new passengers boarded. Among them was a young couple in their twenties, attractive and fashionable. The tension in the air seemed to dissipate. But only for a short time.

"Honey. Look. Here it is."

The young couple took their seats, the man staring down at his iPad. The woman slipped in beside him. Brendan could hear some tinny audio, but couldn't make out what it was.

"Posted ten minutes ago," the young man said.

They both fell silent, staring raptly at the screen. Brendan fidgeted in his seat. After about a minute, the woman said, "My God."

"Yeah," said the young man. "Holy shit."

He couldn't take it anymore. Brendan got out of his seat and walked down the aisle toward the couple. He passed a trio of college-aged girls silently watching their own devices. One of the girls was crying. A man in a gray maintenance-worker suit was staring into his phone, ashen-faced.

The young couple looked up as Brendan approached. "I'm sorry," he said, "I'm a journalist, and like an idiot I left my phone in New York. Can I see?"

The young woman looked at Brendan sorrowfully but the young man was eager to help. "Yeah," he said. "Just popped up on my CNN Alerts."

Brendan stood in the aisle beside them, as the man held up his iPad and dragged back the play button to the start and then tapped it. He pressed a button to increase the volume as Brendan leaned in to watch, keeping his disfigured hand behind his back.

An attractive newscaster stared out at them. "Just this morning in New York City, the destruction of two locations in downtown Manhattan."

The shot changed from the newscaster to amateur video showing smoky ruins. The newscaster's voice continued. "We now know that 66 Hudson Street and 111 8th Avenue were the sites of what the FBI are calling terrorist attacks from a group known as Nonsystem."

The video changed to a still image, a blurry picture of a man in black fatigues, holding what looked like a submachine gun.

"66 Hudson is known as the Meet-Me-Room, a massive hub for the World Wide Web. A similar data center further uptown on Eighth Avenue was devastated by C-4 explosives. More than a hundred people are injured or dead. Several police officers have been shot."

Now a different video replaced the still image. Brendan recognized the man who was speaking. Just a couple days ago, Brendan had head-butted him. There was a small bandage across the bridge of Harlan Doherty's nose. His name and FBI affiliation came up in a graphic along the bottom of the screen. Doherty stood in front of a background of smoldering rubble and flashing police lights.

The newscaster said, "Agent Doherty, what's the story here? Have any arrests been made?"

"This is going to be a case of swift justice, Alice. The FBI has been working with the Department of Justice already to draw out Nonsystem."

As he spoke, the screen displayed footage of a group of young people, like the ones on the train, pulled from the backs of black, tinted-window SUVS. "It's sad to encounter homegrown terrorists like this," Doherty said. "But it's no surprise that they're not completely independent; we believe the terrorist hacker group to be for hire, and under contract from several different foreign anti-American groups."

It was hard to tell where they were — until the camera caught a glimpse of a nearby city police car, with the logo for *Boston Police* emblazoned across the door.

"To answer your question, yes, we now have several members in custody."

Brendan watched the law enforcement personnel, several of them in plain clothes, but with a copious supply of SWAT members surrounding and assisting, heavily armed, parade the individuals up a wide set of concrete stairs into a government building with pillars in the front.

Brendan didn't recognize anyone, until he saw Deputy Bostrom.

The last shot of the newscast was of the pretty anchor, who said, "Our hearts go out to all of the families of the victims in this terrorism crisis. We now turn to the scene of the first attack, where rescuers are—"

The video froze.

The young man held the tablet up and gave it a look. His girlfriend pointed to an icon on the screen. "Lost service," she said.

The young couple fell silent. The young man put the iPad away and the woman chewed her nail and looked out the window. The way she bit her nails reminded Brendan of Sloane.

"Thank you," Brendan said to them. He returned to his seat feeling hollowed out.

Behind him, it sounded like the young couple were arguing. Brendan heard the man saying softly, "Honey, come on," as she squeezed out of the seat. She hurried up the aisle. Brendan could smell the perfume and shampoo on her as she passed, reminding him of Sloane again, and their one night together.

He gazed out the window and saw buildings now, old barns and charming houses with big porches. Tractors in fields. Fledgling summer corn. Apple trees in blossom. He was in the countryside, a couple of hours from his destination.

He closed his eyes for a moment and Sloane's image formed in his mind. He could feel her fingers on his skin. He could smell her, taste her.

But then she began to fade.

CHAPTER FORTY-SIX / FRIDAY, 4:14 PM

The train depot sat on a rise. To the west, two-lane blacktop bisected a huge swath of forest, photograph-still in the dry, late-summer heat. It had gotten warm again while he'd been on the train. Now four in the afternoon, the shadows were lengthening but the temperature remained high. Down the road a mile before it curved out of sight, a lone car approached, skating over the quicksilver that shimmered above the sunburned asphalt. As it neared, Brendan realized that today would have been his trial if he were still in jail.

The taxi pulled into the small parking lot. He'd called it from the depot payphone. He'd been the only passenger to get off the train. The young couple with the iPad were staying on until Montreal, another hour or more away. The taxi, white letters reading *ADK Mountain Taxi* on its side, found a narrow slot lot beside the train tracks.

The driver was a heavy-set woman in a t-shirt, with greasy brown curls. Her sweaty upper lip curled back as she stared up at Brendan. "You called for the taxi?"

Brendan realized there was no air conditioning in the car, a few moments later as they sliced through the heat. It was the least of his concerns, in fact, he was glad for it. His pores opened and the sweat beaded off his skin. Better than the canned, stale, dry-storage cool air of the train. Better than the stink of prison. He inhaled the scents of pine, raveling asphalt, and raspberry bushes as they drove. The driver sparked a cigarette and that alluring smell of tobacco drifted over to him. "You mind?"

"Not if I can have one."

Fuck it.

She shook a cigarette out of her pack. They were a cheap brand, 100s. Brendan took one and lit it with the push-in lighter in the center console. It was an old car, a Plymouth, probably early-nineties model. He'd noticed the rust slowly digesting the undercarriage and wheel wells.

"Careful with that." The driver nodded at the cigarette as the lighter popped from the console. Brendan fed the tip to the glowing coils. "It'll kill ya," she said.

* * *

Forty-five minutes later the cab dropped Brendan off in Lake Placid. The small town was choked with summer traffic along its main street, like a city. Thunderhead clouds shouldered together over a range of jagged mountain peaks. The air was heavy with an impending summer storm, a need to release the heat.

It was Friday evening, and the small town hall, with its chamber of commerce within, had just closed. It didn't matter. He walked along the sidewalk through the quaint retail district, trail baskets and antique snowshoes on display, just another window shopper.

He'd last walked these streets years ago. A village gateway to high peaks, a good place for skiing, hunting, and fishing. Lake Placid had twice hosted the winter Olympics.

He supposed there was some significance in all this, something to the fact that he was going to find closure with Titan in a place calling itself an "Olympic Village." But, he had other things to think about.

The Heilshorns would've kept a low profile over the years. That was fairly easy to do; like most every other place in the world, the rich and the poor didn't mix in Lake Placid. Unless, that was, the poor were changing the linens in their hotel room, bringing cocktails to their dinner table overlooking the mountain lakes, or tending to their wooded grounds while they were away. Or, as was the case with his wife and daughter's truck-driving killer, trying to get the money they'd been promised.

There were a handful of groundskeepers and caretakers in the area. Most of them weren't in the Yellow Pages, and only a few of them had websites. They worked mostly by referral. The people who kept the mansions and Great Camps hidden away in the forests were big on personal recommendations.

A decade earlier he had tracked Damon Cosgrove to Lake Placid after Cosgrove, a long-haul truck driver, had made parole. He'd never given any thought to why Cosgrove had chosen this location. He'd picked up his trail in Westchester and followed him here. He'd managed to keep tabs on Cosgrove for two days, but eventually he'd lost him completely. The man who had killed his family, and Brendan had let him slip through his fingers. Couldn't even find him in a town as small as this. He'd rented a small cabin as far away from the village as possible and set about drinking himself into a stupor. Eighteen months had blurred past in a prolonged binge. He'd had his father's life insurance to live on.

Now, however, he had no money in the bank. He didn't need to check an ATM to know that he wouldn't have any access to funds. His accounts would be frozen. A branch manager would tell him that the Department of Justice, or maybe the FBI had ordered it. Maybe Harlan Doherty had signed the mandate himself. Or John Rascher. That didn't matter either.

He had some cash left. It would be enough. He didn't know if he was going to last through the night, anyway.

Surely Staryles was on his way. He was going to the one place Staryles would know to look for him. Because Staryles knew about Damon Cosgrove. If Brendan hadn't realized it then because he'd been too drunk to see straight, he understood now. Damon Cosgrove had come here because the Heilshorns had a home here. Chances were they'd never paid him and he'd come to collect. They'd killed him instead.

Maybe Staryles had eyes on him right now, but he didn't think so. Not at the moment. For just a precious short time, he was free.

* * *

Within two hours of trolling the local bars, he had the names of three caretakers. It was full dark now as he found the one payphone in town by the public beach and placed his calls. He could smell the alcohol clinging to him from the Happy Hours he'd invaded. But he'd stayed dry.

The first call got him a machine. He didn't bother with a message, and plunked in more change. For a moment, he felt like an investigator again, like the PI he'd been briefly in Laramie, checking for cheating husbands and busboy thieves. The second number he tried got a result. A man with a voice as dry as tinder answered and then immediately broke into a coughing fit. Brendan said hello and quickly went through his spiel, careful not to sound like a telemarketer or someone asking for a charitable donation.

He was new in town, and had recently bought property and was looking for a caretaker. He'd been referred by the Heilshorns.

After a few more minutes of getting to know each other, Brendan got to the point and asked the caretaker if he knew the Heilshorns personally. He didn't, but he marveled at their house on Whitney Road. A classic Great Camp, restored not remodeled, just the way it should be.

Mr. Heilshorn had an impressive collection of Adirondack guide boats.

Brendan said he would be in touch.

He hung up and walked to a nearby hotel. He needed to rest for what was about to come, and he had to time things just right.

He thought he remembered Whitney Road, just around Mirror Lake in the center of town. Over on the other side, far back behind the million-dollar homes hemming the still, glassy water.

It had only taken two calls. He was in much better shape to get shit done sober.

Overhead, thunder rumbled again, sounding close.

CHAPTER FORTY-SEVEN / SATURDAY 7:28 PM

Jennifer was unbelievably tired. She hadn't gotten a wink of sleep the night before — she'd been awake since the morning she'd met with Philip Largo. After the harrowing chase through Cape Cod, once she'd gotten home she'd been too wired up to even think about resting. But after a hasty shower and a bad meal from canned goods in the pantry, exhaustion slipped over her like a shroud, and she'd slept for seven straight hours on the couch without moving a muscle. When she awoke, stiff and groggy, it was just starting to get dark outside.

The first thing she did when she woke up was check her phone. The internet wasn't working, and she had no service, no new voicemails. The flat-screen digital TV in the corner claimed No Signal. She opened up her laptop and attempted to get online, but there was no connection there either.

Her family had a landline. She found the cordless phone sitting in its charger, next to her father's recliner in the den. She picked it up and clicked the talk button. She exhaled relief when she heard the dial tone.

She called FBI headquarters in Washington and asked for Gary Petrino. He answered on the second ring. She could hear phones ringing and burbling voices in the background.

"Agent Petrino."

"Petrino," she said. "I need you to switch to a secure line."

"Agent Aiken. Good to hear from you, too. Give me a second."

She heard a click and a series of beeps. Petrino started to talk but she cut him off.

"What do we know about ICANN?"

"Uhm, okay. I'm fine, you? And so on, is how it goes."

She waited for him.

"That's the Internet Corporation for Assigned Names and Numbers."

"I know what it is. I need a list of names of the people headhunted to be ICANN members."

"Where are you?"

"Safe."

He was silent for a moment. "Aiken, you're in a lot of trouble."

"Petrino," she urged. "Tell me what you know."

"Okay, Jesus. ICANN. Each of the fourteen civilian members holds a metal key to a safety-deposit box. Each of these boxes contains a smartcard. When these are all activated in unison, it creates a master key which reboots the internet."

"Based on what IP?"

"Well, come on, Aiken. That would be ICANN protocol."

"How do they do it? Can it all be done remotely?"

"No. They have to fly to a single location."

"In the US, right? Petrino, I've gotten all the same briefs you have. I've read all the memos. Those are the lines they've been feeding us for three years."

"Listen, You need to come in. You're in danger."

"That's just the limited hangout — members flown to a top-secret US location, blah blah blah. Come on. You know how this works. The master key won't be created by civilians. It's Wick, right?"

Petrino was unresponsive. "Petrino!" she shouted.

"Aiken. Don't do this."

They need me now more than ever. That's why I'm still alive. All they have to go on is my testimony, my case files, my story. They made the arrests based on me. Not on wiretaps, not on forensic evidence. Nonsystem will have encrypted everything. Maybe they'll get nothing from their hardware after all — or, it will take months. They'll lean on those kids for confessions, but maybe the kids won't budge. They'll have to let them go.

Or, they'll keep them right where they are under the NDAA. Maybe they'll send them to Gitmo. They can do anything they want — this is a matter of national security.

"Aiken, Nonsystem attacked a New York City data center this morning, while you were in with Wick."

She felt her throat close up. "What?" She thought of the streetlights dark on route 6. The ghost town Cotuit had become. She pictured Wick, sitting across from her, perfectly poised and equable as the city burned. "What's going on, Gary?"

Petrino was old school, gray and indifferent as a tomcat, not much riled him. But suddenly he sounded like a spooked rookie agent. "It's the end of the fucking world, Jennifer, that's what's going on. It's been fucking chaos. Are you somewhere secure? You say you're safe?"

"I am. I'm good."

"Has anyone tried to contact you?"

"I have no cell service. Internet is out. Calling you from an old landline."

"You're in Massachusetts?"

She felt a pang of fear. "I might be."

"Makes sense. Yeah, Massachusetts is down." He seemed to be calming down some, but there was still an edge to his voice.

"What does that mean?"

"Internet is down in seven states. There are some areas where it's still sluggish, some dial-up, but it's pretty much dead. Cell-phone towers have wigged out, too. It's a major crash; the whole northeast has basically imploded. Bridges, roads, schools, subways, all affected. The President declared a national emergency at three this afternoon." Petrino paused, breathing loudly into the phone. "So, they did it. Your little gang of hackers are pretty beefed up after all."

"Petrino, I spent the night before last cramming internet shutdown information. There's no way Nonsystem is doing this. For one thing, you can't destroy a signal while using it. You've got to cut cables, pillage data centers, demolish root servers — you need analog violence, not just some amped up DDoS strike."

"Are you speaking English?"

"What I'm saying is, this type of destruction is not about hackers. The internet is full of backups, redundancies. Nonsystem knows you can't kill the internet from within; repairs would override damage. This is not coming from them. They warned me about this."

Petrino was silent. She could sense him evaluating her. Wondering if she'd gone native, if she might be a traitor. She knew it was a risk calling the FBI if they were in fact under the thumb of Central Security Service, but Petrino worked mostly on his own as a profiler.

"There have been targeted attacks on data centers all over the country," Petrino said. "So, I hear you. I understand the physical components here. Turn the TV on, regular TV, they're still a couple of stations broadcasting. SWAT teams pushing back demonstrators already surging all over the country; half of them want to fry Nonsystem, the other half of them are calling for freedom of the internet. Liberation of digital currency, net neutrality, all that sort of thing. God, protests used to be simple. You wanted to end a war, you showed some tit.

Sorry. Anyway, if it isn't Nonsystem, or the fucking Islamic State behind them, beg pardon, who is doing this?"

"I don't know." It was a lie. Baldest she'd ever told. She could see Wick's empty eyes, the false charm carefully etched into his features. She could hear Gentian say *we're ready*. He'd wanted this? Were they martyrs?

"Okay . . ." Petrino drawled. "If you don't know, or can't guess, you got any idea for motivation? I can get you those ICANN names, but it's going to take a while. Things are totally jacked here. Got a number I can call you back at?"

Jennifer closed her eyes. She'd grown to like Petrino. He was about her only friend in this thing for the past couple years. But she was about to lose him, too.

"No," she said.

He exhaled with frustration. "Alright. Listen. You need to be careful. Stay somewhere safe. There's been looting and rioting in Boston, and it's a total nightmare in New York City. Too many traffic collisions to count, people jumping from buildings, shootings right out in the open."

She felt cold.

"Okay." She looked out the window at the azure blue of Cotuit Bay in the distance. She realized there was no one left she could trust. "Thanks, Gary. I gotta go."

"Okay. Stay safe."

She hung up and stood motionless in her family kitchen for a moment, her mind just spinning wheels. She then dialed a number from memory. She heard a series of chimes and a prerecorded voice saying that "all circuits are busy now." Her parents weren't reachable. Her mother had upgraded everything in their Ramapo home to digital a couple years before. A bundle of internet and phone. This house was the only place her family had with old technologies.

She remembered the TV they used to have. A picture-tube with rabbit ears on top. Jennifer went into the hallway. She pulled the string and the compartment swung down in the ceiling. She reached up and unfolded the stairs down, waving away the dust. She climbed up and looked around in the attic. It had to be a hundred degrees. There it was, the old Zenith television. Grunting and gritting her teeth against the pain flaring in her back and her neck, she wrestled the TV out of the small space and down the rickety stairs, nearly slipping and dropping the whole thing.

She found an outlet in the fake wood paneling in the living room and plugged it in. She fumbled with the rabbit ears for a moment, making sure they were still connected. She pressed the power button and stood back as the screen slowly came to life.

CHAPTER FORTY-EIGHT / SATURDAY 6:08 AM

The rain came hard and fast, turning the world the color of cinder. A tethered dinghy bounced in the waves and thumped against the dock. The lake turned choppy, the water gray and frothy in the downpour. The trees shook, their branches silver, beads of rain slicing through the thick boughs. The trees surrounded the large Adirondack Great Camp, it too colorless in the storm.

The bad man's past already conforms to his badness and is filled only with dreariness.

Brendan stood in the driveway, his jeans and sweatshirt soaked through, looking at the Land Cruiser parked at the end of the driveway in front of the single-bay garage. The garage was built into the ground, part of the basement of the large structure. Alongside the garage door was an entrance, the door white with chipped paint. The iron knob squeaked in his grip; it was open. Brendan slipped inside.

The basement was dark, musty, and smelled of earth. As his eyes adjusted to the weak light coming in through the ground-level windows, he saw bags of potting soil stacked up and other landscaping and gardening equipment. Near the back was a workbench and a wall of tools. An old rotary-dial phone was fastened to the wall. Deeper in, a large object sat covered in a tarpaulin. He lifted the canvas covering and peered underneath. A restored boat; a guide boat, Alexander Heilshorn's prized possession.

Along the far wall were stairs going up, with boxes stuffed beneath. The place was littered with old chairs, bicycles, shelves with canned food, camping supplies.

Pounding from above. Thuds against the floor that moved quickly from one end of the house to another, like running. It sounded like a child. Brendan looked at the ceiling. The footfalls shook the dust from the underfloor.

He started up the stairs.

The wood groaned softly beneath his weight; one stair creaked louder than others, and he froze halfway up. He waited. He heard the pounding again, reverberations of a child running, back in the other direction. He quickly went up the rest of the steps, while the child was in motion, using the sound to conceal his movement.

He faced the narrow door at the top of the stairs. It was locked.

Made sense, he thought. Keep a small child from wandering downstairs. He paused, listening to the noise of the rain outside, the distant banging of the dinghy against the dock. As he considered his course of action, he heard a different sound.

The latch of the door at the garage entrance. Someone was coming in behind him from the outside.

He stood still, his soaked clothes dripping, wetting the strip of worn carpet that ran down the flight of stairs. He felt the rain in his hair trickle down the sides of his face. He kept his breathing shallow, straining to hear more.

He thought he detected the scrape of a foot. As he hesitated and listened, the pounding suddenly resumed as the child in the house ran back across the floor again, covering the whole breadth of it. *Thump thump thump thump*

thump. The sound sinking down towards the other end of the building.

The stairs rose into an alcove where various bags and jackets hung from pegs in the wall. Where he stood, on the second step from the top, he was hidden from below. If he took just one step down, his feet would be visible.

He was trapped in between. Door locked to the house, someone in the basement.

Another rumble of thunder. The deep bass of it, like a stone rolling across a hard floor in heaven. There was no turning back.

Brendan launched himself at the door, throwing his shoulder into it, giving it every ounce of strength he had. But there was no leverage. He heard a splintery crack of wood and the door seemed to give way some but it didn't open. His stomach went oily. His heart seemed to stop beating for a moment. A flare of heat around his ears, in his armpits, his groin. His whole body pulsed with the beating of his heart, his skin tingled with nerves and blood.

From below him came the distinct sounds of shoes on concrete, a figure running across the space towards the stairs.

He threw himself at the door again; his shoulder, the palm of his hand, even the side of his skull thwacked into the wood. There was a crunching sound, and a groaning of metal as the latch bent slightly and sheared away from the wood casing and the door exploded open and Brendan tumbled through.

He was on his hands and knees. A linoleum floor. A huge kitchen connected to a huge dining room with cathedral windows.

A woman standing by the sink turned to look at him, her eyes wide, her mouth a grim, determined line.

Greta Heilshorn.

On the far side of the enormous open-plan room, hidden beneath the curved legs of an antique dining table, a little girl peered out at him, like a fawn through the trees.

Her eyes, the shape of the nose and mouth, he'd seen those before. He'd seen them in the reflection of a bedroom mirror. The little girl, Leah, looked at lot like her mother, Rebecca Heilshorn.

Brendan got to his feet, watching Greta. The women held a spatula in her hand. The air smelled of onions and garlic — she was cooking an omelet on the stove. Her wrinkled lips parted for a moment, and Brendan heard a hiss, but it could've just been the rain, and then he turned as Staryles bounded up the stairs after him.

The little girl, Leah, cried out, "Ma'am!"

Ma'am, Greta Heilshorn, didn't move. She stood still, eyes locked on Brendan as he lunged further away from the mouth of the basement stairway, clattering into pots and pans hung on the wall. She kept her eyes on him amid the chaos. He distantly realized that the water was running in the sink behind her.

Staryles exploded through the doorway, and immediately swung around to Brendan, who hurled one of the pots at him. Staryles ducked, but didn't get clear entirely, and the handle of the pot clipped him across the ear. He yelped and put his hand to the side of his head, raising the semi-automatic handgun with the suppressor. He pointed it at Brendan.

"Enough," shouted Great Heilshorn. Her voice was commanding.

Staryles' head snapped to the left to look at her, his expression reading, *You for real? I got this guy dead to rights.*

Brendan remembered the face. Movie-star looks. Lifeless eyes. The last time he'd seen Jeremy Staryles, he'd been sitting across from Brendan in a New York City jail, giving Brendan one hour to either join him or rot in hell.

"Not here," Greta responded. "You'll make a huge mess."

From where he was, sitting on his butt, surrounded by cutlery, Brendan could only partly see the little girl on the other side of the room. Just her hand and part of her foot from where she was on all fours beneath the table.

"Come on out, Leah," Greta said. She turned away for a moment and calmly removed the pan from the burner on the stove before the eggs burned.

Leah looked right at Brendan as she went to her grandmother. In that stolen moment, he no longer saw Rebecca's face, but an expression carved from the experience of living with Greta Heilshorn. He only hoped there was still some innocence left in her, some part of her unspoiled by the wretchedness of this life. He felt a pang of guilt for being a part of it, for bringing the violence of the day.

"Come here, child."

Leah came out from beneath the table and once again disappeared from his view, blocked by the kitchen island.

Leah crossed the room to Greta, who put her arm around the girl's shoulders.

"Get him up," Greta said to Staryles, her eyes locked on Brendan.

"Do it," Staryles barked, and Brendan rose to his feet, and then Staryles laughed.

Brendan stood shaking, his breath coming in jerky gasps. Greta wriggled her lips for a moment, as if tasting something. To Staryles, she said, "Take him out back and kill him there."

"Move," Staryles, and pointed behind him.

Brendan started that way, slowly, keeping his hands out in front of him, palms out. He swiveled his head to look at Greta across the wood block as he walked.

"When you're finished," Greta said to Staryles, "you may quarter him, pull him apart, and send his pieces to Jennifer Aiken at the Justice Department."

Staryles shoved Brendan forward. He entered another massive room, with couches arranged around in squares, with a grand piano, and a large river-stone fireplace. An entire wall of rear-facing windows, floor-to-ceiling. These provided a view of the back lawn sloping up and away to a border of evergreens. There was a long, rectangular garden there. Even from here Brendan could see corn stalks.

Greta's voice floated in from the kitchen.

"Do it in the garden," she said. "Just like he killed our Kevin."

CHAPTER FORTY-NINE / SATURDAY, 6:13 AM

NBC was on the television. A reporter stood in front of a scene of mayhem in Manhattan. The message scrolled beneath the reporter on the screen: *Emergency Broadcast System urges you to stay in your home. Do not attempt to drive or to enter populated areas.*

The TV had been on all night.

Jennifer watched from the couch. She rubbed her arms for comfort while she listened to what the reporter was saying.

". . . A hospital that is unable to get fuel oil this morning, forced to relocate nearly two hundred patients. Police and fire departments are having difficulty communicating as internet services are still down, or have slowed to a crawl. All commercial flights at JFK and LaGuardia are still grounded. The Department of Transportation has reported multiple motor vehicle accidents due to GPS failures. Rioting continues in the Bronx and in Harlem, and spread overnight into Midtown and Downtown Manhattan. The Metro Transit Authority has suspended all subway travel."

The shot cut from the reporter to hand-held footage that was shaky and blurred. It was like watching video from Benghazi. People were breaking windows and pillaging businesses. Armored vehicles prowled the streets, whole garrisons of National Guardsmen formed phalanxes. The battle scenarios at Camp Edwards had come to life.

The reporter was looking more and more uncomfortable in her position along the West Side Highway. A caravan of police vehicles raced past behind her, lights blazing. She was about to speak when the camera filming her jostled and went dark.

After a few seconds of blank silence, the news anchor came on screen. "We seem to have lost the feed from Shelly. We have an expert on domestic terrorism standing by, Max Kamber from the Department of Defense. We're unable to get a satellite feed from Washington, but we have Max on our landline phone connection."

There was a headshot of a gray-haired man in his fifties, suspended in the corner of the screen.

The anchor tilted her head. "Professor Kamber, we've heard that this is the work of the cyber hacker group for hire. That the group was contracted by anti-Americans, possibly ISIL."

"That's right," came Kamber's disembodied voice.

More headshots now filled the image, one after another, among them many of the people she had met the previous night. She saw Gentian. She'd been standing beside him just twenty-four hours ago.

Jennifer let go of her arms started moving about the room. She began looking for supplies, anything she could find; her mother kept some money in an empty baking soda box in the kitchen. It was time to get moving.

She entered the kitchen. She riffled through the cabinets for food, dumping anything she could find into an old gym bag, and found the cash. Not much: a hundred and sixty-four dollars. The anchor's voice floated from the other room. "What makes a group like this willing to turn on their own country? The anti-American agenda is clear,

303

but many of the Nonsystem members are American citizens. What's the allure for them?"

Kamber responded: "This group is responsible for the proliferation of identity-concealing software such as Dark Wallet. But the government has consistently shut them down, and they're frustrated."

Jennifer checked the date on a jar of peanut butter, didn't have the patience to find it, tossed it in the bag anyway. "The internet is just like the financial system," Kamber continued. "And they're becoming entwined more and more — we've designed all the parts, but no one really understands how it operates."

Jennifer stepped back into the living room to look at the screen.

"Since they are truly unable to circumvent all regulations on the flow of currency, libertarian extremists like Nonsystem resort to this kind of domestic terrorism. This is an act of desperation. An attempt to send a message, that if they cannot be completely free to do whatever they want to online, they'll try to topple the internet itself."

Here it comes, thought Jennifer. It was just as Gentian had said it would be.

"But, they can't. Not completely. American counter-cyber-terrorism forces are too strong. And we have backup systems that even groups like this are unaware of. You're going to hear about that soon, I'm sure."

Back to the anchor. "Police are on the hunt to round up remaining members of Nonsystem, including this young woman, revealed to us just moments ago as Sloane Dewan."

Sloane's face appeared. She was smiling in the photo, which looked a few years old — eyes were bright and alive. Jennifer felt something knot deep inside of her. It was the same image she had used at her presentation in Washington just a few days ago.

"Dewan was known as the infamous 'Baby Sloane,'" an infant who miraculously survived an ad hoc birth in an alleyway and was rescued by heroic cop, Seamus Argon. Dewan is the adopted daughter of . . ."

A knock at the front door startled Jennifer.

CHAPTER FIFTY / SATURDAY, 6:25 AM

The garden behind the great camp sloped up towards the line of trees edging the property. It was enclosed by a split rail fence.

Staryles pointed at the latched gate. "Open it. Go in."

Brendan swung it open and stepped through. Staryles followed him.

Brendan said nothing. He walked further into the garden. He noted the vegetables. It brought back memories, from three years before, of Olivia Jane's garden, where Kevin Heilshorn lay fatally wounded in the dirt, taking his last breaths, staring up at the sky.

Brendan stopped and turned around, facing Staryles who was just a few yards away.

"Is this where she wants you to do it?" Brendan asked. "Right here?"

His heart rate had steadied. He remembered how he'd strived for a calm spirit before taking the Rebecca Heilshorn case, how his peace became disturbed during the course of that investigation, how it had taken three years to get it back.

Overhead, the sun was behind a thick smudge of clouds, temporarily withholding the rain, but ready to deluge again any moment.

"Thing is, Greta is no longer in with the right people," Brendan said. "You think she's calling this, you think she's in charge. But you're wrong. You're off the winning team."

Staryles lifted the gun higher, aiming at Brendan's head.

"What are you talking about?"

"Everyone has enemies, Staryles. And my enemy's enemy is my friend."

He lifted up his hands to either side of him, without thinking, turning his palms up, waiting for the rain.

Staryles' usually handsome face had become contorted, a thing from nightmares. He stepped close to Brendan, exuding evil.

Brendan thought of the book *The Great Divorce* and remembered the final line in the passage:

And that is why the Blessed will say 'We have never lived anywhere except in Heaven,' and the Lost, 'We were always in Hell.'

And both will speak truly.

Brendan looked past Staryles, to the house, where Greta Heilshorn stood watching through the windows.

"Oh well," Staryles said. And his finger moved against the trigger.

CHAPTER FIFTY-ONE / SATURDAY, 6:27 AM

Jennifer's father kept some old guns in the house. Turkey guns for the spring hunt on the Cape Cod National Seashore. One was an antique "long fowler" .75 caliber flintlock. The gun was a preposterous six feet long, used in colonial times. It hung above a framed picture of Marilyn Monroe in the back den.

The rest of the guns were locked in a gun cabinet in the den, and Jennifer didn't have the combination.

A shadow darkened the door behind the curtained glass. The knock came again. Jennifer froze. Not knowing whether to call out and ask who was there. The vehicle she'd borrowed — stolen, really — was in the driveway. Whoever was out there knew someone was inside.

The curtains were drawn around the rest of the living room except for the windows behind the couch. She snapped out of her paralysis and moved quietly to the couch, leaned on her knee and pulled the curtains closed. Her heart was pounding so hard she felt her throat closing up. The blood sang in her ears. She felt hunted by her own side.

But could she be sure who was out there? It could be a neighbor, checking on the house or wanting to discuss the crisis. Her first thoughts had been to arm herself, when the visitor could be totally harmless. It was a pattern of thought previously unfamiliar to her. Now she was wondering if the gun cabinet was something she could bust her way into. She needed to stop, get a grip. People needed to band together in times like this, not fall prey to paranoia.

More knocking. The way the doorframe rattled, it was not Eleanor Beech from two houses down Old Post Road. The dark shape loomed, the door shook; this was a man. And as she stood near the couch where she had drawn the blinds, she saw a figure pass. Another man, moving around to the back of the house. The shadow of the second figure slipped along above the couch.

She halted again. Her breath became fast and shallow. She was panicking. The shape at the front door suddenly dropped out of sight. She watched as a hand pushed through the black rubber cat door. The hand was closed in a loose fist. Then it opened, and something fell out. Her breathing stopped altogether. The hand withdrew, leaving sunflower seed casings in a small pile on the floor. The shape — Delaney's shape — stood back up on the other side of the glass. And then the glass shattered.

Jennifer broke into a run. She bounded down the short hallway which fed into the rear den. She grabbed the flintlock from the wall. It was a huge heavy beast of a gun, and she wielded it like a battering ram. She charged the pine gun cabinet with it. The first impact made a splintery crack. She drew back, gathered herself, and rammed again. The butt of the long gun burst through the wood. Yet she realized from the size of the hole she'd made it would do her little good like that. She needed the whole door open to get the shotgun out — her father kept an H&R Single Shot 10 in there, and that was the weapon she needed — and she had to get the ammunition and load it. But there was no time.

"Ms. Aiken?" The voice floated from the living room. A sing-song voice, a man enjoying himself. "Ms. Aiken."

She stood motionless with the flintlock in her hand. Nowhere else to go. This was a bungalow. There was only one door, and Delaney was there now. The person who'd gone around the back could come in a window, but that was it. She was trapped.

She turned the giant gun around in her hands so that she could point the barrel. Her heart pounded. She placed her feet shoulder-width apart and raised the barrel to point at the door to the den. She heard the creaking of footsteps of Delaney as he moved further into the house.

"Ms. Aiken? We need to talk."

What was he doing here? Delaney was an investigator from Oneida County. She was sure Bostrom had lost them during the chase two days ago, but it was certainly possible he had gone into the system and found her father and the address. Why ride all the way out here to Cotuit Bay? He had no jurisdiction here. There was only one answer. He meant to kill her.

"Ms. Aiken . . . Come on out from back there."

She couldn't take it anymore. Her entire body trembled. She stepped forward into the hallway and swung the big gun towards the living room. Delaney was there, his own weapon in his grip, a semi-automatic rifle. He looked at her for a moment, expressionless. He took in the sight of her, the flintlock she was holding, and then he broke out in a maniac grin.

"Holy shit," he said.

He stepped forward, smile faltering, and aimed the rifle at her. At the same time, she heard a noise from outside. The sound of engines approaching, the crunch of tires over gravel. Then, shouting. The other man out there was yelling something, trying to get Delaney's attention. He cocked his head to the side, listening. Then he locked on her with his dull, torpid eyes, and started to back away, returning to the living room.

Jennifer stepped back into the den. She rushed to the window and looked out at the driveway. Two black SUVs were pulling in behind what must have been Delaney's dark sedan. The doors of the first SUV opened. John Rascher stepped out.

"John!" It just burst out of her. He heard her, he must've heard her, because she saw his face tighten, alarm light up in his eyes. Then Delaney, probably back at the front door now, opened fire.

CHAPTER FIFTY-TWO/ SATURDAY, 6:33 AM

Staryles was standing a few paces from Brendan when his head whipped to the side. There was a burst of blood, and then Staryles toppled over. The sound followed a second later, a cracking gunshot from the treeline beyond the garden that rolled off the distant mountains.

Brendan moved quickly to where Staryles lay. He kicked the gun from the fallen man's hand. Half of Staryles' face was gone, leaving a twisted gristle of tissue and bone. Yet he was still alive — one eye ruptured, the other looking around in bewildered fashion.

Brendan turned his gaze to the trees surrounding the property, as they started coming out of the woods. He stood, just watching, expecting this, grateful for this, but momentarily paralyzed with a sense of complete unreality.

They were Argon's men. Ex-cops, firemen, highwaymen, carpenters, contractors, even a Best Buy manager — Russell Gide emerged among them, no longer wearing his striped tracksuit, but decked in cargo pants and a camouflage vest over a stained white t-shirt. Gide was also brandishing an automatic rifle. One man wore a bandolier of ammunition and was holding a video camera.

Above them, the storm approached over the mountains, ready to heave.

At Brendan's feet, Staryles gagged and sputtered. A blood bubble formed at his lips and burst. With his one eye, he looked up at Brendan and moaned as he strained to move. Staryles, with half his face in ruins, was trying to get up. The blood spurted from his neck, his carotid artery shredded, as he tried to stand.

Brendan stepped back from the gory spray of blood.

He realized he felt sorry for the crumpled man at his feet. Staryles was pure psychopath and a murderer. Yet Brendan found himself thinking about what could have led him to this, what turned his neural pathways to the electric pulses of a killer. It had to be more than loyalty, or a code. Staryles' drive was to be on the winning side. Maybe he thought the Heilshorn legacy was that side, and that Titan, and all of the multinational overlords like it, was the future. Or, maybe there was more. Brendan wondered if Alexander Heilshorn had been some kind of a surrogate father for Staryles, Greta a perverted mother figure.

She was being pulled away from the window now — Argon's friend, Santos, held her in his massive arms, dragging her back into the house. At the last second, she kicked against the glass. The reflection of the outside world shuddered from the blow as Santos hauled her away.

There were other men in there, too; hopefully one of them had Leah and was looking after her, keeping her safe.

Argon's men came down the hill, some of them stepping over the fence and into the garden, others walking towards the house. Eight of them, by Brendan's count — and he had only called Russell Gide. Gide had been his third of three phone calls following his release from Rikers. He'd called Sloane, Jennifer, and the man in the tracksuit. Not only had Gide been willing to help Brendan, he'd acted as if he'd been patiently awaiting the opportunity. Brendan's plan had only involved the need for a couple of men, to stop Jeremy Staryles and subdue

Greta, but even Leonard Dutko had shown up, the tall guy with his thick mustache, who'd been reluctant to go any further the previous year, citing the vulnerability of his wife and kids. They'd all turned out to help Brendan and kill the man who had haunted their lives.

Staryles was still trying to get up. He got one foot beneath him and then fell forward over the knee of the other leg, his obliterated face mashing into the mud.

"Where are you going to go?" Brendan's voice was quiet, almost a whisper.

A moment later and the rain came down, tap-tapping the pea plants, the beans, pattering against the large fronds of the zucchini, until it fell harder, filling the air with a riot of noise, like static turned up on an old TV.

Hopelessly, Staryles tried to crawl away through the mud. The men gathered around and Brendan turned his attention to them.

"Shovels are in the basement," Brendan said. He turned and swept his hand over the garden.

The men glanced at the plants, then down at Staryles.

"We calling in EMS for him?" It was a gray-haired man who spoke. Brendan didn't know his name. They all watched Staryles, who was now hardly moving. He had managed to get over onto his stomach, one arm outstretched in front of him, as if reaching for the house.

His body went limp.

"Alright," said Brendan.

He squatted down and looked into Staryles' face. Staryles was dead.

Brendan rose to his feet. The rain was soaking his clothes — the jeans and sweatshirt get-up. Brendan blinked away the moisture, but the rain beat at his scalp and ran down his face in rivulets; he felt one runnel coursing down his nose. The rain washed the bit of cover-up from his face, revealing his scar.

"This is crazy," said Russell Gide. His lanky body was like a livewire. "I just fucking shot that guy."

Gide bent forward and threw up on his shoes.

CHAPTER FIFTY-THREE / SATURDAY, 6:38 AM

She saw Rascher get hit. The impact of the bullet threw him back against the SUV. The men with him were soldiers from Edwards. They spread out and returned fire on Delaney and his associate. The rounds exploded like fireworks. *Pop. Pop-pop-pop.* Jennifer dropped away from the window and rolled her body against the wall. It was like being in the middle of a war. Amid the cacophony, she worked her way back to the gun cabinet. Lying on her back, she was able to reach up with her feet and start kicking at the door, working the ragged hole she'd made with the turkey gun into a larger opening. She kicked and thrashed at it with her feet, gunshots popping all around the outside of her house, the rattle of automatic fire issuing from the living room. Her ears were ringing. In the middle of it all she realized she was screaming.

One last sharp kick and the piece of wood bearing the latch gave way. She spun herself around on the floor and, on her belly now, reached up and jimmied the door all the way open. The bottom of the cabinet was a row of cubby bins. She sifted through the boxes of ammo until she came up with the 10 gauge shells. She shook a few out of the box. She could only use one at a time in the H&R.

Shotgun shell in hand, she hoisted herself to her knees, reached up and released the heavy weapon from its bracket. The thing weighed a ton, more than the flintlock. She laid the gun over her thighs. The H&R was a break action. She thumbed the release to drop open the barrel. There was no safety. No half cock. You pulled back the hammer, aimed, and destroyed. Her father would go on and on about it. Referring to it as the "kitchen door gun." She shoved the shell into the barrel and snapped it closed. The gun was loaded.

The firefight continued. Delaney was still in the living room. His partner must have fled into the woods between the houses, because the shots seemed to concentrate in that direction. There was a path in those woods that led to a small creek. She remembered crossing the creek as a little girl. Just a few feet wide, it had seemed like the Mississippi.

Jennifer got to her feet. She stepped out into the hallway. Not wasting any time. She walked to the end and into the living room. Delaney was right where she'd pinpointed him in her mind, just inside the door, squeezing off rounds into the driveway, lips pulled back and teeth bared in a death mask. He didn't even see her as she came into the room. She didn't announce herself, didn't make a sound. She only breathed, once in, once out, and took aim. She saw the face of the little girl in the back of Stemp's car, saw Delaney turn the gun on that little girl's mother. She squeezed the trigger.

The one thing her father had always pointed out about the old single-barrel shotguns was that while they were simpler, and cheaper, than the double-barrel, the kickback was much more severe. The second the shot exploded out of the barrel, the massive 10 gauge recoil threw her back against the wall. She almost dropped the gun but managed to keep her grip on it as she hit. She kept her eyes open, too, watching as the shot buried into Delaney's shoulder, his neck, his jaw. The automatic rifle fell out of his grip. Blood immediately started running from his busted arteries. He fell against the recliner just inside the doorway, his eyes wide, his mouth gasping like the last catch of the day.

CHAPTER FIFTY-FOUR / SATURDAY, 7:14 AM

Brendan watched the men pitch dirt over their shoulders. After a short time, he moved along the edge of the house. He rounded the far corner of the building. This was where he had arrived. He slipped into the garage, the same way he had done just a half an hour before.

Back in the basement, he made his way over to where the tools were, squinting to see in the gloom. Santos was upstairs with the girl. Brendan paused, listening to the piano playing softly under the chatter of rain — the music silken even as it was muffled by the floor. Leah, her small fingers dancing over the keys. Santos had made her feel secure and comfortable enough to play. That was good.

The Heilshorns had legal custody of the girl. She was theirs. No judge or social worker in the world would turn Leah Heilshorn over to any of Brendan's people, nor to him. He was a fugitive. And in a matter of hours, he wouldn't exist. It didn't matter what he knew or what he'd been caught up in — more importantly, what he'd been trying to extricate himself from.

Leonard Dutko and a fireman named Chris Kelley had brought Greta Heilshorn into the basement. They had lashed her hands behind her back and tied her to a chair.

Brendan found it fitting, as he imagined Jennifer Aiken once in a similar position, on Alexander Heilshorn's orders.

Brendan stood looking at the older woman.

"You're going to lose Leah," he said.

Greta's mouth twisted into a rind of silence. Her pewter eyes drove at him, the whites wrecked with red capillaries. She still wore her apron, pale brown with lace edging. An ankle-gray skirt beneath. Not a run in her stockings. Soft, comfortable shoes on her feet. Her teeth clicked together. She was biting at the air, which he wondered if she was aware of.

He jerked a thumb towards the back of the house. "Right now, outside, men are digging in your garden. I know what they're going to find. *You* know what they're going to find."

He searched her face. He could hear Leonard Dutko behind him, the air whistling through his nostrils, standing with his rifle in his hands.

Brendan went on. "Greta, one way or the other, you're going to lose her. She's not yours — she never was; you're all done. I know who her father really is, who has a legal claim to her. And that's Philip Largo."

There was a glimmer in her eyes. He could feel her resolve, hardened and refined over years of stubbornness and secrecy. He couldn't expect to break her in just a few minutes.

"Think about it, Greta. It's the chance of a lifetime. A man who was smeared by a sex scandal after being lured by one of your own pros. He finds out you've been keeping his daughter all these years? More, the press find out? I know that you've got all kinds of faith in Titan. I know your husband struck his deal — years ago — with the government, with the FBI, with the Federal Reserve, and their CSS army. But you're forgetting about the public. You're forgetting history. Marginalized people come back for their revenge. They come back with pitchforks. Or, you know, shovels."

He waited. The two of them stared at each another for almost a minute before he spoke again. His voice was soft, his hands were steady. In the distance he thought he could hear the shovels breaking ground in the garden.

"You have a chance to do something, Greta. Help yourself. Help her — help her so she grows up never having to know what kind of a monster you are. Somewhere, you have the names; all of the women who ever worked for XList. All of their children you use to keep them working. All of the businessmen and politicians who are their fathers. All of the ways in which you and your husband have manipulated the system, buying legislation, the judiciary, funding everything with your black-market enterprise. You're going to send out the order, Greta, to let every one of those women and children go. From the top of your pyramid, you're going to send the information down through the organization. Because you're not going to bury me up there like you wanted to. I'm never going to stop."

Greta remained stone-faced. Her acidic words were delivered calmly, "Your family is cursed and dead. Your mother, father, your wife and child. You have nothing."

Brendan took a step towards her as the rain intensified outside. He'd put a pistol to her husband's head seven months ago. He'd gunned down her son long before that. He'd stood in the bedroom of the farmhouse in Remsen and looked down at her bloody, cut-up daughter on his first and only case as a county detective. He thought of telling Greta these things — that she was only seeing a reflection of herself — but he didn't need to.

Instead, he turned and walked to where the old rotary phone hung on the wall next to the workbench.

He listened for a dial tone, then stuck his finger in the plate and rotated the old spider-spring assembly to enter in a long distance number. He hoped the Heilshorn's had long distance. Their home wasn't exactly cheap, he thought, glancing at the restored guide boat and thinking of the cathedral windows above, the grand piano, Heilshorn's buildings in Manhattan, his house in Scarsdale, his billions in investments.

Probably they had long distance.

Yeah.

He turned and watched Greta where she sat framed in the gray light seining through the garage-door windows as the line on the other end rang. Did she look curious? Maybe. Perhaps, mildly.

"Hello?" said a voice.

"It's Brendan Healy," he said, still looking at Greta.

"Brendan. I'm glad to hear you." The connection was scratchy.

"Where are you getting this call?"

"This is a SAT phone," said Didier Lazard, sounding a bit like a child describing a favorite toy. "This is the first conversation on this phone, and there is no way to tap the line, unless it's on your end. Is everything well?"

"Yes. How does it feel? You're out."

Greta kept her head turned away, but he knew she was listening.

"Oh, most definitely out. Most definitely." The word *definitely* was hard for Lazard to pronounce, as though he had marbles in his mouth. There was a whirring white noise in the background. It sounded like Lazard was flying. "I will take care of everything now. Philip Largo is my first call."

"That's good. And you've visited the garden?"

"Just about to."

"Is she cooperating?"

Brendan felt a smile curl the edges of his mouth. "Not really."

"Well, you tell her. Tell her Didier says hello. I have the best law enforcement money can buy all set on this. And a racketeering charge requires the proof of multiple predicate crimes, so we've got plenty of good prosecutors, too."

Brendan listened, watching Greta. She couldn't feign complete apathy now. She was definitely showing some agitation, her teeth still clicking, and now rubbing her bony fingers together. Brendan said aloud for her benefit: "That's right. Separate murders, extortion, prostitution, human trafficking. They'll need to prove at least two of those beyond a reasonable doubt. To show how Greta was part of this enterprise that was committing all these crimes for the past twenty-five years."

"You know why she plays it cool, yes?"

Brendan stared into her. "I do."

"Huh? Right, my friend? But money talks, bullshit walks."

Being associated with someone like Lazard wasn't easy. But these were dirty deeds, and he was the man for the job.

"You don't have to worry," Lazard said from faraway, "I am the one calling the shots . . . Now that I have left the IMF, I have more power and influence than I'd ever dreamed." He chuckled, a sound scattered and broken up by the remote connection.

"Thank you, Didier."

"Oh thank *you,* my friend. We'll be in touch again soon. Your flight is all prepared."

Brendan hung up the phone slowly. The bell inside made a light chime as he set the handset in the cradle. "That was Didier Lazard," he said. He turned to face Greta again.

"I know who it was."

He nodded. He looked down at his feet, and scuffed a shoe against the gritty basement floor.

"Then you know that the biggest worry on Lazard's mind is that the BRICS nations — Brazil, Russia, India, China and South Africa — are going to set up an international bank to rival the IMF. His former organization. And that the US petrodollar will be out of the world market as the number one currency for buying oil. To Lazard's thinking, the US dollar will collapse in a short time and the BRICS nations will be in place to take over with either a gold-backed Ruble or Yuan. He wants to be where the future is, Greta. It seems everyone does. You know all this because your husband was willing to do anything to keep the power for himself, for Titan, to wage war in the Middle East for decades to come, if necessary, and to suppress any populist ideas about money, like Nonsystem's ideas. That's why Lazard has been covertly funding Nonsystem for the last three years. Philomena Argon came to him with the information she had on Titan. And he's prepared to spend unlimited sums of money on the Justice Department and the FBI to ensure full cooperation in prosecuting you and XList to the fullest extent of the law."

Brendan crossed the room and crouched down in front of Greta.

"Personally, I don't care about all the geopolitics. I just want those women and children — and the men too — I want them free. And they will be. Because, well, Greta, Lazard has more money than you do."

CHAPTER FIFTY-FIVE / SATURDAY, 7:14 AM

The breeze coming off the bay rustled the trees and raised the dirt and gravel. Her hearing was returning to normal after yet another deafening round of gunplay, and the birds resumed their singing.

Rascher looked up at the sky. "You're coming with me," he said, and offered a wan smile. There was blood between his teeth.

A soldier came trotting up behind them. He took a knee beside Rascher. "I'm alright," Rascher said to him. Jennifer and the soldier helped Rascher to his feet. There was a dark, growing stain on his crisp white shirt. Blood pooled along his belt and pattered to the dirt driveway, turning the light brown dust black. He leaned against the SUV and looked off at Jennifer's family home where two other soldiers dragged a man out of the woods. Delaney's partner.

Delaney himself was still in the house. With the front door part way open, she could see the soles of his shoes. He'd fallen over like that when she'd shot him. His feet jerked with the spasms of his body. A soldier inside the house stepped into view, holding a rifle. He stood over the fallen investigator.

Jennifer turned away from the scene. "I have to check on the neighbor, Eleanor Beech. She's old."

She let go of Rascher and started off in the other direction when a hand caught her by the arm.

Jennifer looked down at the hand holding her. She could see every detail in that moment. The skin split over one of the knuckles. The blood spatter pattern along the inner ridge and the thumb. Then she looked up at the soldier. His eyes were iron blue.

"Let her go," Rascher said.

The soldier released his grip and Jennifer walked away from the house.

She passed by the small cherubim statues her mother kept flanking the front driveway. The morning was warm, already high in the seventies. She turned onto Old Post Road. She'd walked this way many times as a kid, often in bare feet, heading down to the water. The rising sun winked from behind the maples. A squirrel darted across her path. Her mind was nearly empty, her thoughts some kind of background noise, far away.

Behind her came a loud crack; a single report of gunfire.

She turned down the driveway to the Beech home, which was nestled among the trees. Wind chimes dangled over the front door, tolling crystal sounds. The house was dark, no vehicle parked in front. Luckily Eleanor Beech was not home today. Still, Jennifer walked to the door and sat on the single step. She stuck her legs out in front of her. She saw that her pants were torn around the ankle and she was bleeding there. She'd cut herself kicking in the gun cabinet. She dug out a splinter embedded in the flesh. She felt the stubble on her skin and realized it had been three days since she'd shaved her legs. When the tears came, she was barely aware of them. She let go of her leg, placed her palms on the stair, tilted her head back, and closed her eyes.

The wind dried her face. She heard the gulls calling over the water. She opened her eyes and got up. She dusted off her backside and walked away from the Beech home. Back down Old Post Road, back to her family's summer home, back to the soldiers from Camp Edwards and a wounded John Rascher, back to her life.

There was no more running.

She reached them as two soldiers were hefting Rascher into the SUV. She glanced at the front door. Delaney was no longer there. She thought she could hear the soldier who'd executed him drag him deeper into the house. Delaney's partner was no longer outside. Jennifer guessed he was in the house, too.

When she saw the first flames lick out the den window towards the back of the place, she felt nothing. She only stood and watched the fire grow until the soldiers came out. This time when they hooked into her armpits and walked her to the SUVs she didn't pull away or protest.

She let them place her in the back of the vehicle. Rascher was back with her, holding a compress to his side. His color was bad, his lips already waxy, but she thought he would make it. For some reason men like Rascher always made it. The soldiers got in. The two SUVs backed out of the driveway and drove off.

CHAPTER FIFTY-SIX / SATURDAY, 7:33 AM

A ghost, Brendan thought, and splashed water on his face in Greta's lavish bathroom. There was a vanity with a basin sink and blackened brass features. Lantern-style sconces on the wall. Wicker baskets piled with pristine white towels. In the center of the room was an antique copper tub. They were the kind of touches he remembered from the newly renovated room at the Bloomingdale house where Rebecca Heilshorn had been slain in her bed.

There was a noise downstairs. He listened and heard Leah playing the piano. A moment later it stopped, and then there was thudding across the floor. More bounding around the place like all six-year-olds probably did. Then the muffled call from Santos, more thumping, and the piano playing resumed. Leah had seemed healthy enough, normal enough, but there was no doubt in his mind that whatever Greta Heilshorn had been cultivating the girl for, it wasn't a normal life filled with piano lessons and tap dance recitals. There were these things, but then there was the darkness of the life Greta Heilshorn was running. A brothel madam — XList — and the legacy of Titan.

A few moments later, slightly spruced up and feeling a little more together, Brendan stood in the living room as

Leah played. She glanced at him, giving him a quick once-over. She didn't know who he was, nor would she ever. She would come to know her father, though. Philip Largo would be the only one who would have the chance at custody now.

Brendan left the main room and went out the back door, through which Staryles had marched him an hour ago, towards his death.

The rain had slackened off some, but the men were drenched as they dug into the wet heavy earth. It might take hours with only the five of them working. Brendan found a shovel and joined them. Dutko followed suit a few minutes later, leaving Greta behind with Chris Kelley. A half an hour later, and they had found their first body. Dutko was able to ID him as a medical examiner from Westchester County.

Twenty minutes after that, and the second body was found. Brendan knew who it was. Though significantly decomposed, Brendan was sure the buried man was Wyn Weston, the Justice Department agent missing for months.

They unearthed two more, one nothing more than bones and cloth. It would take time in the lab to verify dental records, but Brendan was sure the corpse would be revealed as Damon Cosgrove, the truck driver who'd killed his wife and daughter. The other, a more recent addition to the cemetery in the garden, was sure to be Lawrence Taber. Brendan recognized the body type, the man's size and athletic build. His heart was heavy with the family's loss; Taber left behind a wife and son.

Russell Gide turned to Brendan, smiling in the rain. His anxiety seemed to have worked itself out through the hard labor. His gaze wandered over the graves. "Crazy. Right on their own property. Why not burn them? Sink them in the lake?"

Brendan didn't know. Heilshorn had always been right out in the open. Hiding in plain sight. Maybe Greta was the same way, with a macabre twist. Growing food from dirt holding the dead.

The men gathered around and looked down at the shallow graves.

There was one more body to add.

Staryles didn't exist. Not on paper. He was designed to disappear. But his body was here.

Gide handed Brendan the package Brendan had sent him from the Sheraton in New York. Brendan opened it and took out his old identification. His wallet with his ID — even his badge from Oneida County. He placed these in Staryles' pockets. He dragged Staryles' body into one of the graves recently emptied. He held a gardening tool from the basement in his hand.

He thought about Argon as he knocked out Staryles' teeth. Argon's body had been tampered with as it lay on the morgue slab. The anger helped Brendan keep back the gag reflex as he removed one of Staryles' fingers, snapping the digit like a twig.

He thought about the near future, how money would pass between key hands, and how nearly all of the individuals Alexander Heilshorn had ever marked for death would be accounted for. At least in the eyes of the law.

At last he climbed out of the grave and gazed down through the rain at Staryles' unrecognizable face.

Gide passed Brendan the can of kerosene.

* * *

Brendan rode in the ADK Taxi to the small airport. He smoked a cigarette with the woman driver, the same one who had picked him up from the train.

The airport was tiny, out in the middle of nowhere. Commercial flights were grounded due to the total disintegration of the internet. Air Traffic Control wasn't allowing charters until further notice. But, as Lazard said, money talked. A lone Cessna commuter plane sat on the tarmac in the sheets of rain. From inside the lounge, looking at the plane through the glass, Brendan spoke on a payphone to Russell Gide.

Gide described the scene at the Heilshorns. The police had arrived — both local and state — and exhumed the remaining bodies from the garden. Prior to their arrival, Argon's men had taken video of the entire scene, and then placed their anonymous call, taken Leah, left Greta Heilshorn in the basement, and disappeared.

Within a short time, as expected, the whole property became the exclusive domain of the feds. There would be nothing in the papers about Wyn Weston's body, or any of the others, or of the Heilshorns. Maybe the local paper, the Adirondack Daily Enterprise, would try to write something, but the editor would receive a call from a no-nonsense FBI agent issuing a gag order. The editor would probably put up a fight, if she had any salt, about the right to free speech, and the federal agent would remind her, *this is a matter of national security.*

But Philip Largo would get his daughter back, and XList would be soon be over. The internet wouldn't be down forever, and even if Altnet emerged and was everything CSS hoped it would be — a completely regulated and government controlled internet, there was no way the people could be silenced, no way the truth could be stopped. Brendan felt like he was proof of that. He felt like Argon's men were proof of that.

CHAPTER FIFTY-SEVEN / SUNDAY, 10:42 AM

The private charter plane descended over the Cayman Islands on a Sunday morning. Brendan looked out the window at the bursts of palm tree tops and turquoise water with its frothy white fringe.

Lazard met him at the gate. He looked completely at home in a short-sleeved shirt and linen pants, and sandals. He greeted Brendan warmly, shaking his hand with both of his large mitts. Then he stepped back, his eyes lingering over Brendan's pale complexion.

"You need some sun," he said.

Outside, the heat was like a sudden hug. The tropical breeze ruffled the Cape Rush surrounding the tiny airport terminal. He watched the birds cut silhouettes through the blue sky. He turned his head in the direction of the surf. He gazed out at it as they walked, Lazard chatting away about the weather and the sights.

Brendan realized he'd never been to a place quite like this. He'd never even been to Florida. He'd spent his entire life in the north, even those four years he'd checked out of society, he'd never wandered south.

"Hey," he heard.

They were in the parking lot, shining cars lined up. Lazard was standing by a convertible.

"You good?"

Brendan nodded.

* * *

They drove down the road with Lazard's dark hair blowing about his head. He finally took to clamping down on it with one of his hands.

Brendan looked over. Three days of beard stubble matched his shaved head. "Too much wind?"

Lazard grinned. "I love it," he called back.

"How far is it?"

"Couple more miles," answered Lazard. He then cut Brendan a sideways glance, taking in his altered appearance. "What do I call you now, huh?"

Brendan stared up at the blazing sun. "William Chase."

"William Chase? Can I call you Billy?"

"No."

"How about Will. 'Will Chase.' That is appropriate, huh?"

Brendan smiled, but his mind was elsewhere. He thought of Donald Kettering, the hardware store owner from Boonville, father of Rebecca's one other child. Rebecca Heilshorn had named their daughter Aldona, which was an anagram of Donald.

Ever since he'd first laid eyes on her, Brendan knew Rebecca had had something to tell him.

* * *

The Ugland House was a building containing thousands of safety deposit boxes. Over 18,000 corporations from around the world were registered. Many of the corporations would claim to have offices on the premises, though there was no economic activity at The Ugland House. It was a place solely for the books.

"The bulk of corporations in the registry are your US corporations," Lazard said as they neared. "Using the international tax rules to shift profits out of the US, a high tax rate country, into this, a low tax rate country." He glanced at Brendan. "The tax rate here is zero percent."

Lazard's large fingers wrapped around the steering wheel at 10 and 2. "You allocate as much as possible of your income to low rate countries, keep as much of your expenses on the books in your high rate countries, and hey, bingo. Or is it Yahtzee? But by any reasonable standard, when most of your business is in the US, most of the know-how, the research, the production is there. The profits that are taxed should also be there, yes?"

"Yes," Brendan said. It wasn't a political answer. With everything he had seen over the past ten years of his life, it was the only answer.

"Seventy billion a year in potential revenue lost to offshore tax shelters," Lazard said. "And the CEOs come down here and eat dinner at the Westin Grand and look out at the ocean like gods."

They turned into the parking lot outside The Ugland House. The space was surrounded by Royal Palms, tall and bent, like sleepy sentinels. The high sun hit the fronds and threw long, crisscrossing shadows over the weather-bleached pavement. There were only a few cars in the lot, parked far away.

"But," said Lazard, "there's no real money here. From a few private individuals, yes. But the corporate dollars, any physical dollars, are in the US onshore."

He zipped into a parking space, put the convertible in park and seemed to sink into his seat, the engine still purring beneath the expansive hood.

Lazard settled into a contemplative silence, rubbing at his face. Then he killed the engine and turned to Brendan and smiled, his jowls lifting into creases of skin. "What's here is even better."

* * *

Lazard had a key to one of the boxes. He withdrew the contents and brought Brendan into a small room designated for box owners to view their inventory in private. Along the way to the room, a pretty, dark-skinned clerk smiled at Lazard, who grinned back and gave her a full up-and-down appraisal with his eyes.

Once in the room, Lazard stood in front of a wall of security boxes with a certain reverence, as if the boxes themselves were holy artifacts.

"There was a finite supply of bitcoin to begin with, but it is expansionary," Lazard said. "Just like the money we spend every day that we think runs the world, it is completely faith-based, imaginary; it only has value based on the value that we give it. As long as people believe in it, whether it's paper or it's digital, it's a viable means of commerce. But, by hiding your online transactions, being able to do whatever you want without Uncle Sam, the IRS, or the banks involved?"

He reached up and ran two paw-like hands through his thick hair.

"'Oh boy,' you say. That is terrifying to your US Government, more of a threat than they would ever let on publicly." He dropped his hands to his sides and turned to Brendan. "So, what do they do? How do they stop it? Take out the new libertarian frontier? But the internet is not something you can just unplug, yes? Not unless there is a major attack. Something to blow it up and chop it up. And then, all of the executive orders kick in. The country is yours to control without anyone saying differently."

He stepped in so close that Brendan could smell the suntan lotion on his skin, the sweet *café con leche* on his breath.

"But really you have generated this attack yourself," Lazard said. "You have a frame-up for a group of hackers, libertarians with high digital IQs, but not actual terrorists. So what? You say they did it; they did it. Meanwhile your own Cyber Division under the CSS has been running around sabotaging the data centers and cutting the sub-oceanic cables and setting C-4 explosives and leaving behind the clues that Nonsystem is responsible, killing anyone who knows otherwise."

Lazard then held up his hands in mock alarm, making his eyes wide for effect. "'My God. Look what these cyber terrorists did! But don't worry." Then he reached out and threw an arm around Brendan, miming a good buddy, lowering the pitch of his voice. "Don't worry everybody, rest assured, because we, your government, we have a surprise for you. We have a backup internet! Well, it's completely regulated by us. But, you'll be able to do all the things you love to do like shop Amazon and check your email and post pictures on Facebook and go to Etsy and get knitted booties for baby. This is going to be a lot better for you. A lot safer. Because it's your safety we have in mind.'"

Lazard stepped back and shook his head, incredulous at his own words. Then his eyes, dark around the edges, but afire in the center, homed in on Brendan.

"But that's just the icing on the cake, you see. Because really in doing all of this you've managed to spoil all the encryption applications which have been developed over the past twenty years for civilian privacy." He slapped the back of his hand into his palm with a loud crack. "You've eliminated privacy in the digital world. Gone. There is no more *Silent Circle* or *HTTP Everywhere*. Project Bullrun becomes a success by default. There's no more deep web, no Dark Wallet, nothing left enciphered or stealthy. It's total exposure for the people, complete access for the government. The exact, and I mean *exact* opposite of how it was intended. Congratulations, Mr. William Chase, your country has come full circle."

Lazard walked to one of the boxes and slipped a key from his loose pants. He opened the door and withdrew a long slender metal box. He brought the box to the table in the center of the room and set it down. The room was refrigerator cold.

"Of course, you'll never be able to prove that," Lazard said. He looked from the box on the table to Brendan. "No one can. Some cases, as your US Attorney General might say, are too big to prosecute."

Brendan folded his arms in the cool air. "But Greta Heilshorn will go down. That's what you wanted, Didier. You're not a martyr. You wanted the Heilshorns trashed, XList revenue clamped off, and Titan to take a blow because they'd been moving in on your own turf with bitcoin enterprises. And you want to watch the global petrodollar fail."

"I'm not hiding it."

Brendan stepped away from the table and dropped his arms. Suddenly he wanted a drink. He hadn't felt such a craving since he'd been at Rikers. It was sudden and powerful, rolling up through his nervous system like a flash fire. But then it dissipated as he brought himself under control.

He had to make peace with this. Within himself. It was hard to love your country and to see the truth behind the lies at the same time. But, it was possible. They didn't have to be mutually exclusive.

Since he'd looked Heilshorn in the eyes that day at Roosevelt Hospital he'd understood that he was looking into the face of something which had taken seed in the country a century before. An exploitation of the love and faith of the people, a manipulation of the system that cost lives. He'd known even then, without proof, Heilshorn had been working with the government. He'd almost blurted it out to Jennifer Aiken when she'd come to Rikers. But he hadn't. He'd tried to keep her safe. It hadn't worked out too well, but at least she was still alive. And Sloane? There were mixed reports. Some indicated she'd been captured. Others speculated she was still at large. If Lazard knew, he wasn't saying, not even to Brendan. If

Sloane was free, she'd be deep underground. Never to come up again.

There was some strange relief in that.

Lazard had fallen silent. It was all on the table now, like the security box. Out on the table, but enclosed in this room, within the walls of The Ugland House. Where the world kept its secrets. While the titans dined, as Lazard had said, at the Westin Grand.

"Like we discussed," Lazard said finally, opening the box, "Philomena Argon and Sloane Dewan were always working with me. I was personally helping to finance Nonsystem. Even now there are Nonsystem hackers all over the world learning the protocols of the Altnet, how to get past the firewalls and logins. But, I've come to know you, Mr. William Chase. You don't care about any of that. You want this. More, you want this because *she* wants this. Aiken."

He pulled a smooth, black storage drive from the box and held it in the air in front of Brendan.

"But you also know, as does she, that proof of a private equity firm funding the collapse of American freedom, and the rise of totalitarianism, will never see the light of day. How does the government prosecute itself? This is your American conundrum, yes? But, all that said, this I give to you. The backup of all Philomena's data. Everything she was working on while with me at the IMF, and with her brother, and with Sloane. You can send it to your friend in the Justice Department, to Ms. Aiken. But, like I said, it won't do you any good. You'd be better off dressing in some cargo pants and going door to door with a fine-toothed comb, Mr. Chase, and going down this list one name at a time. Maybe that's the only way left."

He paused for a moment, giving Brendan another look. "Keep you from drinking, anyway."

CHAPTER FIFTY-EIGHT / MONDAY, 9:12 AM

In the Russell Building on Capitol Hill in Washington DC, the Senate Select Intelligence Committee on Current and Projected Threats to the US had assembled in a massive room. From her desk on the floor in front of the broad dais, Jennifer looked up at the senators and *ex officio* members, their names on placards in front of them.

Seated along the platform were the National Counterterrorism Center Director, the FBI Director, Director of National Intelligence, and the Director of the CIA. There was also the Defense Intelligence Agency Director, and the Assistant Secretary of State for Intelligence and Research. So many ranks, so many departments.

Conspicuously absent was the director of the NSA and the CSS. In his stead sat Brigadier General Wick, seated behind the FBI Director. Where the other men wore their crisp suits, Wick was in full formal military attire, his medals glinting in the bright overhead lights.

Their names, ranks, positions — these felt pointless. She found it hard to concentrate on them, on who they were, men she had come to know over the years, but men she had never really known at all. She found it hard to keep their names straight in her head, when there was only one name she could think about.

He had been listed in a department brief along with the other bodies discovered at the Heilshorn mansion in the Adirondack Mountains of Upstate New York. One name in what the media, with what little they knew, were calling a tragic shootout over the sinister black market enterprise known as XList. Brendan Healy, once a cop on the case of the murdered escort Rebecca Heilshorn, was counted among the dead, his body badly burned.

The men and women on the platform were sworn in, raising their right hands in the air. The *ex officio* group was composed of the same individuals — save for Fogarty, the CIA head — who had served on another recent committee that had found that the CIA had misled the government and the public concerning its interrogation program during the long wars in Iraq and Afghanistan. The Department of Justice had been involved then, too, to testify that the enhanced interrogation tactics employed by the CIA were effective in obtaining unique intelligence helping to disrupt terrorist plots and save lives.

Now the CIA sat on the panel, represented by Fogarty, and it was a former agent of the Department of Justice who was about to be questioned. It was a game of musical chairs. A puppet show.

"Ms. Aiken, thank you for being here today," said Robert Cole, the Director of National Intelligence. Cole was the ad-hoc chairman of the committee, a handsome man in his mid-sixties with kind eyes.

Jennifer leaned towards the microphone. "Thank you very much, Mr. Chairman. It's a pleasure to be here."

When in Rome, she thought.

* * *

Thirty minutes later, and the pleasantries were a faint memory. Jennifer was out for blood.

"Mr. Chairman, the face of propaganda is complex. The problems of our country are systemic — most every one of us believes we're working towards some version of the greater good. And we have a balkanized media to support our worldview."

She took a nervous fumbling sip of her water, then steadied herself.

"What ultimately brings everyone here today is not some nefarious secret plan. It's been right out in the open. We have a sort of critical obliviousness as a society, and are prone to the fallacy that everything as it is, will *stay* the way it is. Yet everything around us has evolved and grown. Population, technology, our laws. We normalize it, acclimatize to it, until the next thing comes along. Like cell-phone interceptor towers. Police responding to demonstrations with IRAD sirens and BearCat armored cars and Sky Watch towers. Surveillance that has people detained in airports for their tweets, cops knocking down doors for Facebook posts, FBI investigations launched over 'Un-American' sentiment. Or maybe, if you will, Article 215 of the Patriot Act. Liberty's at a tipping point, Mr. Chairman."

She took a breath and pressed on.

"The people know they're being monitored. Some of them consider these instances of detainment as 'taking one for the team.' In the interest of that greater good, to disrupt terrorist plots, to stop the next mass murderer or respond to the next Waco. But to anyone who takes a look, there is little to justify these measures. FBI stings that lure in potential threats, aid them in obtaining materials to commit acts of domestic destruction. CIA interrogation tactics not yielding vital information, and then dissembled about. A US citizen today is nearly sixty-times more likely to be killed by an officer of the law than a terrorist. The conspiracy theorists are called paranoid, but I have to wonder, Mr. Chairman, if the paranoia isn't on the other side? The side that says we justify all of this with the 'known unknowns' — the threats we consider possible but have no evidence of. Is it probable that we might actually be contributing to some of these threats? Alexander Heilshorn was out to make money, something obviously sanctioned — practically considered a holy endeavor — in our culture, but perhaps he believed he was serving his nation by aiding in the proliferation of a militarized police force, by contributing to an event which—"

Cole held up his hand and cut her off. "Ms. Aiken, I appreciate your overview of the situation in America. Let that be sufficient. But meandering as deep into conjectural territory as you are about to, you're implicating the American government in a . . ." He glanced down at his notes, which, Jennifer felt, was purely for effect, ". . . A false-flag event." He looked up. "Ms. Aiken, we're not here today for an ethics lesson. We're here because a terrorist group known as Nonsystem staged and executed a series of cyber-attacks and ground-based attacks on US soil to incapacitate the Internet and wreak havoc on municipal services, to endanger the lives of innocents. An attack on the homeland. Now, you're sitting there talking about how ineffective our intelligence community is, how despite all our efforts we only glean useless information. But didn't this intelligence community help to prevent what could have been an even worse attack?"

Jennifer's heart raced. She glanced to the side and thought she saw General Wick smiling faintly. He was gazing off into the room, as if he couldn't be bothered to look at her.

"Mr. Chairman . . ."

The hand in the air again, and Cole was bobbing his head as if to say *We've heard your story, and we're finished with it.*

"Ms. Aiken, you should feel proud to have been a part of something that was able to keep a disaster from becoming an apocalypse. And I choose that word with no intent of hyperbole."

"Mr. Chairman, you make it sound like this is a debriefing—"

"Well, it's not a *trial*," he said with sudden force. He glowered at her as his words reverberated throughout the cavernous space.

His outburst had an unexpected effect on her; instead of flustering her or scaring her, Jennifer felt her pulse easing, her breathing relax. Meanwhile, Cole was frustrated, bordering on irate.

"Mr. Chairman," she said softly, "in discovery, I described how I will be able to show how Titan was laundering its income and channeling it into the —"

"This committee is not acknowledging such evidence. We have no way to identify its source or validate its authenticity, Ms. Aiken. As a former prosecutor, I'd think you would be able to understand the painstaking evidence threshold of jurisprudence. Those documents could've come from the moon."

No. Not from the moon. From the dead.

There was a ruffling of the committee as the other delegates began talking to each other, some of them chuckling. Cole put his hand over his microphone and leaned towards Bradley Gallup, the FBI Director. The two men spoke briefly. Jennifer could see FBI Agent Harlan Doherty, with his distinctive mustache, sitting towards the back of the dais. He shrugged at her and smiled.

Jennifer's lawyer leaned in and whispered to her, "I'm advising you to comport yourself. Back down, Jennifer. You're going to wind up in jail."

So what, she thought instantly. *Send me to jail. Or drag me through court for a few years; I don't care.*

But despite this sudden burst of freedom fighter spirit, the calmer, more rational voice of reason continued to assert itself.

That doesn't do anyone any good. Not you, not anyone. Maybe only the people — like Wick — who will gloat over your crucifixion. Don't give them the satisfaction.

And, one other thought. An image, really, and a feeling. A face. Brendan Healy's face, his humane eyes, his scars.

Brendan hadn't wanted to make a deal with the DOJ. He'd had his own way out. And now he was gone.

But, you're somewhere, aren't you? Bombshells like a backup copy of all Philomena's data — everything that was seized by the FBI — don't just fall from the sky. You sent it to me. But why? It's useless here.

Cole sat upright again, facing the microphone, looking down at Jennifer for a moment, then into the room, at the faces of the other attendees; the media working its angles, the denizens of Capitol Hill, a scattering of concerned citizens.

"Ladies and gentlemen, the purpose of this select committee is to examine and interpret the current and projected threats to our nation. Currently, through the combined efforts of the Department of Justice and the FBI, we were able to stop, in the process, a domestic terrorist attack on multiple levels. An attack cleverly made to appear as something to which those subscribing to conspiracy theories and wild conjecture might draw false conclusions. But if this was the case, as former Special Prosecutor Aiken claims . . ."

He was cut off by Korey Ramsey, who flanked Cole on the other side. Jennifer watched Ramsey's jaw move as he spoke directly into Cole's ear. She didn't have to hear the exchange to know what was being said. Ramsey was advising Cole not to mention a false-flag event again, even in the context of it being a unfounded rumor, a paranoid conspiracy theory. It was far better left unstated. She watched Cole pull away, nod, and reiterate his sermon.

He cleared his throat, and it echoed in the room. "Nonsystem tried to implicate others in its attempt, to throw blame elsewhere," he said. "They knew that. . ."

He continued to drone on, but Jennifer found herself tuning out. This was how it would go. She'd been naïve to think otherwise. There would be more posturing and rallying. There would be some obligatory rolling of heads — someone would have to take the blame for the casualties that had occurred. It wasn't the CIA's turn, so it was more likely that the FBI would be witch-hunted on this go-around. Flaws in their investigation. Connections that hadn't been made sooner. The DOJ would emerge victorious, holding up XList as their victory, John Rascher gloating like a hunter with his kill. Former special prosecutor Jennifer Aiken would be a footnote, if noted at all.

Gentian had known it, too. He'd claimed he was ready — and she knew now what he'd meant. Ready to take the fall for this, to be the scapegoat. Why? Perhaps he believed in people. He believed that people would see the truth. Because here, in this forum, truth was like poison.

There would be no mention of the IMF or the Central Security Service. The IMF was not a US government body, of course; there was no representative on the dais. And the only representative of the latter organization was Wick.

As the committee continued to chew its way through other witnesses — Rascher taking a turn, Doherty answering questions, the US Attorney General reading a shaky statement — Wick got up and left. He was simply there one minute, gazing out over the room, only once making eye contact with Jennifer after she'd returned to the main seating area. Then he was gone.

At the end of a twelve hour day, with only two relatively short breaks, she was tired, her body achy. Yet her mind remained calm and alert, clearer than it had been in days, weeks, maybe months. She was coming out of the aftermath of New York. Her faculties were returning. But things weren't the same; she didn't feel the same. She hadn't since that first night in Cotuit Bay.

She felt reborn.

CHAPTER FIFTY-NINE / MONDAY, 5:22 PM

Jennifer sat and watched the television in her Washington townhouse apartment. From the windows you could see Gangplank Marina, still under construction. Word was that the work would be delayed even longer as attention was focused, both in the private and public sectors, on restoring and augmenting the internet. Altnet. It was a big payday for private companies involved in internet security and infrastructure, and a launch pad for a new crop of politicians crowing about terrorism as they ramped their campaigns up for the next cycle.

Philip Largo was one of them.

On the screen, Largo cut a solemn figure as he walked through the gaggle of reporters and took the small stage. He stepped in front of the podium and the lights flashed on his pale face. He looked calm and determined.

The crowd fell silent.

"When I was a young man, I made some irresponsible choices. As you know, I had an affair with an escort. She called herself Danice."

The crowd murmured and then settled itself for more.

"Danice worked for the escort service known as XList. A sinister enterprise that is now, thanks to the efforts of our outstanding investigators and prosecutors, in an unprecedented joint effort of the FBI and the Justice Department, dismantled."

Whistles and cheers from the crowd and extended applause.

Jennifer snuck a quick glance at the two agents in the room with her. Men in her own home, watching the TV with bored expressions. She refocused on Largo.

Largo gazed out over the reporters and photographers. He looked into the television camera, peering right into Jennifer's eyes, it seemed.

She waited. If Philip Largo, who now had the attention of the spotlight again, were to tell the world about Titan, about the secret building of the data center, about *why* he had been targeted, it would blow open the cover-up: why Heilshorn and Titan were funding a data center as a backup to an internet attack, and why Nonsystem supposedly wanted to bring down the web. The applause quieted.

Largo stared into the camera, then dropped his eyes for a moment, and furrowed his brow in sorrow.

"In my position as State Assemblyman at the time, and in my race for governor, I became weak." He lowered his head, his face lost to the watchful crowd, the photographers eagerly snapping pictures of his shame. Jennifer imagined one of those shots of Largo's downcast head would be all over the papers and web.

The headline would be: *Former Assemblyman Expresses Deep Remorse. Now Running for State Comptroller.*

He raised his head, his face the picture of penitence. Then, he carefully built his expression into something else; a mask of resilience. Nobility. She had always thought Largo was meant to be in politics. She couldn't have been more right.

"But I don't regret it," Largo said with a talk-show-confessional tone. "I don't regret it for a second, because of this — because of her."

The crowd stilled, lights flashing silently as three armed guards walked up onto the platform. They reminded her of her own security detail, and she felt a wash of pity and gratitude for the three men who had given their lives for her. And Eddie Stemp — his honesty with her, his role in bringing some of the truth to light. She'd made discreet inquiries, but hadn't gotten very far in determining what had happened to Stemp's family. The Oneida County Sheriff's was now under investigation by the Justice Department, she knew that. The entire incident had been smothered by the Department and the FBI.

One of the guards, a woman, was holding the hand of a girl. She led the little girl across the bright stage to Largo, who picked her up in his arms. The girl looked at him, smiled, and then turned her small, sweet face to the crowd.

"This is my daughter," Largo said to them. "This is Leah."

The crowd gasped. Largo's lawyers had probably laid out this narrow course. Largo was clearly sticking to the line, but there was a painful truth in his eyes he couldn't entirely hide with his rhetoric. It was welling up in him, this need to express the truth.

That his daughter had been hidden from him for almost seven years by the Heilshorns. That they ran XList, which dealt in prostitution, human trafficking, blackmail and murder, while they kept his little girl. And that revenue from XList fed Titan, which in turn fed Heilshorn, who had financed politico-military endeavors, such as Altnet, such as the framing of Nonsystem.

The audience hadn't seen this revelation coming. Largo waited for them to calm down and settled Leah on his hip. There had been a deep rift between those who had supported Largo despite his indiscretion and those who felt he was scum — the majority of voters had written him off. Now, seeing Largo there with his child, Jennifer realized the brilliance of his strategy. Leah represented justice, forgiveness, and the American dream. Largo would come back into favor again. He already was.

"I will forever have to live with what I did. But, looking at my daughter, who came out of that, I wouldn't change anything. And I never solicited sex. Let that be clear. I had an affair, yes. But, like Lawrence Taber, we were both under the impression that the women we were with were . . . that they weren't professionals in the trade. I was entrapped, and by the same man and the same organization who blackmailed Lawrence Taber . . ."

This elicited a fresh wave of excitement in the crowd, and Largo was grabbed by one of his slick-suited attorneys who whispered something in his ear. The lawyer's eyes were wide, his jaw working. Largo nodded. Then his eyes closed. For a second, Jennifer wondered if Philip Largo was going to lose it. But he composed himself and turned back to the press, holding Leah, looking like a man bracing for impact.

The world held its breath.

"Thank you," he said.

Jennifer exhaled in a burst. The press conference was over. She watched Largo take his daughter in both arms, hugging her close as he exited the stage. Then the station broke for a commercial.

Jennifer sat back. Largo was a disappointment. But at least Leah was safe. Her care would be scrutinized. She would be raised by some top-notch nanny. And she would be out of the Heilshorn's world.

Jennifer flipped aimlessly through the channels, watching out of the corner of her eye as one of her guards, who had been making himself a sandwich in the kitchenette, walked out of the room. She heard the agent open the front door and caught the noise of a car engine. A moment later and the FBI agent was leading John Rascher into her living room. His arm was in a sling and he was still pale from the shooting.

Jennifer frowned at him. "What are you doing here?"

"I'm going to drive you."

She had another battery of debriefings at the DOJ headquarters to look forward to that evening. With any luck, she'd be through it all by the time she was old and gray. Maybe have a few good years left to take up sewing.

"That's nice of you. But I have my private chauffeurs right here with me."

She indicated the two impassive agents, who, she knew, resented the hell out of their babysitting detail and wished they could be anywhere else but stuck here with her. Rascher glanced at them briefly and then found her gaze and held it. There was something treading water behind his eyes — fear? A kind of potential energy.

"Yeah, well, I'd like to drive you. Have a chance to talk. If that's okay with these gentlemen."

The two agents looked at each other and murmured consent. Jennifer continued to clock Rascher. What was he up to?

He led her out to his vehicle and he opened the door for her. He had his own personal driver, a kid who wore a suit one size too big and an expression like he was ready to lay down his life for the DOJ. They just kept coming, she thought.

Before he closed the door on her, Rascher turned to the two agents getting into their own vehicle.

"Hey, do me a favor? She's going to need that box of files by the kitchen counter. You grab that for me? Sorry, we're actually running late. Just meet you there."

* * *

For a gangly young man in a too-big suit, the kid drove like they were at a NASCAR rally. Before she knew it, the townhouses were far behind them and they were rocketing past the Gangplank Marina, and through the touristy fish market, where the drive had to slow. She could smell shrimp through the open window.

"Where are we going, John?"

350

He was silent, looking out. She watched him trace a finger over his lower lip, back and forth. They made their way through thick traffic. Within a few seconds, they spanned the Washington Channel. On the far side, Jennifer caught a glimpse of the magnolia trees with their white blossoms, lining the road down to Hain's Point. Then the trees and the golf greens vanished, and they were swallowed up into the rushing interstate.

They looped through a coil of off ramps until they'd left behind 395 and were on George Washington Memorial Highway. When John Rascher finally looked away from the window and turned to her, she saw his eyes were red. And at last she understood.

"I'm sorry," he said. The lip he'd been polishing with his finger was now trembling as he tried to hold back the emotion. She watched it work its way through his system, saw the single tear escape, which he quickly swiped away. He gathered himself and lowered his voice. What would come now would be the regretful speech, but he'd already communicated everything she'd ever wanted to hear from him.

"I know I was . . ."

She leaned forward and put a hand on his knee. He stared back at her for a moment but then broke the eye contact. He was apologizing for who he was, not easy for a man to do — not easy for anyone to do, man or woman.

She turned away and looked out the front window as they sped down the highway towards Reagan International Airport. Past the co-op buildings hazy in the distance, towards the air traffic control tower penetrating the gauzy white sky.

The driver looped them around to the departures. They drove past the commercial airlines' departures to a separate hanger off the main concourse. A small white jet waited for them.

"I don't know who William Chase is," Rascher said. "But anyone willing to go to such lengths to get a hold of you . . . I guess they deserve you."

The driver got out of the car and held the door for her. She didn't have anything with her. No clothing besides what she was wearing. Not even a toothbrush. The plane engines were thrumming. The steward was walking over, his hand in the air in greeting.

Jennifer gave Rascher a hard look, but she was suppressing a smile. "Did you make some money out of this?"

He turned away and tried to hide his own betraying expression. "I meant what I said."

She shook his hand, gave it a squeeze, and then she turned to the steward. The steward led her to the plane. She glanced back at John Rascher, her old college boyfriend, his suit jacket off his shoulder because his arm was in a sling. And she realized she would never see him again.

EPILOGUE

Brendan stood on the hotel balcony overlooking Grand Cayman Island as the sun came up. Far below, the waves broke the coral reef and slid over the rippled white sands up to the beach.

It was nice to watch the sun spread light over the ocean. It was good to inhale the salty air. But he didn't care much about the hotel luxury.

His parents, before they split up, had often dragged him into uncomfortable situations as a boy. Parties and functions his father enjoyed, affluence that his mother didn't like. She relied on the wine to get her through, while Brendan would find places to hide. His father would invariably find him and scoop him up to meet someone. His father, laughing, showing all those teeth, hair swept back, while his mother would sit at the dining table. Brendan had inherited her dark hair. Also the dark introspection, the aversion to crowds, the tendency to chase it all away with alcohol.

He had loved both his parents.

He turned from the sunrise and looked into the room. White linen billowed in the breeze. Cozy furniture sat with bright cushions, a hutch with Aztec molding, a kitchen with blond-oak cabinetry and marble counters. The place smelled of oiled leather and sea air. On the stone table was the black, portable storage drive, caught in the light of the rising sun. Daybreak illuminated the device containing information on more black markets, human trafficking, malfeasance, corruption. There was much more to be done, but that could wait for another time.

He lit up a cigarette.

* * *

The Westin Grand was ridiculously opulent. She knew Brendan was indulging her for a few days before they left for the Maldives, to simple stilt-houses over turquoise lagoons. That would suit her just fine, too.

Jennifer walked through the door adjoining their suites, made her way through his room, and came up behind him. She handed him a cup of coffee, which he took, wordlessly. The two of them drank and admired the view. She couldn't believe that less than forty-eight hours ago she had been sitting in her townhouse in Washington. Under constant watch. It worried her — she couldn't lie; it worried her to disappear the way she had — but she couldn't deny that it felt good. Free. It didn't feel like running away, it felt like moving towards something. She just wasn't quite sure what, exactly.

She stood beside him. He reached over and put a hand on her lower back. Still looking out into the morning, he asked her, "How are you feeling?"

"I'm great. Head is clear." She watched a boat coming into the small port. "My room-phone rang last night."

He turned his head slightly, looking at her out of the corner of his eye. "Yeah?"

"Yeah. Someone looking for Hanna Becket? Asking what I wanted for my in-flight meal tomorrow."

"Huh," he said. "What did you decide? Chicken or fish?"

She raised her eyebrows at him, trying not to smile. "Hanna?"

Brendan stepped away from the railing and spread his arms. "The names get chosen at random. But, hey – Hanna's got a ring to it."

He took a sip of his coffee, watching her over the rim of the mug. *Not Brendan*, she thought, *William Chase*. And she was now Hanna Becket. He had set her up with a new identity. Yet, looking into his eyes, she thought that the more things changed, the more they stayed the same. Names didn't matter. She knew who she was, she knew who he was, too. Or, she was learning.

They'd been here for two days now, and she hadn't so much as kissed him. She would fix that tonight, she thought.

"Yeah the name's not bad," she said.

She glanced into the room at the storage drive on the table. She had a feeling there was more in store for her in the Maldives than volcanic islands and overwater bungalows. She turned back to him, and he winked.

They both moved up against the railing to take in the full view.

He slipped his arm around her waist and pulled her closer.

THE END

TJB
6/23/14 - 6/25/15
Elizabethown, NY

Acknowledgements

This book would not have been possible without the help of some incredible people.

My main man, Geoff Pierce, helped me through the darkest doubts and pointed out the shapes in the inkblots. Jasper Joffe personally edited this entire trilogy with ruthless precision and indefatigable patience. Dava Clement-Brearton listened, allowed, waited, responded, supported, and knew intuitively how to deal with my chaos each step of the way.

Thanks to early readers Bob Sirrine and J.V. Manning. To everyone at Joffe Books, including the other writers who have inspired and cheered me on. And to you, for taking this trip with me.

Thank you.

Thank you for reading this book. If you enjoyed it please leave feedback on Amazon, and if there is anything we missed or you have a question about then please get in touch. The author and publishing team appreciate your feedback and time reading this book.

Our email is office@joffebooks.com

www.joffebooks.com

Made in the USA
Monee, IL
23 September 2020

43202180R00215